DETERMINED

SOUL SEER CHRONICLES, BOOK 7

S.J. CAIRNS

Black Thumb
Publishing

Cover design by Getcovers

Logo created by S.J. Cairns

Logo image by CNuisin depositphotos.com ID 265803116

Tree vector by Loca depositphotos.com ID 16818659

ISBN 978-1-7782611-8-3 (Ebook)
ISBN 978-1-7782611-9-0 (Paperback)
ISBN 978-1-998875-00-9 (Hardcover)

Black Thumb Publishing
Ontario, Canada
www.sjcairns.com

 Created with Vellum

To Bosco:
Unfortunately, my pug buddy passed away during the makings of this series. I will forever remember days and nights spent listening to his snoring, soaking in his unending cuddles, avoiding soap in his eyes as he insisted on sharing my showers, and watching him grow from a tiny little puppy mill survivor into a distinguished old man.
Always loved, forever missed.

ACKNOWLEDGMENTS

I tend to acknowledge the same people each book. Kind of hard not to when their support is a constant fuel for my creativity and drive to put words on the page. If I have never thanked you for lending an ear, answering a silly question, moaning about how difficult this whole process can be, or just for enjoying a pleasant banter about this indie publishing world I have found myself in, I thank you now. I am no one without my family, bookish comrades, and loyal readers.

1

STRAPPED AND PREPARED

Sophie

Nothingness. No Caine or Gareth, no blood-soaked battlefield, no black sky or screams of the dying, nothing.

Nya knows not to panic. The drop into bleakness is a trick meant to isolate her from her long-lost love. Gareth is still in front of us, still trapped like Nya, his spirit a wavering overlay of Caine's body until the Illusionists blinded Nya and Gareth from their reunion.

Too bad, so sad, bitch.

Pain ripped through my legs. They gave out. Nya screamed with my voice; my lungs filled the field with her cries. Biting cold cut into my hands as I crashed into melting snow and tried to grab my legs to grip the pain.

My hands. I can feel my hands.

I flexed my fingers. They moved with my thoughts, shocking me with the control.

A piercing spike of pain shot through my skull. Nya fought me, trying to shove her way into taking over again.

Someone was yelling my name, telling me to hold on. Donovan? I couldn't see him with Nya closing my eyes against the pain. We shared in the agony until it somehow doubled in my legs.

More bones broken. Snapped too fast to heal.

Another crack was my arm. I screamed. Nya screamed.

Who's doing this to me?

Nya opened our eyes enough to showcase Donovan with his hand stretched out towards me.

He knows I'm in here. Why is he doing this? Hasn't he hurt me enough?

"*Stop! Please stop, Nya! Get out of me!*"

"*No. I've wandered too long! This is not how it ends.*"

Warmth cradled me. A voice spoke. Donovan's voice? What is he saying?

Fuck! My head snapped back. A rush of energy rolled through me.

Fire.

Fire blazed between us, dancing with the surrounding trees. The face of my lover alight and smiling across it, gratitude thick in his mind. Not for the futures I will create for us, but for the simple invitation to share this life. It will end early yet a sliver was spent with me. He would perish happily if that were all there was to offer.

It was not.

The magic soaking the air will release us from this life to gift us breath in others, to love in others, to ensure wherever the fates send us our paths will forever cross.

No.

The fire has grown. I cringed away from pain in the bottoms of my feet. My shift is ablaze, the smell acrid in my nostrils, the stink of it dizzying.

See beyond this torture. See beyond the cruel stares. Chanting in my head is frantic, praying for release, though a release with no true death. A momentary sacrifice in exchange for the ultimate survival, confident in the spell and from whom it came. Loring proclaimed its success, so it will be. The words continued in circles until the fire stole the breath from my lungs and enveloped my body. The screams of my love threatened to upend my focus. I am capable. I will see him again.

I scrambled, mid-scream, fleeing the flames. Something caught around my feet and I went down. My head and shoulder bounced off something hard. Flat, grey cement chilled my palm.

A man stood a few feet from me, his hands out towards me, lips moving. I couldn't hear anything.

"Don't...Don't...Don't touch me...." I raced away from him, a wall stopping me. More cement. White.

The man glared down at me, his face familiar.

Donovan?

What was he doing? Fuck. We're in a cement box. Tobias caught us. He must have dragged us back to the Sorrel Compound cells.

Why was he in here with me? Part of Tobias's torture? Last time we were in separate kennels. Caveman said Donovan was never in my cell. Nothing but another trick.

Rage surged at the nightmare the Sorrel cells burned into my memories. The son was not so different than the father after all.

Panting breaths came in punches as hate made me dizzy. Hate for ending up in a cell, hate for Tobias, hate for Donovan, and hate for myself for ever loving him.

"Are you real?" The restraint in my voice was necessary if I wanted answers. He may lie. If I caught a hint that he was, no one else was around to stop me from tearing off his nose and ripping his testicles through the bloody facial cavity.

Donovan's lips parted, his brow creased, but he didn't speak. He kept his distance, watching.

I righted my feet beneath me and slid up the wall. "Where am I?" The edge in my tone was freshly sharpened by impatience.

Again, he didn't say anything.

"All I need from you are answers. You don't bother talking, I'm going to start swinging."

His eyes glittered like black tar in the sun. Was he going to cry?

How dare he get weepy. No way was I volunteering for comfort duty. He could soothe his ragged edges with the vaginas he roughed up days ago.

After a throat-clearing grunt he answered with strain. "These are the cells of Vincent's new Prison Creation."

A cell was easy guesswork. It being Vincent's was confusing. No telling if these were any better than Vincent's family-operated cells considering they devoted centuries to tweaking their system.

Faith in your oldest friend didn't count for much, until he asked you to tear down the most powerful establishment of our race. Especially since he had a history of failing.

Did Vincent take down the Sovereignty this time?

I needed to know more.

"Why am I here?" Could Vincent have imprisoned me for things Nya did? I was hijacked by an ancient with fantasies of rom-com happy endings. How could I be held accountable?

Donovan straightened, inhaled, and crossed his arms in what seemed like a stall tactic. "Because it's better than being slaughtered by my parents' covens, or the Sovereignty, or Loring, or any number of devotees. Or even the others in the Mother Coven who disagreed with reopening the Creation and now see us as traitors."

"Do I get details, or do I have to ransack your brain for them?"

"Try it. The cell's magically bound. No power works in here."

Same as the Sorrel cells. A flash of those days hit so strongly I smelled the ham sandwiches I refused to eat and never would again.

The memory piggy-backed its uglier and meaner friend, reminding me of how Donovan spent his time in lockup. Every drawn-out orgasm he shuddered through meant he was having a hell of a lot more fun than I was.

"I didn't want any of them." His voice splashed like ice water.

"I thought you couldn't read my mind."

"Don't have to. I can see it on your face."

I glared, not hiding anything he may be seeing.

"You can hate me, but I tried—"

"Not hard enough, evidently."

He exhaled and his shoulders slumped. I never brought up the topic and didn't want to talk about it.

Though, I did have questions, even if they were of an unexpected variety. "Is Caine alive?"

He licked his lips and stared at the floor a moment. "Yes, Caine is alive. Both Nya and Gareth are dead. Loring fled, but I took out Evaristus."

"How?"

"I injected Nya's soul into him and then ripped him apart."

"Caine and I already tried tearing him up." Actually, we riddled his body with water-bloated blades of grass that sliced him to bits.

He shrugged. "Can't kill a soulless man. Adding a soul changed the rules."

Hmm. Maybe some truth in there. None I could verify in here.

If Loring was alive, I could still shove him through a wood-chipper *Fargo*-style. He escaped with murdering Aunt Lacey for far too long.

"Where's everyone else?"

"Survivors are here, too, in different cells when they want to be. Caine was out cold, like you, when Gareth was pulled from him. He's awake now." This was said with a slight twitch of his lips as if he wished differently.

Not long ago, I would have bet my left ass cheek that Caine was my future. Instead, I shacked up and played house with Donovan because of the Soul Magic that connected our souls hundreds of years ago.

No wait. The broken connection between us meant we no longer felt every minute brush of sensation anymore. Which left my options open.

Huh, good detail to remember.

I listened to the rest of Donovan's explanation of the Creation imploding, nearly killing us all if Graham, the demon Gualichu inhabiting the body of a young portal creator, hadn't gulped the excess energy blast like a free lunch buffet. Leftover enemies scattered; survivors came to the Prison Creation.

"Where's Olive?"

"Here. All the Ballards survived including Adam, Serena, and your mom."

I didn't think to ask about them because none of them should have been there in the first place. "Whose bright idea was it to let them fight?"

"They didn't have a choice." Exhaustion bled into his words. "Your mom didn't fight and she's not here. She and Bosco are safe."

Without saying more, Donovan turned and headed towards the wall behind him, disappearing through it.

What the fuck? That's it? Unlike the Sorrel cells, these didn't have a door. The wall *was* the door?

Could I leave?

I sprung to stand where Donovan once stood. I took a few hesitant steps forward with my hands in front of me, my arms going straight through the wall. Cool air encased my skin wherever they ended up.

"Okay." I rolled my shoulder. "Let's do this."

Bracing for what might meet me on the other side, I was ready for anything from a trick where I end up in another cell to miraculously waking up in my own bed with freshly washed linens.

I took another step and passed through the wall.

Light sheared my eyes.

"Fuck me!" I spun away from the onslaught and hit a hard surface behind me, pressing my hands into something rough and unyielding. Leaving the cells must mean not entering as easily.

I blinked through tears. Reddish-brown brick scraped against my palms. I pressed into the most pristine brick I can remember seeing. It stretched out along both sides of me and upwards high above my head. Cold marble under my bare feet—shit, I have no shoes on— reflected overhead light, yet not the light that blinded me when I came through the wall. No, that was a barrage of soul glows.

Last time a soul glow sucker punched me in the retina that hard it was Aunt Lacey's minutes after I first released my power. Crowds of Magics drove me to tears, especially in the beginning. This was like seeing souls for the first time.

I am still powerful. No matter what Nya did to me or how different I may be without her, I was still a Soul Seer.

A pinch of healing power directed to my eyes soothed them as I listened to voices behind me, finding no demands or shouts of war, all conversational. I didn't clock any Tainted souls, though the others hit me too hard to notice. And if Donovan lured me into another cell or if I were in the Sovereignty cells, every soul I saw could be a part of some elaborate torture plan.

An inhale and a swipe at the tears on my cheeks, I faced whatever was behind me in the same way I braced myself before going through the wall.

Holy shit. The second dose of soul glows was no better than the first beyond knowing to expect them. A little bit of healing power helped me see the Magics beyond their bright glows. None of them spewed any Taint...at least none in front of me.

Dripping from molded ceilings, forty feet or more above me, were ornate chandeliers throwing light off of the gleaming marble floors. Everything around me shone, except for the brick wall. A courthouse feel was somewhat cold and clinical, yet stylish wood accents reeked of money. A decor I remembered well from 'Bring Your Child to Work' Day with Mom in grade school. Though, Serena and I were mostly bored amongst a sad audience sitting through far too many Theft Under $5000 cases.

"Sophie!" A body slam, a strangling squeeze, and an ear-piercing squeal in my ear was a telltale sign of Kim's overbearing excitement. Her soul glow crowded me. Was it brighter than before? I couldn't concentrate through her bouncing us.

Over Kim's shoulder stood Caveman, his immortal soul glow unmistakable and a tad murky as it was the first time we met. Not Tainted, but something lurked or hid within. It took me a moment to remember his real name was Hall, but I only thought of him as Caveman. He exchanged a guarded look with Donovan who responded with shrugged shoulders.

Before I could interpret their likely telepathic conversation, Kim held me in front of her by my shoulders as if to get a better view.

She rubbed the skin of my arm peeking from large, scorched holes in my shirt where, apparently, I had been on fire at some point. "How do you feel?"

Kim's question was clear, but I wasn't tracking. My mind was stuck on the convo between Donovan and Caveman that was no longer silent. Caveman asked Donovan if he was serious about joining the Tactical Team Vincent headed.

"Are you?" Donovan returned.

"Yeah."

"Really?"

"As a Recondite Magic without an undercover gig, this'll keep my skills sharp. I'm not much of a team player and until it stops me from doing what I want, I'm in. You?"

Donovan didn't hesitate. "Fuck yeah."

I pushed by Kim. "I'm in."

Caveman's eyebrows lifted and his gaze shifted to Donovan.

What the fuck? I didn't need his permission. "He doesn't own me. Plus, Vincent already promised me a spot."

Caveman raised a hand. "Fine by me, Soul Seer. Once suited up, we're headed out. I recommend footwear."

The chilled marble reminded me of the boots Vincent gave me after they rescued me from the Sorrel Compound. They were mine and someone—probably Donovan—removed them.

"How do I get back into the cell?" If this was some kind of fake scenario conjured up in some Sovereignty cell, it was as real as they came. It was better than sitting around.

Kim touched my arm. "Wait a sec, Soph. You just woke up. Your family wants to see you—"

I pulled away, uninterested in anyone's sympathetic attention. "Wherever we're headed will require more than boots, no?"

Caveman glanced at Kim and then at me again. "Gear, yes. And plenty of it provided for the Team. The mission is a supply run to The Chiff and then to check on some safe houses. Not exactly working in the danger zone, but with Loring free and pissed off Magics everywhere, you never know."

It took a second to remember the underground safe haven for unTainted Magics beneath the mall had been infiltrated around the same time they plucked us from the Sorrel Compound. They weren't gabby about the details, but it sounded like a massacre.

"What about the field?" Kim touched Caveman's arm to regain his attention. "So many of our own were left there to rot."

Caveman huffed. "The barrier spell protects them from the Blind stumbling onto them—"

"Try." The plea in Kim's eyes was tailor-made for Caveman.

Did the poor bastard realize he was being manipulated? For a good reason, but still, those blue-greens of Kim's were working him over.

Caveman placed a heavy hand on her shoulder. "You don't need guns to bury bodies, kitten. Others can pull grave-digger duty."

"Anyone pulling grave-digger duty still needs protection. The longer the bodies are left there, the longer the enemy could return for their own and possibly mess with who was left behind. Families need to be notified. We can't let people think their loved ones disappeared without explanation and I—"

"You can't come."

Kim balked at Caveman's interruption and apparent order.

Maybe he wasn't so easily swayed.

Caveman stared down at her with mischief in his glare. "Don't play dumb, kitten. It doesn't suit you. I know that's what you're playing at, and I'm not about to expose you to potential threats this soon after dodging a literal war. We are in hiding for good reason."

"You don't get a say here, Viking. The level of threat exposure is up to me to decide."

Wanting to knock their heads like antagonistic siblings, antsy impatience wound me up. Judging by Donovan's bleary-eyed irritation, this was a regular thing for these two.

Keyed up and ready to get on mission with the Tactical Team, I gave a mental "fuck it" and left in search of another Team member to kit me out.

Without ever palming one before, I was surprised by how comfortable my new gun felt in my hand. Gregor, the first Tactical Team member I roped into helping me, explained the Beretta PX4 Storm Compact was perfect for a first-time user while still packing some punch with 9mm rounds and a fifteen round magazine I loaded and unloaded to familiarize myself with the process.

Magics didn't need weapons, though the Team seemed to love them.

Blind weapons were seen as beneath a Magics' complex abilities. Realistically, they made a big impact. Vincent was smart enough to know this and insist the Team be strapped and prepared for combat in instances where our abilities would expose or put ourselves and those we protected in greater danger.

Seeing the Tactical Team for the first time in the mall as they went after Gualichu, the Blind surrounding them, I sure as hell thought they were badass. And no one would assume they were anything but a specialized SWAT team.

Whether or not it was responsible to give me a gun was another question no one was asking. As far as experience, mine was limited to shooting out the middle of Toonies at my Uncle Dave's with small rifles. Illegal, but cute on a keychain.

With the weighed magazine in one hand and the gun in the other, I was thrown off balance as something smacked into my legs, buckling my knees, and sending both the gun and magazine flying to the marble floor before me or Gregor could snatch them up.

I wheeled around and extracted the little body from my legs with force. "Hey! Watch what you're doing."

Andy's whole body steeled, shock and fear colouring his eyes. I released my too-tight grip and stepped away from my anger. "Sorry. I was holding a gun."

The apology sounded weak because it was. He smiled if only because he thought he should.

Behind the kid stood a short blonde with a perfect high ponytail, Andy's mom, Bridgette. Last I saw her, Bridgette was doing what earned her the nickname 'Jet' and was flying over the battlefield when we originally trapped Evaristus and Loring inside of the Diluculo Creation. Caine jumped in after her, resulting in being trapped. Besides the loss of too much weight, she looked great. Too perky for me to match without serious self-loathing, she was rightfully excited to no longer have the hand of a Puppeteer controlling her every move.

With a strength Jet couldn't match before, her soul colour glowed yellow as usual, yet hit the gym and was flexing with pride. My seemingly flabby resiliency to see soul glows may have been the cause, though I guessed if you were ridden like a mule and used for your power, the least you could walk away with is a power bump severance package.

Behind Jet was another broad-chested Magic with a blue soul glow I knew all too well, except I couldn't make myself speak actual words to him or manage to look at him straight. While Gregor picked up the clip and gun, Jet made ignoring the broad-chested Magic easier when she pulled me down into a tight hug and thanked me for taking care of Andy while she was away.

'Away' was a tame way of dancing around the fact I stole Andy from Jet's parents who enlisted Tainted friends to try and release Jet and Caine from the Creation, they instead releasing a demon. Super tame.

With too much to say and eager for a weapons lesson, I itched to bolt from the conversation.

I closed my eyes to avoid Mr. Broad-Chest, searching for the last good memory of him before he dove into the water outside of the Creation instead of how I saw him through Donovan's eyes during the transference spell. Inside Diluculo may have been it, us walking hand-in-hand and talking about better days ahead if we survived. Or before that, at Ranlyn's, talking outside of the bathroom and finding common ground. That may have been it.

A true reunion could wait. Heading out on mission didn't work when my eyes were tear-swollen. After all the effort put into getting him from the Creation, I needed more time to deal with that mission being over and how it ended.

Chasing another objective was what I needed right now.

Maybe Jet was done dealing with my awkwardness or maybe Caine tipped her off to move along. Either way, she took Andy by the shoulders with a gentle "See you later, Sophie." Andy kept checking until they gained some distance, but I couldn't make myself give him the attention he deserved. Or maybe he saw spots on me portending my death.

Teaching the kid how to pinky promise, and the gratitude on his face when we broke into his bedroom and took him away, pounced up from my memory banks to add a dash of guilt to the mix.

Kim and Caveman's voices overruled my churning thoughts. Whatever Kim was doing broke the man down. He promised to scope out the abandoned battlefield if she established a burial party that didn't include herself. I didn't have to see through the pissy look on Kim's face to know she enjoyed every moment of Caveman's overbearing nature keeping her in the cave. With or without her boyfriend Frog in the picture, being the focus of a man like Caveman was never a bad thing.

With my Beretta tucked into its holster, a five-inch stainless steel black blade on my hip, a mini flashlight in a tactical vest pocket along with black gloves and a synchronized water-proof smartwatch strapped to my wrist, I was ready to face the worst of it. I hadn't been in control of my body for quite some time. Geared up afforded me the sense I could take on anyone, be it with my innate abilities or a blade, and was a lesson in true empowerment.

"Here." Ismail grabbed my attention holding a small pile of black fabric towards me. "Standard issue. Boots also required."

I took whatever he handed me and searched around at how to re-enter the cells where I assumed my boots were. Ismail waved for me to follow him and showed me the cell console so I could change, it somehow knowing even though I wasn't in the cell, that my belongings were in there.

Leaving my cell covered in blacked-out tactical gear—ecstatic to see it included socks and a hair tie—since my hair was a loose and tangled mess—and feeling more badass than I ever thought possible, I waited an agonizing twenty-three minutes, sweat soaking the back of my neck, before the heavy clunk of the Team's steel toed combats sounded across the floor. I kept track on my fancy new watch.

An armed guard telepathically called to the security desk to confirm our clearance before we were ushered inside an elevator. Apparently, we couldn't leave our hideout whenever we wanted like Donovan claimed. Surprise, surprise.

Clearance or not, some guard in a crappy uniform was not stopping me from leaving and I doubted Vincent's Prison Creation's ability to challenge all the Magics within it if they arranged a coup.

Did everyone even know how tight their leashes were?

Unlike similar rides, these elevators didn't come with the sickening sense of motion that sunk my stomach. Even if it did, I was distracted by the jeebs Donovan standing in my personal bubble gave me. Six other Tactical Team members layered in weapons, squished inside the metal box, equalled sweat beading down between my shoulder blades.

Flash-sweats were enough, his hard-bodied presence causing me to burn internally in a non-sexy 'I need to escape you' kind of way. My only save was inwardly superimposing the memory of those gyrating hips of his into a scene illustrating a more pragmatic version of him being a cheating prick so those jeebs didn't morph into masochistic fantasy.

"Bastard."

Jessabelle squinted at me. "What?"

Oops. I shook my head, unable to form an explanation.

When the metal doors slid open, I shoved past Bronya. The thick sole of my combat boot caught the gap of the elevator, and I flew forward.

I stopped short of a face plant, a snicker sounding behind me.

I looked over my shoulder and saw Donovan's hand extended, telekinetically catching me. Bronya laughed and shook her head in a way that made me want to kick her in the tit.

"Let me go."

Donovan's expression hardened. He dropped his hand and I hit the ground, my chin cranking off of the parking garage pavement.

Bronya let out a whoop of laughter and stepped over me, her sleek ponytail swinging behind her. The others didn't comment as they moved passed me towards a blacked-out Yukon Denali.

Echoes of Bronya's laughter bounced off of the parking garage's walls, setting my anger to boil. I popped up to my feet. Someone grabbed the shoulder of my tactical vest before I rushed forward.

"Leave it, sweetheart." Caveman's growl in my ear was too close. I shook him off. "You attack one of your own and you can kiss the Team goodbye. Then how would you purge all that delicious rage?"

"Fuck off, Caveman." I headed towards the Denali.

Caveman followed. "You saved my life outside the Sorrel Compound. Any part of me that needed healing you saw to it and more. So, this is me thanking you and returning the favour, if only to prevent the waste of your talents on such a woman would be. Bronya wins her childish games if you take off her head."

"Bronya dies if I take off her head. It's called decapitation. I bet you've even done it a time or two while pillaging feeble towns for peasant women and livestock."

He laughed. "That I have. And have met many insecure women

like Bronya willing to throw themselves at uninterested targets. They only succeed if they know you see them as a threat."

"Please. That's what over-indulging mothers of ugly teenagers tell their daughters, so they don't kidnap the popular girls and bury them alive under their school football field."

"Why would they do that?"

"Because there are more plain-looking teenage girls than pretty, popular ones."

He grabbed my shoulder, forcing me to face him. "What does any of this mean?"

I shook him off again and continued on. "It means don't talk to me if you can't understand my language."

"Have you buried teenage girls under your school football field?"

"No." I stopped at the open vehicle door. "My school didn't have a football field. And you're welcome for the ass-saving." I climbed inside to the sound of Caveman laughing behind me, having no idea why we bothered with the convo or where it was going, besides it stopping me from attacking Bronya. Caveman was right in that they would likely kick me off of the Team if I did.

The Denali was a typical luxury vehicle with grey interior, yet something told me they didn't choose the vehicle for its gleaming grill. This one was different than the SUVs we drove the first time I met the Team. The memory of Nya taking over my body in the back of one of those SUVs rushed forward before I shoved it aside and stuffed it in a proverbial closet as my hands began to tremble.

Lincoln was a testy, heart-sick, driver and Team Lead. He took off before Ismail was comfortable in the open trunk, hitting the gas, and throwing him into the dark, tinted window. With his ass planted in an anchoring position, Ismail checked his weapon was loaded, ready to pop open the trunk and shoot like an action star.

Leaving the garage, I recognized we came from the Carlisle Street parking garage across from the downtown bus terminal. A place I knew well before I bought a car.

The question of where my Barracuda was hit me. I couldn't

remember the last time I drove it. Did Nya? Would she know how to drive? Cars weren't invented yet in her time. Thinking of her behind the wheel of my car started my knee bopping, hitting the seat in front of me as I was stuck next to Caveman in the furthest row of seats.

"How does Vincent expect to keep the Creation a secret when it's accessed by a public elevator?" Lots of people hung out in this lot. Not all of them savory characters, but even if some of them were high, they could still track seeing the same people come in and out and tell something was off about them. It was an office building, and we weren't exactly dressed for a cubicle.

"It's a Creation." Caveman's tone said this went without saying. Donovan told me as much as well, but I wanted to hear it from someone else.

"But we didn't go through the veil." I was prepared for the pain of one.

"The elevator took us through it."

"Really? My memories of veil-jumping involved the feeling of being eaten alive by a bear and then sizzling in its stomach acid."

Caveman smiled. "Diluculo is old. Creations nowadays come with the technological upgrades of a new millennia. No painful side effects."

I made an impassive "Hmm," thinking it's still an elevator also used by the Blind. Not what I would consider high security.

"Higher security than a group of cars driving into the middle of nowhere and then disappearing into a field, like with Diluculo. In order to access the Prison Creation from outside you have to know the proper access procedures. When leaving, it's the same as any elevator since you're already within the Creation. Plus, it has the advantage of around the clock access where cars are expected to be anyway."

His answer to my inner thoughts meant Caveman read my mind. When did my mental walls slip? Maybe they hadn't been up at all. It was instinctual before. Before what, I didn't dwell on, but it used to take little to no effort. Was my power weaker now?

I looked out the window as we drove around town, not focusing on storefronts or meandering pedestrians, too preoccupied with the pieces of missing data Nya's presence scrambled. Discombobulated was a good way to describe it. Was this what Alzheimer's patients felt like? Enduring vague memories that don't connect while knowing there were holes where memories no longer were and somehow feeling the hole's presence?

So fucking frustrating.

Darkness covered the Denali's windows. I recognized the underground loading bays beneath the Pen Centre mall to the hidden entrance of The Chiff. Unlike my first visit to the underground fortress there was no spell to usher us inside, no Magics directing us, or searching IDs and giving the all-clear to enter. No Magics were in The Chiff anymore so we parked the vehicle and prepared to fall out.

Before we did, Lincoln ordered everyone to perform a weapons check.

I palmed my Beretta ready to check it over like Gregor taught me.

"Keep it holstered, Sophie." Lincoln crapped in my cornflakes. "And I want you on Donovan's ass the whole time."

Pfft. "Why doesn't fuck-face get the newbie rules?"

Lincoln laughed without humour. "Donovan's far from a newbie, sweetheart."

"Watch it." Donovan warning came with a snarl.

Suppressing a growl at his territorial response, I already knew about Donovan's combat training. Kind of expected when you've been preened as heir to a Tainted Coven, I assumed his training didn't include weapons. Tobias would see them as beneath Magics, though it was practical for them to train on how to use them.

I shoved my Beretta into its holster. "This is fucking bunk."

"Stop complaining. Keep it tucked away or go shopping." Lincoln left like he didn't care which option I chose.

I resented the fact they were untrusting even though Vincent recruited me himself. Cowering behind Donovan's ass was the last position I wanted to play. And why Donovan? Caveman would have been a sufficient mentor and at least one I didn't contemplate killing and blaming it on an accidental discharge since I was *such* a trigger-happy newb.

Filing in behind Donovan's tight cheating ass onto the first level of The Chiff, I was surprised the lights were all on, expecting blackness illuminated by LED flashlights or spells, awaiting bad guys to pounce from dark corners like a zombie game.

Yawn.

The lights saved us from tripping over the dead. Not a few, not dozens...easily hundreds of bodies covered the ground like autumn leaves. Blood pooled beneath some, while others showed zero signs of injury and appeared to be sleeping. Regardless, the stench of decaying bodies reminded me of meeting Loring inside the barn in Pario with the tortured and deceased Elders. The stench of death clung to my sinuses.

Even with the innumerable dead, I expected more. A good indication of many survivors. Niches were ransacked. Items were knocked over into walkways for the sake of destruction. No one was allowed to return to clean up, though many were likely too scared. The Chiff was no longer a place of safety.

Row after row of cubbies were still filled with magical items, wares, and sleeping bags where families slept, leaving the majority of everything they owned behind.

Lincoln used hand signals to direct the Team. I noticed Donovan watched and listened as we split into two groups: Lincoln, Gregor, Arden, and Bronya in one group, and Ismail, Jessabelle, Caveman, Donovan, and me in the other. I followed Donovan as directed, but Caveman watched my back. In front of me, Donovan moved with the stealth of a cougar. His size twelve steel-toes landed each step with feathered whispers, a sleek predatory gait, alert, scanning every nook with intensity.

Not long ago, Donovan claimed he didn't enjoy killing and warned against doing so unless a last resort as it would weigh too heavily on my conscious. Seeing his profile from behind as he searched his corners, his steely, focused gaze called him a liar. He would have loved to come across an enemy Magic and put them down. He enjoyed controlling me too much and someone with his background carried a kill-count beyond what he admitted to.

Maybe he's a trophy keeper. Aunt Lacey gifted him a big house. For all I knew, he stashed a box of pierced earlobes or pinky toes in the attic.

He did look different than he did even a couple of weeks ago, maybe not serial killer different, but different. I couldn't pinpoint why.

I dropped the endless mental garbage and refocused to clear niche after niche, working our way deeper into The Chiff.

On my last visit, we used doors that opened to whatever levels you wanted. Vincent didn't tell me how they worked, but now they didn't, so we were relegated to the stairs for access to the lower levels. Members filled backpacks with items. I couldn't tell what they chose to take or what the importance of any of it might be. My kit didn't include a backpack, my judgement not trusted with this either.

With no backpack and no gun, I was an honorary ride-along because Vincent ordered it and no more, they giving me the power of a two-year-old with a plastic mallet on their parent's construction job site. Useless with the illusion of utility without the permission to inflict true damage.

Such bullshit.

The lower we went, the more the stink became too much to ignore. Lincoln ordered us not to use magic to rid ourselves of it in case enemies were nearby and could sense our presence if we did. Valid, but I wanted to yak. It was stronger than anything I smelled in Diluculo, even with all the rotting bodies Evaristus left lying around in the sun.

About thirty levels down we hit water. It rose above our toes the entire floor. Arden said the safety nets regulating ground water was removed in order to kill the most Magics possible in one swift action.

According to him, there were countless levels below this one with too few exits.

An image from the movie *Titanic* came to mind of people scrambling to escape the frigid water, while others accepted their fates and refused to leave their cabins. Cruel way to go, though clearly effective.

The lights on this floor weren't working. We switched to spelled night vision safety glasses I have never seen on any TV show before.

Again, nothing but the dead manned the level, though they floated in garbage, the water so dirty you couldn't see through it. The smell was all the floaters no one saved from their watery grave.

Like all of the others, we left them to continue to rot, our objective not including body retrieval as too many would overwhelm us. Donovan mentioned he and I could disintegrate them if they wanted, but Lincoln said they needed to be catalogued first and one level would take days.

I didn't like being volunteered, but I would have loved to dust some bodies and let my power free for a few minutes. All of this tension keyed me up for action.

The level below was submerged in rancid water floor to ceiling. No one was going in there without some type of special suit or contamination spell, and we weren't devoting time to swimming.

Well, not all of us were.

Ismail handed off his weapons in exchange for a spell before he dove into the fetid water and disappeared. No one said why he did this. No way he could clear all the remaining floors on his own, but no one shared with me why he took the plunge. The rest of us were at the ready, weapons drawn—except for me—in case we were ambushed. Since Ismail used a spell the enemy could detect, we braced for attack.

When ten minutes passed, I itched with impatience. When twenty minutes passed, I was fuming. All I saw was floating garbage to guess at and the others to ignore when they defaulted to telepathic conversations, Caveman and Donovan included. No one attempted to chat me up, not that I cared.

A splash brought us around in a panic. Ismail came out of the water, and he somehow remained dry. Guess that was the spell's work. He didn't have an oxygen tank, so that was probably another spell. Maybe underwater breathing was a part of Ismail's power. His soul colour was bright, yet uncoloured, so no sign of a specialty skill.

Ismail and Lincoln nodded at each other as if Ismail obtained whatever item or information he needed down in the lower levels and then Lincoln headed up the stairs away from the water-logged level.

I glared at Caveman as if to say, "Are you fucking kidding me?" since we weren't given any information on what Ismail gathered and clearly weren't going to be filled in.

Caveman gave a sly smile, expecting nothing less, the man clearly used to blindly taking orders from bigger fish than Lincoln.

Returning to well-lit stairwells, we didn't stop at each level as we ascended. We took the stairwell all the way up without stopping, the sweat and muscle aches getting to me. I pushed myself to keep up, not about to be the weak link. A tingle of my power reacted to the stress and kept me going until we reached the ground floor.

Pretending not to wheeze like an asthmatic child or be soaked like I followed Ismail into the body-soup levels, I followed in step until we reached Nora's office. Familiar with the room, I was not expecting to see the woman dead, still seated in her office chair with her throat slit open.

No one else reacted to seeing her, expecting her presence. Another thing the others knew that I didn't.

Arden took an office chair from the opposite side of the desk and used his boot to scoot Nora, still in her chair, off to the side. Her body slipped down onto the floor, no one commenting on her death.

"Nora sold out The Chiff to Chase." Caveman's voice was alive in my head, again, diving in like my mental defences didn't exist.

"Why would she do that? She ran the place. So did her family, for

generations. The niches were shitholes, but she probably had a cushy set-up."

Caveman shrugged. *"Not for nothing, that's for sure. Chase must have brokered some promises he never planned on delivering. The Sovereignty's good like that. It's how the lower levels were flooded, and their access doors shut down. Chase couldn't have pulled that off on his own and relished in relaying the details to Vincent before we scooped you from the Sorrel Compound."*

"What if Chase lied and Rodney or his son gave Chase the key? She was fucking the son." I couldn't remember his name. *"Maybe the father-son duo was angling for their own Sovereignty deal."*

"Maybe."

If Nora did set up all the Magics here, she deserved to die bloody. I didn't like the woman and understood why Arden pushed her into the corner like even in death she inconvenienced him from accessing her computer.

The rest of us kept watch as Arden got to work. I paced, wondering what his clicking and searching entailed as it wasn't outlined to me. Assuming it was as important as Ismail's secret mission underwater, I would think infiltrating The Chiff's inner workings included some highly sensitive information which may be of benefit to us in some way. Whatever it was, Nora never handed it over willingly when she was alive, and it was safe to assume Chase found no use for it or didn't have someone with Arden's hacking skills on hand or he would have taken Nora's hard drives.

Bronya's annoying tone brought my focus around. I didn't hear what she said, but it was directed at Donovan.

He let out a bored sigh. "Your desperation's seeping through your thong."

Guess he wasn't in the mood. Or didn't appreciate Bronya putting them on display, too public, too soon, trying to keep things on the down-low. Whatever it was, he walked away from her, leaving her to man the door as he found another spot to fiddle with his shiny new blade.

Being on the sidelines was demeaning. This was an opportunity to teach me something useful and the others couldn't be bothered.

I stared through the broken windows overlooking the dead outside of the office and remembered something Nora told me when I met her. "Evil seeps in and destroys as children. You are a fool to believe he can be anything more". She was talking about Donovan. In hindsight, maybe she was also talking about herself.

Shattered window glass crunched under my boots as I marvelled at the destruction one person's deceit could cause. I felt it in my bones. And no matter the attempts to erase or explain away the damage, it would never be the same.

2

UP TO SPEED

Caine

Nothing beat indoor plumbing. Hiding behind a bush and hoping you didn't get picked off by devotees with your pants around your ankles was something I could do without for the rest of my life, even without the cells having lockable doors. How I ever chose to do it while camping with the guys was a mystery. Now, a single flush, toilet paper, and soap and water to top off the experience, was enough to make a guy emotional and humbly grateful for those who risked everything to rescue us from the Creation.

In second place for things to bow at the feet of was Vincent for creating this prison and the spread served the first day here. The staff arranged a buffet they weren't prepared for, or maybe one of them found a magical solution to feed the sudden hoard of people, it replenishing when the warming trays were empty. The first thing I grabbed was a croissant. I damn near choked on it when the buttery sweetness hit my tongue and brought a bubble of emotion to rival my first bathroom trip. Oh, and the meat. Breakfast sausage and bacon and some kind of beef something I didn't bother to read the label of. Even cutlery. Anything was better than chowing down with dirty hands and blood-packed nails. No more stringy squirrels for me.

I was so fucking lucky to have made it out. And without Gareth riding my ass. Damn. I owed Donovan for that one.

I assumed Sophie felt better to be rid of Nya, but clad in tactical gear, she was ready for a fight as if Nya was still a threat. I was told Nya was as gone as Gareth was. And while inside, Donovan said Sophie was waging war to free me, but when I saw her, she did everything to ensure she didn't catch a glimpse of me.

In fact, her thoughts focused on us in the Creation together before we fought Evaristus and Loring the first time, and then at Ranlyn's when I told her I didn't hate her for being with Donovan once I gained a handle on their connection and how my time in her life next to her was not meant to be.

Why was she thinking about that? And why could I read her mind at all? Her mental walls were as thick as fortified steel before.

Nya hadn't possessed her for that long, but it seemed like she'd been ridden as long as Jet was. Not to belittle the experience, of course. It just seemed so much more happened that I hadn't learned about yet. Not everyone loved recounting everything I missed while inside the Creation, though I was worried about her.

She was too skinny, for one. An important five-to-ten pounds that left her cheekbones a tad too sharp, accentuating the bags under her dark eyes. Something about her stare was detached. She didn't want to feel how she did, and her cold glare was meant to scare away the common question of her well-being. Maybe that's why she wouldn't look at me.

Was she angry at me for going in after Jet and getting trapped in the Creation? It's not like I planned it or particularly enjoyed the vacation. Her thoughts didn't say so, though we took off quickly.

Seemed like she wasn't particularly happy with Donovan, either.

Things were deep-freeze level frigid, but then she was cold towards everyone, snapped at Andy with only a half-assed apology, was barely cordial with Jet, and shook Kim off like dandruff. She didn't even wait for her family to catch up with her before she took off.

Needing to catch up on all I missed while inside, Kim was the one to ask.

After a big hug from her—she was giddy I was still breathing—we sat in an empty office. I missed those hugs. Physical contact in the Creation was mostly violent and no one quite strangled you with love the way Kim did.

"So, Kim. Not begging to join the Tactical Team?"

"Please. While Donovan's fulfilling his G.I. Joe fantasies, I'm up to my armpits in Sect Leader duties. You not interested?"

I half-shrugged. "Seems like a Sophie-Donovan thing. Plus, I could use a break from fighting." My laugh was strained even to me, but she gave a slow nod, not blaming me for wanting to take a beat. We were still in hiding, so further battle wasn't far away, but I was enjoying sleeping on something up off of the ground, even if my nights were a blur of nightmares and waking up in blind panic thinking the camp was being attacked.

Before she could say anything, I focused the conversation. "I'd have to be an ostrich to miss the fact something's wrong with Sophie. What else happened while I was in there?"

Kim took a breath. "You sure you have the time to hear it? It's not pretty."

"I was going to take another hot shower until I turned into one big wrinkle just because I can. It can wait. The hot water never runs out. I've tested it." I settled in the chair. "Catch me up to speed."

Kim smiled at such a simple thing I saw as a luxury these days, but her smile was sad when she sat forward and braced her elbows on the desk to talk all things Sophie.

Some details I knew from when Donovan visited the Creation with that spell connecting him to Gareth, but since half of the time Gareth was in control, I didn't remember everything I should.

Kim recapped all she could in the simplest way possible, focusing on the sex ritual Donovan's sick fuck of a dad treated his coven to and how that impacted Sophie and their Soul Magic connection.

No wonder Sophie dropped noticeable pounds and disconnected her smile.

When Kim finished, I regretted not taking notes on all the twists and turns and who was kidnapped when and by whom. Also explained why the Apporter wasn't around. Olson was always glued to the Elders, and I hadn't seen him.

"Even if it wasn't Donovan's fault, Sophie would feel like Donovan fucked around since they escaped the connection. Hence one of the biggest inconveniences of my life."

Kim lifted a brow in agreement.

"With all the bullshit Sophie went through with Brock, it'll take a lifetime of Donovan grovelling to bring her around."

Kim pursed her lips. "You know, she's never told me about Brock. Donovan mentioned something about him leaving her. I figured she was too embarrassed to talk about it."

Oops.

She laughed at whatever guilty expression I made. "I won't rat you out. I just need some insight for when I talk with her. Which is happening whether she listens or not."

I groaned. With how bad Sophie was, I didn't feel like keeping the secret would help, so I told Kim about Sophie's druggy ex, the prick that held her heart and fucked around on her, sold her dog, and left town without a word.

Kim kept blinking as if having trouble absorbing what I told her.

"They were engaged," I added as an aside.

Her eyes widened. "Engaged?"

"I know, right? And with a stolen ring. Guy was a real winner."

She sat back in the chair, arms crossed. "Huh. Makes perfect sense."

"I assumed you knew."

Kim shook her head.

"It took a lot for her to move on from him. Which is why I know she wouldn't have cheated on me if the connection thing hadn't basically forced her. She cared about Donovan even with me around, but if she thought it was beyond that, she would have ended us before moving on."

She sat forward again. "She really would have."

"I know. I still think Donovan manipulated the situation to his advantage, but I was too pissed at the time to see the whole picture."

Instead of getting into it, Kim changed the subject. "How is it without Gareth squatting in your body?"

I laughed. "Better." I paused trying to find the words. "I tried to work with him when he gave me no choice, but I felt insane most of the time. Every decision, every thought came with an internal commentator arguing about the right way to hunt, to fight, to lead... everything. Ness could bring me back once she knew what was happening, though it was a daily struggle."

Kim nodded with narrowed lids.

"What?"

"I like her."

"Do you?"

She gave a one-shoulder shrug. "I only saw her through the Nexus Transference spell when Donovan went in, but she doesn't take anyone's shit. Gotta respect that. Plus, she's protective of her brother so she's not completely heartless."

I laughed and nodded. Kim's assessment was completely Ness.

"No details, eh?"

I raised empty hands. "None to tell. We haven't broached the subject of being together since we've been free. She's been scarce or busy or not alone, probably by design. Not one for the heart-to-hearts."

She laughed. "I get it. What about your powers? Are they different?"

"Haven't tested them. I'm assuming I'd have all my original abilities."

Thinking an easy test was in order, I awakened my power to a low hum along my skin. The surge was immediate, controlled. "Good sign."

I lifted my hand and telekinetically reached for a black office phone on the desk. The receiver flew into my palm so quickly I almost dropped it.

"Lord love a duck!" Kim brought a hand to her throat in shock. "'Kay, I think you're golden."

We laughed as I returned the receiver to its docking station. The successful test was a relief, though I bet Gareth's specialty powers involving water were gone.

"Have you talked to Frog?" It was still weird to think one of my friends knew about Magics and was dating one.

When I said the guy's name, she looked almost taken by surprise.

"Are you not dating anymore?"

"Oh no, we are. Umm, I haven't exactly called him since we got here."

"Okay."

She fiddled with her hair. "Yeah, I don't know what to say. He knows about my magic now, a whole story I'm sure he'll have opinions on, but I may have fudged how bad it's gotten. Before the battle to reopen the Creation, I tried to lessen the seriousness. I didn't want him freaking out and trying to find me. He'd get himself hurt or killed."

I nodded. "I can talk to him first if that's easier."

She straightened. "Really?"

"Sure. I've known the guy since I was eight. He deserves to know I'm still alive."

Happy for me to take the heat, Kim dialled and thrust the receiver at me almost as forcefully as I did telekinetically.

When Frog picked up, I dove right in. "Get off my girlfriend, beefcake!" Kim's brows scrunched but I shook my head. Over the years, we amassed a treasure trove of inside jokes.

"You motherfucking donkey-face!"

I laughed. "Love you too, buddy."

I gave Frog an update, trying to stick to enough details to include him and be assured I was okay. Frog sounded carefree through the rough topics, but I knew the guy enough to hear his overwhelmed tone. I gave him credit for keeping it together.

"You weren't even you when I saw you in there." Frog tried to describe seeing me through Donovan during the spell.

"I'm all me now, bro."

"And what about Kim? My girl's a walking sitcom who could probably kill me with a twitch of her nose."

I laughed trying not to tip off Kim. "You better believe it."

"Any chance we can pretend you're just a tech nerd with a Star Wars obsession?"

"Is that what you want?"

Frog paused. "What I'd like is to tell the guys about this crazy shit without that dick Donovan coming after me. Douche bag doesn't fight fair."

"I'd be pretty pissed myself."

"What? You two are buddies, now?"

I clucked my tongue. "More like in understanding of each other's positions. This life isn't easy."

"He's still a dick."

I chuckled. "Yes. Yes, he is."

When I said enough and was updated on the rest of our friends, I passed the phone to Kim. Her cheeks flushed red while she sat listening to a barrage of whatever Frog unloaded.

Mouthing a "thanks" for the talk that made a bigger impact than the one with Frog, I bailed to give Kim some privacy and walked into Blake's path.

The guy was with Jared and some other Coveners all exploding in congratulatory hugs and high-fives for surviving before they hit up the cafeteria.

Jared and Blake hung around a second. I knew what they wanted. "I'm sorry, guys. I used you as pawns and persuaded you to be my muscle so I could jump into the Creation and look for my cousin. I'd like to say I regret doing it, but Jet's breathing free air and reunited with her son. I probably feel less bad about how it went down than I should, but know, without your involvement, I wouldn't have been able to get my family back and I'll be forever grateful to both of you for that."

They glanced at each other with impassive expressions, still pissed off I put them in the position I did, and then broke into smiles and patted me on the shoulder and extended hugs, welcoming me back to reality. Both looked a tad battle worn yet retained their senses of humour.

"Ranlyn was raging at first." Jared pulled a face indicating an understatement.

Blake hit Jared. "Sophie was worse." Jared nodded with widened eyes in agreement. "We're lucky she didn't cut our nuts off right there and then. Though, she might now. I heard she's not finished fighting and pulled a gun on the kid?"

Oh my god. "No, dude. That's not at all what happened." I filled them in on my first-account details to ensure they spread the word on the truth. Sophie wouldn't care what people thought, but who needed the rumor mill activated for stupidity when there are more important things to worry about.

Spotting Sophie's brother Adam in the crowd of the lobby, I told the guys I would catch up with them later and I went to find out anything more about Sophie.

Adam confirmed as much. "No clue, man. Apparently, she's dressed up like some warrior princess and bounced. Like, what the fuck? I get she's stubborn, but she attracts bad luck like mosquitoes and thinks strapping on a gun is going to fix things? Doubts."

"She's got the rest of the Team. She'll be fine." I said this as not to worry her brother, but I agreed with the guy. Sophie running around with a gun didn't add up.

Adam nodded and cleared his throat. "Sorry about, y'know, you two." When I looked at him, he added, "With the whole awkward breakup thing. I don't know all the details, but we all kind of heard more than we wanted to through things like your convos in the Creation and whatever." I was surprised and didn't respond before Adam went on. "At least fate sent you a nice shake of sass and ass to replace her."

Oh geez. "Ness isn't a replacement."

"Whatever." Adam rolled his eyes. "Still hot and probably exactly what you need since she's nothin' like my sister."

"You really want me to get into how hot your sister is?"

"Umm, yeah-no. Keep that to yourself."

3

____

ON THE DOCKET

Vincent

Before me stood the oiled and buffed twelve-foot African blackwood boardroom table my father shipped from somewhere remote...the Sahara Desert, if I recall correctly. The grain of such an illustrious piece kept my fingers busy as I traced nature's laugh lines, letting my mind wander far from the multitude of rubbish my brother peddled from across the table.

While my pedantic brother, Chase, maintained the role of daily management and fancied calling himself the leader of all, our father, Alasdair Llewellyn, manned the helm like an old-world king presiding over his loyal constituency, lending his signature and overruling my brother's orders whenever it suited his needs. Unwilling to relinquish full reign to anyone, retirement was absent from the Sovereignty's true leader's vocabulary.

The counsel in front of me protected their own. Handpicked and replaced as necessary, Alasdair was never far from whomever wore the political crown, snuggled within a behind-the-scenes capacity, and whispering sufficient lies to ensure pre-designed outcomes from the governing seat-warmer.

Steel eyes stared down the blackwood at a board member five seats away reviewing a high-valued client file. In the latest slot, a scoundrel of a Magic with the power to manipulate air who had slain another Magic and his family by sucking the oxygen from their home as they slept for the purpose of capital gain, an immense bore for Alasdair, mass murder holding no intrigue or challenge.

Alasdair slid aside the dossier to me at his left. "Vincent will try the case."

"Sir," the silver-haired member interjected doing his best not to anger his employer, "Mr. Westmore has requested—"

"Mr. Westmore is lucky this matter is being addressed at all. If Mr. Westmore requires representation, then he will gladly accept Vincent as his counsel and will thank us with every cent he earned while killing the Gullifords."

"Yes, sir." The man nodded and cowered without further objections.

I left the dossier between us. "Father, I have not presented in court in more than three decades." Addressing him as Alasdair caused more problems than were worth, so even though I held no love for the man, "father" is what I stuck with. Favourable to "Master".

"You will take the case and you will prevail. Next?"

A call to move on may have been enough for the other syco-phants, however, I would not have earned my rebellious reputation if I did not make my protestation clear. "Why?"

The attention of the council members and anticipation of retribution hung in silence.

"Because I am leaving you with no other choice."

The leaded tone and locked gaze my father gave me ended my dissent. Nevertheless, my response resulted with little impact beyond informing the others I was not above questioning my position within the fold.

Settling into my high-backed chair, I resumed a dissociative state while Alasdair, again, motioned for the next issue on the docket to be addressed.

I mulled over my father's motives for assigning me the case.

Cora-Lynn. Must be.

The only way Alasdair knew to trap me was to use my dead wife's soul as the end-all bargaining chip. I took it as it was...desperation. Cora-Lynn was claimed by an unjust death centuries ago. I would have given my immortality so that she could live a full life. My father stomped all over that by ending her and knew she was his lone bargaining chip.

A weighted clap on my shoulder shocked me back into notice of my surroundings.

My brother's manicured hand squeezed my shoulder as if to intimidate. "Have fun with Mr. Westmore. You're precisely his type."

Whether Chase was using a sprig of homophobic posturing to unbalance me or meant something in which I would soon learn upon meeting Mr. Westmore, I did not dare guess at, and refused Chase the luxury of engagement.

Briefcase in one hand and the dossier in the other, I headed straight for my father's office, entering without knocking. The overwhelming scent of expensive leather and stale cigar smoke greeted me.

"Is this what your tactics have dwindled to? Dossiers of no-win cases as future excuses to destroy Cora-Lynn's soul when I expectedly fail?"

Alasdair refused to pause his writings, whatever it may be, his gaze cast down at the papers in front of him. "I don't require excuses to end what is of no importance to me. My excuses lay only in reasons of why I should keep her soul alive." Alasdair finished what appeared to be his signature and then looked at me, hands folded. "You will win Mr. Westmore's case because regardless of what Charles or Chester or Chase or whatever your brother is calling himself these days believes, your talent in the courtroom is an artistry that far surpasses most if not all other firm employees including Chase himself and rivals my own. The fact that your woman's soul hangs in the balance may give you incentive if that's what you require, however, my goal is for you to see you are exactly where you are supposed to be. Cora-Lynn's continued survival is your payment for your victory. Though the status of her existence is unimportant to my cause."

Alasdair's courtrooms were exponentially detached from where I belonged. The ability to weasel any rat-bastard out of facing true justice is no talent, only a deviance I inherited. A black scar ingrained on my soul unerasable no matter the amount of healing ability I possessed and beyond the reach of Sophie's Soul Seeing gifts.

"You have Mr. Westmore's case file. Pay strict attention to his recorded statement and find loopholes to construct—"

"I grasp loopholes."

Alasdair shone what passed as a smile. "Yes, you certainly do."

Leaving Alasdair's office before I stated something that would further jeopardize Cora-Lynn's soul, I dwelled on my father's words. Snaking a Sovereignty client's way out of paying for their crimes was the cost of protecting that which could not protect itself. A cost rendered before and one I was willing to pay again even if it haunted me.

4

FANNING THE FLAMES

Sophie

I almost cheered when Arden finished with Nora's computer. It took far too long, and I was sick of pacing around on lookout duty while most spoke in hushed voices without sharing with the group.

Equipped with whatever Arden found, plus the backpacks of supplies and whatever secret thing Ismail nabbed, we made our way out of The Chiff and into the Denali to continue on to our next stop.

Ecstatic to be free of The Chiff, but sure the stank of decaying bodies followed us, I was beyond pissed with all the secrecy.

"'Kay, ass-cheese." I grabbed Lincoln's arm and stepped in front of him. "Whether you like the fact I'm on the Team or not, I refuse to be treated like a snot-nosed cadet ride-along. Since everyone else gets to know super special things including the plan, so do I. So, where the fuck are we going and why?"

Jessabelle was the one who answered. "Safe houses." She earned a sharp glare from Lincoln as she walked up behind us, pokerfaced and continuing on as I followed. "In Long Beach are safe houses where some of The Chiff survivors are hiding. We head there, check in on how they're doing, see what they need, as well as visit some cabin-regulars all in one trip. They're Mother Coven members with far-reaching contacts who we hope will have further information about Loring or any of his people."

Giving her a nod of appreciation, Jessabelle smiled and climbed into the Denali as Lincoln already started the vehicle like he might leave us behind.

I actually knew the location of the safe houses. Not the exact address, but they were down the street from my Uncle Dave's where I shot out the middle of Toonies with small rifles, swam during the summers, and camped in his backyard far too close to a bonfire burning whatever he could rummage up, mostly heavily-used furniture.

Thinking back, I realized I hadn't been in a few years and wondered when I may ever get to go again without risking his life and the lives of anyone with me. He was my mom's brother, but he didn't display a soul glow at the family reunion, so he wasn't tapped for a coven application and wouldn't know about the family's role or the players on any side of this war.

The hour drive was interrupted by a quick gas station fill-up and washroom break as Lincoln called into Ranlyn to update him on where we were on the journey. I got the feeling it wasn't protocol, but in Vincent's absence Ranlyn requested being kept in the loop and Lincoln was obliging. Ranlyn wasn't even on the same plane of existence and knew what was going on before me.

Anger simmered inside of me since I woke up, and nothing I did dialled it down. No deep breathing coping skills, no distraction tactics, I was primed for chaos whether I decided to create it or felt justified in fanning the flames. My insides were a melting pot of anxious paranoia and seething resentment, and I wanted to start moving again.

Back on the road, the anger rode sidecar in case it was needed, though all I had was a snowy scenery to glare at. Lake Erie was beautiful in the summer. Nothing ocean-adjacent, but the cold water was refreshing when the temperatures soared over thirty Celsius with a dash of stifling, breathing-in-water-anyway humidity. The sand may burn your toes and the sun may scorch your shoulders, but the beach always equalled fun.

Passing my Uncle Dave's quaint house, the neighbouring mini-putt and attached stationary fry truck that served the greatest French fries and ice cream closed up for the winter, I found it hard to become excited for the next sun-soaked season. Even if I made it to the beach, those fun times would be spoiled by outings like this.

Since December brought in high, frigid winds, effectively closing the beach, most of the neighbouring cottages stood empty. With no one around to question suspicious activity, the safe house cabins were a luxurious set of six that dotted the lakeside, their road-side access covered in thick coniferous trees disguising anything townies might accidently wander into.

I was always jealous of the people who lived in those cabins, assuming they were deep-pocket vacationers. Guess not.

Some survivors of The Chiff attack still trickled in, presumably too scared by what they might find if they took the chance and sought sanctuary, ultimately left with no choice. The Chiff was supposed to be impenetrable. Most would never trust their safety no matter how hidden they were, but once the Magic community found out about the breach, they sent the word through contacts that they would take in anyone who required refuge.

The Team parked inside the cover of the heavy trees and began at the source of the call to assistance at the owners of the cabins, a brother-sister team, found in the largest cabin second from the right. A monster of a two-storey lake house with a white stucco exterior, floor to ceiling windows everywhere, and screamed professionally designed interior in no way announced, "Magics hiding from evil found inside".

Max and Tamara agreed to speak to any refugees from The Chiff to see about properly burying the dead before the time came when retrieving their family and friends would involve a squeegee and bucket, though they were surprised the place hadn't been looted to the bare shelves by now. A lot of money in goods sat on those shelves.

While Lincoln, Ismail, and Jessabelle went cabin-to-cabin speaking with the survivors and learning all they needed, the others were on guard detail, sweeping around the buildings, checking that the beach was clear of suspicious activity or, I don't know, anything. I wasn't completely sure, so I kept an eye out.

Finding nothing of note, we returned to Max and Tamara's cabin, thanking them for their cooperation.

I was annoyed I still hadn't seen any action. Restlessness crept in and I found myself pacing the windows near the water hoping the enemy would pop up out of the waves and give me a target to focus on. If shit went down, no one could tell me what arsenal I was allowed to use. Gun or powers, it was happening.

The sensation of Donovan watching me jacked-up my restlessness. What does he think I'm going to do? Steal the Denali and go on a rampage? Showing up to the Sorrel Compound and gunning Tobias down wasn't a bad idea. A few others I could think of earned a spot in my crosshairs. Donovan would do well to remind himself that I wasn't his to keep tabs on.

Dealing with Nya caging me like a dog who pissed on her carpets whenever she wanted was enough. Letting him think tagging along on the Team meant something to me was not on my agenda. At this point, he was stalking me. All I needed was for him to back off. Refusing to give in to Bronya as a distraction was his version of proving to me he didn't want anyone else but me. Give it time. He would cave because it's who he was.

Done with the mission, I watched the world go by in the Denali's window and tried to ignore my gut churning. I couldn't stop fidgeting. I couldn't stop the incessant thoughts of time buried within Nya and the blanks in my memory or countless hours spent on the Sorrel cells floor. Donovan being close enough to smell was infuriating.

"Pull over!" I tried to unlock the door and fumbled a couple of times, getting it, but the vehicle was moving too fast to jump out.

"What? Why?" Lincoln called with clear annoyance.

Fuck it.

I pushed on the door and gained a few inches of fresh air as Lincoln skidded to a stop on the gravel shoulder before I hopped out and rushed to puke in the ditch.

The ground went sideways. I put my hands down in time not to face-plant into the gravel, my palms taking the brunt. Closed eyes did nothing to stop the sway of dizziness, though the cold air helped a bit.

Low voices behind me complained or gagged. Blocking them was easy when I threw up again and the buzz of traffic sped by.

Fucking motion sickness. Of all the things to put me down, being in a car did nothing but make me look weak.

Footsteps crunched gravel behind me. I didn't have to see who it was to know who they belonged to.

"Go suck a dirty dick, asshole." Talking was impossible, as was thought projection. The guy was probably spying on my thoughts and would hear it for himself. As if I needed the added embarrassment of Donovan doting on me and making me the weak link on my first mission.

"No one thinks that. It's just motion sickness—"

"Stay out of my head, lice-licker. I don't want your help."

I retched again, all dry heaves. You needed to eat food in order to have something to throw up. No one informed my stomach of this.

"You don't have to wage war to—"

"You don't *have* to keep talking but you keep fucking going." I spat acidic saliva dangling from my lips and braced myself on my knees, gulping oxygen, and fighting to find my equilibrium.

"Dish out whatever you want, I can take it. Just know, now that Nya's gone, your mental walls are flabby."

I glared at him over my shoulder. He stood with his arms crossed, looking down on me from a position he probably enjoyed.

"Hate me all you want, but don't use me as an excuse for your self-destruction. Next time you're strapped down and raped by a small village, some you're genetically related to, so your seed can fill the ranks of your enemies, then you have license to be self-destructive. Me? I'm keepin' my shit tight to watch your ass. Your appreciation is too much to expect right now but I'd think you could relax the cursing of my every breath."

He didn't deserve an answer to a rant meant to force guilt.

"You done chucking?" He held out a bottle of water.

I took a deep breath of winter air, stood, snatched the bottle from him, took a swig, and spit it near his boots before climbing into the car.

"Stubborn, but not broken. I carry the flag and know what it's like." He slipped in, pretending like he wasn't still lecturing me. *"Listen or don't, I can't make you see straight or look at me like I matter more than your new boots. I'm still all-in. Consider me handcuffed to your fate whether you like it or not. You'll get it one day."*

Sending a lick of healing energy through my body and muscling up a mental barrier was exhausting. Keeping the window down a crack to let the cold air wash over me didn't garner any complaints, though I didn't ask.

Riding the elevator through the veil into the Prison Creation, all I wanted was to soak in a burning hot shower.

"Hold up." Lincoln grabbed my arm to stop me as I did with him outside The Chiff. "I need your weapons."

I eyed him like he stole my wallet and pulled out of his hold. "Is everyone else handing theirs in?"

"Yes."

I looked to the others who started divesting their weapons after a second's consideration. By their hesitation and careful positioning, I gathered the distinct impression that handing over their weapons after a mission wasn't protocol.

Fine. It's not like I got to use my gun anyway. I unholstered and handed over the weapon and blade from my belt, then stripped off the tactical vest.

"You want my clothing, too?"

Lincoln huffed with annoyance. "Usually, they're washed so we don't have to smell your stank-ass cooped up on the road."

Right. "Fine."

I whipped my shirt over my head and tossed it at Lincoln, keeping eye contact in challenge, exposing my black bra, and ignoring Donovan's closeness and discomfort at everyone else seeing what he no doubt thought he had a right to be possessive over. Then I let my cargo pants pool at my feet, kicked them up into my hand, and thrust them at Lincoln.

"The boots are mine." Even if they probably smelled the worst from stepping in decaying body soup, no fucking way was I handing them over.

Lincoln could keep what he wanted if it fuelled his big-boss ego.

When cat-calls came from somewhere, I threw out the middle finger on my way to the cell console, and then disappeared into a cell as Lincoln and Donovan were talking too low to overhear. Anyone who hadn't seen me in my near-nakedness would know about it within the next twenty minutes. Not like it mattered. The Team should get a locker room, or the rest should grow the fuck up.

I sat on the edge of the bed, wishing my mouth didn't taste like ass, and feeling the impact of my healing power being cancelled out by the cells. The remnants of my motion sickness crept up, and it felt too much like being in the Sorrel Compound cells again.

I ran to the toilet and heaved some more.

5

BRUTALLY WRETCHED

Sophie

Shaking off the motion sickness took a bit. Pacing the cell, furious at Lincoln and his extra set of Sophie rules. Anger permeated my every breath. It didn't matter that my knees ached with every step and my shoulder muscles tightened so close to my spine it felt like someone was knifing me, I kept pacing to the rhythm of my racing thoughts, getting nowhere.

"Shit! Sorry!"

I spun to see Caine's back, he having turned around and stared at the floor. I realized I was still wearing nothing but underwear and combat boots.

"What are you doing here, Caine?"

"Sorry, I just wanted to talk. I'll go."

"No, wait. Give me a sec." I struggled with jeans I found in a bag I didn't pack and was forced to restart as they wouldn't fit over my boots.

Caine faced away from me as I scrambled to dress. "Nice tattoo by the way."

I yanked at my pantleg, my fingers slipping. "What?"

"The huge back piece. A beetle or something? Wasn't there last I'd seen." 'Last I'd seen you naked' went unsaid.

"Firefly. It's new." Details weren't necessary and I forgot it was there. Finishing pulling my shirt down and smoothing my hair, I left my boots untied. "Okay. Decent."

Caine turned around slowly. "Sorry."

"It's all good." I fiddled with my twisted shirt sleeve.

"Wow. You're that pissed at me."

I glared up at him, confused. "Who said I was pissed at you?" Did Donovan? I would expect that from him.

Caine shrugged. "It's the first time you've acknowledged me or even looked straight at me, and we haven't seen each other in months."

I huffed and rocked on my thick-soled heels, trying to find the words.

"I had to go after Jet. I couldn't leave her."

A cheerless laugh fell from my lips as I shook my head. A sob escaped me. I raced to cover my face and dropped down to sit on the bed behind me.

Caine called my name. I couldn't answer him. I couldn't concentrate on anything more than existing in the same room with him after all this time.

The mattress next to me depressed. The weight of his arm around me and the tight squeeze of my shoulder unravelled me, and I fell into his embrace.

Too much time passed with him rubbing my arm and doing his best to console me while I lost my shit. I don't know how long we sat like that, but I forced myself to pull it together and straightened in my seat before going and snapping off some toilet paper from the roll.

"Vincent coulda sprung for two-ply, the cheap bastard." I wiped my face and nose, getting more to take care of the snot and tears, and keeping Caine from seeing it.

Caine laughed. "One-ply beats dirty leaves any day."

I froze and realized what I said and to whom. Compared to what Caine endured, my complaints were petty.

Trying to finish up quickly, the paper caught and ripped on the ring Aunt Lacey gave me, Nya's ring. The beautiful piece of white gold, teardrop smoky quarts, and diamonds was enough to make my hands tremble.

Caine was at my side. "I guess we don't need these anymore." He lifted his own hand, the matching priceless piece still on his finger before he took it off and held it in his palm. "I can get rid of them."

I grappled with the ring, finally getting it off with a hard tug. He took it and pocketed both. Whatever he did with them didn't matter to me as long as they were gone. Those rings meant more to Aunt Lacey than anyone, and not even she was around to see her mistakes.

Feeling another wave of emotion hit me, I went for more toilet paper and caught the tears I could. A second or two passed before I could face him.

"I know you had to do it." I cleared my throat, my voice strained. "I tried to go after you, but the Creation closed. We didn't know how—"

He tilted his head. "Kim filled me in."

I nodded and ran a hand over my tightly tied ponytail unsure what to say next.

"She also told me about the broken connection with Donovan."

The name caused a sound of disgust to burst forth. "Umbilical cord needed to snap at some point. Slap that ass, this baby is overcooked."

Caine smiled but retained a look of concern. "Can you not feel him at all?"

I shrugged and played with the toilet paper in my fingers.

"It will kill both of you if you don't forgive him."

I dropped my hands and glared at him. "Since when are you on Donovan's side?"

He laughed and sat back on the bed. "No, no, no. Believe me, I still think he's a douche, but if you hating him means Tainting your soul, is it really worth that?"

"That dick-squeeze wanted—"

"Tobias made him see you."

This time I looked straight into his grey eyes, seeing that he believed what he was saying. "What are you talking about?"

He sat forward, elbows to knees. "Kim told me that during the Conception Rituals, both of them, that Tobias tricked Donovan into thinking he was physically with you because his body wouldn't...participate...without a little incentive. Whatever Donovan did or felt as he did it, was only because he thought he was with you."

Donovan's mention of being strapped down and raped fit that theory. I understood what the ritual was about, but I still didn't want to believe it. Plus, how would Kim know when she wasn't there? Is that the story Donovan told her? Because if it was, I didn't believe the lying bastard for a second.

"What else did Kim tell you?"

Reluctance coloured his expression. Whatever he saw in mine, he had to know I wouldn't let up.

Nothing he said came as a surprise and aligned with what Donovan told me when I woke up. Donovan's, Kim's, and now Caine's accounts matched, except for the Conception Rituals. Donovan didn't detail those.

Could Tobias really do that to his son? After knowing the torture he put Donovan through as a child, the man was capable.

Things fell quiet once Caine finished the retelling. Feeling the pressure to engage, I dug for something to say. "Ness seems cool, not that she and I have officially met."

Caine gave a small laugh. "Yeah, she is."

"Is that going somewhere?"

Caine rubbed his hand over his face. "I don't know."

"You don't want it to?"

"It would be nice, I guess."

"Riiight. Make sure to sound so enthusiastic when you talk to her about it. She'll be swooning like a Disney princess on Molly."

Caine laughed again and paused before saying, "I'm sorry for what I said before. You know...before confronting Evar. I meant it when I told you I'd be with you if we found a way around your connection with Donovan, but it was a lot to put on you. I should've kept my mouth shut." I shrugged having nothing to say about it. "With the connection severed now, it would be an opportune moment to step in if I really wanted to. But...." He stopped and exhaled.

"What?"

"You're miserable."

"What are you smoking? Did you miss the sunflowers growing out of my nipples when you barged in here?"

He laughed. "No confession on what I saw and didn't see. What's clear is your misery. You're brutally wretched. Say any different and you're a damn liar. Or delusional."

"Wow. Fucking Christ, Caine."

"I admit I was in denial about you two from the beginning. I was in love with you. I didn't want to think about my life without you. Now, I'm pretty damn sure even without the connection you still would have wanted him, and we would've ended badly."

I levelled my stare at him. "The connection is lost right now, and I'd rather remove my eye with a melon baller then let Donovan touch me. He can five-knuckle shuffle it for the rest of his life for all I care. Go blind while he's at it."

"Only cuz you're pissed right now."

I rolled my eyes.

"You haven't had enough time to wrestle with the fact that Donovan didn't betray you like you thought."

"*Pfft*. That's not it."

"No? Then what is?"

I shrugged. "No clue, but that's not it."

"You're freaking out about something. My guess? This ties to

Brock and you're too scared Donovan will turn into him, or you'll turn into the same person you were with him, so you won't give Donovan a chance."

"Or maybe I just don't wanna knock boots with the guy anymore. Why is that not a possibility?"

"Because you're in love with him."

"Look it, buddy," I splayed my hands in front of me, "this visit has been enlightening and all, I'm ecstatic you're finally free and Andy has his mother, but I'm done talking."

He looked at me a sec. "Really?"

"Really."

"Okay." Caine gave a hollow laugh and stood. "Maybe later."

I nodded as was truly done talking, not saying a word, or trying to stop him when he left the cell.

Whatever Caine's motives were for trying to get Donovan back in my bed, it didn't matter. Donovan knew how it was. He said he was still all-in regardless of my self-destruction. I wasn't destructing, I was trying to keep things together and everyone trying to unpack all of my baggage onto the cement in front of me did nothing but leave me exposed. They didn't come at me with solutions. They came with judgements and a mirror to shove in my face when they were the ones refusing to see things as it was now.

Donovan would get over me, in time, yet would most likely move on quickly to Bronya or anything remotely like her. We went through some shit together and a trauma bond was no reason to stick it out. Donovan and I getting together started a downward spiral I was happy to jump off of. Centuries of this rollercoaster was enough to expect from anyone.

6

FACING UGLINESS

Kim

The sound of disappointment and frustration in Frog's tone as we ended our conversation lingered in my head. I couldn't tell him everything. Simple things, like where I was could pose too much danger for him and translated into us not seeing each other in person for a bit.

He said he felt powerless to do anything about it, and he was. Plus, he wanted to be with me, and didn't understand why he couldn't be since he knew all he did already.

Frog may be a six-foot-five brute, but he didn't know what he was up against and would likely be injured or killed. Saying this was a hit to his ego that ended the conversation on a sour note. Still with wishes of seeing each other soon and worry for my safety, but the sentiments were layered with regret on my end and resentment on his. So much for normal.

A tug on my arm was Caine having come from a cell hoping to speak with Sophie. It took a while and Donovan was waiting, primed to jump into the cell to ensure all they were doing was talking.

Caine waved me aside. "Have you spoken to her?"

"Not as much as you, apparently."

The look in his grey eyes was daunting.

"What?"

Caine side-eyed Donovan across the way speaking with Hall who was trying on some kind of vest too small for his chest. "She's not okay. Not even after I told her Donovan was forced to see her during the rituals. She knows the truth and still hates him."

That's not right. "Maybe her anger is about something else."

"That's the problem. It *is* something else. She knows it is, but doesn't know what."

"Well, she's been awake after Nya possessed her for only a hot minute and has spent most of that time in mission mode. That's not long enough to process anything. She's probably not ready yet. Give it a couple of days. It's Sophie, she'll talk."

"I don't know, Kim. When she and I first met, she was solitary, closed-off. Something tells me this is more than that."

They had a heart-to-heart and Caine knew Sophie in ways I didn't. I was worried, but after what she endured, I'm not sure if we were expecting too much of her.

Olive approached me and Caine. "Sorry for the interruption. Do either of you know where Sophie's disappeared to?"

"Her cell," Caine answered her.

"Do you mind fetching her and meeting us in the large board-room? We're having a Ballard meeting and I need to round up the others."

"Yes. I'll get her." Volunteering gave me the chance—

"Kim." Caine called my name, stopping me after a single step. "Don't push. She all but physically threw me out of her cell. She's not up for it right now."

"What? I'm not going to push."

"Yeah, yeah. Watch yourself. She's not fucking around and is in no mood for it."

No mood? I was in no mood for it either, but Sophie was my best friend. Letting her avoid me was not happening.

When I popped into the cell, Sophie was sitting on the bed with her head in her hands.

"You okay?"

Sophie's attention snapped up, ready to fight.

"Whoa, tiger."

"Jesus, Kim." Sophie popped off the bed. "No, I'm not okay. Without a lock, I'm a zoo exhibit for all to see and expected to pose for a selfie."

"Sorry. Olive's holding a Ballard Coven meeting in the larger boardroom and wanted me to let you know."

Sophie started towards the wall to exit.

I stepped in front of her.

Sophie met my stare and a couple beats passed in silence. When I didn't move, she rested on her heels. "Are you really coming at me like this?"

Damn. That look. I saw it before in others and pushed myself to follow through. "You feel like a rape victim, don't you?" The glare I earned was better than a punch. "I know this is pushing it, but I would understand if that's how you felt, because you are one. What was done to Donovan was also done to you. He was raped. And he is just as much a victim. Only you couldn't see who raped you, only felt it without the ability to fight back or understand what was happening."

Sophie took a couple steps away without wavering from a solid mask I never saw her wear.

"I won't bring it up again unless you want to. You can run missions with the Team and slaughter Tobias with your bare hands, but in the meantime, none of this is Donovan's fault, so why do you still hold it against him?"

"You too? Jesus Christ!"

"I don't care about Donovan. Well, I kind of do. He's like a mole you end up naming, but ultimately would rather not stare at every day. Regardless, you hating him means you lose more of yourself. So, take the time you need to purge the idea of Donovan's betrayal from your head, stop looking at him like that ex of yours, and figure out what you need to do to find the best friend I know."

"My ex? Fucking men. Of course, one of them told you about Brock. Because why not share with the whole fucking Coven, right?" She shook her head as if contemplating murdering someone.

"Whatever about the ex. I'm here for whenever you have to vent, no different than before. The worse this connection tear gets, the harder it will be to empower your Soul Magic back to what it was. Neither of you deserve what losing the Soul Magic will cause. Not even asshole Donovan."

I got the sense Sophie was listening even if she played it off like what I said took a quick slide through one ear and out the other. The words hadn't processed yet, but Sophie heard them. She told me lots of things, but she didn't want anyone talking about this and was scowling at me like the enemy for making her face the ugliness.

I expected Sophie to shut me out. This didn't mean I was giving up; I had to pick my moments.

"I'll show you to the boardroom." I ended the conversation there and left the cell feeling Sophie following, who may have already known where the boardroom was, but it was the exit I was taking.

Walking at a brisk pace, the thump of Sophie's boots behind me was unsettling. Sophie didn't talk, yet didn't rush by me to find the room on her own or to run away from me. I thought about what I said in the cell and crossed my fingers it was enough to break into the rigid cocoon Sophie wrapped herself in.

I stopped at the boardroom. Sophie wasn't paying attention and almost barrelled into me, cursing before taking a step back.

"There you are." Olive's singsong tone rose above the others talking as they waited. I went to leave. "Please, Kim, stay. You might have something to add if I forget."

Sophie didn't indicate if she wanted me hanging around or not.

She didn't look at me at all. I stayed at Olive's insistence and was pretty sure Sophie wanted the opposite.

As everyone settled, Olive and Lewis stood at the front of the group as we remained near the door we came in. I was ready in case Sophie made a run for it.

Olive put a hand to her chest. "We were lucky not to lose anyone in this fight and I'm sorry some of you were involved against your will—"

"Yeah, what the hell was that?" Sophie's Uncle Dwayne stood, angry as always and with his hands on his hips. He may appear to be a gritty cowboy with his wide brim hat and tall boots, but he was a non-joiner. "One second we were in the attic, the next something blows through and recruits us for battle? You tellin' me you had nothin' to do with that?" He shook his pointed finger at Olive.

Olive pursed her lips and glanced at Sophie like she was prompting her to speak up, though Sophie kept her head down like she was attempting to turn invisible.

"Why are you looking at me?"

This dropped Olive's jaw in astonishment of Sophie's tone. I wasn't sure she knew what her uncle was talking about.

"That was Nya," I filled in for her. "With our enemies surrounding the estate, we would have all died without her keeping them at bay. When she couldn't hold them off any longer, she saved us by rushing everyone through the portal to the field."

"I'd be god-damned grateful you're not bull chum." Kassie, Sophie's bitchy cousin and fellow Soul Seer, surprised me by speaking up.

Dwayne's hard edges softened from anger to a simmering suspicion, his eyes swinging to Sophie in what might have been thanks, but he wasn't going to say it.

They hated Nya for what she did to Sophie, but she did also save them.

Whatever Sophie was thinking, she was hiding it behind a stone façade. Shut down or about to break down, one of the two or both would happen any moment.

"Is there anything to return to?" Sophie's cousin Shannon questioned near the left of the room. I watched Sophie for a reaction of potentially losing the Ballard Estate, but her eyes were on the floor again.

"We don't know," Lewis answered. "We have to assume that the estate has fallen or that if it hasn't, our enemies know where it is, making it no longer safe. We may never be able to return."

"But there was so much there," Chelsea spoke up. "Maybe they didn't breach the attic."

"Did you see them?" Ronny was looking at Chelsea like she was literally blind not to. "There's no way it's still standing."

The kid was probably right but his callousness erupted into arguing. Some wanted confirmation of the estate's condition. Others thought they were seven shades of stupid or suicidal for considering it. And others didn't think it mattered if they weren't going back to it.

"I'll find out." Sophie's voice was lost beneath the crowd's arguing.

I heard Sophie speak, but no one was listening to her, and she didn't look like she was up for repeating herself. Twisting her head a bit to the side with her eyes closed spoke of a headache. Something actually normal of the Sophie I knew. Maybe everyone being so loud was overwhelming her? I could yell for everyone to shut the fuck up, but they ignored Lewis's baritone and Olive waving for them to quiet down.

Through it all, Sophie stood, eyes closed, forehead scrunched, before she pressed her fingertips into her closed eyelids. Definitely a headache, or a building one. I wasn't exactly in love with the noise either, but it wasn't my meeting or my coven.

The room dropped into silence.

Everyone stood staring at each other. A few were moving their lips, but I didn't hear them.

Were my ears messed up?

Wait. People were moving around and the sounds of their shoes and creaking of their chairs was normal, their voices were the only thing not working.

Oh shit. This was Sophie.

I shook Sophie's shoulder to get her to open her eyes. When she finally did, she squinted and scowled.

I tried to mouth "What did you do?" but she didn't understand. I pointed to my throat and to everyone else, but charades wasn't her game in the best of moods.

"What are you doing?" Sophie's voice was loud in the room. Others heard her and knew she did something to silence the group since she was the only one with a voice.

She looked around at everyone, the recognition of what was going on crossed her expression. "I...I'll get the Team to check out the estate." With that, she spun on her heel and raced from the boardroom.

I chased after Sophie, she trying to navigate slow-moving people and knocking into most of them.

She reached Hall and Donovan before I could catch up, but I saw her grab Hall's arm and drag him along with her.

They managed two-steps before he planted his feet. "Hold up, tiger. What's going on?"

Sophie and Hall were looking at each other, neither speaking, so I assumed they were communicating telepathically.

"What happened?" Donovan asked me.

For fuck's sake. My voice was still gone.

Sophie and Hall left, making a quick stop at the cell console, and then disappearing into a cell.

"Are you fucking with me, Kim? If you are, know I'm not in the mood to take your shit."

"I don't know!" My voice echoed. "Jesus Murphy." Of course, my voice roars to life when I'm yelling. Now everyone in the lobby was gawking at me.

"Kim, tell me why Sophie just dragged Hall into a cell. I know he's got it bad for you, so it's not what it looks like, but a few blanks filled in would be really fucking nice." The control in Donovan's voice was paper thin.

"All the Ballards were arguing, and I think Sophie got overwhelmed or triggered or whatever, and suddenly none of us could talk. She didn't know what she did, it just happened. Then she promised them she would have the Team look into the estate's condition and took off to get Hall."

"Okay. That's messed up, but Hall isn't the Team Leader. Lincoln is."

"As if Sophie cares about hierarchy. She went to someone she trusts. No offence." Though he definitely appeared a tad hurt by the fact Sophie went to a virtual stranger instead of him.

"And going off books. Shit." Donovan raced for the console. I followed closely, understanding his worry.

We entered the same cell as Sophie and Hall. Hall stopped talking as soon as he saw us.

"You could've come to me," Donovan directed at Sophie.

She just looked at him. Not averting her hard gaze, not speaking at all. This was her unapologetic stubbornness showing she was sticking to her decision and not requiring his opinion on the matter.

"She wants to—"

"I know what she wants," Donovan cut Hall off without looking away from Sophie. "I would've taken you myself. Without informing the others."

No one could read each other's thoughts in the cell, though you didn't need to to know Sophie didn't trust Donovan with much of anything.

Sophie continued to stand and stare at him as if she were cursing his existence as Hall and I glanced at each other, dreaming about being elsewhere.

"I can't stop you from going," Hall interrupted their staring contest. "You've asked me to provide protection and I will, with a few conditions."

Sophie finally concentrated on Hall.

"Donovan's included, non-negotiable. He knows the area as well as the property. Next is a shit-tonne of gear and weapons, plus a promise we operate at night. If you can work along those terms, I'm in."

Hall held out his hand, letting it hang between him and Sophie to give her the opportunity to shake on it. Sophie shook Hall's hand, solidifying the deal without complaining or discussing terms.

"I'll let you know when I can secure the gear and weapons." With everything ironclad, Hall moved towards the exit only to grab my arm and drag me out of the cell with him.

"Why'd you do that?"

"Because you don't want to be in a confined space with those two any longer than necessary. No magic abilities doesn't mean no danger."

"Yeah, okay. They're not going to kill each other."

He tilted his head. "Donovan wouldn't kill her, no. As for Sophie, she would push it as far as her anger would allow her and she's packing a lot of wrath in such a small body."

I didn't want to think of them hurting each other. Sophie hated the thought of abusive relationships. Maybe them doing this mission to check on the estate would help convince Sophie Donovan was on her side.

7

INVOLUNTARY SILENCE

Sophie

When Hall and Kim left the cell, Donovan kept quiet. I didn't move or accommodate him in any fashion.

"Everyone's voices were restored when you came in here," he finally spoke. "The cell's binding cancels your power."

I remained silent.

"So, you're willing to talk to everyone but me?"

No answer.

"I'm the one you're pissed at. Get it over with."

He thought antagonizing me would get him what he wanted. Too bad.

"I didn't want it."

I took a deep breath, not interested in hearing it.

"Tobias forced me to see—"

"I know!" I cut him off from what I'm sure was a long-winded explanation I didn't need to hear again.

He straightened, his brow creased, shaking his head a little. It took longer than normal to find his lips. "You know?"

"Yeah. Caine told me. Then Kim told me. Somehow, you've won them over."

"Won them? Wait a second. You know what Tobias did to me...and you still hate me?" The muscles in his face flexed with his clenching jaw.

This was the perfect moment to break the dam of silence and let the bastard chew his cud, but I couldn't make myself. Every muscle in my body was flexed, prepared for immediate action, and I couldn't force an inch of relaxation in order to get my tongue moving.

I wasn't blind. Devastation shone in his now glassy eyes. Maybe it was anger or sadness. Whatever it was, it tripped him up. I could understand the fact that what happened, happened to him directly and not second-hand like with me, but none of that mattered. If he wanted to pretend what occurred was no big deal and move on with his life as it were nothing but another visit to dear ol' dad's place, that was on him.

"Do you understand that I will have children?" His words brought him a few steps closer to me. My fists fell at my side by some innate reflex. "That I likely fathered bastards from the first time the Conception Rituals were forced on me? Now, I'll father a whole new generation of little fuckers I may one day have to kill when they come after me as my enemy. They might not be told who I am to them or why I'm supposed to die, but they will still be forced to come after me. You have no idea how much it hurts me that you were pulled into this, but I won't let you make this my fault. This isn't another of life's traumas we carry around and joke about through social media memes. This is a dog shit sandwich rotting in the sun that I've been force-fed my whole life!"

By this point, he was yelling pretty damn close to my face, and it took everything in me not to break his nose. Every syllable forced my fingernails to cut into my palms.

At some point I stopped hearing what he was saying, focused on all the rage in his expression. I saw him act like this towards most others but couldn't believe his audacity to direct it towards me considering all I went through because of him.

"Say something!" he demanded from me, he now so close I felt his angered breath on my cheeks.

Talking was a luxury I couldn't activate. Articulating how I felt and why I felt how I did was stuck somewhere inside of the swirling tornado of emotions in me. He didn't get it. I harboured so much I wished I could unload on him, so much I wanted him to hear, but it wasn't accessible right now and him yelling at me was locking it down tighter.

"Fine. I'll be around when you decide to stop acting like a brat."

This was said in a way that meant he wasn't holding his breath. Donovan was pissed and couldn't force me to talk, and he knew it. For some reason, this made my involuntary silence all the much sweeter. If we were outside of the cell, he could read my mind. I wasn't sure how much he already read, hoping for only glimpses, but I still hated thinking he could read me at all. Yet another example of me being too weak when it came to defending myself against him.

I could accidently silence a room of people like a Seedling, but no, protecting my brain was too much. As was stopping Nya from taking over and stopping Tobias from fulfilling his sick breeding projects. I may not be able to control any of that, but I could control how and when I talked about it, if I did at all.

Too much was out of my hands. The loss of control almost crippling as I struggled to regain order over any aspect of my life I could manage.

For now, the Tactical Team solved part of the problem and I knew with Caveman's specialty as a Recondite Magic he would be my best chance at working under the radar. A quick mission required a few people, not the whole Team. Not that I would ever go to Lincoln for a favour. Caveman bringing in Donovan was overkill. Some bullshit 'guy code' he was pulling, like Caveman would be stepping on Donovan's toes without extending the invite. I went to Caveman for a reason and didn't go to Donovan for an equally justifiable reason. If it wasn't such a worthwhile cause, I would have dropped the whole thing, but I wanted to check out the estate's condition.

Hours passed as I waited for nightfall, checking my watch every few minutes as time stood still. I spent the endless minutes staring at the ceiling. The dappled cement a better view than whatever was outside of the cell where I was mauled with unwanted advice and invasive questions about my fucked-up life.

I knew what they all wanted me to do, and I was resolved to do the opposite.

8

DECADENT PLEASURE

Vincent

Out in the darkness is nothing short of invisible prison walls in the form of lush foliage.

I sipped a sixty-five-hundred-dollar glass of stocked Irish whiskey in boredom and submission looking through floor to ceiling windows into that darkness. My father's guards remained under cover yet vigilant to ensure the boss's rebellious son complied with the agreed upon rules in his luxury cage, a portal-ride into the middle of nowhere, when not at the office or the courtroom. Short, guarded excursions to the diner included.

A simmering anger seethed as I sunk into a high-backed chair in front of a crackling fire. I was content with denial instead of the dreadful admission that of my father's accuracy or potential foresight. As Alasdair foresaw, I unearthed a loophole in Mr. Westmore's murder case, relinquishing the Magic of all charges while simultaneously compromising my morals. Was Cora-Lynn's soul worthy of breaking long-standing personal ethics? As selfish as my answer was, no reservations hindered success when answering my conscience with a resounding "Yes".

The affected family of Mr. Westmore's crime would have no memory of the death of their loved one once they died and moved on from this life. A luxury far more than Cora-Lynn was afforded.

Another issue forcing my hand to assist the murderous bastard was having no inkling of where Cora-Lynn's soul was held. In a container? A vial? An empty can of specialty coffee? For obvious reasons, Alasdair never revealed her location. If made common knowledge, this would give the enemies of the Sovereignty information needed to move forward with infiltration strategies.

Unaware of if my father knew of my involvement with the Tactical Team and the cases they took on, underestimating Alasdair's reach would be to my detriment.

With a silent apology and another tip of my glass to the family I ruined, I recalled my conversation with Mr. Westmore to relay the good news regarding the win without ever stepping in a courtroom.

A triumph even for me.

After explaining how the win came about, Mr. Westmore expressed no qualms with the injustice, he giving a smarmy "Excellent" before I hung up in the midst of the man's promises of referrals for other such cases and extending a "special dinner" invitation in appreciation, lending credence to Chase's comment regarding me being Mr. Westmore's type. Last thing I needed was to busy myself with dodging advances of any kind regardless of sexual interest.

I possessed no need for more cases involving others of Mr. Westmore's grade, certainly not today, and retreated to my cage. With how my father spoke, any future cases would mirror the last and leave me draped in the filth of the win.

Sitting within a mansion amongst antique and opulent furnishing with everything one could hope to create in a home, my thoughts moved away from my dirtied soul to thoughts of Sophie.

Her eyes remained closed last I saw her. Alive, or I would have been notified otherwise. With the Sovereignty personnel tailing my every movement and reporting them to Alasdair, high reliance weighed on inside contacts to provide timely information about anything requiring my attention or express knowledge. Someone would have informed me of a death of such importance.

Meetings between myself and these contacts remained sparse as would mean the death of the contact or imprisonment for their treason, while I may incur no true consequence, their unfortunate ends would be my punishment.

The fact Sophie and Donovan were alive in the world without me, their supposed Overseer, was enough to escape from under my father's hold. And yet, I remained, taking chances with lives I had no hope of providing recompense while representing a greater danger to themselves and their families.

I downed the remainder of The Brollach and placed the tumbler on the floor between my feet, staring into flames as they danced. With Mr. Westmore's case a check mark in my father's win column, I needed a plan. Killing Chase or my father would be a decadent pleasure. Collapsing the Sovereignty completely would forever be the prevailing goal and I refused to wait for another decade to pass before creating this opportunity.

9

RECLAMATION OF DOMINANCE

Kim

"No stubborn redheaded beauties allowed." Hall selected, checked, and packed away weapons into their holsters, pockets, and clipped onto his belt as if he geared up for war every day. "While your scowl is fearsome, the plan includes a focused objective of survival. You're a lovely distraction, kitten, but still a distraction. And if you're in need of one, you only need to ask, and we can find a room and dip into my private thoughts again. You can choose the location we visit this time. Remember, I've been almost everywhere."

I glanced out the door at passing Magics to see if anyone heard him. No one reacted like they did, though they couldn't have missed his wolfish grin.

Last thing I needed was people knowing about Hall's gift of bringing you into his headspace and allowing you to fully experience all he has in any location he's been before. With him present. Or that I indulged in the escape too many times since I was accidently pulled into it with Vincent when they were strategically planning to get Sophie and Donovan out of the Sorrel cells.

The details were so real, the ultimate immersive experience no VR set-up could reproduce. After we escaped the battlefield, I needed to getaway and was stuck in the Prison Creation with everyone else. I probably shouldn't have indulged, especially knowing how it reenforced his intrigue, but it was a tad addicting.

Right now, I needed his intentions away from luring me into his private world and into the ultra-real one around us.

"Let's be honest, Viking. You can't stop me from going. I was there the first time Sophie ever saw the estate. I want to be there. And I will be."

He stood close and peered down at me in softened challenge. "The invitation is open-ended and lady's choice. As for this mission, it's just a house, kitten."

I peered around again. He wasn't exactly lowering his voice, but his tone was sultry enough to gain suspicious glares I didn't need rolling around the rumour mill if anyone happened to stop by the office we were in.

"I'm not commenting on anything other than the mission. And, no, The Ballard Estate is not *just* a house. It's an ancestral home. The last time Sophie saw it, it had pretty things like walls and antique furniture and an attic full of irreplaceable magical items and even a torture chamber in the basement. If she shows up and finds a pile of rubble, it may be her Jenga. Sophie's on the brink of a meltdown. I'm going."

He pulled up a leg onto a nearby chair and bent forward—the shift bringing his face far too close to my chest—and tucked his back-up gun into his boot before straightening and peering down at me with those ice-blue eyes for a long, lingering second. "I'm not so out-of-touch with the concept of family as not to understand Sophie's predicament, though I would assume a breakdown of such magnitude would occur over her damaged connection to Donovan and not a stack of stone."

I gasped. "Do *not* call it that in front of her!"

My stern finger in his face made him smile. He closed his lips around my finger, his reflexes quicker than mine.

Taken by surprise, I hesitated before pulling out of his mouth, his lips making a smacking noise as I did.

The tip of his tongue grazed his top lip, his smile returning.

"Are you kidding me?" I held my finger up but away from him, not about to wipe it on my pants. "You're like a starving goat at a petting zoo. You don't get to slobber all over people whenever you want."

"You're not just any people."

"I'm people enough."

His brows cinched. "People enough?"

"Yes." Damn this guy. Amazing what he thinks he can get away with. He must try tactics like that on every woman he thinks he can make bat her eyelashes and unzip her jeans.

"Alright, people enough, you were saying."

A small growl in aggravation caused his smile to grow. I couldn't win. "I was saying..." I paused and exhaled, "...that Sophie wouldn't turn to Donovan for a papercut, let alone a shoulder, and you're useless with anything but a gun or whatever that is." I pointed at the handle of some kind of curved blade sticking out of his tactical vest with my damp finger, settling on drying in on my pants anyway so he would stop looking at it.

"I have other talents, kitten, karambit included." He palmed the weapon and spun it around on one finger and then gripping the black metal in his fist in a practiced way, not even bothering to look away from me as he did.

A flash of him gripping the karambit naked—both of them since I noticed another in his vest—skittered across my brain as the purr in his voice probably intended. I pushed it aside. "Exactly. Which is why you need me."

He leaned in closer, retaining eye contact. "That's not why I need you, love." I narrowed my gaze, and he straightened a bit. "I can definitely bring the hardware if the thrill of danger is your thing."

"*Ugh*! Get your mind off your dick for two seconds and realize I'm going on this mission. You wanna leave me without a weapon, which is why I came to you in the first place, then fine. I can take care of myself."

"Why go in it alone when I'm happy to oblige?"

"Stop that."

He laughed and sheathed the karambit. "Okay fine. We can momentarily forget you crave to delve into my luscious brain and have your way with me. For now."

I narrowed my eyes at him again, shaking my head. I didn't have my way with him in the way it sounded, though he was a tad handsy while I indulged in his brain, and he enjoyed my unapologetic requests of what I wanted to experience and how.

He tucked his thumbs into the arm holes of his vest. "What about Caine? They've communicated at length—"

"Are you trying to make things worse?"

In place of an answer, Viking lifted his hands in surrender and tightened the already tight straps of his tactical vest across his broad chest.

"You're not coming." Donovan came up behind us into the office meeting spot.

I hid a yelp in surprise and hoped he didn't hear anything we said. "Really, asshole?"

"Don't bother," Hall warned Donovan. "Already visited the argument and lost. She's in." He winked at me and passed Donovan a gun with matching ammo.

Donovan shook his head and strapped on a vest and holster Viking also handed him. Whatever training Donovan had with that crazy, Tainted, family of his, it included handling weapons I never pictured him holding let alone doing so with familiarity. Aunt Lacey's Sect was so different. He must have thought we were all children when he first joined. I suppose we were. Some still are.

"I'm in because I said I was in, not because you gave me permission." I felt the need to clarify, even if I wasn't so proficient with weapons. "Sophie may need me—"

"Sophie doesn't want anyone's help. Not yours, not anybody's." Donovan didn't bother to look up at me as he continued to ready himself.

"She talked to Caine." The dig was purposeful, and he stopped and zeroed in on me as it hit home.

Hall redirected. "You know, Lincoln told me they don't normally take member's weapons at the end of a run."

Donovan was holstering some kind of fixed blade of his own. "No shit."

"She's disconnected. Weaponizing her while surrounded by these people in here...." He raised a brow and shook his head. "Find a way to pacify her anger before you're at the end of her Beretta. A rogue mission like this with limited witnesses may not be smart."

"Killing me means killing herself."

"You think she cares about that right now? Death is freedom to some."

Donovan exhaled with concern and flinched at the sound of heavy boots entering the room.

Sophie entered, lack of sleep or stress darkening her blank eyes. Robotic drive landed her here and she was oddly comfortable with the gun Viking passed her, even though I know she hadn't been logging hours at a gun range in her free time.

"We ready?" Sophie addressed only Hall.

He nodded and then hit me with a subtle glance that said, "Told you so," I could only roll my eyes at.

"How are we leaving without people seeing us?" Sophie posed the question, which I was happy for, though I saw it as her preparing to fight her way out if anyone tried to stop her.

"Not an issue," Hall answered.

Donovan finished tightening his boot. "Because...?"

Hall grinned as he pulled his hair back and fastened it. "Because it's not."

No one questioned him again, trusting him completely. When we exited the office into the main room, the guard was asleep, head down on the desk, though his arms hung down at his sides as if he passed out. Any passersby would have thought we were taking off on a mission. As long as no one else on the Team saw us, we were fine.

Hall made a deep chuckle as we left without being stopped.

10

NO MORE, NO LESS

Sophie

Sitting tight for the hour drive to the estate in Dunnville caused anxiousness and a hyper-fixation on wishing Olson the Apporter was in front of me so I could shoot his face in. His travelling ability was his lone redeeming quality and would have come in handy instead enduring this ride. Portals weren't my thing. Ranlyn was good at creating them but letting him in on the plan was not an option. He would stop us and things would get ugly.

Stealing weapons and gear was required in case enemies waited for us, though grand theft auto was essential. Donovan hotwired a car, showing off like it's something to be proud of. How could I have thought that brand of showmanship was sexy?

I guess because he got the car up and running, Donovan appointed himself the driver. I sat in the back of a dark, four-door family car. Thankfully, no car seats to trip us up.

The others chatted about strategy or the Coven and our enemies. Pissing away time instead of sticking on the radio for everyone to ignore.

The car bumped and shuddered, and I realized we were at the Dunnville cemetery on Elegy Road that led to the estate.

Donovan pulled the car behind some trees. "We walk from here."

Hmm. Not a question, a directive as if this was his mission.

Donovan glared at me in the rear-view mirror. "If we drive right up to the estate and they're waiting for us—"

"No fucking kidding!" He must have read my mind. My stupid mental walls betrayed me again.

A low growl escaped him as Donovan popped open the door and jumped out of the car after me, everyone behind me in a few steps. I wasn't waiting for them.

I slipped along the tree line, creeping closer, scanning for potential enemies. When I didn't see any soul glows, I stepped more into the open road. I heard my name from behind me on the edge of a whisper and then again telepathically, both attempts ignored.

Relief soared through me. The estate was still standing. A small light illuminated the front seating area and lighting the porch through the window. Lights in high, round, attic windows shone as well. I needed to see inside. I needed to know my family's sanctuary was still intact.

Last I saw this place was through the tunnelled vision Nya afforded me as she held off the Tainted at the property's boundary wards, locking Donovan inside and away from interference.

I sprinted a few yards up the steps and grabbed the front door handle. My hand ghosted through it, the cold bronze causing no physical sensation.

What the fizz?

Stunned by confusion, I left my hand partway through the door, wondering why I wasn't allowed inside. Did the estate still think I was Nya? The aunts did state the house bore a consciousness all its own, maybe this was it protecting itself from whomever it thought I was?

The door disappeared. A pile of rubble towered over my head and stretched out for what seemed like a football field.

No. No, this had to be a trick.

I stepped away from a heap of charred, melted, and smoking wood, bricks, and once-upon-a-time furniture. Most of it was unrecognizable, yet the sink from the attic bathroom was cracked into chunks and resting on more rubble, its twisted plumbing sticking out of it with chicken wire and plaster from inside the walls.

Someone was hiding the damage. Not Olive, she didn't know its condition.

A bloom of crippling hopelessness grew in my chest and tightened the muscles until I wanted to crawl into myself and burrow beneath the debris. Not mine. The estate's. It brought with it stinging tears and a choking sob.

While surveying the wreckage, I stepped over the usual threshold of the estate and stumbled on whatever consciousness lived here. What was normally an excited greeting was now undiluted despair. I never knew what lived within the estate that made Olive and me feel this way or how it could be conscious enough to choose the Ballard Estate's heirs over the years, but it was more real than any other's emotions I ever felt, more than Donovan's, more than Nya's, and the estate was shattered by its destruction and left among its historical rubble to grieve alone.

A flash of light and the chaos of rushing Tainted power levelled a legacy.

I *will* find a way to fix this.

A hard hit from behind snapped my neck back. I flew into the heap of debris, and it dug into my flesh.

I flipped over, ready to attack. Donovan grabbed my hands before I hit him. A vision side-swiped his defence. He gasped and closed his eyes against whatever he saw.

"Off me, asshole!" I shoved him away as the despair from the estate consciousness bled away from my chest.

Shouting on the lawn overshadowed the sound of Donovan scrambling to gain his footing in the wreckage. Someone was fighting.

I shifted to my stomach and peered over some shapeless piece of wood and saw Caveman and Kim in the midst of a fight. A Magic against Caveman went down hard, dispatched with a shot of energy and a swipe with a knife. The bloody spray in the moonlight shone black and dappled Caveman's cruel smirk. Kim faced another, using a defensive push-back ability of her own without the brutality of the man at her side.

Donovan prattled off a plan I wasn't listening to, a plan no doubt forcing me to remain behind while he plays the hero so he could use it to manipulate me later.

With rage in my veins, I surged to race off into the fray.

Donovan forced me down. I spun to grab his hand and torqued it into a painful angle, shoving him onto the wreckage, and climbing on top of him with my forearm pressing into his windpipe.

"Sorry, Donny-boy. I'll fight my own battles." Using his father's nickname for him was an extra dig.

I wretched the twisted hand still in my grasp beyond its natural limit until his wrist snapped, his lips opening in a silent scream.

Up and off of him in a swift movement and on my way to find a target, I added a mental, *"Stay the fuck outta my way,"* as not to leave any room for misinterpretation.

He could heal in seconds. Any inconvenience was my own.

I pulled my knife, locked onto a target, and pounced on the first Magic I reached. A battle cry flowed with the arc of my arm as I grappled them and I plunged my knife into their shoulder and held on, his roar in pain echoing.

A twist of blade and the target belted another cry as they fell to their knees. I wrenched my blade from their flesh in a splay of blood reminiscent of the Caveman's attack. Before the body fell, it disintegrated into a heap of ash and sprinkled the snow in dust, my innate power switching on as easily as a microwave and acting as an incinerator.

I sought out my next target and saw Caveman trading blows with another Magic, the smile on his face ghastly yet free. Kim fought with a mix of shields and attacks, holding her own, though Donovan was still behind at the wreckage staring at me with shock widening his eyes.

Another ten or so Magics came at us from the treeline and parking lot where the dropped illusion revealed bombed out cars, one shell looking too much like my Barracuda.

Another piss off amping up my rage.

A woman rushed me, teeth gritted into a snarl, arm outstretched with building magic.

I unholstered my Beretta and squeezed the trigger. The gun kicked in my palm. A vibration rang up my arm as the shot was a punch to the eardrums. The woman's momentum flew her to the ground at my feet as she grabbed her gut where my bullet landed.

I spun with an elbow up at a sudden presence behind me, crashing into their face. Donovan grabbed for his nose and fought to remain upright, a knee hitting the ground, blood dappling the snow.

"I told you to back the fuck off." Why he was coming up behind me at all earned him a broken nose. The fucking nerve of the guy.

Soul glows raced from the same spot in the trees as the woman had. I aimed and pulled the trigger a few more times, keeping them at bay, and retaining my hold on my weapon. When they toyed with coming for me anyway, I grabbed the writhing woman on the ground and pulled her to her feet, using her like a shield.

A lick of power helped me hold the woman upright and fight gravity. "Cut the shit or she dies like the guy soaking up the snow! I might even heal her if this ends right." Then I said for the woman now groaning in pain, "Guess we'll see how much loyalty they have for you."

A Magic stepped forward with his hands up in surrender, the bearded man looking worn yet familiar.

"Miklos. Are these others from Rosemary's crew, the half of the Coven that hates us, or did you scrounge up your own band of rebels? Can never tell what side you're on."

He lowered his hands but kept them visible. "I've always been on the side of good and wager my soul is left unTainted. Surely, your power can attest to that."

"Try again. For all I know, the brightness of your soul is blinding me from your Taint and you've cleansed the others with a layer of goodness to hide behind." I tightened my grip on the woman. "Regardless, you betrayed your Coven, tried to off me multiple times, fought against co-Elders, and set up shop with Tainted who interrogated not only us but hurt a little kid and a defenceless dog, and likely had something to do with The Chiff infiltration. So, as far as I'm concerned, you can go fuck yourself."

I lifted the gun to the woman's head, her mewling and Donovan calling my name from behind me went ignored as I focused on Miklos.

The ex-Elder lunged forward. "No. Please."

I held the woman tighter until he settled. I wasn't going to pull the trigger, but he was convinced I would, which was what I wanted. The fact he was more worried about a bullet instead of my disintegration power was stupid on his part, but I wasn't in the position to play around. Bullet or power didn't matter to me.

"Sophie, please. Re-uniting the Mother Coven will require a miracle. If they see that you and I can settle our differences, then we may have a chance with the others."

"You tried to kill me. How exactly do you make up for that 'difference'?"

He shook his head. "The Apish Coffer misled me. It bound me to a promise to do everything in my power to keep the Creation from destruction. With the premonition calling for you and your mate to do the opposite, I knew your deaths would keep such a promise. Now, I am all too aware that this tactic was nothing more than the coffer's desire of self-preservation."

"And Hinapouri came along for kicks?"

"No. Hinapouri would use any occasion to fuel a war. Yet, she too believed as I did and acted with ruthlessness to obtain what was needed to ensure success."

I pointed the gun at Miklos and pulled the trigger, shooting him in the thigh.

Kim shrieked, as did the woman in my arms. Other voices rose as Miklos fell to his knees.

"No!" Miklos raised his hand to order his people against retaliation.

For an immortal like Miklos, a bullet wound was an inconvenience and far less than deserved.

"Read me." Miklos panted and fought to stand, managing one knee up, and leaning into it. "Read me and see the truth."

Pausing while deciding, I let go of the woman and pushed her towards her comrades. One of them could probably heal her so I didn't waste time doing so myself.

"Stay on your knees."

Miklos nodded, gripping his bleeding thigh. I searched to Caveman to gage his readiness to handle the others if they charged while I was mid-reading.

"Oh, now you need our help?" The Caveman's quip went ignored as he moved closer to Miklos's people.

Donovan followed Caveman, wiping lingering blood still trickling down his face, giving Caveman a nod as an answer to a telepathic question. Caveman looked at Kim. Another telepathic conversation must have passed before she rolled her eyes and followed along, landing a concerning glance on me.

The three of them stood behind Miklos between him and his comrades, Donovan erecting a shield they could still see us through.

Miklos scanned the shield, lifted a hand again to his people, and turned back to me. "You're not who you used to be."

"I'm more myself than the last time we spoke." Faint memories of him and Nya conversing lingered. I couldn't decern what exactly they did beyond talk of infiltrating the Creation with Tobias at their side, but he understood and nodded as if afraid of what that meant for him right now.

Still not trusting Miklos, I took a pair of zip ties from my vest and moved to bind Miklos's hands.

"Ensure the backs of his hands are touching and tie above the wrist behind him. Do the same to his ankles. I'll do a quick binding." The helpful remark came from Caveman. I didn't face him as he remained focused on the enemy.

I didn't see Caveman do the binding or witness a change in Miklos so I had to trust he could pull it off without interacting with the guy. The one he did on Olson during our Sorrel Compound escape didn't hold, so it may mean nothing.

Unbuttoning Miklos's wool coat and then pulling open his tie and doing the same with his dress shirt, I wished I could have read his soul by touching his face, but I was unconfident in how it would work now without Nya's power on board. A false start would signal Miklos of weakness and possible attack. I didn't need that.

Looking to his chest, the hair there wasn't much thinner than his dark beard and in order to read him I had to sift my fingers through it to hit skin. Thankfully, he was tall. Since he was on his knees, I didn't have to bend much to make contact.

Keeping my eyes open, I plunged into Miklos's soul. He grunted with the invasion.

Knowing how Nya used her power, as I felt it when she did, left an imprint on me. I thought without her power I was weakened. If anything, I was knowledgeable of Nya's centuries of experience and could now stretch my powers to fill out the empty spaces, leaving me with a newfound arsenal without the arduous learning curve.

Perfect.

Inside of the Hungarian's soul, I skimmed to the Apish Coffers, gaging this by conversations since I was unconscious at the time. I ignored Miklos's grunts and anguished protests, focusing on following him through opening the coffers with his group. After dispatching a few Magics guarding a coffer, one of Hinapouri's tribesman in Miklos's group lost their sense of touch.

The next coffer asked for something specific from Miklos. When the coffer was dug up from the ground, I confirmed that this little box of horrors forced his bonded promise to keep the Creation intact at all costs or Miklos would perish along with it.

I was privy to his inner monologue recounting the premonition I didn't even know existed at the time and the process of him being at odds with betraying his Coven, a Coven he pledged his devotion to for the better part of a Millennia. He made the mistake of conferring with Hinapouri, and I watched as the now dead Maori Warrior's grin twisted and she took advantage, volunteering to uphold his promise alongside him. He tried to consider alternatives before following through with the promise, using Hinapouri as a soundboard, asking if the promise would still count if the Creation and Apish Coffers were rendered useless. She insisted they couldn't afford that chance and must stop anyone attempting to do otherwise.

Zipping ahead with more ease than with past soul readings, I found his memories that brought us to my current reading. Miklos and his people arrived at the estate thinking my family and I would return at some point, and he planned to negotiate a Coven reunion when we did. When he arrived, the estate was a pile of sticks and stones. One Magic in his group knew an illusion spell that would solve that problem as long as one of them saw the estate fully intact before. Miklos offered his memory to be used as the construction of the image that gave me false hope my family's history survived.

I continued to read on until I saw myself waltz up to the door and freeze as the con dropped and displayed the devastating scene. "Jason" went to move forward. Caveman spotted him and magic went flying from both sides.

I watched as I sprang from the wreckage of the estate and sliced "Eddie" down in a spray of blood before he erupted in a shower of ash and heard it as Miklos realized he was not looking at the same Seedling he met months prior. This war had changed her.

The replay of the kill cast me out of Miklos so quickly the air in Miklos's lungs broke free and he fell forward into the snow in a garbled complaint with his hands still tied behind his back. I saw the blood on my hands and arms as it glinted in the moonlight against my black gear.

When I had sunk my blade into the shoulder of "Eddie", the gush of blood meant I hit an artery. If I knew more about anatomy, I could have pinpointed which and claimed the bullseye was intentional. In actuality, my brain told me that spot was critical to incapacitating prey and would grant me time to work other magic and break him down to ash. No way did I think that process would be a blink before it was all over.

Miklos was right. I wasn't the same person.

I took out my knife still layered in Eddie's blood and the others as well as Miklos tensed as if I was going to kill him while he lay immobile. I sliced through the zip ties, releasing Miklos's hands and feet. He took a second to register his freedom before standing.

"You're a moron." Miklos's eyes narrowed as I called him out. "Being an Elder should come with a test. With the Creation destroyed, the Apish Coffer would be destroyed along with it, cancelling your consequence. Though you were telling the truth. You didn't destroy my family's estate or you'd already be dead."

He didn't have anything to say to this.

"Once you stole the discus, didn't it seem odd that Hinapouri handed it over to Tobias who also wanted the Creation opened, meaning your own supposed allies could still destroy you?"

He stood slowly and straightened, healing his leg wound, swiping snow off of his coat, and doing up his shirt against the cold. "By then, the situation grew beyond my reach."

Sure. That could happen. All to save his skin. Miklos's self-preservation would be his ultimate drive and his downfall. I would remember that.

"Drop the shield," I told Donovan. "He's good."

The shield fell and those from Miklos group came forward, but not right to us.

"You'll have to search for your weapons. I don't play fetch." Apparently, Caveman either tossed or ordered them to throw their

Blind weapons into the trees. Magic could do worse but may as well remove all the ordnances you could.

Two in the group went off to find them, and I patted myself on the back for bringing Hall.

The mention of fetch reminded me of Bosco. I hadn't seen him since I woke up, though Donovan said he was safe with my mom. I wondered if he would see me as a different person like Miklos did.

"I need a meeting with the other Elders. We have much to discuss." Miklos's demand was expected but that's not what we were here for, nor did he know we were hiding inside another Creation.

"There's only two Elders right now," I informed him.

Caveman explained where Vincent was and why.

"Hmm. I have my own contacts within the Sovereignty. I can contact them if you need, however, I would still request that I see Ranlyn and Veata in the interim."

I holstered my knife. "We're not the Elders' messengers. And we sure as hell don't speak for them."

"We'll put forth the request." Hall was far nicer than he needed to be. "We own no responsibility for the outcome."

With that being the best he could presently hope for, Miklos handed over a piece of paper with a secure contact number on it for us to use when a reply was given. "I also have ears for whispers of Loring or his future plans."

The name filled me with an anxious need to palm my Beretta again. "It's safe to assume he spent his stint in the Creation doing more than pumping iron and cozying up to his cellmate. He'll have a plan."

"The guy has nothing to lose," Kim added. "Guaranteed his plan includes a body count, starting with anyone responsible for slaying his Master." Everyone agreed, knowing we were all on that list with stars of priority scratched in red next to our names.

Before we left, Miklos promised to do a spell on the rubble of the estate to keep it from further weathering and so my family or I could return to sift through the remnants for salvageable items. I appreciated the gesture, but he was overdoing it. His eagerness to prove he wasn't the bad guy was already annoying.

We parted ways while he began the spell.

On our return trip to the prison, the car was completely quiet. Caveman took the driver's seat and I waited until Donovan chose his seat then climbed into the back with Kim.

She broke the silence. "What did you see while you read Miklos?"

I shrugged. "He was telling the truth. After the coffer made him promise to keep the Creation standing at all costs, things snowballed."

"I still don't trust him," Caveman interjected.

"Neither do I," I assured him. "This all happened because he's too attached to his immortality. His intentions appear genuine, but I know what I read. Whatever he has to talk to the Elders about it's probably some assholeian favour of self-interest. I didn't read everything, like what his role was during infiltrating The Chiff, but Miklos's in it for himself and probably did whatever Hinapouri told him to. Let the Elders sort it out."

Silence thickened quickly.

"Are we going to talk about how you took that guy down?" Caveman glanced at me in the rear-view mirror.

I didn't answer.

"Props to you for the kill. Swift, crippling, executed perfectly, but if what you're saying is true and Miklos was innocent, then you just killed an ally, not an enemy."

I remained silent.

"That strike a chord with you at all?"

I met his ice blue stare. "I wouldn't think I'd have to explain the concept of casualties of war to you, Caveman."

"I'm intimately familiar with the term, but judging by how these two freaked, they've never seen you do that before."

"Oh, we have," Kim said, "just not that quickly. That dude's body broke down like a dry sandcastle. Usually it crawls."

I shrugged.

Donovan gave a hollow laugh and shook his head. He didn't turn to the back seat.

"Fuck you." His little laugh irritated me.

This time he did turn but didn't say anything.

Everyone decided conversation wasn't so important after that.

———

Pit stops at our homes was encouraged since we were already on the road. Mine and Kim's apartment building was still standing.

The comforting relief I waited for as I stepped into my apartment left me empty when it didn't rush forward and embrace me with familiarity like the estate did. Every room felt foreign and vacant like someone pulled a midnight move and left all their belongings behind. Ones that just happened to be mine.

The feeling was unsettling. I couldn't pinpoint why I felt the way I did. Every time I expected to feel a certain way and didn't, I was forced to reorient myself, not knowing what to expect the next time someone pushed me to react.

Grabbing a bag for extra underwear and clothing, I saw a Post-it Note on my dresser. Caine wrote on the little yellow paper that he would walk Bosco in the morning for me after the first night he spent on my couch. That was a big deal back then and I remembered feeling sentimental enough to keep it. What saved me from chucking it was something I couldn't connect to anymore, couldn't understand or rummage up even if I wanted to.

"Please let me help you."

I spun to find Kim in my room. The bedroom door closed behind her.

"I already know what's wrong with me." This wasn't true and maybe she knew it.

"That's scarier than if you didn't. You brutally killed an innocent person and act as if it doesn't affect you, which I know can't be true. I get you need control of the things you can right now, but this is a whole other level of self-destruction, and you know what it'll do to your soul."

"I feel different," I finally said. Kim kept quiet until I was ready to fill the silence. "I know what happened wasn't Donovan's fault." I put the Post-it Note on the dresser, now keeping it for a different reason. "It doesn't matter. I can't look at him and not want to smack him around or worse. No one forced me into this life, so you can stop feeling guilty." Kim tried to interrupt. I pushed on. "I chose this, so I'm dealing with it. Now isn't the time to self-reflect. It's time to gather the Elders and plan to reunite the Coven, if that's even possible, plus take down the Sovereignty and get Vincent back so the prison can be used how it's supposed to be instead of a hotel. Loring's also out there doing damage no matter where he is whether or not it's filtered down to us yet. Let's leave the head-shrinking for when I can handle it."

Kim nodded. "Can you do me a favour in the meantime? Please talk to someone, even if it's Caine, even if it's screaming at Donovan. You're holding too much in. You know what it looks like when someone's on the verge of a breakdown and you've been wearing that mask since you woke up."

"Can you honestly say none of this has fucked with your head? Because if it hasn't then you're worse off than me."

"Oh, it has. But I'm not the one going all scorched earth." She tried for a laugh that didn't sound right. "I also wasn't the one in the Sorrel cells." I marched off towards Kim, going around her, and into the hallway. "Nor was I taken over by some ancient—"

"Walking away means you've pushed too far, after you said you wouldn't. You do shit like that all of the time, which only makes your word untrustworthy. Now, since I generally like you, maybe shut your trap before that changes."

Caveman and Donovan stared at us from the tiny entrance of my apartment, the men squeezed in shoulder-to-shoulder, yet more uncomfortable at overhearing me and Kim's conversation. I shooed them all outside into the hall so I could lock up, though why I bothered was more of a habit than a move to protect anything inside. A part of me wished I did pocket the Post-it Note, if only to connect to something from that time and re-establish a baseline for how fucked things had become.

When we returned to the Prison Creation many were awake and pissed off after finding the sleeping guard. Edson and Ranlyn approached us, yelling. As did Lincoln since the guns and gear were taken from wherever he stored them. Likely another cell, which were open anyway.

I didn't stop to defend the choice in leaving for the estate. Caveman drugged the guard and stole the gear from Lincoln's armory stash. I didn't tell him to go about it that way.

"If you could stop bitching for a sec," I raised my voice above the others, "then you could join the rest of the Team and the Elders and find out what happened with Miklos while we were gone."

"Miklos?" Ranlyn said the name with surprise and confusion.

"Yeah, Miklos. Dark hair, bird's nest of a beard, Hungarian accent...How many Miklos's do you know, Jeeves?"

"Quit with the attitude, Sophie." Most of the time Ranlyn doesn't pull that with me. His patience was low today.

Rounded up and curious, the four of us stood in the boardroom recounting the conversation and reading with Miklos to Ranlyn and Veata.

After what Miklos claimed had sunk in, Ranlyn's hesitant gaze shifted to mine. "Can you always trust what you read?"

"Believe me, I wish I read something that meant I could dust him on the spot." I motioned at Caveman, Kim, and Donovan. "These guys are spoilsports, gettin' all uppity about killing innocents. I see what's happened whether or not the subject wants me to. No more, no less."

Ranlyn looked to the others in confusion of my explanation but didn't ask questions.

"Show up to the meeting," I said to distract him.

, Veata's clouded eyes turned to me. "You are not an Elder."

"No kidding, chicky-poo. Though I could've probably done better than Miklos since he started this bullshit."

"Another reason against reconciliation."

"That's not a reason, Ranlyn, it's an excuse. Miklos doesn't have to return as an Elder. If anything, this is a prime opportunity to suss out information you can't gather with your asses hiding in a Creation like Evar and his sick pals. One of which who is gallivanting around the world and simmering on how to best fillet our bodies for dinner. You have the upper hand here. Select the location, the terms, the players, everything. Don't make promises. Pick their brains and leave 'em hanging. Plus, reach your contacts in the Sovereignty so you can bring Vincent in on this, too. You know he'd want to be there and may be able to offer info with his insider access. And you," I turned to Donovan, "need to contact your mother in case she has other info about Loring or anyone who might be able to find him."

I ignored his surprised reaction at me addressing him. "You know I have no idea how to do that."

"You're so fucking smart, you'll figure it out." With all the coven contacts and spells available to find the woman, he wasn't trying hard enough, and I couldn't tolerate his laziness.

11

GOOD FORTUNE

Donovan

I watched as Sophie left the boardroom having said all she needed with no room for backtalk. For someone with no specialized training who knew nothing about this world, Sophie sure knew how to light a fire under the Elders' asses. Once she left, they were going to do pretty well what she said and worked on getting in touch with Vincent and finding a contact for Rosemary.

Leaving the Elders to do their jobs, I headed to a cell and opened a bottle of Jack I snagged from my place. The big house felt painfully empty. The last time I was in it, Sophie and I were on the same team. The bed was still unmade. So was Andy's. We had woken up from the nightmare that was Hinapouri and Miklos, plus a few other Tainted, interrogating and torturing, then stole the discus in order to control when to open the Creation. If I returned to my home, it would be me alone in a big empty mansion. No one else would be there, not even Bosco, unless it was for a Coven meeting and Sophie might not even show up.

I sat on the too-hard mattress and took the first swig, turning it into more of a guzzle, and followed it up with a second. Getting comfortable wasn't an option, neither was trying to forget the sight of Sophie killing like a sociopath and what led to her getting like that.

No matter what Hall tried to drill into me, my guilt over everything happening to her wouldn't disappear with justifications of "external factors beyond your control".

Pfft. Good try.

No matter how many years the big guy lived through, nothing he said could dissolve the rank accountability I felt.

When Kim brought Sophie to that first Coven meeting, Sophie was a wholly different person. Even through the split with Caine and us shacking up, she was still herself. Now, she was so far off from the person I knew, it scared me to venture months in the future and think of who she would be then.

Legitimate fear stopped me from too many things, too scared to make a wrong move and send her further over the edge.

She dusted a man, shot a woman to use as a bargaining chip, not to mention broke my arm and my face without a hint of pause or remorse. Phantom pain from the breaks had me taking another swig.

What was even scarier was what I would become to save her from herself, and she spent her days cursing my existence.

Back in The Chiff, Bronya shot her shot with me again and, when turned down, pointed out I wasn't on Sophie's mind at all and was wasting my time trying. Taking the high road where my footprints didn't previously exist, I walked away, but it needled me. Invasion of privacy was not my thing, it used against me too often, but I couldn't help seeking thoughts of myself in Sophie's mind. It took a grey matter archeologist to find any sliver of me, but I was there beneath the tornado of crazed inner dialogue and countless layers of worries and thoughts of family—missing the holidays and the future of the Ballard Family Estate, friends and Coveners including Kim and Hall's closeness, and Gregor's quick weapons lesson. Every thought of me was slight and negative tangents of not wanting to think of me. She buried me, and I couldn't think of anyone else but her.

A few more tips of the bottle and the warmth of J.D. heated me up right down to my toes, settling in my bones and loosening my muscles. I slid down the wall, repositioning the pillow behind my head as the weight of the drink settled in and threatened to pull me away from coherent thoughts.

After a few more gulps, the walls began to waver, so I closed my eyes, thinking over and over about how I had lost her.

A shove at my shoulder shocked me awake. Fox stood over me. "The sauce hit you hard I see."

He pushed my feet to the side and sat on the edge of the bed managing a grin though the guy looked like shit.

I moaned, rubbed my head, and sat up, wishing healing power worked in the cells. The bottle fell at my side. I rushed to right it. Nothing spilled.

"Sophie getting to you?"

"No." My voice was rough from the booze and head aching. "The non-Sophie replacement is getting to me. It's worse than Nya taking over. At least then I knew it wasn't her."

Fox nodded.

I focused on him when he didn't have a snappy reply. "What's going on?"

He shifted and pushed up the right folded cuff of his plaid shirt to his elbow. "I'm not getting better, kid."

"Okay. Your healing powers are better than mine. I don't think I can—"

"Nah, you can't help me. Not why I'm here."

The look on the guy's face was enough to set my heartbeat to stutter. "Why *are* you here?"

Taking in a deep breath that expanded his chest and gut, Fox braced his hand on his knee as if it were keeping himself upright. "I'm gonna stay with a friend. Another Druid. He might be able help."

I didn't want to ask but the question tumbled out. "What if he can't?"

"Then it's curtain-time for me, kid."

My gut yo-yoed as things came together in my head. "You're sick because I made you fight. You said you couldn't handle it and I still talked you into—"

"Stop. Don't worry, Van." Fox placed a hand on my shoulder and squeezed like he didn't have the energy to come after me if I bolted. "I knew what I was getting myself into and harbour no regrets or resentments. Don't you dare be thinking you have enough influence over me to make me do something I don't want to or let this be another reason you snuggle a bottle until you pass out, 'kay? What happened needed to happen."

I felt as hollow as a jack-o-lantern. Fox was the first person to protect me, the first one to force me to sit still for more than a day, gave me a job, a bed, and some money to get by. Now, because I was selfish enough to—

"Fuck, man." I pushed my back against the wall at the head of the bed, knees pulled up, elbows resting on them as my fingers turned to fists pulling at my hair. If I didn't puke or pass out, then I wanted to punch the piss out of someone.

Perfect night for a bar brawl.

"Don't do anything stupid, Van."

Fox said this as if he could read my mind. He's seen me like this a few times so he didn't need to slip into my head to see what would come next if he died.

"I know this is heavy, but I swear, if you get reckless or off yourself, I'll find you in the afterlife and administer more punishment than Tobias could cook up. We clear?" I couldn't even look at him. "Besides, I'm not dead yet. It could be a simple power drain—"

I surged forward and wrapped my arms around Fox's thick neck until my shoulders ached. The guy reciprocated, holding tightly as I fought to keep my shit from exploding into tears.

After a minute or two, he patted my back. "Focus on your girl."

"Sure." I pulled away. "Right now, Sophie's not mine. I think it'd be easier to heal you with the power of my good fortune."

Fox chuckled. "She's always been yours. And you hers. The girl is messed up. You've been there, I've seen it. Keep Sophie from killing herself or anyone important, and she'll realize you were there even when she did her damndest to drive you away."

I sniffed the snot threatening to escape and cleared my throat. "This is Soul Magic, Fox. Broken Soul Magic. You know what that means."

He gave a tight-lipped nod. "Yes, I do. It means you have a connection deeper than anything I'll ever experience. That'll count for something when she's ready. Do your best not to be her enemy between now and then and remember she's working against what the Soul Magic is doing to her. This isn't her fault either."

"I'm in this, too, but I don't feel things the way she does. Shouldn't it be equal if it's the Soul Magic?"

He shook his head. "Not the way it works. She severed the connection. Soul Magic's unforgiving. Conceivably you could be like this the rest of your lives, except chances are more likely that tear will only expand. It poisons her which in turn poisons the relationship as it changes her into someone you barely recognize and forces you to turn your back on her. I've seen you hold a grudge against someone for stepping on your boot." I laughed and Fox smiled. "Apply some of that stubbornness with her."

"Yeah." Things quieted a moment. "This is why you can't die. Not even Aunt Lacey's around to keep me straight."

"Nah, you don't need us now. You've heard every lecture I can give and whatever I missed Lacey covered the rest. Just don't fall into old habits. The bottle's step one. You hit a club and Sophie's good as gone. You know that."

"Yeah, I do," I muttered.

"And don't be hittin' the club trying to evoke a reaction from her either. That'll backfire far worse, and she'll still be good as gone."

"I got it. No clubs."

"Good." Fox grinned, satisfied with himself. "Look, Van, I gotta hit the road. I'll keep in touch if I can, but don't expect anything for the next couple of days."

We stood and embraced again, this time without as much reservation in case it was our last.

"Promise me you'll find a way to call me if you know you won't get better. Please."

"Will do, kid." He slapped my shoulder, gave a tight smile, mashed up my already messed hair, and left the cell.

Left standing alone, I was surprised I was upright at all considering I couldn't feel my legs. Nobody makes Fox do anything, but he wouldn't have volunteered to fight in the field if I hadn't pressured him. And now the only person I considered a father might die because of my selfishness.

I rushed to the seatless toilet and retched until I had nothing left.

12

DIRECT RECALL

Sophie

Since Donovan and Kim's Sect were meeting, I guess I was supposed to show face. We filled the chairs of the large boardroom as Donovan stood with the familiar green and clammy gloss of a hangover, and let Kim take the lead—typical of him to flee from responsibility—as she recounted information we learned from seeing Miklos in the middle of last night.

"Fixing this clusterfuck is great and all, but when can we return to real life?" Denise's old BFF Jamie melted back into her attitude that Denise partially shed when she hooked-up with my brother. "Or at least let people know we're not dead? They're gonna start calling the police if they haven't already."

This was a popular question. Most prayed Kim would give permission to leave since the elevator guards were ultra-vigilant now that Caveman dosed one of them.

"You're all antsy, and I sympathize. I have people I miss and a boss who's probably written me off by now. We have access to a secure phone, but you still can't leave or tell whoever you call where you are or why you can't return. Create whatever story you want: a last-minute vacation, visiting people out of town, stuck in the hospital, anything that makes sense for you. Understand that leaving could mean leading our enemies to us. And remember, there are also Blind here. They survived the Creation, but they're in more danger than ever at no fault of their own."

People grumbled, the consensus being that they were in enough trouble already regardless of fallout from leaving.

"You're all lucky you're not dead," Donovan interrupted people's complaints, he half-lidded and irritated. "Whine that you're a prisoner all you want, but it's keeping you breathing and stopping our enemies from following you home and slaughtering you and your families in your sleep. It's temporary. Get over it."

Narrowed eyes and shifting seats illustrated a great dislike for everything Donovan after that, but they didn't grumble as much as with Kim.

I hated to admit it, but Donovan was right. They're all alive. Revel in it or line up and let the Elders' end them now for being ungrateful.

Kim fielded more questions: would Miklos return as an Elder if he was forgiven being the most popularly discussed, plus complaints of food and general lack of amenities for being stuck in a magical pocket. Donovan taking another back seat as his co-Sect Leader could do nothing but placate the crowd. Edson wasn't about to make things comfortable for people and Vincent wasn't around for temporary approvals so Magics could manifest things like rock-climbing walls or whatever inane ideas people suggested.

With that said, Kim ended the meeting, the Coveners leaving while the Ballard Sect took its place. Instead of Kim and Donovan at the head of the table, Olive and Lewis told the Sect what transpired with Miklos and how he may not be the enemy we assumed, including all the details I lived firsthand, causing me to zone in and out of attention.

When a question of the estate's condition came up, I was called out of my trance. "Umm, the estate's a collapsed heap of wood, scorched by power along with whoever's cars were outside, including mine." I didn't have it in me to beat around the bush or lie to them, and their gasps and moans in disbelief and shock displayed the impact. "Miklos didn't do it. He did do a spell to keep things weather-tight and hidden until someone can search the wreckage for anything salvageable."

Olive looked to me like I birthed a two-headed eel right there on the conference table.

Lewis gasped. "It's gone? Completely gone?"

Olive held a hand to her chest and felt for a chair she narrowly missed as she sat down.

Everyone started asking questions, talking over each other. Was there anything left? Was the attic untouched? On and on.

Like, really? How could the attic be left untouched in a "collapsed heap of wood" scenario? I raged inside. Instead of repeating myself, I reached inward and projected the image of the estate the last time I saw it into everyone's brain.

Direct recall. Far more efficient.

The tears started as the image broke any lingering denial of the estate's condition. The building was gone. Finished. Unless you wanted it in different languages, it was all I could say.

I had to admit that seeing Olive with tears running down her cheeks was difficult, but my aunt stayed glued to her seat as Lewis and his wife Priscilla comforted her, and I did everything I could not to focus on their grief.

In the back of my mind, I knew it would be a bigger deal to Olive than it would be to me, and that it was a shock when I saw it first-hand. I had only a short time with the estate. Olive knew it as a child and grew up within it until her institutionalization ripped her away. And even then, she dreamed of stepping through its doors again. Now, there were no doors left to step through.

Lewis went on to fulfill his brotherly role as Olive fought to collect herself. "Remember everyone, be thankful you have your lives.

Without Nya rushing us into the field, we would have all been a part of the debris. Even though it will never be the same, once we can return to the outside world, we will rebuild, and everyone present will be a part of reclaiming the estate's history."

For some, this reassurance seemed helpful. For others, they didn't believe they were leaving the Prison Creation anytime soon and if they did, would have to stay far from Dunnville and the remains of the estate.

If most were expecting a procedural run-down of events, they got a kick in the jaw. Being a small Sect, the Ballards cared mostly for what directly impacted them. Miklos wanting a sit-down with the Elders was low on their 'stuff I care about' meter and when I was done with the update, tears were dried and re-dried and they left to find whatever distraction they could from thinking of their beloved estate still smoldering.

Olive hung back. Adam and Serena lingered as well. It was the first time they were chatting me up since at the last meeting where I took their voices from them.

"I hadn't had a chance to ask how you're doing, Firefly." Olive held onto a saturated handkerchief. Her dark eyes a shimmer of black water.

"I'm fine."

"I beg to differ." Olive's eyes did a once-over me. "Your soul colour has changed."

Changed? "Tainted?"

"No, not Tainted. Sickly."

"Dull," Adam added when Olive struggled for words.

"Everything looks dull behind sunglasses, asshat."

"I'm afraid he's right, Firefly," Olive defended to Adam's smug delight. "Definitely not Tainted, however, it seems your Seer green is faded or in a fog."

"My Soul Seeing hasn't changed." I surveyed the soul colours in the room seeing them the same as always. At least, I thought they were the same. "Even my Soul Reading is fine, or I wouldn't have read Miklos. If anything, my power is more responsive." I didn't mention my weak mental barriers.

"Oh, I'm sure it is. Just to our eyes there's an obvious difference."

"Maybe it's because of whatever's happening with your lover-boy." Serena's attempt at help was definitely the opposite.

The expression I shot her was reflected back, Serena not in the mood for cowing-down to my attitude. "Whatever. I'm fine."

Serena gave me a look that said, "Fine, princess."

"I'm going to call Mom. Maybe Dad, too. No clue what to say to him, so maybe not." Adam let me know. "He'll be pissed we missed Christmas. And a shit-tonne of Leaf's games. Maybe once the meeting with Miklos happens, we can return to life. Get me to band practice."

"You're worried about hockey and your shitty band when you have people on your tail willing to snap your spine like a guitar string without a second thought? Nice to know your priorities are in check."

"Twat," Adam shot back.

"Dick-fart," I replied, devoid of the usual playfulness.

"You don't care if you return to your life?" Serena asked. "To work, to Bosco—"

"I don't have a job or a career or an education to return to. And Bosco is safer with my mom. More important things are going down. I don't have time to divide my attention with people who are fucking up their own lives while I'm dealing with others who aren't asking to be hunted down."

"Geez, 'cuz. Come on," was all Serena said as she pushed Adam out the door with her.

The look on my cousin's face was familiar as the expression she shrugged on when she needed to remove herself from a situation before things got real serious, real quick.

Last thing anyone needed was Serena and me getting into it.

13

SEMBLANCE OF HARMONY

Vincent

The first case with Mr. Westmore was long gone, the rigors of court adrenalizing after a three-decade hiatus. Another win, another chip at my moral compass as it was smashed with every fall of the gavel. Words left my mouth and ruined lives, while those committing true evil walked away with further reasons to remain the wretched humans they were.

With Mrs. Chet off the hook for killing yet another husband and his heir for full control of their fortune, I ached for a break at the diner down the street for space from the oppression that was the family business. As expected, my appointed guards filed in behind to keep watch of my movements. Weeks of their presence and I refused to dawdle to accommodate Marcus and Gregory's pace.

Before reaching fresh air, a familiar face among the Blind stood out, Sophie's mother, Lucinda. It took a moment to recall Lucinda worked within the legal system of the Blind. She entered a mediation office. Given the time, and the group of tense individuals following in behind her, she may be some time.

I pulled my double-breasted tweed overcoat tightly in anticipation of the chilled winter day. In the reflection of office windows was Gregory's sculpted goatee struggling through the downtown crowds of the Blind, yet ahead of his cohort as I quickened my steps.

A low muttered spell created a wake of walking space, the Blind stepping away from my path without knowledge of why and reconverging behind me in my guards' way.

Abandoning my route would only highlight Lucinda as a target, so I stayed the course to the diner I visited in order to feel closer to Sophie and memories of time spent together.

Inside the diner, I headed straight for the bathroom and slipped out of a side emergency exit, quieting the alarm with a snap of power before it sounded.

A little juvenile, but Gregory and Marcus were fooled by the tactic as I backtracked to the courthouse and knocked on the door Lucinda entered. When the door opened, I asked Lucinda to come and answer an important phone call about her daughter.

My presence set a panicked look upon her face as she excused herself from her red-faced clients, deferring them to a co-worker.

"*Sophie is fine,*" I sent telepathically. "*I need to speak with you.*"

With the quick comment, her alarm eased.

Only a few feet away was another mediation room, this one empty. I led Lucinda inside and shut us in.

"Sophie's fine?"

"Safe, yes. I would receive word if either of my Charges were hurt. I assure you Sophie is presently fine."

"Charges?"

With no time to explain, I hurried. "Please, Lucinda." I motioned for her to sit in one of the office chairs and I did so as well. "When you speak to Sophie next, I need you to tell her that I have no choice but to play my part in retrieving Cora-Lynn's soul, that I have not forgotten about her, but that I still need her help against the Sovereignty." Lucinda's eyes were too wide. "Are you capable of delivering this message?"

Lucinda swallowed with a hand to her chest. "Are you in love with my daughter?"

Her question took me aback. "I do love your daughter, yet not in the context you suggest. This message is important, Lucinda. Sophie will understand what I refer to and needs to know I have not abandoned her or the cause. That I—"

The door burst open, causing us both to startle and Lucinda to squeal. I sprung from my seat to shield the woman.

The middle-aged man now looking at me and then around me closed the door behind him; familiar dark eyes of a friend were daggers of judgement. "Are you suicidal? You can't be sneaking around meeting with Sophie's mother here."

The shock that this man also knew her daughter registered loudly as Lucinda's mind was an open theatre.

"John, I know—"

"Your guards are searching for you, and this is hardly the place. Too much is on the line—"

"I am aware of the risks."

"They're already trying to call you in."

"Who?"

"Your co-Elders."

With Lucinda present, John went ahead to detail an altercation between Sophie and Miklos, one that involved her killing one man, shooting a woman to use as a buffer from the enemy, and even Miklos himself before reading his soul.

"My daughter murdered someone?"

John continued on without addressing Lucinda, knowing full well it was far from the first life Sophie had ended. "He claims Hinapouri and a bound promise to an Apish Coffer while breaking the webbing around the Creation misled him."

I rubbed my bottom lip in thought. "And this meeting is for what purpose?"

"To reunite the Mother Coven. Or to establish the beginnings of reconciliation."

I turned to Sophie's mother, her brows crimped in thought, her mind stuck on her daughter ending another's life.

"Ranlyn has reservations about Miklos's true intentions," John relayed as he stroked a short, tailored beard as dark as his hair with the beginning of grey revealing his age.

I nodded with reservations of my own. "Lucinda…" I waited for her to acknowledge me. "I need you to speak with Sophie on my behalf. Confirm the meeting with the Elders and let them know I will attend once they have solidified details."

"You—"

"Are too closely surveyed and cannot risk exposure. Getting away to attend the meeting will pose risk enough. I need you to do this."

With a quick breath in, Lucinda clenched her jaw. "I can do that."

"Thank you." I reached into my pocket for a business card. "Return to your meeting and call this number when able. It will connect you to where Sophie is. Please deliver my message."

Lucinda managed to take the card with shaking fingers and nod before I rushed her out of the room with my continued thanks.

This haphazard plan was a risk to both myself and to Sophie's mother, but a part of me found it impossible not to snatch the chance. Seeing Sophie in her mother's eyes made staying away from her harder than expected.

"You happy?" John chided. "That human has no control over her thoughts. A passing Magic could—"

"Consider it done, John." I reached for my friend and Sovereignty contact's shoulder. "Attending this meeting is priority. If the Mother Coven has a chance of re-establishing any semblance of harmony, my presence as Coven Elder is required or the Elders will appear divided."

"Fine. When the time and place are set, I'll make sure you get away. Try for a heads up. I need more than an hour to coordinate your absence."

I smiled. "No promises."

We left the room and went our separate ways, casually losing each other in the crowd as hopes of my message making it to the right people through Sophie's mother worried me.

I pitched forward, my hands catching my fall by reflex, yet my chin bounced off of the marble flooring and gnashed my teeth into my tongue. Others travelling through the courthouse stopped to gage my wellness and assist, all Blind and unaware a Magic engineered my fall.

Upon rising to my feet and thanking my helpers, I sought my guards through the moving crowd and spotted them striding towards me.

Readying myself for whatever they planned to do next, I rooted my gait into a discrete fighting stance, swallowing the blood from my bitten tongue, and healed before the men reached me. The only evidence of the fall was a couple of droplets of blood blotting my white button-down. Another dry-cleaning expense my father would incur.

Gregory stopped a few feet from me. "Your father requests a meeting. Now." Marcus remained silent wearing a look which said he would ensure I made it to Alasdair's office alive regardless of any wayward plans on my part.

Without calling them out on their obvious misuse of power within eyeshot of the Blind population—an offense punishable by imprisonment in their employer's cells—I straightened my clothing on the way to my father's office and added Gregory's name to a mental list of those I would cut down without remorse when the time came.

Alasdair Llewellyn sat at his desk, arguably the most influential Magic in existence as he double-talked some poor shlub on the phone with a guilt trip regarding an issue Alasdair fumbled. In my father's world, the man does no wrong and no one is brave enough to force him to face those wrongs.

Taking the liberty to make myself comfortable, I poured myself a drink of Alasdair's most expensive scotch option from a vintage decanter, visible from my father's eyeline when I allowed it to drip onto the expensive finish of his Mid-century, two-tier butler's cart.

As expected, Alasdair did not mention the lack of respect in wasting such a fine product while damaging another. I took a seat and gulped down the glass instead of savouring it.

When Alasdair dismissed the person on the line, their voice was still heard shouting before the receiver dropped.

"A successful cover-up, I presume." I plonked down my crystal glass onto my father's desk ignoring the coaster.

Without looking at the travesty that would soon be a ringed reminder of his son's pettiness, Alasdair folded his hands on the desk. "Another successful day. I was certain this one would have sullied your winning streak."

Lifting a file off his desk, Alasdair extended it between us.

I refused to accept the file. "Another case?"

Dropping the file, it knocked the crystal glass to the floor. The carnage went unacknowledged as the glass smashed into a hundred tiny diamonds at my feet.

Alasdair re-folded his hands. "A client requires your set of expertise."

"I have tried and won over a dozen cases in the last week alone. How many more of your friends do I need to ignore the law for before I have compiled enough to win my freedom?"

"Freedom is a condition I never agreed to."

A point of future negation to ruminate over. "Cora-Lynn—"

"Is a trapped soul. You are a trapped Magic that will continue to do your job successfully until the day comes you are fit to run the firm."

"I will never run the firm." My voice was eerily calm to my ears.

"You do realize you could run it as you please once in power, yes? Try cases you enjoy while shifting the law to your will."

"Neither you nor Chase would allow that. Additionally, I do not need the Sovereignty in order to live the option you defined."

"Right." Alasdair settled back in his chair. "Your rebellion comes with an end goal once you kill me and the board."

"Yes, it does." At this point I felt righteous in confirming the rumour.

Alasdair gave a slow nod. "My justifications of the decisions I make on a daily basis are beyond the scope of your understanding. If your rebellion ever follows the future you have designed then I will sit from my perch in the afterlife and watch as you learn what it means to be in my position. As I witnessed from your performance in the courtroom, I have no doubt that you are exactly where you should be. You will be needed now more than ever since Loring has escaped and will be leading many others in crimes we have not encountered in this decade."

"Do you know of his location?" I thought this a better question then replaying the same "you are right where you are destined to be" speech.

"There's not much that doesn't cross my desk."

"And yet, you are not sweeping him up?"

"Why would I? What is his crime?"

"You cannot be serious?"

"Produce evidence against him and he will be tracked and punished."

"Right. This is precisely the problem with your system. Turning a cheek when it suits you regardless of harm to innocents. You need Magics to continue to apply for your services and most would not look upon you so kindly if you imprisoned their Master. Loring living life as a fugitive keeps you in business."

"That is simply not the case, though I do admit that Loring's release conveniently provides an interesting scope of probability in terms of future cases. You of which I can partially thank for that."

"That is how you view Loring's escape into the populace?"

Alasdair leaned forward with a whine of leather from his chair. "Do you understand how much grief I am catching for having you at the table? Fulfill your role and you will reap your reward. Until I say you have earned it, you will uphold your oath to the Sovereignty and its laws.

"Also, stop dodging your guards. Next time I am updated with another of your attempts to flee there will be consequences that others you care about will pay in your stead since you care not if you reap them yourself."

Always my father's way. Alasdair knew me enough to know that I cared less about myself than I did of those I loved and that would be the easiest way to cause me true pain. After the threat, I refrained from more argument, seeing the immoveable force in my father's eyes. This fight was like countless others I was destined to lose, so I grabbed the file from the desk and left, the crunch of broken crystal beneath my loafers.

14

PROBLEM SOLVING

Caine

Being a messenger boy wasn't exactly my calling, but it gave me an excuse to drag Sophie out of her cell. She was always in there, alone, isolating from everyone unless on a mission or grabbing food before taking it back to her cell, which didn't happen all that often either.

I found her lying in bed staring at the ceiling. Was that how she spent her time?

"Hey—"

She shot up in a panic, eyes wide, fists tightened.

"Shit, sorry!" I raised my hands. "It's just me."

She didn't relax.

"You've got a call."

She finally blinked and inhaled, checking herself a moment before following me out into the lobby and into the office where her call came through.

Across the crowd of people walking around the place, Ness stood with her brother and Derek and giving me—or maybe Sophie the stank-eye.

When Sophie picked up the receiver, I left and approached Ness and the others, focusing on Ness. "How're you doing?"

"Fine."

She was lying. "Sophie had a phone call."

Ness shrugged. "Good for her."

I stopped myself from laughing but a slow grin escaped. "You're not jealous, are you?"

"Oh, course she is," Derek added with a laugh I knew was the opposite of helpful.

Her dark eyes narrowed at Derek. "Of what?" She turned my way. "I'm not your girlfriend."

Ouch, even if accurate. "Neither is Sophie."

"Again. Good for her." She started towards somewhere, leaving the conversation and my vicinity all together.

Felix and Derek shook their heads in annoyance as I took a few quick steps to catch up with Ness.

"Where are you going?"

She motored onward.

When we passed an open and empty office, I took a chance, and pulled her into it.

"Excuse me." She brushed me off and crossed her arms.

I ignored her heavy glare. "You know—"

"I know nothing, apparently."

"You know Sophie's with Donovan."

She made a small laugh. "Not according to her she's not."

"You talked to her?"

"*Pfft.* Right! Like I'd ever. They're not staying in the same cell, and she'll barely look at the guy let alone talk to him, If you believe the rumours, half of which are straight from you, so unless you're exaggerating—"

"I'm not."

"Right, of course, because she has no problem talking to you."

The dig proved her point, even if her conclusions were way off.

"Don't give me that look, Caine. Not after you admitted to telling her you'd be with her if she wasn't with Donovan. Well, Miss Perfect-Who's-Saved-Your-Ass-A-Million-Times is single and chattin' you up. This is the chance you've been waiting for."

Remembering that day, I meant what I said to Sophie, but it wasn't fair, and since then I had a lot of nights to understand why I was wrong.

"If Sophie and Donovan aren't together, their Soul Magic will eat them up and they'll turn on each other and themselves. Become husks of the people they are. Just because Donovan's an ass and Sophie and me are no longer together, doesn't mean either of them deserve that fate."

"You sure? Cuz I'd think her fucking Donovan while you guys were together would be a good reason to see her crash and burn."

I inclined my head and took a step closer, but Ness held her ground. "I'm never getting back with Sophie. Not ever. I'll repeat it until you believe it, but it's not happening regardless of whatever fantasy you think I'm harbouring. She and Donovan are messed up right now, but they're stuck with each other. And as someone who cares about her and now sees her as a good friend, I'm not letting her ruin her life and her future lives, just like I'm not going to let my history with her ruin us."

"Be real, chump. There is no us."

"Hmm...." I took a step closer and watched as her breath hitched while she desperately tried to hide the rush of pink in her cheeks. "You sure about that?"

"You're suddenly cocky."

I enjoyed the breathiness in her voice. "I'm confident in what I felt in that hell and was too scared to act on and potentially lose. Where not facing death every second we breathe anymore. Gareth's gone. And I'm not pining for anyone else."

After slight hesitation, her lips parted. I gave a mental "fuck it" and leaned into a kiss before she could say anything. For a half-second, I felt no reciprocation and went to back off, thinking I'd really misread things. When her lips began moving, matching my pace, and then driving into it to bring things deeper, I had a moment of shock this was actually happening.

Ness's arms snaked around my neck and pulled me against her as she backed into the wall before she was yanking my shirt over my head.

Panting as more clothing hit the floor, her teeth biting my shoulder and her nails in my back severed months of sexual tension. Perfect skin warmed beneath my palms, the sound of her low moans exquisite.

A hitch of power closed and magic-locked the door. No fucking way did I want anything interrupting.

Power still buzzing through me, I grabbed hold of her thighs and hefted her up. Her legs wrapped around my hips, eliminating the height difference. She clenched her thighs and drove me into her wetness. I stilled and pressed my weight into her. She tightened herself around me and rolled her hips.

With months of build up, I nearly broke a speed record, the feeling of her around me heavenly.

I opened my eyes, wanting to see that flush in her cheeks again, and was shocked to see the office was gone. Trees surrounded us. Ones that looked far too much like the Creation we escaped.

She clenched her thighs as if to get me moving. I ignored the near nighttime setting of the Creation forest around us and dug my fingers into her plush ass, finding the punishing rhythm she insisted on. The reward of her squeezing me inside of her was almost overwhelming.

Sweat beaded our skin as if we were enduring the heat of Evar's Creation, so real the sensation of tree bark cut into my palm as I braced myself to drive deeper and faster.

She let out a gasp and a cry that tightened her grip on me. I kept pace as long as I could before I lost it, my knees nearly buckling as I fought to keep us up and let her ride this out for as long as possible.

Unable to take any more, I braced my body against hers and the tree at her back as we panted.

Forehead to forehead, I reached up to graze my finger along her luscious lips, and the forest around us disappeared in a snap, her power draining as she shifted to unravel her legs from around me. When her feet hit the floor, she reached for her clothes and started shoving them on. Picking up my own, I couldn't help but suddenly realize she didn't look me in the eyes, not now, and not during.

One-night stands happened too frequently in my past before the coma and sleeping curse. The aftermath was always brutally uncomfortable, but the bliss usually lasted more than ten seconds. Now, I was getting the silent treatment.

"Wasn't expecting that." Shit. I sounded ridiculous. Why was that the first thing out of my stupid mouth?

"Yeah." She pulled her jeans up over her hips, still without looking at me.

She smoothed her hair and walked out the door without responding. Wait, didn't I lock it? Maybe she quickly unlocked it?

"Ness!" I tore my shirt on and raced after her.

"Gotta check on Felix." Again, she didn't look at me.

She was walking too fast for me to catch up and not look like I was chasing her, which she clearly didn't want. Checking on her brother was an obvious excuse.

My zipper was still undone. I situated myself, realizing neither of us thought of protection. Dammit! I got what I wanted only to gain exactly what I feared. Things got out of control and fast.

With her brother or Derek in the mix as a buffer, she would make sure I couldn't say anything to address what just happened. If I tried going at her telepathically, she would just be more pissed, guaranteeing our office romp to be a one-time thing. Or forest romp. Why did she choose that backdrop? She could have chosen any place she wanted. Did she think that's what I wanted?

Sophie and Ranlyn's voices drifted over from another office, talking about Vincent getting her a message through her mother. Something that sounded pretty dangerous for Sophie's mom.

Her thoughts were open and a mash of focusing on her and Ranlyn's conversation and fighting to disconnect from how she felt while speaking to her mom and hearing Bosco in the background of the call. The guilt in Sophie's mother's voice as she cried into the phone was enough to break Sophie down. At least the Sophie I used to know. Not a tear dropped, and she felt sadder for not feeling the need to.

Damn. Something was so wrong with her.

I stepped into the room and joined the conversation to take my mind off of the Ness situation.

Ranlyn nodded, agreeing to something. "I won't waste time. The meeting will be arranged for tonight."

Sophie straightened. "The Tactical Team has to be there. The Elders need security and I seriously doubt Miklos is gonna show alone."

Ranlyn was listening, but it took some convincing for him to agree to bring along the Team. When Sophie's shoulders noticeably relaxed, I got the sense her desperation for involvement was an excuse to see Vincent and nothing to do with protection detail.

"I'll make the calls and speak with Veata." Ranlyn looked to me. "Will you be a part of the meeting? I don't see us requiring your persuasion, yet it's always a possibility."

"Ah, no. I'm not on the Team. Call me in if you need me, though."

Ranlyn smirked. "Kim isn't on the Team either, though I understand she was present when Miklos made his claim."

"Off the books mission. She invited herself." Sophie's justification bordered on rude. Why would Kim bother if Sophie didn't ask her along?

Ranlyn turned to her with a hard stare. "Yes, it was off the books. And the last mission off my radar, I promise you. Always keep me in the loop, Sophie. I've backed you until now because I trust you and so did Aunt Lacey." Sophie shifted uncomfortably. "I wouldn't have stopped you from going even if you wanted to do so without Lincoln's knowledge. I would have even gone with you...without the need to drug the guard."

Sophie met him straight-faced. "Good to know."

Damn. They drugged the guard? May have been a mission worth being a fly on the wall for.

Ranlyn surprised me by stepping forward and hugging her. To my even greater surprise was Sophie's lack of hesitation in hugging him back. He whispered something to her too quiet for me to over-hear but caused a curt laugh from her in response.

When he pulled away, Ranlyn smiled a smile all for her, nodded to me, and excused himself.

I knew they were close, but I didn't quite grasp their relationship. They met before he was an Elder and survived some shit together. Maybe something borne in that.

When Ranlyn left, I stopped Sophie from doing the same. "Can I ask you something weird?"

Her left eyebrow arched. "If it burns when you pee, I can heal it, but I'm not touching it and you didn't get it from me."

"Ha ha. Happy you found your sense of humour. Though, my question is sex-related." She waited for me to go on. "If you have sex with someone and they bolt afterwards, it's always a bad thing, right?"

I watched Sophie's lips part in pause before saying, "You slept with Ness, I take it."

I braced my hands on my hips still feeling the drying wetness in my briefs. "Yup. I realize telling you this is six kinds of crazy, but it literally just happened, and I'm thrown off. I'm not usually on this end of things."

"Karma for the dip and ditch. Sounds deserving." She took a second to work out an actual response. "Was everything fine until the money shot?"

I laughed. "Classy."

She shrugged.

"Not really. We were arguing and it just sort of happened. She wouldn't really look at me and used a questionable illusion...I don't know. It was amazing, but something was wrong."

She smirked. "From personal experience, I'd say your technique isn't the problem."

"Umm, good to know. Thanks."

"So, I'm gonna assume she thought having sex would solve whatever problem you were fighting about. Clearly it didn't."

I ran my hand over my stubbled chin. "She thought...she thought I didn't want her. You'd think sex would solve the confusion."

"*Pfft.* All you proved was that you wanted to have sex with her. Any guy can stick their dick in you. Unlike her, some vaginas are insecure enough to believe that counts for 'happily-ever-after'."

Quick footsteps sounded in the hall. Ness, Felix, and Derek walked by, returning from the direction of the cafeteria. Ness's chin was level in that purposeful way of ignoring who you were walking by, but she never turned our way. However, Derek did, giving a direct glare at me in warning without stopping.

"Think she overheard?" Sophie asked with blatant sarcasm in her tone.

"If she only caught the end of what you said than I'm royally screwed cuz she thinks I still want you."

"Caine!" She punched me in the arm.

"Ouch. What?"

"What do you mean, what? I have enough enemies. I don't need Ness as another one. She could blind me with an illusion and take my ass down before I saw her peach-coloured soul glow."

"She doesn't hate you. Her soul glow is peach?"

Sophie scoffed. "Of course, you would deflect. Yes, as is her brother's, so it's likely an Illusionist thing. And more on topic, you're ten pounds heavier carrying around all that bullshit. I can precisely imagine what she's thinking right now when seeing us standing here." She shook her head. "You have a lot to prove and are far too good at digging and decorating your own grave. Plus, remember how you felt thinking I only wanted Donovan even though I was with you?"

I gave her a look.

"Okay, bad example, but in the beginning, I actually decided to be with you and not him because that's how I wanted things to be. The jealousy is what I meant. It turned you into a pissed off bull with an extra shot of testosterone and you hated yourself and the situation for always feeling like that. You should be reassuring Ness by being there with her, not here talking to me. What we had and everything with the stupid fucking Soul Magic drama is more complicated than anyone could expect to deal with when questioning if the guy they like still wants their ex. Orgasms aren't going to convince her you want her for more than to cure your sexual frustration."

I let out a heavy sigh, rubbed my hands over my face, and paced a step. "Are you gonna take your own advice or be happy making the rest of us feel stupid for not taking yours?"

She made a throaty noise. "Do whatever you want, but instead of chasing after the hot piece of ass you just plowed, you came to me, your most recent ex, with questions about next steps in your current non-relationship. I'm here for you if you're brave enough to listen to me about anything these days, but this screwup is all yours."

"Right. Thanks."

"No problem, dumbass."

"So, do I get to hand out some advice?"

She dropped her head to the side. "Seriously, man? Kim's already taken a run at fixing me. No advice is going to solve what doesn't need to be solved."

"Maybe not. At one point, you actually loved Donovan." She rolled her eyes at me, so I hurried on. "Maybe if you plugged into the memories of how you and he fell in love in this life, it'll help remind you of why."

"Plug into?"

"Yeah. You know...read your soul. You're the only one I know who can do it, why not take advantage? You hate how things are, but complaining and carrying a gun isn't solving the problem. And while you're in your soul, check out the days when you were miserable and find when you suddenly weren't." Ignoring her distracted stare, I continued. "I hate to admit it, but you had a spark of interest for him even before I was awakened from my sleeping curse. I saw it the first time I was in a room with you two and it never went away."

"That was the Soul Magic."

"Nah, it would've been easier if it were. The Soul Magic isn't the issue. Tobias and Loring fucking with your lives is. Direct your anger at them because they sure as fuck deserve it."

"What do you think I'm doing with the Team?"

"Hey," I raised my hands, "no need to get defensive. Don't forget Donovan is a part of that Team, too. He may be an arrogant jerk, but he's loyal and doesn't deserve what you're dishing out."

"Yeah, yeah. I'll print up your Team Donovan jockstrap ASAP."

"I'd say have sex with him, but apparently that problem-solving method is an epic fail."

"Well, sorry, Caine. You're not the Santa Claus of dicks. Your unit isn't a gift, it's a tool. One Ness can buy online with less hassle and in whatever pretty colour matches her nail polish if she wants. Now, go find her and expect her to blow you off in the non-happy ending sort of way."

"Very funny."

"She helped you when you struggled with Gareth and all that. Now she'll get to see if you want her for more than sex and how easily you scare off when she refuses to make things easy for you, since *easy* could result in her getting hurt. She's a survivor of that place, too."

Taking a page from Ranlyn, I hugged her, stopping her from saying anything more. I didn't receive the uninhibited embrace Ranlyn did, but after a quick pause, she reciprocated and held me close.

She gave me what I needed when speaking about relationships at all was not her favourite topic these days. Ness's reaction made more sense. I wouldn't have given up on her either way, but having some understanding created a resolve to ensure she knew exactly who I wanted.

15

VICTIM AND SURVIVOR

Sophie

I didn't anticipate the set of long, strong arms around me, and it took a moment to tell myself to hug Caine back. First Ranlyn and then Caine. Nothing lingering or sexual, simply a comforting embrace from a friend, one I needed from him but would have never asked for.

He stepped back and smiled down at me as if he were unsure how I was with the body contact.

I gave him a small smile. "If you strike out with Ness, I might even talk to her myself."

He smirked. "I'll let you know when I get that desperate."

With Caine equipped with some insider knowledge, I went to find a Team member to let them know about the Team's role in the meeting with Miklos. Caine followed until he saw Ness and Felix near the lobby and split off to meet them. Ness met my eyes, not attempting to intimidate yet in passive challenge and taking notice of who Caine was with. I tried not to take it personally, but Ness needed to retract her claws.

I wanted Caine to be happy. When reflecting on how Caine and I met and how we ended, it was the only time I enjoyed the prospect of staying friends with an ex. If Ness harboured doubts of where we stood, I would make good on my word. If he and Ness weren't going to be together, no damn way would it be because Ness thought Caine was still up my skirt.

I spotted Bronya. Any lift in attitude from interacting with Caine nose-dived into a pool of loathing. Since she was the first Team member I crossed, it made sense to relay our new mission details to her.

Why couldn't it be anyone else?

Bronya was chatting up another blond Magic with an old break in his nose. His blue-black soul colour shone like oil yet was white where it counted. More gothic than Tainted. A memory hit when I focused on his face, stoic as he conducted the dead outside of Diluculo. He was a Necromancer. Something much more interesting than a palm tree shaped birth mark—the hot topic they were chatting about. He seemed more interested in Bronya's lips than what they were saying, unable to keep his eyes off of them.

I approached the two and forced my way into their inane conversation like a battering ram. "I need to talk to you."

Bronya side-eyed the Necromancer, and then adopted a challenging sneer. "Is that so?"

"Privately." Restrained as my voice was, the contempt was loud.

We stepped away from the death dancer and I wasted no time in explaining the meeting with Miklos, as well as the need to notify the other members.

"Now I'm your messenger monkey?"

I gritted my teeth until pain struck my cheek bone. "You're the first Team member I saw since I spoke with Ranlyn and figured even though you're a bleached asshole of a person, I'd make a professional attempt to bring you up to speed. Stupid me."

Bronya still didn't respond or indicate what she planned on doing with the information.

"Fine. Since normal speed is beyond your comprehension, I'll find a crayon. Maybe I'll act it out like an E-list actress on a kid's show. No? Awesome. I'll find someone capable of basic conversational skills."

I left to find Lincoln or Caveman. Anyone but her.

"Is Donovan single?"

The question stopped me dead in my tracks, muscles steeled from head to toe. Energy flared to my skin, salivating to be used at the audacity of Bronya trying to rattle me. The princess's upturned nose begged to be fucked up and healed in time to fuck it up again and again until someone peeled me off of her. It wasn't about Donovan. Bronya wanted to get to me, and Donovan was her low-road to do it.

Someone grabbed my shoulder and spun me away from her.

Denise was staring at me; another blonde and nearly as irritating. "Donovan's hot, but not worthy of being homeless over, since Edson promises to evict anyone who brawls. Unless you've got a safer place to be. If so, have at her."

I moved to go around her. "Go away."

"Oh, I'm sorry. Was getting kicked out your plan? Next time I'll remind myself you're an ungrateful twat and take sideline bets."

"What's your beef, sis?" Adam sneered at me from behind his sunglasses, his soul colour settling into its Seer green, while he was still hiding behind his dampening crutch.

I should have seen my brother right away or at least assumed they would be together since they were still rocking the relationship vibes.

"No beef."

"Please." Denise laughed. "As soon as blondie opened her mouth your aura turned toxic. Something's brewing."

Bronya walked away with the Necromancer, she sparing a side-eyed sneer for me as she passed.

God, I hated her. "Blondie can suck it. Have either of you seen Lincoln?"

"Who's Lincoln?" Of course, Adam was clueless.

Denise waved him off. "Eating, as of an hour ago. No idea right now."

"And Caveman. I mean...Hall?" I had to remind myself of the guy's actual name.

Adam looked to his girlfriend again to fill in the blanks. Denise rolled her eyes at him. "Probably in a corner somewhere steaming it up with your bestie."

"Excuse me?"

"Can it. Like we don't all know what's going on with them."

Sick of her and her inability to give straight answers, I walked away.

"You're welcome, bitch!" Denise's voice echoed across the lobby behind me.

Since there were only so many places a Tactical Team member could be, I went on a hunt hoping to walk some anger off and ignore how quickly I went from annoyed to utterly enraged when Bronya tried to goad me into a fight.

I was never a flip-a-switch kind of person. What the fuck was wrong with me? My days and nights were filled with seeping anger into every tensed-shouldered interaction I could manage. My skull pounded thinking of my hair-trigger temper at such an insignificant comment I would have normally let roll off my back.

Right now, I wanted to fuck Bronya up and could almost feel the sensation of relief and righteousness for following through with the ways my brain was cooking up.

Finally, I saw Caveman standing with Lincoln and Donovan going over the meeting with Ranlyn and Veata. When I approached the group, they didn't stop their conversation a beat, and explained the meeting with Miklos would convene at Pearson Park in St. Catharines.

I knew the spot well, the expanse of grass across the street from my old high school. Ranlyn believed the location worked in our advantage as it was a large open area with some outbuildings including a library, a playground, and a splash pad to hide reinforcements in case things turned ugly.

Ismail, Gregor, Jessabelle, and even the antagonistic twat Bronya showed as Lincoln had sent Ismail to round them up. As soon as the perky twat-face walked over, my power swelled like a hot flash.

I tried to force it to retreat, but it was a brick wall. It shouldn't have been such a hard task. I kept my eyeline down knowing if anyone gave me so much as a side-eye for the energy flare, I wouldn't be in control of my triple-charged reaction.

"Are you okay?" The soft voice in my grey matter was Donovan's.

Again, he glided inside my head, uninvited, as my mental barriers must have collapsed as my control slipped. I focused enough to snap up a barrier that shut him out, still without looking up as Ranlyn went on about the contributing players and their positions during the meeting.

"I don't wanna waltz onto that field with an army," Ranlyn said as Veata gave a small laugh that went unchecked, "so it'll be your seven Team members, plus us Elders and Vincent."

I thought of the last time I saw Vincent before Nya took over and remembered the feeling of safety and contentment that came with lying against his strong shoulder in the SUV after the Sorrel cells. He piggy-backed me away from all of that, most of the way through the woods, and in the end it didn't matter. Nya took over anyway.

Seeing him that day was close to divine. I may not remember all the lives that starred his face, but my soul experienced a homey familiarity whenever I was with him, and it amazed me how much I craved his presence over the last couple of days.

Nya tore him away and I hadn't seen him since. With my emotions set to unpredictable, I had no idea how I would react when I finally saw the man again and focused my racing thoughts on gearing up for the meeting before I popped a tear duct with an audience.

Kim stood aside as the Team was loading and holstering their gear. "I don't mind being sidelined on this one."

Caine nodded in agreement, standing next to her, though his gaze lingered on the table of guns and ammo like he wanted to squeeze off a few rounds.

Caveman clicked a holster into place around his thigh. "Only because we don't need to appear like we're waging war, not because you're inept, love."

I looked at Kim. Love? Since when did he call her that? It reminded me of Donovan calling me "babe" while I was still with Caine. Denise's mention of Caveman and Kim stealing some private time made me wonder if Kim had slept with the guy. A peek at Caine showed me nothing, as he wasn't taken aback by it even though Kim was supposed to be with one of his best friends. Maybe she and Frog weren't together anymore.

Kim's cheeks reddened in embarrassment, not as comfortable with his open affection, yet her contradicting scowl didn't convince me she didn't enjoy it.

Something might not have happened yet, but it was brewing, and Caveman was confident in where they were headed.

———

The group arrived at Pearson Park thirty minutes early to scout the area. This park was nothing like the one across my apartment where Caine was trapped or the field outside Diluculo. Two full-sized soccer fields spanned the manicured grass now covered in a layer of snow. The playground and splash pad were void of screaming little brats pissing their swim trunks. The largest building housing a library and swimming pool was dark and empty, though we double-checked in case staff was working late or someone was hiding out.

Regardless of the time, the field was lit up by stadium lights that illuminated the meeting far greater than the brightest full moon. When considering how untrustworthy Miklos was, a field with minimal hiding places and sufficient lighting was as close to perfect as our luck got.

We waited on the outskirts of one of the fields behind some pines and a concrete box with bathrooms inside, the stink overriding the crisp winter air and hovering in the slight breeze.

Nothing better than a shit-flavoured snowy night to cap off the day.

Lincoln sent Ismail, Gregor, and Donovan to create a perimeter spell to ward off interruption from the Blind, as well as warn us of Miklos's arrival.

I hated never being chosen for anything important. As a kid, popularity was never an issue. Now, the aggravation of others' distrust was infuriating. Why should I give a crap about what anyone thought about me? I shouldn't but did.

Considering the park was huge and flat, I hated to admit that once Donovan was thirty feet away, as he and the others maneuvered through shadows created by the stadium lights, I couldn't see him. Could I work a cover spell so seamlessly? At one point, maybe. I wasn't so certain of anything now.

Squinting into the darkness for a sign of Donovan or anyone else, I heard Caveman say, "Got my money, Lewy?"

Vincent walked out of the shadows of the neighbouring Children's Discovery Centre in an expensive suit under a thigh length wool overcoat.

"I actually do." Vincent's green eyes sparkled and radiated something within his smile.

Caveman laughed. "You do not."

Vincent reached into an inside coat pocket, produced a thick envelope, and passed it to Caveman. "You can thank my father. Figured it appropriate to use his money instead of my own."

Caveman took the envelope and slapped it into his palm. "Dirty money still pays for drinks. Round on me on the other side of this?"

Vincent gave a laugh filled with mixed emotions. "If only."

Caveman sucked his teeth. "No kidding. That prison of yours is dry. I suggest stocking the staff fridge with some spirits."

"Stock it with belly dancers if you prefer. Until the day it becomes a working prison, it is yours to enjoy."

"Mmm. Even the priciest belly dancers around here would never be the same as Tunisia."

"No. Nothing close." Vincent laughed again, this time with more joy at whatever memory they shared involving Tunisian belly dancers.

With his hands deep in his wool pockets, Vincent's loafered feet were nearly hidden in the snow though he didn't seem to care.

He peered around Caveman to me. "How are you doing?"

I didn't say anything. Didn't move. Didn't even blink.

Seeing something in this, Vincent's smile disappeared. He glanced at Caveman, then back to me. "Come."

One word and I was following him towards the Discovery Centre.

He stopped and turned to me in the shadows a good distance from the others.

Silent seconds ticked by.

He put a hand on my shoulder. "You can cry if you need to."

Fuck me. I took in a harsh breath and fought against my buckling knees. Until he said something, I didn't realize how much I was holding in. His words pulled the plug on my restraint, my hands over my face doing nothing to stifle the shuddering gasps.

His body was against mine, warm arms holding me steady, and I allowed myself to be held. Elegant cologne emanated from the soft wool of his coat against my cheek as I soaked him in, feeling the crush of his arms and the weight of his head atop mine.

Breaking the embrace, completely sick of all the tears and borrowing strength from others, I straightened. Vincent kept his arms around me, locking himself to me, and looking down through his glasses I knew he only wore out of habit, his green eyes still visible in the dim light.

"I hate this." I reached between us to swipe at my tears, realizing

I wasn't wearing makeup. I never went without my liquid eyeliner and mascara. Not that he cared or commented on how shitty I looked.

"Hate what, precisely?"

I shook my head not knowing where to start. Now wasn't the time or place to delve into it.

"They have yet to arrive," he said in a soft tone. "Use the time we have."

A sob stuck in my chest like I had eaten rice too fast, the emotion settling where it shouldn't, and refusing to dissipate. After the meeting he would leave again. Regardless of the reason, I wasn't okay with that. "I guess...I assumed going into hiding meant you'd be with us."

He nodded. "I would be given the choice. My family ensured to trap me in an inescapable bind."

"Can we help you out of it?"

"Not yet. I am uncertain of the location of Cora-Lynn's soul. Once I can release her, I can run with you. Not until then. If I do, my father will destroy her. I cannot let that happen. You will be okay. Trust your Coven."

I made a stout laugh.

"What?"

"You were the only one with the experience to get us through everything this far. Now...." I didn't know how to finish that thought without hitting the downslope of a rant I could breathlessly rage on for a healthy hour. When it came down to it, even with the Coveners around, I was alone.

"My presence in the prison will not cure your loneliness." He must have heard my thoughts, and he tried to smooth over my frustration with this by moving those comforting hands to my shoulders with a squeeze. "People care about you." He glanced to the side. I followed his eyeline as Donovan, Ismail, and Gregor returned from their perimeter check.

"Don't imply him." I took a half-step away from him, but my

clipped tone wasn't enough of a warning, and Vincent stopped me from creating distance between us.

"I am implying more than Donovan. Things are different now. Nya is gone so there are holes in your abilities. There will be things you will need to relearn and others that will surprise you by being too easy. Nevertheless, I am most worried about *you*. Your mental shields are weaker than before you knew they existed and there is a lot of troubling background thoughts you cannot hide. Push Donovan away all you like. You know you will have to face him soon."

"He's an asshole."

"He is a victim and a survivor, as are you."

I didn't want to hear it.

"I can tell by touching you that something is off with your soul. Has Olive mentioned any changes?"

I twisted then stepped back, and this time his hands dropped. "I'm not Tainted!"

"No, I do not sense the Tainted, yet something is off. The Soul Magic has sustained damage. The overwhelming conflict within you proves as much. I know you still love him."

I flinched and exhaled in a chilled stream of oxygen. "Don't be gross."

"If love did not remain, you would not feel so wounded. This damage has fractured that bond, what you feel is from the fracture. The truth of Tobias's hand in the Conception Rituals should have changed your outlook. And the feral inner recoil I felt from mere mention of this proves you still have much to process that has nothing to do with Soul Magic and everything to do with the fact the instant you started dreaming of Caine, your life has been one heinous event after another. Each out of your hands and forcing decisions you should not have been placed in the position to make."

I couldn't argue that.

"Tobias's ritual sought to humiliate his son while bloating his ranks. Taking you away from Donovan was Tobias's greatest accomplishment. He knows of the Soul Magic, knows what losing it will do to the both of you. Anyone who knows an inkling about either of you before you met in this life, knows you need each other."

"Right." I crossed my arms, a little awkward around the gear. "Need because I'm a moron and however many god-forsaken centuries ago decided Soul Magic was the answer."

"Soul Magic cannot be created or held over so many lifetimes if two souls do not truly care for one another. You deserve happiness and you deserve to unravel this. If you keep blaming him, you will remain stuck. That is too lazy an approach for you. Control your emotions instead of letting them ruin you."

"And if this damage to our Soul Magic won't let me?"

"I will find a way to heal it," he said with an air of promise. "In the meantime, remember you can read your soul. Find where this all started and feel what it was like before Tobias wedged his way into your path."

I was reminded of how Caine said the same thing. I didn't answer or say anything more.

Judging by the crinkle next to his eyes, Vincent considered our talk a success. I wasn't so certain, though I didn't want our time to end.

Without adding more on Donovan, he must have known I was done hearing his name. I didn't need the guide of *101 Ways to Fix Your Life*, I just needed Vincent.

He pulled me into another embrace that I welcomed. His arms wound tightly around me as I burrowed myself into his open coat and breathed in his comforting scent. Never had there been sexual attraction between us. More like he was an older brother or mentor or something. One with wisdom beyond his many years, who was loaded, and could kick major ass.

"I told you we need you."

His chest rumbled against me.

"Well, what kind of Overseer would I be if I let my Charges murder each other? Especially since I equipped them with state-of-the-art weaponry." I actually laughed this time, though was clueless of what he meant by Overseer and Charges. Was it an actual role? Or a weird off-handed comment? "You look formidable, by the way. The gear suits you." He cradled my face on both sides. "Now channel that anger. We need to meet the Hungarian bastard so I can return to being grounded." Vincent put his arm around my shoulders as we strolled back to the others.

"Are you sure there isn't more we can do for you? Help you search for the location of Cora-Lynn's soul? Someone other than your dad has to know."

"I imagine no other does and an assault to force the information now is impetuous. Timing is everything. A move at a Sovereignty takeover cannot occur until we are certain about the location, not a moment before."

"I know she's your priority."

He stiffened and stopped walking.

"It's fine...she should be. After watching my back forever you're entitled to do something epic for yourself."

"Thank you." He started walking again and pulled me close to lay a peck on the top of my head.

Why I couldn't manage this ease with Kim, Olive, or any of my other family right now was beyond me. Something about them all felt judgemental.

I still had an arm around Vincent's waist when we reached the others.

"Donovan." Vincent gave a nod in greeting.

I noticed the severe look he returned, his brows expressing confusion. A silent exchange passed between the two of them, one that had Donovan's features in a mash of emotions before Vincent let go of me with a "Be right back" and moved to speak with Ranlyn and Veata.

Whatever their telepathic conversation involved, I didn't appreciate Donovan running him off. Obviously, Vincent's Elder responsibilities were paramount, but since my mind-related powers were on the fritz, both of them knew I was left out of the convo and meant to keep it that way.

Lincoln approached the group. "Gregor and I will flank the Elders during the meeting. Ismail, Hall, I want the two of you sweeping the perimeter during the exchange in case slugs creep up on us and the perimeter spell doesn't hold."

All of this was delivered like a seasoned squad leader, the others treating the instruction as a direct order, ready to execute every measure of their mission like it would save the world.

I wasn't ignorant to the fact that this meeting was an olive branch that could dictate the future of the Mother Coven. If this ended in battle, we could kiss a whole division of people on the enemy's list goodbye, resigning them to hide like in the Prison Creation forever. And if that happens, we will never see the end of the Sovereignty reign. They will continue to rule, and the Mother Coven will continue to hide like rats.

Vincent returned. "Instead of taking the stage second, we will make our presence known immediately. Miklos and whomever accompanies him may have remained out of sight. Since he called us here, we should be the ones to proceed first in a show of confidence." Vincent spoke to Lincoln. "Everyone aware of their positions?"

"Yes, sir."

Vincent looked to me, and I returned a slight nod knowing Vincent wasn't worried about his Team as a whole. Probably not even for Donovan since he'd been down this road before. This was routine for the rest of them, not so much for me. Tactically speaking, I was the weakest link and needed to prove I was worth the effort to train.

At a leisurely pace, matching Veata's gate since she and her cane would be the slowest, we made our way into the open. Ranlyn took the lead in the middle, Veata to his left, Vincent to his right. Jessabelle flanked Vincent on his other side while Gregor and Bronya were at Veata's side.

Donovan stood to my left as we all positioned ourselves behind Ranlyn. Clearly Donovan's placement was a planned preventative measure to ensure my safety. This wasn't explained, but I could connect the dots. Another silent conversation I was kept out of since no one gave me a designated position as with the others. I tried to shake it off, refusing to address Donovan or embarrass myself by asking where I should stand and be useless for anything other than a show of force and another familiar face for Miklos.

As we waited ankle deep in snow in the crisp winter night, I noted that I couldn't see Caveman and Ismail as they circled the perimeter. Not their breath, not their footsteps, not a sound, though they no doubt never stopped moving.

Miklos and his people stepped out from behind the trees. They must have been waiting for the Elders to move first as Vincent presumed. We should have seen them among the sparse trees dotting the lawn, plus the multiple perimeter checks with no mention of a portal, something that would have caused enough of resonate magical hum to give them away.

Miklos led the same group we encountered outside of the rubble of the Ballard Estate, plus one new addition to replace the guy I dusted for an even ten on both sides. All of Miklos's people were spaced much like our own group, approaching slow to stow intimidation, any weapons tucked away. Though a bullet would probably do less damage than the bag of tricks each of those Magics possessed judging by the array of soul colours I logged.

"Last we met you ran like a coward," Vincent called across the way when Miklos's group stopped. "Now you wish to shake hands like gentlemen and erase your treason?"

From my position, I saw Ranlyn's head twitch as if he stopped himself from shooting Vincent a dirty look for the unhelpful comment.

Miklos's expression didn't change. "If a handshake could negate all wrongdoing, then I would be prepared to take your palm."

"The guilty are usually so willing." Vincent's tone was steady, Miklos not making any outward reaction.

"Tell us why you have requested our presence." A note of irritation layered Ranlyn's command.

"My intentions for this meeting were never secret. Salix and Wend can attest to that."

I still found it weird to hear my Coven name since the custom was Aunt Lacey's and no one stuck to tradition.

"Granted, but you did not explain why you've decided to reach out. You state you *want* to, however, I'd wager you *need* to. So, what is it you need?" Ranlyn's tone was hard as he confronted his former co-Elder. Turns out Ranlyn hit the nail on the head.

Miklos lifted his chin with smugness, but he was clearly hiding the fact it bothered him Ranlyn accurately read between the lines. "We need to know where you're hiding."

Vincent outright laughed. Not a belly bouncer but enough to make an impact as it reached the far ends of the park, hardening the last of Miklos's soft, hairy edges.

"We are being hunted."

"Is that so?" Veata asked with a bit of sarcastic wit. "And why do you suppose that is? Do you think it's possible this could have been avoided, Miklos? Do you suppose we would have to hide at all if you hadn't flipped sides like French toast? If that beard wasn't so thick, you'd see the egg on your face. We're lucky not to smell your rotting breakfast from here, traitor."

In Veata's usual way she managed to be hilarious while delivering a tongue lashing.

Trying to ignore her, Miklos searched to Ranlyn. "Loring and his flock are not our only enemies. Rosemary's flock and any other Tainted who survived the Creation takedown, even others who only heard of the event, are circling. Not readying to strike, but merely toying with us. Safety is lost. Wherever you hide could save our Coven from annihilation."

"Or would bring the enemy down on us," Ranlyn added.

"Couldn't have written a better introduction myself!" A booming rasp made us all jump. "On second thought, I would think some grander exploits could've been spackled throughout, yet timing was superb."

As soon as Loring spoke and appeared behind Miklos's group, everyone shifted gears and dropped into a fighting stance, his presence momentarily uniting us with Miklos's people against a common enemy. Being the closest from the Team, Bronya and Gregor cried in a grunt of pain, Bronya falling on her side, Gregor collapsing to a knee as a few from Miklos's group did the same.

Loring's boisterous cackle highlighted the fact he had the jump on us, though the Tainted Magic wasn't jumping anywhere while leaning into a cane and harboring the scars and deformations from when Caine and I trapped him and Evaristus underground. He can tailor his suits any way he wants, but he can never fully hide what we did to him, and I was sick with satisfaction over it.

"Please." Loring tried but uncontrollably laughed before saying, "Please try and access your abilities again. Your first attempt was so successful."

Using their powers is what put them down? How was Loring doing it?

While we stood impotently, unable to react at our seething hatred or end up mewling in the snow, the vibration in the air told me everyone's power was still enacted. Since we hadn't acted on our power rush, it may be what left us standing.

Energy raged, begging to be released, promising it could make me proud to punish Loring in the most delightful ways as well as ease the discomfort of my power revving its engines without letting it ride. Retreat wasn't an option. Loring may not have put me in the Sorrel cells, but he was the first person I can claim as a true enemy. He stole enough. By extension, he was responsible for everything since he laid eyes on me at Aunt Lacey's.

Wrath kept me strapped in a hyper-vigilance, everything in me instinctively drove me to protect and avenge Aunt Lacey and all the Magics he caused suffering against.

After making light of our members down in the snow, Loring glanced over his shoulder and at least twenty members of his flock popped into view, hiding under a spell the whole time in wait for some cue for a masterful reveal.

Always with the theatrics.

No one moved. Bullets didn't require magic, but no one palmed a weapon yet, waiting for Loring to reveal his next hidden rabbit as was his character.

"Thank you, Miklos, for guiding me to this magnificent stage." Loring held out his arms to embellish his thanks, the scars accentuated in the stadium lights, casting off his skin like it had been removed in slices and pieced back together like a grotesque puzzle.

Miklos stared at our scarred enemy in bared hate. He should have expected a tail and taken precautions to lose them.

"My Master has passed, yet I have as many Puppets to keep eyes on those who broke the world rightfully ours." Ours being himself and Evaristus. "Not that your travels are any more secret...Firefly." Loring crooked his head to the side to look at me around Donovan.

An impulse of power blew through me as his stare locked onto mine. A strike of agony blazed through the top of my head and landed me on the ground. Pain tingled through my extremities, undulating with wringing intensity.

Hands grabbed my arms. I pushed them away, knowing they were Donovan's before seeing him. I didn't need him making me appear weak when I was doing a splendid job of it myself.

Flexing to my feet as the lingering tingles of pain railed through me, the blood rushing from my head to my heels blotted my vision. I stood low and held on, praying I didn't faint, and ecstatic when the Magics around me came into full view. Vincent was close as if he too had rushed to me when I went down. All I heard was that nerve-humping laugh of Loring's. His perverse enjoyment evoked my magic again, it simmering instead of lashing out.

"Firefly's a hissing dragon and no longer a fan of her soulmate. Huh, intriguing. I see my deceased acolyte's heir is also missing." Loring smiled at the mention of Caine. "Ditched the men and gained yourself some protection. Suits you well, girl."

A growl in my throat escaped.

Another bolt of punishment spanked me, laying me out. This time it was the pre-emptive thought of attack while my powers were engaged.

Stars glistened above, the glinting sparks of light having nothing to do with the sky.

I heard a snarl from Donovan as he knelt at my side and fought his own over-reactions. He worked on control for years, and I was showing off my Seedling tendencies—impulsive, quick-tempered, easily goaded by meaningless meddling comments spouted from some shrivelled prick with a god complex.

Cold winter air rushed through my lips and the return of my power simmering piggybacked the pain of Loring's spell or whatever he did to us. I cursed to myself, the cool snow seeping through my clothes, my hands clawed into my forehead trying to block everything as Loring continued to mouth off.

"*Sophie....*" Vincent's soft yet firm voice came into my head. Before he could tell me to calm myself, I told him to fuck off and tried retreating into myself to find the reins of my magic running wild on adrenaline and revenge.

I managed to tone it down a notch and then tamped it further when I heard Kim's name. The confusion of Loring mentioning her was enough for me to drag myself into a seated position as the spell connecting my power to every nerve tingled.

"Welcome back, Firefly. You wouldn't want to miss this since you were part and parcel of us discovering the little gem." Loring looked over his shoulder to his flock. "Gents, our gem, please."

Two other Magics blinked into existence, each holding the end of a thick piece of curved wood that lay atop the shoulders of a man, his arms strapped to them, their hold keeping his large frame on his knees in the snow.

Loring chuckled like a sadistic child. "Medieval, I know. None-theless, with a Blind specimen so large, this method certainly keeps him contained. The male was trying to find you Firefly, and Kim.

Showing up at both of your squalid dwellings. How could I pass up the opportunity?"

With his head down, I didn't recognize the big guy until he lifted his head like it weighed one hundred pounds.

Shit! Frog.

His light hair was darkened and matted with blood and sweat, more blood dripping from his lips. His eyes were swollen, one nearly shut. And judging by how he found it difficult to keep his balance or straighten without Loring's men holding him in place, there was plenty of damage under his clothing.

Thankfully Kim and Caine weren't around for this. Not that it didn't strike me as heinous...it was. The guy had been worked over, but they were closer to Frog than anyone else present. The Tactical Team was likely ignorant of who Frog was, and Vincent maybe met him once at Donovan's.

When we decided to swing by our places, it should have occurred to us that it was too easy without being trapped or swarmed by the enemy. By that time, we were gone, and Loring's guys must have already apprehended Frog and didn't stick around.

Something else occurred to me. How much did Frog know about our world? Dammit, definitely more than he should. Enough to be a threat? Not of the Prison Creation, but enough to put himself in danger or to be used as leverage.

"I have no desire to own this whelp." Loring sneered at Frog like he was vermin. "My flock has had their fun and he served to prove my point. No one is beyond my reach and everyone responsible for the death of my Master will suffer or their loved ones will suffer in their stead. Any others will not be in such good condition to be released. Needless and cruel? Indeed. You can surrender and accept your warranted penalties and, if I happen to find something redeeming, may even show mercy and grant you position within my flock."

His tone should have evoked generosity since it was what he was going for, though came across as condescending. If Loring kept his word, he would choose few to join him when killing those responsible for his Master's death was much more satisfying.

The Magics holding Frog disappeared while Frog remained. The wood in their now invisible hands still held high, so those magics hadn't fully disappeared as Olson could do. They were hiding behind the spell that smuggled them in.

As Loring talked on, more of his flock blinked out of view. "Since no one is willing enough to surrender now, I look forward to seeing you in the future, as of course I expect a coup. And if I do not see you, you will see evidence of my presence around the region and beyond to wherever necessary to attain what I want. Let this simple human be a lesson."

With his warning delivered, Loring disappeared, and Frog fell face first into the snow. Pouncing forward, the Team, Elders, and Miklos's flock didn't have targets to attack or shoot, yet knew they were still useless as they felt the reverberation of magic in the air keeping their powers impotently caged.

We could have searched the park for hours. No matter the foot work we put in, Loring was gone, and we were lucky to remain standing.

I sprinted to Frog, for some reason wanting the first face he saw to be familiar. A few others helped with the leather strapping him to the wood across his shoulders, though I couldn't have recalled who as my attention was monopolized by the sight of his injuries as I palmed his face, trying to keep him conscious and above the snow. Frog's eyelids were too swollen to open completely but what I saw was splashed with blood surrounding his blue eyes.

"Where's Kim?" Frog's voice rasped like he had been screaming for hours.

"She's fine."

"They have her—" He was cut off by a mucus-y cough ending with blood drooling down his lips.

"He's a bastard liar. They never took her. Kim's perfectly safe, I promise you."

Frog's second arm was released, neither he nor I able to brace his weight. He slumped to the ground in exhaustion but didn't stay down long. He pulled himself up onto all fours, wobbling and straining for strength.

"Hold up." I tried to stop him as he stood and staggered.

"I wanna see her," he slurred, the blood from his lips dripping to mix with his already saturated shirt front.

Vincent shook his head at me, knowing I wanted to bring Frog to the Prison Creation. Frog pulled at my Tactical vest forcing me to face him. Donovan grabbed the guy's wrist, it falling easily from me in his weakness. Donovan let go quickly as the contact sparked a vision.

"I wanna see her," Frog repeated. "I need to be sure and I sure as shit don't trust your word."

For some reason that stung. "Fine."

"No," Vincent's voice clipped.

"Not a chance." Caveman jumped in with his two cents as we turned to see he and Ismail return from their scouting position during the exchange. "You being there puts Kim in danger." He spoke directly to Frog.

"Who the fuck're you?" Frog shot at Caveman, wobbling again as he refused to lean on anyone.

"The fucker protecting her from Blind idiots like yourself."

Their territorial responses weren't getting us anywhere.

"Look it," I snapped, "we will take you—"

"Sophie...." Vincent tried.

"—if you agree to be bound and hooded and be subjected to any other measures we can possibly think of including only seeing her in a private room so you can't see other people or know where we are." I turned to Vincent and the Elders. "Will that work?" Vincent was being protective of his baby, the project that had brought him the closest to a solution against the Sovereignty rule, so I understood Vincent's hesitance and wouldn't do anything to jeopardize all he worked for. The protection of the Coveners in general was important, but Frog wasn't going away, and we needed to know what happened and anything else that might be important about his time with Loring.

"Hood me." Frog grabbed my arm again and dropped it before Donovan could make him. "I don't give a shit what you do. I need to see her."

Vincent surrendered.

"Are you fucking kidding me?" Caveman stepped up in Vincent's face. "Ismail and I couldn't reach any of you because when Loring showed up, you all disappeared, and then you come through with a Blind human wanting to waltz into the—"

"Enough!" Ranlyn yelled above Caveman's ranting not wanting him to inadvertently reveal to Miklos and his people where we were. Caveman stopped but continued to glower at Vincent. "Control yourself. We are all aware of your true concerns and they have nothing to do with safety." Caveman turned his glower on Ranlyn. I was surprised Ranlyn knew about the Caveman and Kim connection. Everyone saw more than I did.

"We will bring the man with us, implementing the agreed conditions," Ranlyn said with finality.

"We still need to go with you." Miklos lobbied for continued protection, and we were brought around to the reason for the meeting. "Go ahead and bind us. We don't care where it is as long as we can be there in safety."

"Not a chance," Ranlyn responded without pretence.

"You—"

"Owe you nothing," Veata jumped in. "I don't trust you, Hungarian. A hood won't save you from pinpointing our location and Loring can easily track you, proven by his attendance here. You're a danger to the whole of us. I'm sure you have contacts willing to service you."

"This does not help the Mother Coven's division. We came here in good faith."

"You came here in desperation and led our enemies straight to us." Ranlyn already sounded tired of him. "If survival of the Mother

Coven is truly your goal, then going with us would only endanger it more, meaning you're in it for yourself. We have accepted your olive branch. Now use your brain and find refuge somewhere in the world that won't jeopardize the rest of us. We can be reached at this number." He pulled out a card and extended it. With hesitation Miklos took it. "It's untraceable but if we need to be contacted or if you need immediate help...call."

Miklos and his crew still weren't satisfied. Ranlyn was firm and Miklos was dismissed, his crew leaving as everyone refocused on Frog and what to do next.

I offered to heal Frog, but he wouldn't let me touch him, so I didn't push. If he wanted to be in pain akin to a cleated kick to the nuts, then that was his prerogative.

I saw Vincent and panic hit. "You're coming too, right?"

"I am."

My shoulders relaxed.

"I need to speak with Edson and cannot remain long."

I gave a tight nod, taking what I could.

The others had already started walking back to the vehicles, Frog leading a staggered path as Donovan dragged his feet trying to stay close to me. His presence annoyed me to no end, as I walked with Vincent.

Vincent put an arm around my shoulders as we walked. "Worry not, my father will not kill me yet. He still needs me." He knew him leaving and me never seeing him again was on my mind.

"He could still throw you into the Sovereignty cells."

"Nah, Alasdair would choose ending me over imprisonment." I scowled and he chuckled. "I jest, Sophie. However, if I do outlive my usefulness, I will be disposed of which is why I bother to win his crooked court cases he throws at me."

"You have to win court cases?"

He nodded. "Unfortunately, though I try my damndest, I have my father's blood in my veins, and this affords me great ability when considering the law. Something my father is lording over me."

"Until you find Cora-Lynn's soul?"

"Only until then."

I nodded through a sigh.

"After we deal with Frog, will you do as I suggested?" I squinted in thought, eliciting a laugh. "Forget already? The Soul Reading to discover and re-establish your connection to Donovan."

"Oh."

"Yes, oh. Please consider the possibility that all of this will pass if you give the tactic honest effort. I know those feelings are presently elusive and though he is not everyone's cup of tea, he does deserve you even if he does not think himself worthy."

I unabashedly pointed at Donovan's back as he walked some distance in front of us. "He deserves me? I'd like to hear your definition of worthy—"

"Stop!" His voice rose as he stopped our progress and turned me to face him, placing both hands on either side of my face.

I saw Donovan turn and tense as if he expected Vincent to kiss me. Noticing this, Vincent moved his hands to my shoulders. I didn't want Vincent to kiss me, but even if he was going to, Donovan had no right to bitc—

"Listen," he said to grab my attention away from Donovan. "We have covered your current emotional plane. Please, promise me you will endeavour to search yourself before Nya took over, before the horrors at the Sorrel Compound, and find slices of your love for Donovan and for who you were.

"After years at your side and playing witness to the incredible romance the two of you share, I refuse to be a bystander as it crumbles." He paused with a fear in his gaze I rarely saw. "If you allow the tear in your Soul Magic to grow, you will be without the Team... and without me." He held me tighter to prevent me from pulling away. "I will not give up, but you would be without yourself. You and Donovan will both be lost. If it takes me to convince Caine to persuade you into injecting yourself into those memories and keeping you there until you have changed your mind, then I would travel such lengths to ensure it is done. Please, Sophie. Please try."

Vincent never looked at me like this. I wasn't sure if he could convince Caine to use his powers to overtake my free will, and I couldn't promise anything, but whatever he heard in my weakly shielded mind must have reassured him. A small grin crinkled his green eyes, and he resumed walking with me tucked under his arm, Donovan proceeding as we did.

On the way to the Prison Creation, Caveman sat next to Frog. Instead of a hood, Veata removed his eyes with a temporary spell, and they disappeared in a creepy-ass way along with his hearing. He wasn't happy about it, but a hood could fail or be removed if Frog managed to free a hand. An alternative route to the entrance was also taken in case he was directionally gifted.

Caveman suggested we knock him out, the option argued and lost. He stayed as close as a wart, the two looking like the beginnings of a Scandinavian Olympic team with their large bodies and blond hair. Caveman was not on Frog's team and couldn't contain his aggravation the whole ride. I couldn't read his mind, though I guessed his thoughts contained worry for Kim's safety as well as a rundown on his opinions of Frog.

I could slip into Frog's head still and all his thoughts were consumed with worry for Kim, convinced she was kidnapped.

Caveman pushed Frog ahead of him once we were inside the Creation, gruff and moving too fast considering Frog couldn't see where he was or who might be in his way.

Once settled into an office, Veata returned Frog's sight and hearing as the Team broke off, Vincent to find Edson, and I stayed in the office and told Donovan to find Kim. He didn't look happy for the directive, but someone had to fetch her, and I wasn't leaving Caveman with Frog since the guy was set on making Frog feel unwelcome by landing a hard hand on Frog's shoulder and shoving him down into a chair.

Frog pushed Caveman's hand off of his shoulder. "Yeah, okay, Thor. Go fuck yourself."

Caveman leaned on the table with an intense glare at Frog. "Watch your mouth, son."

Frog popped up to his feet, blues-to-blues challenging Hall, even though Frog was still beaten bloody. "Calm your steroids, pal!"

Caveman snarled. "You better be worth it."

"Worth what?"

"Putting her life in peril." Caveman leaned closer. "I'll see the icy reaches of Nifheim before I allow your ignorance to endanger her. And I will end you and ensure you'll remember your death for lifetimes if you do."

"Hall!" Kim walked in with Donovan.

Damn. Things were just getting interesting.

16

IN THE DARK

Kim

"What's the matter with you?" I pushed around Sophie who decided to do nothing while Hall and Frog were about to beat each other up.

Hall faced me. Good. I needed to deal with him first.

"Don't pretend like you don't know what my problem is. You're wasting your time with this human."

"I can waste my time anyway I want, Viking. Leave." The impact on Hall was harsh, his jaw muscles clenching, his blue eyes jagged icebergs threatening to rip the whole place down. His broad, bull-headed shoulders were set, his body obscuring my view of Frog. Whatever he thought was going on between us, it didn't make this macho man display okay.

"We'll be here, man. Time for you to bounce." Donovan was the voice of reason. Or maybe he didn't want to have to fight the two of them.

Disengaging all that anger, Hall took a sharp breath in through his nose, straightened, and left without looking at me or Frog, taking his overbearing assumptions with him.

I didn't miss it when Donovan gave Hall an expression that said he felt sorry for the jerk as he clapped him on the shoulder before Hall left the room.

Egomaniacs unite.

Closing the door and remaining inside, Sophie and Donovan kept their distance, not only from us but from each other.

I could finally focus on Frog. "Oh, shit. You're hurt."

Splashes of blood were drying to all of his exposed skin. His already plush lips were swollen and split against a tooth, his cheek plumped up like a hedgehog burrowed beneath it, and both whites of his eyes were dappled with blood. And that was the injuries I could see.

"Who the fuck is that guy?" Frog was glaring after Hall.

"It doesn't matter."

"He sure thinks it matters."

"Stop." I gained his divided attention by pulling on his arm, making him wince. We sat in two chairs facing each other. "I don't understand. What happened?"

"I was trying to find you, hanging out by your work, your place, and thought maybe you'd go home at some point. I left to hit a sub shop. When I went back, your mail was gone from the mailbox, so I knocked on your door. Some assholes rushed me and knocked me out. When I woke up, I was surrounded by a bunch of people I've never seen before who thought it'd be fun to beat some info outta me. I didn't tell them anything."

"I believe you. You wouldn't have had to say a word for them to get anything they wanted from your mind."

Frog rolled his shoulders, uncomfortable with the reminder.

"What did they ask you?"

"They wanted to know where people you knew were hiding. Sophie, Caine, and others I've never heard of. I kept telling them that. Not that it mattered. They kept at it and..." He paused. I reached for his hands, his knuckles bloody like he put up a good fight. "They convinced me they already had you. I don't know why I believed them, but I did. Still, they wanted to find others. Even said they would let you go if I told, but you never let me know where you were so I couldn't have told them if I wanted to."

I got the impression if it meant me or the others, Frog would have spilled in a second to ensure I was safe and I was conflicted on if that was a good thing.

Regardless of his loyalty, Magics with Loring wouldn't need to torture for information. The beating was a message and for kicks. Frog was probably a constant annoyance for their surveillance, and they figured they would have some fun with the poor Blind human.

"I'm so sorry." I couldn't apologize enough for getting him mixed up in all of this. I turned to Sophie at the end of the room. "Can you heal him?"

Frog grabbed my wrist too hard. "I don't want her help."

I snuck a glance Sophie's way and saw Donovan straighten in his leaning chair, ready to act if needed, but Sophie was still staring at the table with no notice of what was happening.

I turned my arm, loosening his grip. "People will ask questions when they see your injuries. They'll want to know who worked you over and why. People like Dom who will expect revenge on your behalf." Bringing one of Caine and Frog's best friends into the mix was supposed to change his mind, but he was too stubborn and shook his head no. "How are you going to explain the bruises, Frog? A mugging?"

He shrugged. "Happens to people every day."

"Without a police report?"

"She's not touching me." He wasn't budging.

"Would you let me heal you if I had the ability?"

His glare was hard, only a second of hesitation before saying, "No."

This was a lot more than him playing tough guy. I shifted away from him. "This is who I am."

"No kidding, but you're not like them." He cast a judgemental glare towards Sophie and Donovan with no qualms about talking loud enough for them to overhear.

"The only difference is that they're much stronger than me. One day I *will* be them. Or at least I want to be."

"Why?"

"Why not?"

"For starters? They're miserable." When I went to object, he leaned in like the closeness could convince me. "Look, I'm in the dark since I'm not trustworthy enough to know simple details, but I definitely know enough about them that I know I never want to be them," he said, pointing at Sophie and Donovan.

"Hey!" I swatted his arm down.

He went on like I didn't do anything. "Besides the fact Sophie jumped into the guy's pants before Caine was on the back burner, you can't seriously look at them and see a future. That homey-hopper and her prick boyfriend may deserve each other regardless of this magic shit, but what about what's happened to Caine? He's awake from his coma now, but he's had nothing but shit shovelled at his doorstep. Sophie woke him up, but she also broke his goddamned heart and still expects Caine to stick around and do his bidding. He doesn't see his mom or his friends. All of this magic shit has consumed his life."

His tone softened but only slightly. "When can things get back to normal? Cuz I'd really like to chill with my girlfriend and my friend without checking over my shoulder for some cocky d-bag trying to take us out."

I sat in a long silence absorbing all of what Frog dropped on me. "You're mad and in pain, so I can forget half of what you just said, but let me straighten something out for you. That homey-hopper over there is my best friend and she couldn't control how things went down with Caine. And, yes, magic fucked that up too, but if Sophie and Caine can move on from it than you can suck it up. Plus, don't you think I'd like to go to work or have a date night with you without worrying?"

He raised a split eyebrow as if to ask, "Would you?"

"Of course I would, but this is my life right now. Accept it or give up and let me know now so I'm not wasting my time trying to iron out your prejudices."

His nostrils flared, his anger simmering.

"If you want to keep the pain of the beating like some macabre souvenir, so be it. You were brought here for your protection and to reassure you I was alive. They could have dumped you outside of the hospital or left you where they found you. Right now, we have enormous protection issues of our own, so although I'm ecstatic as a monkey in a banana pit that you're alive, I have a Sect to run and other peoples' lives to try and save before they're completely decimated. I didn't think mine was amongst those I had to Krazy Glue together, but you've painted a vivid picture of what you think about this 'magic shit'."

I sprung to my feet, Frog trying to follow, barely lifting his ass off the chair before I shoved him back down, his damaged shoulder the only reason it worked. "You can't leave this room, so I'll fetch Caine for you. Maybe he can answer some questions about his homey-hopper situation."

Bull-with-his-nuts-tied mad, I stormed out with blood pumping adrenaline to find Caine, pretty sure that Sophie and Donovan got an earful of the topic-ender to our conversation, but I was so pissed I didn't stop until I found Caine in the cafeteria.

He stood as I sped-walked up to him, his grey eyes bracing. "Go check on your bastard bestie in the main boardroom." His thick brows scrunched. "Quickly. I left his stupid ass with Sophie and Donovan, and they probably aren't too happy with him right now."

With Caine calling after me, I stalked off as quickly as I came in. I needed to check on the Coveners. They were probably fine, and I was so angry I had bypassed most of them anyway, unable to speak with my chin trembling, and hid in the staff bathroom until my blood pressure lowered.

Was Hall right? Was I wasting my time with Frog? He had the crap beat out of him and was now captive by people he was supposed to trust, when clearly he didn't even trust me. The mood swing could be forgiven, but did he really think about things the way he said them?

Frog had been through a lot and was mostly in the dark, but I was angry too, and wasn't about to let anyone spew all that hate and not stand up for myself and my friends.

If Frog couldn't rise above his prejudices and make peace with the fact I wasn't about to change who I was for him, then I was going to have to cut him loose, and didn't that prospect let the tears in beyond the velvet rope.

17

LITTLE UNDERSTANDING

Caine

When Kim blew through and said my "bestie" was in the boardroom, it took me a couple of moments to think about who she meant. Could only be Frog, right?

Kim was generally uptight. This time the redness of her cheeks and the bulging vein in her forehead said she was mega pissed.

"Guess you're needed," Ness said when Kim and her bulging neck vein ran off.

We had been talking, or at least I was talking, and Ness was absorbing, though she hadn't said anything while I tried to be calm about our relationship going from nothing, to having sex, and her seeing me talking with Sophie.

After all that work, I really didn't want to leave her.

"I guess. Do you want to come with me?"

Her forehead creased. "Why?"

"I guess I don't have a non-cheesy answer for that."

"I don't know Frog, and chances are you'll talk about stuff I already know about or has nothing to do with me."

"Hmm. Too soon to meet my friends, eh?" She huffed but didn't answer, making me laugh. I leaned down and pecked her cheek. "I'll find you afterwards."

Her brows hitched up as she surveyed who witnessed the PDA, but again she said nothing.

Ness may be abrasive and outwardly cold, but I knew better. We jumped in too fast after staying at arms' length for months, allowing that sexual tension to break us, and now had hazmat level damage control to contend with.

What a joy.

Inside the boardroom, I saw Frog across from the door sitting at the table looking like someone worked him over. Walking into the room farther, Sophie and Donovan were at the far end of the long table. No one was talking, though all eyes flipped to me as I entered.

Frog stood as I came around the table and we hugged quickly before sitting. "Damn. Who used your face as a hacky-sack, bro?"

"Fucked if I know. Rest of the body ain't so hot either." He rolled his shoulders like even my hug was too much.

"Loring and his flock had some fun," Donovan called from across the room and went into the Team accompanying the Elders to Pearson Park and what happened there. When he finished, he settled back, leaning his chair the farthest it would go, and went quiet. Sophie never offered a word.

"Wow, man. You have no clue how lucky you are to be breathing right now and still with all your body parts intact. Loring is no one to fuck with."

"So I'm told." Frog sat, covering up a jolt of pain by clearing his throat.

I sat in front of him. "I can heal you."

He shook his head. "Don't need it."

"Fine, tough guy. You wanna talk about why Kim's pissed at you instead?"

Frog clucked his tongue. "Maybe because I called your ex over there a homey-hopper? I'm sure that didn't help."

"I bet." I leaned forward in my chair. "First off, to set you straight on the topic, me and Donovan were anything but 'homey's'."

"You bromancing now?"

I ignored him. "Secondly, Sophie didn't mean to—"

"She fell on his dick? She thought it was a free pussy-polishing device? Chick seems rock solid enough for a SWAT team to mistake—"

"You wanna talk about the big issue or we gonna have a problem?" I couldn't help my tone was hard as nails.

Frog leaned in to match my posture, the blood on his whites making his stare more intense. "Why are you always sticking up for that chick? The old Caine woulda dumped any dick-eating ho-bag and left her in a puddle of her own tears. She's not sp—"

I snatched Frog's will with a hitch of power, controlling his ability to speak long enough to read the realization and panic in his thoughts before letting his will go.

Frog straightened. "Yo."

"You done with the commentary about Sophie?" He didn't respond, this time by choice. "Do I seem like the old Caine to you? I'm not concerned with how you see things with your little understanding of a shitty and complex situation. Kim is dealing with enough—"

"She wouldn't be dealing with any of it if all this magic shit wasn't fucking with her life."

"Magic shit? You called it that to her, didn't you?" Frog's lack of response confirmed it. "Understand something, bro. There is no Kim without that 'magic shit'. She's been in it long before Sophie or me, so settle with that or leave her. You're not the only guy on her radar and we've dealt with enough Blind making us feel guilty for being who we are."

"What do you mean on her radar?"

I saw a flash of Frog's thoughts, and he was thinking of Hall muscling him into the room when they showed up and how the guy acted around Kim. "You know exactly who I mean given the way the big, blond Viking-looking dude dragged you in here."

He huffed. "I'm not afraid of that poser. Plus, Kim wasn't born this way. It doesn't have to be like this."

"That poser is the real deal. I'm sure the cutlery the guy used as a kid is in a museum somewhere. As for being born this way, Kim wasn't, but I was. So were the majority of the people in this place where you shouldn't even be allowed."

"You know what I mean."

"Yeah, I do. So, if you can't stop your big mouth from chewing the foot kicking your gag reflex, then simplify life and live it far away from Kim. You being here is a huge risk that could kill a lot of people. You're my friend, but don't kid yourself, I have no problem locking you down if it means saving those people's lives."

Without waiting for some smart-ass response I knew Frog had raring to go, I turned to Sophie and Donovan. "Does he know anything useful?"

"Fuck you, buddy."

"Nope," Donovan responded. "Loring snatched and questioned. Beating was for fun."

"I coulda told you that," Frog interjected.

"Yeah, but he—" I pointed at Donovan "—could tell me without you speaking a word. As could Sophie or me, plus I can persuade you to think you were in a bar fight or conveniently make you forget Kim ever existed." Frog did some more glaring. "Your thoughts aren't your own here. So, keep them clean of your bigoted opinions if you don't wanna piss off a lot of people, every one of them able to literally obliterate you." I wasn't sorry for talking to him like this. Hard lines had to be drawn.

The door swung open. I sprung to my feet since Frog wasn't supposed to see the other Coveners.

18

CONTINUED EXISTENCE

Sophie

The Elders entered the boardroom, Caine, Donovan, and I all spooked to attention.

Ranlyn turned to Donovan. "What do we know?"

"Loring gained nothing cuz nothin' special's going on in that kid's head." Frog shot him the finger and Donovan shot back a double dose of his own.

"Good. Now you have to leave."

Frog's attention swung to Ranlyn. "Excuse me?"

"You were permitted entry so you could confirm Kim's safety since you were caught up in Loring's flare for the dramatic. You can't stay."

"He doesn't know our location," Caine argued over Frog.

"And it will remain that way."

Donovan approached the Elders. "Loring promised to go after people connected to the ones responsible for killing Evaristus since his true targets are all in hiding. This chump is patient zero. Guaranteed he won't be the last."

I recognized they didn't need me and would be arguing about Frog's stay in a back-and-forth tennis match before someone gave up. Alternatively, I had some important calls to make and went to slip out.

I stopped next to Vincent. "Don't leave without saying goodbye. I'll be across the hall using the phone."

He nodded. I left, closing the door behind me.

First call was to my mom. I would have liked to avoid it all together, but I had to warn my family. Mom was not happy, and raising my voice was the only thing to stop her when she went on a tangent about not knowing where my brother or I was and her talk with Vincent at the courthouse...it was too much in one phone call.

Normally, I would grant my mom room for this, validate her worry, but I couldn't fill that role right now. I needed to know my family was safe from Loring making an example of them. I told her to go to Dunnville with my grandmother. The old woman may not be the Grandma Lizzie I loved as a child or the most devout Magic, but she could protect my mother whether she acknowledged her power or not.

Mom couldn't argue with that.

My father was a bigger hurdle. Thomas Saterlee wasn't an easy one to scare and he wouldn't dare uproot his life without full disclosure. I wasn't about to out myself and put more family in danger. Besides, that's not the kind of bomb you can drop over the phone, even if a cowardly part of me thought it would be a lot easier than a face-to-face explanation.

"I will assign guards to his residence."

I looked up to find Vincent leaning into the door jam, still with my mother in my ear. I smiled in thanks as Mom was saying, "I'll work on something so I can take a leave from my position. I'd like to be of help, but the courthouse isn't as safe as I always thought it was."

"No, it's not."

"Please promise me an update call from you or your brother or even Serena at least once a day so I know you're all okay."

"We can do that. If you haven't heard from one of us, call the number Vincent gave you. I'll tell them to expect you."

I heard a soft whine in the background and realized Bosco must have been on my mom's lap. A familiar complaint said he needed her attention more than whoever was on the phone. He wasn't my child, but I missed that pug face and couldn't imagine him at my grandmother's. She hated me and not Bosco so he would probably be safe, but I wished he were with me instead.

Letting my mom go was an extra ten-minute affair, Mom not wanting to say goodbye in case it was the last time she heard my voice. Without having kids, I couldn't fully sympathize, but only so many promises of being as careful as possible would be enough to make a mother feel secure of her children's continued existence.

With Mom and Bosco safe and Vincent's goons guarding my dad so I didn't have to come up with an excuse to get him out of his house, I could focus on getting revenge against Loring and maybe rest easier.

"I have to return." Easier until Vincent said that.

I sighed. "Can you hurry up with this plan of yours?"

Vincent gave a small laugh. "I will certainly try."

We hugged tightly. He refused to let go when I asked, "When can you skip out again?"

"Not sure." His eyes apologized when he finally pulled away. "Being discreet means I have to govern these visits sparingly."

"Can you call?"

He smiled and peered over his glasses. "You *will* be okay, Sophie. Listen to your Elders, learn from your Team, and remember what I said in the park. I worry about you, and I need you to be okay so I can focus on my role within my father's domain."

"I know." I hugged him tightly again.

I wanted to walk him to the elevator but didn't trust myself not to break down. The unforgiving audience would be on me with questions and punching people was frowned upon. Instead, I watched him leave and felt my stomach drop when he disappeared from sight beyond the office door.

19

RECKLESS WRATH

Donovan

When Sophie left the boardroom, my concentration on trying to convince Ranlyn to keep Frog in the prison, if only until Kim got a chance to speak with him again, shifted and left the room with her. I was attentive enough to hear them argue and Caine agree to *persuade* Frog to talk their friends into a last-minute vacation. Frog tried to argue against this but since he couldn't leave the room, he knew what was coming.

Unlike me—if I had Blind friends to worry about—Caine would probably feel guilty, but he would do it, and Frog seemed like the kind of guy who could find a way to convince his pals a week or so on some beach baked in sun and bikinis was exactly what they needed.

The Coven even agreed to deposit money into Frog's account to pay for it, while Caine would persuade him believe it was pay his work owed him. He would still call Kim frequently and retain the memory of the beating and his trip to the boardroom since he didn't know he was in a Creation, but he would listen to Caine's directions to a T.

Seemed simple enough to me, though Kim would be more pissed than she already was.

Since my role was unneeded, I excused myself, heading for the office Sophie was leaving. Features drawn, arms crossed physically holding herself together, the bags under her eyes swelling then reddened like her cheeks like she might cry any second. Seeing me changed all that. Every softened edge hardened in a transformation that made her look mean.

Distracting myself from forcing Caine to persuade her to being herself again, I watched her walk away, waiting until she was gone before phoning Fox to check on how he was, praying to hear good news.

No such luck.

After hearing the gravel in his tired voice, Fox didn't need to say it for me to know he was getting worse. Fox was the foundation I landed on when I most needed it. Without him, Tobias would have killed me by now, or I would still be running. Also, I wouldn't have met Aunt Lacey who brought me Sophie.

Due to the Soul Magic Sophie and I may have crossed paths eventually but who knew what condition I would have been in by then. My growing sex addiction and substance dependency would have worsened. Not to mention the compulsive stealing.

I found a sliver of happiness while Caine was still locked in the Creation. Sophie came to terms with our relationship, at least to a certain extent. Nights spent watching movies on the couch were more satisfying than any club crawl.

If Fox died, what I would be losing was more than I could fathom and there was no reproducing that man, no matter how many lifetimes I lived.

Hanging up with only a "Talk to you later, kid," was not reassuring. Fox's Druid friend was doing everything they could, but Fox let me go because he didn't have the strength to continue the conversation. Another bad sign.

Since I couldn't do anything about Fox, I decided to take on another immoveable force. Sophie. Vincent gave me a good idea; one I was willing to try. Talking Sophie into complying? Tackling that mountain was a mystery.

Checking the console showed me Sophie wasn't hiding in any of the cells. It was late so quite a few were occupied since maintaining a schedule was pointless in here. Checking the boardrooms and offices, I found one that was locked but only by the handles mechanical lock, not magic.

Taking a chance that a couple hadn't snuck away for privacy, I did an unlock spell and peeped my head in, ready to relock it if all I found was skin-on-skin.

Sophie sat alone in the dark at the desk chair, hand on the bare skin of her chest, eyes closed, *reading* her soul. Closing the door behind me without a whisper, I stood and watched as she sifted through her memories, her inability to shield her thoughts was a bonus I took advantage of.

I was surprised to find that she was concentrating on memories involving us together. A scene of us lounging on my couch as the television sat in front of us was a fond memory I was just thinking of myself, except as I watched through her perspective, something was off.

Because of my Psychometry, touching her skin was blinding. At one time, I thought I had it under control, but that was before she became so strong, so I did my best to stay clear so I could stay focused on her in front of me instead of our past.

She knew this.

In this particular memory, my expressions and the physical distance I insisted on made it seem as if I didn't want to touch her, like she somehow disgusted me. No way in hell that was how it went down. It took everything in me not to hold her every second of the day like some love-sick teenager.

In the next memory, she asked me a simple question, one I remembered answering, but in this version my response had such abject sarcasm that the meaning changed completely. That wasn't how I said it in real-time.

I waited as she examined a dozen more memories, all with that same alteration, casting me as a prick who did nothing but treat her like a disposable one-night stand while keeping her strung along and manipulating her into loving me.

Holy shit. No wonder she hated me. The damage to our Soul Magic wasn't an emotion or the state of a traumatized mind. The poison others talked about leaked from our broken Soul Magic and literally re-wrote all of her memories of me.

When her reading slowed on the Sorrel Cells, I had to stop her. I knew what those alterations had her thinking. Revisiting that time and knowing that she thought I truly enjoyed it? No, I couldn't watch that. Being told what really happened wasn't making a difference and this was why.

Vincent's plan may not work but it was better than watching her validate her hatred for me based on bullshit Soul Readings.

"I need you to come with me."

Sophie zipped out of her *reading* with a loud gasp like the ejection was painful. "What are you doing in here?"

"Now. I need you to come with me now."

She was already scuttling her way around the desk. I planted myself in front of the exit with my hands up, ready to make my plea until she grabbed my wrist, and I was injected with a vision of the last time we fought, the piggy-backing emotion so strong it weakened my knees.

As I regained myself, Sophie already made a run for it.

Racing down the hall after her, I called her name to no reaction from her. She ignored me and was lost in the crowd. Standing at the console in front of the brick wall of cells, I entered her name for a quick search, but it hadn't fully registered her yet and I had to redo it. When her name popped up. I pressed the button needed to open her cell and entered.

She spun to me. "Again! Just because there're no locks around here or because you can spell your way into them even if there was, doesn't give you the green light to stalk me."

"I need to bring you somewhere." I was still a little breathless from the vision and running after her.

"I'm busy."

"I saw that, but you can't Soul Read in a cell anyway...Ugh, off-topic. That doesn't matter. You realize your memories have been altered, right?

"What?"

"I saw them in your mind—"

"What's the matter with you?"

"Please, babe." I tried to keep my voice far calmer than I felt. "You could read the same memories from me and see how different they are from yours."

"What? I'm not reading you."

"Look, if you hated me, I'd have to live with it. That's not what's happening. Your hate for me is based on broken Soul Magic that's twisting your memories into something dark and making you think I'm being an asshole."

"Because you are an asshole. You think you've never done anything wrong to justify it any other way?"

"Sure, I can be an asshole, but not to you and not in those memories you were revisiting."

"You told me yourself you weren't made for long-term relationships."

"What? No, I didn't. I said I'd never been in one before."

"I should've listened to you instead of trying to fix you. Now, you're trying to gaslight me into thinking I'm going crazy."

"Gaslight? No, that's what I mean. You're not crazy, it's the broken Soul Magic poisoning you. You're not seeing it right."

"I was there!"

"So was I!"

No. Enough was enough.

I grabbed her arm intent on muscling her out of the cell.

Pain exploded in my eye, her fist connecting, my neck cranking back with a snap.

I didn't let her go. Instead, I fought to shake off the hit and whipped her in front of me to grab her from behind, pulling her against my chest and trapping her arms at her sides. I arched us backwards, lifting her feet off the ground so I could walk us out.

The bridge of my nose exploded as she drove the back of her skull into my face. *"Fuck!"*

Refusing to let her go as tears and blood spilled down my face, my eyesight shot, I heaved her up off of her feet again as her snarls ringed in my ears. A few running steps was all I needed.

She went limp and slipped down through my arms onto the floor.

Effective. Extremely effective.

Wiley and pissed off didn't do me any favours, nor did having half my eyesight as she kicked my knee in the opposite direction with her combats.

I cried out as muscles tore. I bent to grab my leg, fighting to see her next move. She sported a sadistic smile of satisfaction as she tried to kick my other knee and fully immobilize me. Before she could, I grabbed her ankle and knocked her on her ass.

She kicked at my hand holding her ankle. I shook her, screwing with her aim. Another shake gained me a few feet towards the exit, wobbly on one leg as we spilled from the cell into the lobby.

Voices around us raised in confusion and surprise as we exited the cell mid-scuffle, my mug full of blood dragging Sophie behind me like game meat. I didn't give a shit who was watching. None of them gained our attention as Sophie was focused on attacking me while I rushed a shot of healing magic through me to fix my broken nose and leg. This made it harder to keep a hold of her as she swore and flailed to escape me.

Power from her swelled. I palmed the key Vincent gave me, uttered the magic words, and zipped us both away.

We landed in the basement storeroom in Amsterdam where Vincent took me to find the ritual stone.

Outside the non-magic confines of the cell, Sophie's power was engaged. She reared up and booted me in the chest. Pain and free-flying stole my breath. I plowed through piles of boxes and papers before I hit the wall and slid down onto whatever landed under me.

Blink—Darkness, heavy-headed.

Blink—Sophie shoving boxes aside coming towards me with vengeance in her eyes.

Blink—Another voice shifted Sophie's attention away from me. A name spoken in a familiar voice not immediately coupled with a name and face.

"Elysande?"

As my eyesight grasped a stronger hold on the room, I watched Sophie spin to that name and was now stalking the female voice that called it.

"Sophie!" I struggled to my feet using the debris around me. A box collapsed, and I scrambled, off balance.

The blonde woman I met during my last visit was backing away as Sophie advanced, terrified of who she thought was Elysande—Sophie in a former life where we created our Soul Magic, and then later the daughter of the couple who owned and operated the garment and furniture stores upstairs. Though, I didn't know our names in that time.

Sophie didn't remember ever being Elysande and was operating on reckless wrath, directing it at a moving target, anyone available now that she put me down.

Throwing some magic into it, I propelled myself at her, landing on Sophie's back and flattening her onto the floor while simultaneously murmuring a binding spell to keep her listening. I incapacitated her drive to attack everything she saw like a colour-blind bull.

The blonde was against the wall, eyes wide, hand on her chest, mouth open in shock while I took care of Sophie. "Betyn?" My name in a former life, he having started it all with Elysande.

In Dutch I responded, "Please, I won't hurt you."

"E-Elysande was—"

"Her name is Sophie in this life. I brought her here to help her remember who she is."

"Speak English, assholes!" Sophie screamed. My binding allowed her to speak but not to move.

"She doesn't understand English, babe." The nickname coming out like a restrained curse word. "Now shut it!" I turned to the blonde. "Please return upstairs and stay there. Vincent would be upset if something happened to you."

She turned to leave and stopped. "Do you know if Mr. Llewellyn is okay? We haven't heard from him."

"I've seen him. Once I'm done here, I'll explain his situation. Go now. And lock the door." This time she listened, and I waited for the click of the lock.

"Okay, let's get to it, darlin'." I wrenched Sophie up off the ground by the shoulder of her shirt and onto her feet, the binding keeping her from controlling her limbs without hindering her ability to speak, perfect for interrogations, or in this case, getting Sophie to listen without resorting to another domestic.

Stashing her on top of a box, she sat in a prime position for my little show and tell. "I know you're not an idiot." I wiped away blood from my face with my sleeve. "What you're seeing in your memories is a bunch of fucking lies." She opened her mouth. I talked over her before she could argue. "If you continue to mouth off, I'll take away your ability to speak, including telepathically, understood?"

Silence reigned as Sophie fumed, her once perfectly smooth ponytail partially falling out in the tussle.

"Where are we?" Her tone was robotic, the best she could manage as I wrestled with dumped boxes from her sending me on my last flight.

"Vincent's keepsake holding cell. He didn't tell me our names in that time, but in the beginning of all this," I motioned between us, "we were called Elysande and Betyn." Such random useless shit was scattered around us. At one point, they probably meant something. Maybe Vincent thought his memory wouldn't follow his immortality, but holding onto a carved, wooden miniature elephant, I couldn't guess at the sentiment and all I siphoned vision-wise was a blip of the calloused hands who whittled it. "The ones who lived and loved in the time of the store upstairs...They were a young couple who died tragically, as we apparently tend to do." I telekinetically shoved a box aside to avoid more visions. "Vincent's a fucking pack rat."

"So, you kidnapped me to some musty basement, to what? Give me asbestos poisoning? I'm more likely to die of a sneeze attack."

A heavy breath fell from my lips. Could she really think I wanted to kill her? "We're here so I can remind you that you're not a raging bitch willing to kill innocent blondes."

"Blondes?" Her face twisted up as if she already forgot about going after the woman from upstairs, but then remembered and rolled her eyes. "Oh, please. Don't be dramatic. I wouldn't've killed her."

"You sure about that?" Without looking at her while searching for what I came for, I knew by her silence that she wasn't all together sure about anything.

A grunt in effort was Sophie wriggling in her binding before giving up. "Who was she? What language were you speaking?"

"At least you're searching for answers. Good to be on the same wavelength for a change."

I found the album Vincent unburied the last time I was here. Inside wasn't the exact photo he showed me, but there were others taken the same day with slightly different poses.

Longing for their seemingly effortless love to return to me in this time, I fought against a reaching sadness threatening to break through. Whatever her name once was, she peered up at previous-day me with a joyous glint in her eyes, her hands resting on my chest in the light of a sunny day. I was jealous of whomever I used to be. He was fearless and didn't carry the pain of this lifetime.

"The blonde lady and I were speaking Dutch as we're currently in Amsterdam." I knelt in front of Sophie and held up the photo. "This was us. Not Elysande and Betyn who pulled off the original

Soul Magic connection, but the young couple I mentioned. Her, your, parents owned the store upstairs and Vincent retained ownership all this time."

She squinted at the photo. "Do you think he would beat her up and then hold her hostage?"

"Beat you? I manhandled you a little. Act like the victim all you want; you know I wasn't trying to hurt you. *You* were trying to kill me. Another indicator you're not yourself."

"Sure, sure." She rolled her eyes.

I held the picture in front of her face where she couldn't miss it. "Vincent took this picture in 1885, the summer we met. Look at how happy we are."

She glared at me instead. "Them. Not us. They're moronic teenagers."

"Focus on their expressions. We had that."

"Sure, we did. Until I realized what a joke it was."

I sat back on my heels. "A joke?"

"A spell has forced us into being people we're not. Not an asshair's chance would you have ever dated me normally. I have too much of an opinion and expect you to stick around once the condom's used."

I shook my head in disbelief of her bleak outlook on our relationship and reminded myself she knew me better than that.

"And me," she continued. "Would someone like me ever be with someone like you? Fuck. No. You think cuz you've got dimples and charismatic charm it gives you the right to be a manipulative, selfcentered, d-bag who thinks he can stick his dick in anything he wants and does. Why would I willingly attach myself to a person who lives by those standards and has zero ambition to be anything different?" She didn't wait for an answer. "We're not soulmates. We're two people who, in one life, were dumb as donkey shit with zero foresight and the power to trap our souls in this hamster wheel of horrors. Ending this charade saves us from centuries of misery and the misery we cause people around us. We won't meet again in our next lives.

And, if by chance we do, we sure as fuck won't be playing house and callin' it love."

Her confidence was horrifying. She wanted nothing to do with me or the Soul Magic we once created. I had threatened to remove her speaking abilities and now I wished I haven't given her a choice. Her blatant hatred was so shocking I couldn't smooth out my breath let alone remember how to alter the binding spell.

"You believe all that?" When I managed to ask this, I reached into her mind. Before the answer came out of her mouth, I heard it resonate with conviction.

"You're goddamned right I do."

I nodded in defeat, looking down at the picture in my hands with my chest stuffed with grief. The love-soaked smile she once reserved for me was one I needed for myself. I had it and now it was gone, and from what she said, Sophie was pretty clear on never lobbying for a repeat.

Before Fox left, I told him that I needed Sophie in this life, and I meant it. As comfortable with independence as I thought I was, I didn't realize how quickly I was self-destructing. Something Fox and Aunt Lacey only stemmed the consequences of. Thinking of my old life before her, I knew I couldn't go back to that, not without ignoring sobriety and remaining dick-deep in a revolving door of people that would never be her. I wouldn't survive it.

"What's the connection ever done for us?" She kept going. All I wanted her to do was stop, but she kept turning the knife. "I cheated on Caine, it's caused a rift with Kim, and I can't feel any true connection to my family or most other people. We've killed trying to save each other. We feel each other's pain, get trapped in emotional rinse cycles until we're so strung out we don't know who feels what. I became a target of Joelly's until you killed her, a target of Tobias's and forced to endure...." She took in a jagged breath unable to recount the memory.

As I was still in her mind, I saw a flash of her on the ground of the Sorrel cell through her perspective, saw a clawed hand against the hard floor beneath her as she moaned in pain enough to nauseate me as it triggered the memory of my own trauma that caused hers. I saw it once before when she held me down by the throat with dark, wild eyes full of hate and broke my hand amongst the wreckage of the Ballard Family Estate.

"I can't." She heaved a few breaths trying to hang on to her anger before it gave way under the weight of her exhausted despair. "I can't handle a life with you anymore. It's not worth it. All the bullshit, the pain...it's an addiction, not love. I'd rather be alone."

The oxygen in my lungs felt denser than it should, choking me on its way out. When I saw Vincent at the meeting with Miklos, he told me to bring her here, that it would help. All its done was strengthen her resolve to hate me more.

I flexed to stand, barely hearing myself speak when I said I'd be right back. Maybe I didn't say it aloud.

Walking in a fog of disappointment and rejection, I knocked on the door for the woman to open up, needing air unpolluted by what came out of the person I loved and feared I truly lost.

The blonde woman cracked the door, then widened it more when she realized who the knocker was. Sophie would be right where I left her. Even if she broke through my binding spell, the only way out was through the door to the office I was leaning against.

"Is everything okay?"

A response came once I remembered how to speak Dutch again. "She hates me."

Her expression cinched. "No. She can't."

"She can. Our Soul Magic...it's soured."

The woman didn't say anything, but I sensed she understood a little something about Soul Magic. Maybe Vincent explained things.

"She can't see this life clearly. Her memories are wrong." Stopping, I realized I was unloading on a stranger.

She crossed her arms. "Show her the real memories. Make her see the truth."

"Even if I do, she won't trust me. She'll think I'm manipulating them."

She didn't know how to answer that, and I contemplated leaving. I just couldn't get my feet to move.

"Who does she trust?" she asked. "Someone else must know the truth and can make her listen. If not, this could kill you. Not in other lives, but in this one. She won't care about the past, she needs to know what's real now or she'll never care about a future."

So, she did know. Maybe Vincent shared it all.

What she said made sense. I needed to find people who could attest to the changes to her memories. Not tonight, it was more than I could do in Amsterdam or even at the Prison Creation, but I could start compiling people and key memories.

The basement full of yard sale rejects was a waste of time. "I'm sorry. What's your name?"

The woman appeared surprised I asked. "Lotte."

I recognized the name as the Dutch form of Charlotte.

"I'm sorry to drop all of this on you, Lotte."

She shrugged, waving it off like this was an unexpected turn of her day, not wholly unwanted.

I went on to tell her about Vincent and what happened with him. For all I knew, I was telling her things she would never have known or that Vincent would have kept from her on purpose. For her solid advice alone, she deserved to know.

"Thank you for telling me. If possible, let Mr. Llewellyn know everything will be taken care of until he can re-establish contact."

"I will."

A nod and twist of her lips was discomforting thanks, something in her expression hinting at more. She rushed forward and hugged me. I surprised myself by hugging her back, refraining from skin contact until she backed off with renewed blush in her cheeks.

I would have liked to stay, look at the old photos in the shop again, reminisce about who Sophie and I used to be, but I needed to return to the Prison Creation to find people who would buy into my plan. Kim, Sophie's family, some of the Coveners...they would help.

After extending more thanks to Lotte, I descended the stairs to the hate-filled version of Sophie.

"Thank fucking god!" Sophie said when she saw me. "Can we get the hell outta here?"

Without answering, I palmed the key, started my plea to return to the Prison Creation, and landed on the marble floors, freaking out some guards until they saw who we were.

I snapped my fingers to break the binding spell on Sophie and walked away from her without a word. After pausing at the console, I entered my cell where I spent the rest of the night cooking up a plan.

20

___

INNOVATIVE PRACTICES

Sophie

I flipped over and sat up in bed, the remnants of another nightmare in the sweat over most of my body. Checking my watch told me I slept a couple of fragmented hours, not enough for any sense of rest.

"Hey."

I sprung to my feet ready to go after Donovan again.

Caveman raised his hands. "Whoa. Dial it down, soldier. We've got a mission. Meet us in the lobby." He left without further comment.

I shoved on my boots, hit the bathroom, threw my hair up into a ponytail, and was in the lobby with the other Tactical Team members in less than five minutes.

Lincoln was briefing the Team as I reached them, clearly without giving a fuck that I wasn't there before he started. "The lakeside safe houses missed their scheduled check-in call at nine o'clock this morning. This is the second morning without contact. One day skipped causes suspicion, but happens. Two days? Full on panic."

I ignored Donovan as I geared up, grabbing my Beretta and other weapons I wouldn't be allowed to use. He was lucky the second he saw me wasn't followed up with a bullet to his head. Though, that might kill me, too. Maybe I didn't care if it did.

"Hold up." Lincoln stopped me, Donovan, and Caveman before we stepped into the elevator to ride through the veil. "I saw the battle you two had last night before you disappeared." He looked at Caveman. "And since everyone knows everything around here, I've heard of the little Frog getting in your way of the redhead you're so fond of, causing a few public love spats." Caveman shifted in discomfort or annoyance as Lincoln mentioned some kind of confrontation I missed. Or multiple confrontations, by the sounds of it. "I'm saying this to all three of you...Forget your personal dramas so we can check on these people and make sure they're still alive. I don't need you creating further issues. Not for me and not for these people."

"Thanks for the pep-talk, coach." Caveman's tone was devoid of all humour. "I could use a ball lick, you wanna help with that, too?"

"Not in my job description. Use more of your brain and maybe the redhead would take up the position."

Caveman stepped towards Lincoln with a growl.

"Rrriiiggghhtt," I drawled. "And you tell us to quit the drama? Not sure how antagonizing a wall of muscle is supposed to help with that."

Lincoln didn't look at me, nor did he seem intimidated by Caveman. Maybe Lincoln was the one with a death wish.

"You heard me. Now try listening." Lincoln was full of smugness as he left for the elevator. We joined him for an awkward ride.

About an hour later, we parked near the safe houses without bothering to hide the vehicles. A niggling of intuition told me something was wrong before I left the SUV, the others picking up the same vibe. Eerie quiet filled the street. At this time of day, you should hear something.

We split into three groups. Unsurprised when Lincoln stuck me with Caveman and Donovan.

Inside one home, a smell hit me, triggering a couple of memories I would rather never revisit.

Blood was the new decor of choice, the dark red stuff everywhere as if the attackers were having fun and throwing a party.

"*Soul glows?*" I heard Caveman's voice in my head.

I searched the living room, kitchen, and bathroom as Donovan went upstairs.

"Can't have soul glows when you don't have intact bodies." No reason to bother with telepathy when no one around was alive.

Donovan came down the stairs. "Nothing but chum up there. Loring's devotees must have found them."

"Let's regroup. The other cabins might be the same." Caveman led us outside.

We ran into Jessabelle bent over with her hands on her knees. She straightened when she saw us. "There's...." She couldn't finish.

"In there, too," Donovan told her.

"Hey!" Lincoln yelled from a couple of cabins down. "Get in here."

This cabin was no different than the others. Scattered body parts swam in congealed blood. Furniture was saturated. Chaos in every room. I should probably have been more disgusted and spilling my guts, but I wasn't.

Bronya was holding something in a blanket.

Caveman leaned in. "Souvenir?"

"Gross." She motioned a few feet from her where a torso laid on the ground, ribcage was ripped open like a Thanksgiving turkey.

A high-pitched cry rang out. Caveman jumped, making me flinch. The noise came from the bundle in Bronya's arms.

"A fucking baby?" Nothing else could be so far removed from what I expected to find in this place or in Bronya's arms. If she did squirrel away some body parts for a spell or if it was someone she knew that she wanted to bury, it was a nasty way to go about it, but Bronya was nasty.

Donovan bent over the torso. "Oh shit. Neilan."

No longer the weed of a man we bought the Pompeii Worm from for the Nexus Transference spell. All I saw was bone and blood sludge.

"How can you tell?" Lincoln asked.

"I can't, but Neilan's a Phoenix. You found the baby in the chest cavity, right?"

"Yeah," Lincoln said louder over the baby's crying as Bronya handed it to Jessabelle who was trying to shush it and hopefully found a mint for her puke breath. "Thought Loring's people were getting creative, but there're no babies registered here. Kids. No babies."

"Right." I remembered the story Vincent told me. "When a Phoenix dies, it's born again from its own chest. Not invulnerable, but motherless and immortal."

"And trapped inside his own dead body for at least a day. He's probably starving." Jessabelle was trying to rock Neilan, but it wasn't helping.

Caveman went towards the kitchen. "I'll check for milk."

"They won't have bottles," Jessabelle called after him.

"Don't need 'em. Follow me."

She did. Whatever idea Caveman had, he was confident, and the baby quieted quickly.

Donovan lifted his boots out of a pool on congealed blood. "How do you usually clean up a mess this big?"

"Oh, the usual," Bronya quipped and slammed a flashing smile towards Donovan.

"Help Jessabelle with the baby." Lincoln's tone made this an unmistakeable order.

She met his glare in weak challenge before leaving to join Jessabelle and Caveman in the kitchen.

"Thanks," Donovan mumbled.

Lincoln rolled a shoulder. "It's a phase. It'll pass."

"Are we done here?" I was sure ready to click my heels together and land in a cell if it meant moving things along.

Lincoln pointed at the floor. "Do you see the innards at your toes?"

I nudged my boot into something squishy. "I don't know. Is that what innards look like?"

"Clearly, we're not done." Lincoln huffed. "Our usual methods are doable. We have contacts in the city's crime scene cleanup division, like the ones who cleaned up after your innards nearly ended up on the floor of that dive bar you work at."

It took me a moment to remember what he meant. The stabbing from my neighbour's drunk and abusive ex seemed like a whole other lifetime. That singular event awakened my power and the connection with Donovan, cutting into my life and spiralling everything out of control since.

Lincoln continued to brainstorm after casually mentioning my life-changing near-death experience. "With this many victims? It'd be easier to burn the cabins down."

I shook my head. "I've watched enough cop dramas to know bones survive fires. You need us to destroy whatever's left of the bodies."

Lincoln thought about it and then nodded. "Not all healers can do the opposite and ash bodies like you two can. Once you're done, we'll burn the cabins and walk away. Don't leave a pinky toe bone behind and Ranlyn can have the fire chief, another Magic, claim it an accidental total loss of property so the Coven will benefit from the insurance claim."

"*Pfft.* How noble."

Lincoln stared at me. "Would you rather the alternative?"

I stared back. "I'd rather have showed up to find Loring mid-slaughter and killed his ass. Whatever system is in place to protect us in times like this, it blows monkey balls. This shouldn't've happened."

"As a Team member it's not our job to have opinions. We scout, infiltrate, follow orders, but we don't create the law, nor do we form the politics the Elders deal with. If you want control over big decisions, accept more responsibility. You want to fight, shut the fuck up and get to work."

Ass handed to me, I did as I was told and stuck my hands on as many body parts, bones, and muscles as I could find, disintegrating them into a fine dust that settled atop the coagulating blood. I could disintegrate that too, but the fires would handle it, so I wasn't about to waste my time.

Before we did our specialty jobs on the bodies, we identified as many as possible and compared them to the occupant list. Ismail took up making the records, but with so many pieces, we had to hope for a recognizable head or marking, like tattoos.

He noted Moira was missing from the deceased. She must have been with her daughters or maybe scattered before they got a hold of her. She wasn't a quick mover, but others may have portalled out and took her with them. Either way, someone needed to tell Vincent. If anyone knew where she might be, he would.

I caught Donovan staring at me throughout the process, his expression judgemental while I dusted the bodies of more causalities of this war. He was wasting time looking at me instead of getting the job done, so I moved faster and tried to be in a different room than him at all times.

Jessabelle and Bronya being on baby duty was sexist as far as I was concerned. Caveman sounded like he knew more about child-rearing than both of them combined. Why not hand Neilan over to him? Everyone was standing around as we worked anyway. Except Ismail who was on the phone with as many safe houses as we knew about so he could warn those using them to find safer grounds.

Once every last bit of human remains was taken care of, the last task was to set the cabins ablaze. Moving the vehicles off of the street and waiting an appropriate amount of time before Caveman and Gregor sneaked under cover spells gave Donovan and me time to wash blood from our hands and under our nails in the freezing lake.

Driving away from the cabins in full raging fire, Neilan became frustrated with the cloth dipped in milk he was sucking on, not getting enough as fast as he wanted. The makeshift idea from Caveman hinted at the man being a father at some point, but a pharmacy and department store stop was essential. Caveman made a list and Jessabelle and Bronya were happy to shop.

I refused to take on the squawky Magic purely on principal, so Neilan was handed off to Donovan who was now bouncing him lightly. Give the asshole a prize, Neilan actually calmed, Caveman claiming him as a natural. I hoped Neilan shit on him before they got proper diapers. The ladies were taking so long, it was a possibility. I wasn't the only one getting annoyed at waiting and Lincoln went in after them, finding them immersed in pastel colours and nipple options.

Ugh, babies.

21

WINDOW OF OPPORTUNITY

Donovan

Holding Neilan was odd. I would have been more comfortable disarming a roadside bomb in an active warzone. The women took a millennium to find what they needed in the store. Sophie refused to have anything to do with the kid, making a comment about sexist expectations. Hall found it hilarious when Bronya shoved the little thing into my hands, chuckling until I positioned my hands in the right spot so I didn't drop the bundle of human.

When I tried to pass him off to Hall, he claimed I was doing fine. I guess that meant he knew a thing or two about babies.

It was my first experience holding one. The blue eyes looking up at me freaked me out and had me thinking of the many children I no doubt created during the Conception Rituals. Jesus. The first time was a decade or so ago. They could have been part of the audience during the second round. If the most recent Conception Rituals were a success, the mothers may not even know about it yet. Or maybe they did.

Those kids were clueless to what they were being born into.

Sweat built between my shoulder blades, my body aching as I was afraid to move, afraid to drop him. I was a father, but sure as hell wasn't a dad. I didn't even know what my kids' faces looked like, or who their mothers were, how they've been treated, or how deeply they fell for my father's rhetoric.

When the SUVs doors opened, I all but tossed the kid to Jess-abelle, then put the window down, sucking in cool, fresh air as panic crested and churned my stomach.

The others wrestled with bags of baby stuff, too busy to see me silently panicking.

I forced my eyes closed and stood outside for a bit as they latched a car seat in place and dressed the baby in some appropriate clothing.

Once they were done, I climbed in. Hall slapped me on the shoulder, maybe not so blind to what I was going through, yet keeping his comments to himself.

The cabin massacre was most definitely Loring's work. Someone found out where the safe houses were, or they nabbed someone and were being filtered information. A leak was always possible, though none of the Soul Seers, including Sophie, mentioned seeing any Tainted souls in the Prison Creation or people with blank souls who would be just as suspicious. Which meant someone from the Mother Coven turned on us. Maybe the Apporter, though could be anyone these days.

Those hiding needed to find someplace else to go. Anywhere. Squatting was better than being dead and most didn't want to be anywhere near the Elders inside the Prison Creation, rightfully assuming they were target number one and better off on the lamb.

After stopping for gas, we were back at the prison, and I was stripping off my weapons and heading for a shower. Even with the lake bath, the stink of dead and ashed bodies clung in my nose. Thankfully, I had my own suds to erase the stench as hot water ran down my body before being slurped up by the drain.

My gear was a mess and needed to be washed, so I opted for civilian clothes. The shower didn't energize me. I couldn't remember my last full meal or what I ate, too busy with people dying or being attacked and trying to keep Sophie from ruining every relationship she had and herself while she was at it.

Since Sophie was my main priority, I had a plan to suss out. I found Olive in the cafeteria seated with Lewis, Priscilla, and the aunts and took the window of opportunity for a sit-down while satisfying my hunger pains.

"I need your help," I said as soon as my ass hit the chair.

Before they could tell me to mind my manners, I apologized since they heard what happened with the whole me-dragging-Sophie-from-a-cell thing, mentioning why I did it, what happened in Amsterdam, and about her altered memories.

Lewis sipped something from a small mug. "The Soul Magic damage explains why her soul colour is odd."

"Odd how?" I asked hoping Lewis didn't mean what I thought it meant.

"Shadowed," Olive said.

"Tainted?"

"No, no," Lewis clarified, and my heart yo-yoed into place. "More like aspects of her soul and power are hidden or lost. The colour is dull, almost like someone who has denied the gift in hate, but somehow her power is still strong. I'm not really sure what to make of it."

"Okay." At least she wasn't Tainted, though maybe having a shadowed soul was equally as bad? "Regardless, I need to construct a memory bomb."

The shocked glares I received were priceless. It was an odd request, but I needed their help plus Ranlyn's and every Sect member, but I was doing it with or without her family's involvement.

To my surprise, they didn't fight me. In fact, they were delighted to have found a possible solution they could assist with. Olive felt she owed Sophie for saving her from the institution and helping with the estate and was more than willing to provide whatever I needed.

I rose from the table with a mission, leaving my untouched food behind.

22

RATIONAL AND RESTRAINT

Caine

Ness snapped her fingers in my face. "Are you thinking about her?"

Derek made a smacking sound with his lips and tossed his plastic fork onto his cafeteria tray. "Lay off, Ness."

I *was* thinking about Sophie. The "her" in Ness's question needing no clarification when delivered with that tone. "We haven't really seen her since—"

"Since Donovan dragged her skinny ass out of a cell?" She sipped her iced tea.

"Obviously there's an explanation."

"She coulda hit him first," Felix offered. "His face was all mashed up."

"It doesn't make it okay, Felix." Ness's brother shrugged and leaned back into his cafeteria chair. "I'm all for sticking up for yourself but when it gets bloody, it's just toxic. Maybe he dragged her body off and buried her somewhere."

I sniffed. "He wouldn't do that." Though there was a high likelihood of Sophie starting it. Whatever *it* was.

Derek sneered. "Don't be an idiot, man."

"He wouldn't." I was sure of it.

"Why?" Ness chomped on a fry. "Because he comes from exemplary breeding stock? Because he's the epitome of rational and restraint?"

I leaned into my arms on the table between us. "Abuse is a stretch. Especially when considering it's Sophie."

"And I'm sure Miss Perfect wouldn't beat a guy either, right?" Her slight grin was smug.

"Geez, sis." Felix left for more food, Derek following and giving me a raised brow as if knowing leaving gave me the opportunity to smooth things over.

I responded with an eyebrow of my own, waited for her brother to be out of earshot, and leaned farther across the table. "Are we going to talk about us having sex?"

Why talk about Sophie when we could talk about the core of the issue fueling her attitude?

She sucked in a breath like my bluntness was a physical strike. "We already talked."

"Nope. I talked." I snagged a fry from her plate. "I know why I followed through with it. I care about you, even if you're doing your best to chase me off with this Miss Perfect business. I can't help Sophie's my ex and refuse to regret it since I wouldn't be alive and sitting across from you right now." I pointed the half-eaten fry at her. "You had a huge hand in me surviving the Creation in more than a few battles. Being free and able to focus without Gareth getting in the way was a crapshoot. We made it, Ness. I don't want to waste time with thoughts of the past. I want to move forward and with you. Slow, if need be, but still forward together. How else do I make you see that Sophie and I are over?"

She didn't respond, though it looked like she was chewing over more than her fries.

"And there's no way you can deny enjoying what went down in that office." Her brows cinched and I knew I was right, positively thrilled about the playful direction the conversation took, the rest of it likely too serious for her nerves.

She sipped her lemonade. "Just because I like your dick, doesn't mean I like you."

"True." I chuckled. "Except you do."

My smile grew and I watched her struggle not to return it, the edges of her soft lips flexing. It was enough to threaten to make me hard at the memory of being inside of her with those lips on mine. Felix sitting down with a second helping didn't deter her stare.

Donovan plopped down in the empty spot next to me. "I need your memories of Sophie."

With the mention of Sophie's name, Ness's flirty, subdued smile vanished and retreated into a scowl.

I turned to Donovan. "You're determined to ruin my life, aren't you?"

23

FALSE CONFIDENCE

Vincent

Collecting paperwork from the glossy tabletop as the audience around me dispersed, a few not without a stream of obscenities for the win I earned, I refused to engage with the outraged family when I could only agree with their protests. I managed two or three successful cases a day. More if I convinced a client to forgo trial and settle with promises of a lesser punishment.

As Sovereignty guards emptied the courthouse of stragglers, begrudgingly protecting their employer's son, knowing the damage I inflicted and bored with their postured glances to retaliate, I was cleared to leave.

My father stepped into my path. Unbeknownst to me, he was in the audience.

"How many more?" I posed the routine question, reminding the man with incessant regularity of the primary reason for my presence. "I have won cases others refuse to attempt, including Chase. I deserve to see evidence of Cora-Lynn's soul's existence, or I am best to rely on inside contacts." When Alasdair met my heavy gaze without responding, I repeated, "How many more?"

An obvious bluff, one I willed my father to see through to keep his paranoia focused on staff corruption and gifting false confidence in my continued ignorance of Cora-Lynn's soul location. In my experience, the enemy's opinion of you as weak was a positive. Much preferred over their belief of you gaining ground. Douses their defences in relaxed superiority.

Alasdair stood unfazed, relaxed, hands in his pockets. "Quitting your position would not be in Cora-Lynn's best interest. We just finally got her eating again."

I froze and searched my father's expression for deception as my brain hung in delayed comprehension. "Eating?"

"Yes," Alasdair said plainly. "Food consumption is not a required function for prisoners, however, when the body's processes are neglected for too long, complications arise, and I would prefer not to have to deal with them. We suspend most bodily functions while imprisoned as the cleanup is...messy. Unless it is part of the punishment itself, of course."

"She...Cora-Lynn lives?"

"Yes."

"She cannot...She died...."

"She did, yes." My father spoke as if relaying the weather.

I stood searching the wood panelled walls of the courtroom in hopes they could offer a sensible explanation as I failed to connect my memories of the event to this new information.

"That woman defied our laws."

This snatched my attention. "That woman was a human being with no knowledge of her capabilities."

"You claimed the same then as well. Regardless, laws were still broken."

Boiling rage shook in my hands. "You executed her for it. I remember the day clearly."

"As do I, son. You should know by now that death could not stop justice from being upheld."

The calmness with which Alasdair spoke amplified my anger. "You lie."

"Your wife was executed for her crimes. No lie required."

"You claimed possession of her soul."

"An essence within my custody, yes."

"You implied—"

"I implied nothing. Your assumptions were reached entirely on your own."

I found my words losing strength. "Cora-Lynn has been in the cells since that day?"

Alasdair nodded in lackluster confirmation. "Why would we remove her only to reinsert her later? Of course, since that day. However, it will have been longer for her. Time manipulation has been a part of her correction regiment."

"Correction regiment?"

"Names." Alasdair waved off someone's attempt at progressive branding. "That moniker was not my doing. Punishment is more accurate given the fact we are officers of the Sovereignty Court and officers and courts dole out consequences."

I removed my glasses and rubbed my face, far beyond a collected display of composure, unable to fully grasp the atrocity. In the cells? Cora-Lynn, my wife, hasn't been dead at all, but alive in the cells of my father's prison? Denial surged to the surface. I was unwilling to believe this story was nothing more than a bluff meant to keep me from leaving. Had to be.

"Prove it," I demanded.

With a flicker of my father's lips and a slight nod, I followed Alasdair through the offices, passed the bullpen of Magics into a section of the courthouse I was never before granted admittance. Behind swipe card access, I was surprised to find another large room of bullpens.

Not stopping, all Magics who spotted the two of us stared with piqued curiosity, some with shocked concern as we continued on and exited a set of modern-stylized doors and stepped into an outside courtyard where people lunched alongside their coworkers.

Knowledge of what occurred in the cells was common for the Sovereignty employees chewing their salads like the cattle they were. Mistakes or failure to produce results the company insists on earned you the proverbial 'chop'. Either to the slaughterhouse to be discarded while another heifer takes root in your still-warm plot, or to the cells depending on the amount of embarrassment they caused.

These cud-chewing Magics thought signing their employment agreements meant a steady salary, full benefits, and holidays off without the realization a swipe of a pen locked them into position beyond retirement. Advancement was possible, however, moving up the beanstalk meant greater disposability due to the damning information you were privy to, becoming a potential liability in fracturing the company when you inevitability see beyond the curtain and can no longer contain your bile.

In all worst-case scenarios, the Sovereignty must endure.

The warmth of a balmy day and plush green grass of the court-yard would have been a dead giveaway to the fact the Sovereignty was a Creation, seeing as how it was winter in the real world, but I was having trouble processing and this detail was left unnoticed until I heard birds singing.

Never a company man, my father always forbade me knowledge of the cells' location. Why was this request for proof of Cora-Lynn's continued existence easily obliged? Suspicion set my teeth on edge and most likely would have stalled my willingness to follow my father if I was not too stunned to comprehend probable danger.

As a child, I was schooled in effective torture tactics and interro-gation strategies, shown examples of glorified successes where crimi-nals' weaknesses were exploited and morphed into living nightmares. In an attempt to understand my father and his punitive ways, I sought the law and found comfort in knowing the man everyone deferred to for justice was heinously flawed.

Now I would discover what this writer of horrors had subjected my wife to for an unspeakable length of time.

Through a set of doors, we reached another where my father stopped and waited. Whatever scanning procedure securing the door required, it did so without any outward indications. When satisfied, a hidden keyboard popped out of the wall, containing an old pictographic language—Mycenaean Greek? My father typed in a passcode, making no attempt to hide or disguise the code, one I could not recall in full if required.

Passcode approved and keyboard returned to the original location, Alasdair then placed his hand on a circular padding replacing the keyboard and expelled a pulse of magic my body recognized as a hint of our Soul Extractor power.

I felt sideswiped by the tech involved, verification procedures required, and the unknown location. My contacts were either feeding me enough information to keep up the illusion of knowledge for monetary compensation or were so low-level they did not warrant the type of access needed, therefore were pennies to the millions of what was hidden from me and not worth consulting.

Once through the protected door, a guard dripping in weapons he no doubt never needed or used stood at attention. He was presumably employed to grant visual confirmation in case an infiltrator managed to bypass the exhaustive measures taken or held my father at gunpoint, forcing access. Getting passed "Brad"—as he was addressed, my father earning a nod—would never be accomplished had I arrived alone. And without pretense, my father ensured Brad understood my admittance was a "one time only exception".

Brad stood in a five-by-eight area containing no walls or furniture, the door we entered, and one other door requiring a dual set of codes from my father and from Brad as well as power, voice, and DNA confirmation. I contained the DNA and could alter a voice to the desired intonation, but Brad was certainly an issue, however not one I would allow hindering an escape attempt when the time came.

Access approved, the room on the other side of the door was as unremarkable as the hallway we originated from, making me think I was led right into a trap, or a cell of my own, as we entered a box of grey cement walls.

"What is this?" My voice burst from me, my first words since we left the courtroom.

"No need to be so brash, son. Patience is not one of my many qualities you have inherited, I see."

Standing in the cement room striving to keep my power at bay, my father prattled off a spell I was too distracted to remember, in what sounded like Hebrew, the words conjuring up a figure a few feet away from us. What should have been a man appeared to be more mutation. Birth deformities were common enough, however, this was not from developmental complications, genetic deviations, or trauma at the time of birth. This was a man gnarled by magic.

Human-like qualities remained cloaked with a heavy robe, disguising specific anatomical features beneath despite the fact that if you were to focus beyond a passing glance, you would be hard-pressed to miss facial features that took on the likes of a whole new species. The nose retreated, slivers of nostrils remaining, eyelids over-grown to encapsulate the eye leaving questions to if they existed beneath at all and were rice paper thin. The lips receded and disappeared as if disuse deemed them unnecessary.

The Magic shifted in our direction without fully facing us, either unneeded or it pained them to do so.

"Day of incarceration," Alasdair responded to a telepathic question from the Magic.

The Magic resumed staring at the blank wall in front of us before they lifted a hand baring completely fused fingers that displayed an image on the wall like a projector.

"Cora-Lynn." Her name fell from my lips in a pained whisper. There she was. My wife whom I had not laid eyes on since the day I witnessed her murder.

Seeing my wife walk around the town where we met was a nightmare wrapped in the flashiest bow, a gift that burned like acid. Since she was brought to the cells, it took some gathering comprehension for me to realize what my father was showing me.

All we desired was each other's company into old age, a loving family, and to find undistracted contentment. All the customary things people strive for in everyday life and something I assumed I could never find when considering the ties to my family's business.

Peering at day one of Cora-Lynn's incarceration showed Cora-Lynn in a cell spelled to emulate our town to trick her into believing she lived as she always had, yet no one but herself remained, she encased in loneliness without the ability to leave.

"Vincent!" Cora-Lynn called out for me, confusion crumbled to anger and cursing god for abandoning her until her cries turned hoarse.

My name from her lips brought about bittersweet memories. Countless years disappeared since I forgot the sound of her voice. This simple thing a gift and a torture.

"Run through," Alasdair's command tore Cora-Lynn away.

Before I could question if Cora-Lynn's first day in the cells was all my father planned on gracing me with, the projector-like Magic fast-forwarded through other images of Cora-Lynn as she continued to live on, alone, through days, weeks, and years, all in seconds as I witnessed her lose more and more of herself every passing hour while my father narrated her experience like a bored and underpaid amusement park tour guide.

"As you see, once she became immune to her punishment: accepting her solitary fate, processing nothing but the numbness of her isolation, the next phase was environmental manipulation using foreign stimuli to resurrect an emotional response. Enveloped in foreign surroundings, which as it turned out, is everywhere considering she never ventured outside of the town in which you found her."

The images changed quickly now, our small town replaced, bringing Cora-Lynn to swamplands, forests, snow-capped mountains, and eventually cityscapes with buildings so tall she did not comprehend what they were.

"Since the first phase of completion, she only spends twenty-four hours in any one location. Sleep triggers a new environment, one she would wake up in and live through that day, all the while facing some aspect of fear in any particular setting."

Not only did she suffer morphing environmental manipulation but fear practices as well. Wild animals, heights, fire, suffocation...whatever they found in the depths of her mind they used, and I stood and watched the horrors she endured all because I fell in love with her.

My father's tone remained flat. "Since her incarceration has been quite lengthy it has allowed us the opportunity to seek innovative practices."

Whatever Alasdair said next was lost to me. "Innovative practices" was corporate jargon condoning the use of Cora-Lynn's sentence as a test subject for fresh ideas to torment her and other inmates. Displayed before me was Cora-Lynn's, and many others', version of a true biblical Hell. Fire and brimstone, she in shackles hung from a cave ceiling as demons and monsters ripped apart sinners in lakes of magma below, layers of their relentless screams the only thing she could hear.

Throughout the torture, she sought to see the others below her, they the sole others she saw since her incarceration. No. Not strangers ensconced in their fate, but individuals wearing the faces of anyone Cora-Lynn ever cared for, including myself. For hours, Cora-Lynn hung and watched as her family and friends were tortured, beyond her reach to save them, none of them interacting with her or able to hear her pleas.

A significant change in Cora-Lynn became obvious after her experience in Hell. Her mind unravelling as she bore the onslaught of whatever the Sovereignty cells forced her through. They transformed her into a shadow of the innocent woman who entered the cell. Her soft eyes hardened against that innocence and solidified into seeing nothing but danger and seclusion as she slowly lost her will to retain the person she once was.

Images continued to pass like a flipbook as Alasdair spoke, nothing reaching beyond my concentration on my wife losing herself day by day.

Cora-Lynn's blonde, dirtied, and knotted hair was raked through with her fingers. She developed nervous ticks and pulled on her hair until patches of baldness were visible, continuing to worry her scalp until no hair was left. Caring for herself or her needs was a pointless use of energy she abandoned, doing nothing much more than hiding or running when the shift in environments forced her to.

At some point in her incarceration, Cora-Lynn became wise to the falsehoods of her surroundings and their intent to punish her. She began tearing the worlds around her down by hand, her aggression building and leaving her on the end of a breathless tirade before she would pass out from exhaustion and everything around her would change again.

After countless years of situational awareness and what I assumed was a difficulty to create something Cora-Lynn had yet to experience, she was forced to endure rigorous exercise to survive or elongate the day. Her body lost significant weight, lean muscles now visible once her clothing became scraps and barely covered her skin.

Knowing what my father was capable of, I realized he didn't inflict true physical torture on her. No one carved up her body, removed her organs while awake, defiled her in ways all women fear...nothing so pedestrian. Instead, Alasdair decided psychological torture was more fitting for the woman who stole me away from my station as an active member of the firm.

Cora-Lynn's true punishment was anticipation and restlessness. To be certain she never spent an easy day for the rest of her life. To never have the opportunity of comfort or familiarity, and to forever be sentenced to a fog of distrust for everything so that she would never feel contentment in her own skin again.

I saw myself.

"Ah, yes." My father's tone hit a prideful lilt, attracting my attention in confusion of what I was seeing. "We realized she was too used to solitude. On occasion, we had you visit."

I watched as the images featuring days continued to flip by, some of those images including my face. Interaction between this imposture and Cora-Lynn were unhealthy. Another of my father's perversions. Whatever I said to Cora-Lynn was antagonistic in nature and in the beginning would reduce her to tears until she grew too mad to cry and would attempt to hunt and kill me, never successful, but always left red-faced and full of unchecked wrath.

I failed to turn away from my wife. I continued on as a spectator while heinous images of Cora-Lynn's days were an unending horror film.

As she experienced more and more of my father's creative nature, she turned feral. Teeth coated in grime, gums overgrowing them, wild eyes, no hair, and moved like a rabid cougar. If Alasdair showed me this version of Cora-Lynn without starting from the beginning, I would never have believed the beast in front of me was my sweet Cora-Lynn. She lost everything that made her...her.

A snap and quick turn, and Alasdair's Gucci lapels dug into my fingers as I shoved him into the wall behind us. The crack of Alasdair's skull preceded his eyes rolling, he on the brink of unconsciousness.

I braced my father's weight, keeping him up as his knees threatened to give way. "This. This is why you are undeserving to breathe the air you soil. This is why ending you and your entire establishment has been my life's mission. You ruined her! And for what? To hurt me? To shit in the face of what I stand for because you cannot fathom the evil I see in what you built your empire on?"

Alasdair's eyes focused on mine inches from his, impassive as outrage spurred me on.

"Our world has an alternative to your medieval injustices now." I enunciated my intent as an eerie calm settled over me. "No longer will Magics cower at the mere mention of this establishment for it will no longer stand to benefit from their fear."

"Your lineage is wasted on you." His voice came out as a croak.

Alasdair glanced to his right. The eyeless mutation was at my shoulder, yet I had not seen or sensed its movement.

The cement box around me disappeared, the walls replaced with a tree as wide as I was long, a tropical humidity invading my lungs.

An unforgiving mistake on my part was not realizing the mutation was not the Magic equivalent to a security camera, but the Sovereignty cells' warden. He not only replayed the scenes of those tortured when commanded by an observer such as my father, but was the torturer and the one who ensured prisoners were tucked away where no one could find them.

I had been infused into the unknown with understanding I was precisely where I spent centuries fighting to avoid, a true prisoner at the whim of my father's evil.

Movement caught my eye to my left, too quick to see. A cackle filled the air around me on my right. I spun in a defensive stance in search of my hunter. Without seeing them, I filled with anticipatory dread.

24

DISTORTED APOLOGIES

Sophie

Many were busy crowing over baby Neilan, using the poop factory as a distraction from the brutal dismemberment of a couple dozen of their fellow Magics where they were supposed to be safest from the enemy. The list of the dead Ismail compiled was posted so others would know. And while Neilan was on it, he technically survived in baby-form, born from his previous self's death, and hailed as a lone survivor, earning an asterisk next to his name.

We kept trying to contact Vincent and let him know about the safe house slaughters in case it hadn't made it to him through his contacts, but no one heard from him. Ranlyn and Veata kept trying, though Ranlyn was losing at hiding his worry. Vincent was difficult to get a hold of on a normal day, why this was different, I didn't know. Did no contact mean he was in trouble? No one was sharing and attention was focused on de-escalating fear and paranoia regarding our safety within the Prison Creation, seeking answers and reassurances no one could give them.

People wanted to go home. Others understood why returning to a normal life was impossible right now, but some insisted on a timeline. Morons. Scheduling a war isn't exactly something you pencil in, especially when you weren't the ones waging war in the first place and the enemy was happy to turn family and friends into empty blood bags.

Dead was the only version of Loring that was acceptable, but until then, I was stuck dreaming of his last expression as I ended him. Without proper intel, we may as well invite Loring for a cruller and coffee and then line up for him to rip our hearts out.

Ranlyn handled their complaints and ridiculous questions with otherworldly patience, doling out casual reminders that no one was a prisoner, but how leaving posed a danger. They didn't like it, but they were still alive to complain unlike too many others.

I pushed through the crowd to the cell console. Some got pissy. Who doesn't step aside when you see someone cutting through a crowd? This isn't a concert. I'm not trying to punk your front row view. Slide your ass aside and move on with life or expect an elbow in the ribs on my way by.

Placating people with ribbon-wrapped niceties on blood-soaked topics was Ranlyn's job, I was more hands-on nowadays, and no one wanted to hear my opinions. The safe house bodies I disintegrated to nothing was a necessity to protect our identities and side-step a dumpster load of questions from people who couldn't handle the answers and would give the enemy something to dig for if they were ever captured.

Loring was yukking it up in freedom, god knows where, while we cowered in the cells. He couldn't be far. You can't mind-fuck your prey without staying local.

"Sophie!" I saw Serena waving at me and pantomiming talking on a phone.

I growled and pushed through the crowd, adding some extra energy to move faster in hopes it was Vincent calling, even if I knew the chances of that were slim. Maybe it was my mom. I kept forgetting to talk to her, not exactly in the mood for the inevitable guilt.

Serena went into an office without waiting for me. When I entered the dimly lit room, light in the corner caught my eye. Candles flickered, but their flames didn't look right, neither did the pictures strewn about with faces on them I didn't recognize. The photos were more like a ghostly memory instead of a sharply printed portrait. Some kind of long-stemmed herbs were also tied in a bushel to each frame, the earthy smell in the room likely wafting from it.

"An altar," Serena said as she rounded the office desk, seeing my attention on the photos. "The candles aren't real flames. Well, real, but can't catch things on fire. And the photos are taken from people's memories since no one actually prints pictures these days." Serena opened a drawer and pulled out a couple of mugs and put them on the table. "A group went and took care of the dead outside of the Creation. People wanted a place to mourn them, and this was Edson's compromise."

I went over to the desk as Serena put a pickle jar next to the mugs. She poured liquid into the mugs from the jar and handed me one.

"I take it there's no phone call."

"Nope." She raised the mug. "Make it up to you with alcohol?"

"Considering the hundreds of dead bodies I've seen in the last while, I'm down." An amber-coloured liquid shone inside. "Where's it from?"

"Edson's stash. Drink up. Might be all we get." She lifted hers and we clinked glasses before taking a swig.

I sat on the arm of a chair looking at my cousin, she still the same blonde-haired, blue-eyed alcohol thief ready to have fun no matter the serious shit going down, making sense of chaos by saying "drink up" like our crap-ass situation might improve ounce-by-ounce.

"What?" Serena checked herself over as if I spotted a stain.

"Nothing. Things are just fucked up."

"Word." Serena held up her cup for an air toast.

The taste of the dark liquid was a bit off, maybe spiced, and I couldn't place the brand. "Is this whiskey?"

"I think so. No clue what kind. It's alcohol and it's free, so maybe drinking faster is better."

True that.

I took a bit glug, not enjoying the taste, yet loving the warmth of the drink settling like acid in my gut as I breathed out its heat, my cheeks instantly warming in a nice way.

"What do you think of this place?" A normal enough question, but Serena's tone was off. Edgy.

I gave a one-shoulder shrug. "It's adequate."

My cousin nodded and took another sip from her cup. I followed suit, thinking finishing faster would also spare me awkward small talk.

Things were strained between us. I didn't have the strength to dig deeper into why or face it head on. It wasn't usually required. You piss off Serena she'd be the first to—

Flash! I saw stars and nearly fell off the chair.

Blotches of light burst in front of my eyes, bleeding away Serena until I saw myself sitting across from Donovan on the ground in Aunt Lacey's basement as he held my hand during my first palm reading at the Coven meeting I thought was a tea leaf reading party.

It disappeared and Serena was leaning against the office desk, calling my name, the mug I had been drinking from in her hand.

"What the fuck did y—?"

Flash! More stars.

Donovan and I were in Aunt Lacey's backyard. I was against the wall, my leg up over his thigh, pulling him into me, his hand disappearing between us.

"Whatthefuck!" I screamed, my voice slurred in my ears as whatever that was fell away, bringing me to the office around me.

I scrambled away from Serena, the glow from the fake candles making traces of blurred light in my eyes. Serena was in my field of vision again, Donovan now next to her, both blocking the office exit.

"What'd you do to me?" My question was for my cousin. If Donovan was involved with this, he wouldn't have managed it without her help.

My head swam like I had drunk a few more of those cups. I staggered into another chair and then the wall, trying to keep myself upright as Serena's distorted apologies sounded too far away.

Donovan grabbed my shoulders. "Ride out the memories!"

I sprang forward, catching him off balance. He fell onto his back, my drugged-up weight on top of him, wielding enough fury to wrap my hands around his throat and squeezing until my knuckles ached.

"What'd you do to me?" He did something, made Serena do something.

Flash! Blinding light again.

I scurried backwards until I hit something so hard my skull bounced, adding to my world swimming around me.

A familiar restaurant. I was looking at myself and Donovan hugging, holding each other in the restaurant's kitchen after an attack during Caine's and my first date. The intense attraction was a clear indication of something going on between us.

I clawed at my skull hearing my scream from a distance. A crack on the left side of my brain was another smack of hard floor or wall. My whole body jerked against my will.

Voices rose around me. Hands grabbed my shoulders.

Flash!

Donovan and I were talking but I couldn't hear what we were saying; we too far away for me to catch the conversation. We leaned in close to each other. I laughed as Donovan gave me a cocky grin.

The person looked away, but I saw enough of them to know it was Caine watching us. His memory. He didn't like what he saw.

"Sophie!"

I opened my eyes to see Donovan over me, office walls around me. He held my arms and was telling me to relax.

"Don't fight the memories and it won't hurt."

What? This piece of shit did something to me and is now telling me to sit back and enjoy it?

I pushed him away and sprung to my feet before my knees buckled and landed me on the ground again. Serena stood with her hands over her mouth as if she were surprised by the turn of events when she was the one who helped him.

Flash!

I lost all sense of myself as music pumped in my chest and colourful lights bounced off of the walls around a large group of people. Donovan was flush against me on the dance floor, we in Ranlyn's backyard in the big tent with the Coven around us. I smelled the alcohol on Donovan's breath and then felt the sweat of his slick skin beneath my fingers once we hid away in a small room and let go of all reservations of getting together. The whole coven in the rest of the house accentuated every thrilling sensation as he drove into me—

The office and glowing altar streamed into focus as my pained moans echoed off the walls. The chaos around me was too much. People. So many people stood around, looking down at me. Olive, Lewis, Pricilla, Serena, Adam, and Denise...All too loud, bringing what felt like lightning strikes through my skull, down my spine, and twisted me in memories.

Flash!

A television paused with light in front of Donovan and me as we sat on his couch, then shifted to us chasing each other through his house naked, then someone watching us practice magic together, and then someone watching Donovan whisper something into my ear. I heard "I love you" replaying like background music, Donovan's voice repeating himself over and over as more memories hit in an unending stream and I was forced to relinquish all resistance against them.

25

HONED MANIPULATION TACTICS

Donovan

"You didn't say this would cause her pain!" I swept Sophie up off of the office floor and raced through the lobby to the cell console. Once inside, I laid her on the bed, smoothed her hair aside, and wiped tears from her cheeks which continued to fall even though she stopped thrashing.

"Shoving memories from multiple sources into someone's brain isn't picking daisies, boy." Sophie's Aunt Gloria did nothing but watch as Sophie beat her head against the ground in uncontrollable seizing.

Iris snorted. "With your Psychometry, one would assume you possessed intimate knowledge of how much discomfort visions cause."

Serena pushed others aside in the small space. "Please tell me she's breathing, and I didn't just brain damage my cousin."

"That can't happen, can it?" Adam pushed his dark sunglasses onto his head, none of the Soul Seers in here able to tell me if her soul still glowed while in the cell.

Olive patted and squeezed my shoulder. "She stopped resisting and has settled. Sleep will soothe what the spell roughed up. She may wake with a headache and the knowledge we implanted, but she will be okay."

I wasn't so confident.

"How long will she sleep?" Kim asked what I wanted to, afraid something like this might put her out for days. Kim took some convincing to participate. Regret showed in her crossed arms.

"No more than a night's worth," Gloria answered. "Now, leave her be." Her sister followed as Gloria unceremoniously left the cell.

"I'm staying." No one could force me to leave her side.

Instead, I shifted her to bring her into my lap and wiped away more of her fallen tears, not caring of the others' opinions about it.

No such luck in being left alone. Adam and Serena got comfy. Denise returned a few minutes later with a deck of cards, pulling Kim in with her for a few games of Asshole. Others joined the card games, Jared and Blake as well as a few from the Ballard Coven, filling the tiny space including people sitting on the toilet and the floor.

Ranlyn and Veata visited once Jared and Blake spread the word about what happened, and Olive kept checking in.

Hall came and stayed, standing off to the side, mostly watching Kim. Caine came in as well, in and out, but always returning. I assumed he was probably checking to see if Ness was moping around somewhere.

With the connection damaged, I didn't sleep when she did anymore. The binding on the cells created a rare opportunity for me to touch her without visions and watch her sleep.

I wanted her to see me before anyone else whether the experiment worked or not. If it didn't work, she would hate me, and I would take the brunt for the idea away from her family and the Coveners as I deserved. If it did work, I wanted to be the first to welcome her back to herself.

Gliding my fingers against the smooth skin of her arm, her cheek, and down her sleek hair, I worried what would happen if the experiment failed. Her violent reaction and unconsciousness confirmed she saw what the memory bomb intended her to see, but what if it wasn't enough to fix the damage to the Soul Magic?

I didn't eat, drink, or kill time with the others. I couldn't stop thinking of what she said to me in the storage space in Amsterdam, about living a life without her, and how I royally fucked up everything. By insisting Sophie give in to what we felt for each other, she betrayed Caine and was in danger because of it. Granted, we'd already lost Aunt Lacey, but now Tobias knew Sophie was my weak spot. A sure-fire way to crush me.

I hated myself for what all this has done to her.

Thinking of Tobias triggered thoughts of family and my thoughts drifted to Fox. *Damn.* I might lose him too and would have no one to blame but myself. Again, my honed manipulation tactics perfected from years of self-preservation were never unsuccessful, not even with Fox who saw what would happen and resisted participation in the battle.

Sometimes I wished I didn't care about anything. It was much easier when I was dicking my way through the region and worried about nothing except the next vagina and what it could do for me. That and the Conception Ritual memories made me want to melt my skin off with acid.

"You can't change any of that."

My attention whipped up, surprised to see Caine standing there, returned from wherever he went to placate Ness.

"Stay outta my head." How the hell did Caine even read my mind? Maybe some residual power from Gareth that superseded the cell's binding?

Caine laughed. "Actually, I don't have anything left of Gareth in me, but once certain things are learned, the power can't unlearn them. In the cells or not, some things are still open to me. And what I see in you is dangerous thinking."

"I really don't—"

"Need me for anything? No kidding, man. Besides the side effects, I know what you did here was for her own good."

"We'll see." I looked down at Sophie peacefully sleeping. Much more serene than she did during her waking hours since before we ended up in the cells.

"I'll help any way I can." Caine knelt by the bed. "If it means kidnapping her to a remote cabin and rewiring her fucked up brain, I'd do it if it meant she's herself again."

I appreciated him saying so and planned to use the tactic if this didn't work. "Except she isn't different with you, is she?"

"Oh, she is. She's *too* open, *too* willing to use me as a sounding board instead of talking to whoever she should be. I'm letting it happen because if I don't, she might not talk to anyone at all, and there's so much inside of her she's storing away, it's adding to whatever's poisoning your Soul Magic. She's not the person I fell in love with. Hasn't been since you fucked that up for us."

I almost smiled. "You're welcome."

The sad crook in Caine's cheek was as much of an almost smile as mine was. "But you're still who she should be with. I see why you're so perfect for each other and why the Soul Magic was done in the first place. But this woman—" he motioned to Sophie, "—this angry, vengeful, gun-toting, woman? I don't know her. It's as bad as watching Nya walk around in her meat suit. Which I didn't experience so much but saw in others' memories. It's weird."

I almost laughed remembering I thought the same thing.

"Though, gun-toting Sophie is pretty hot," Blake said, adding his two cents from across the small room.

Caine laughed. "Yes, she is."

"Why are you telling me all this?" It wasn't every day Caine unloaded the touchy-feely stuff on me.

"Does there have to be a reason?"

"In my experience? Yeah."

"Okay. Well, I'm not your dad, or mine for that matter. I see what the two of you are going through and I can't sit back and not offer to do what I can. I loved her. I envisioned sharing an entire life with her. I've moved on because she didn't love me the same way. If not being with you was truly her choice, I'd be calling you a stalker, but it's not her. Whatever's happening with the Soul Magic is calling the shots. We need to restore her so she can make those decisions with a clear mind."

"She hasn't been herself since this magic shit came into it." Serena reminded me of Frog. Was the guy on a plane to sand and sun yet? Better be.

"Remember who brought you into this and only because you begged her." Serena and I always found a way to butt heads.

"Hell, I love this shit." Serena laid down a card. "She knew I would. That's not my point. Ever since she got sucked into this, she's lost herself. She went from being super boring to overwhelmingly over-interesting overnight and doesn't have anything to judge herself by. I'm telling you, this memory bomb of yours didn't work."

"Because you've developed the gift of foresight?" Denise served up the sarcasm.

"No, bitch-boss," Serena bit back with snark, "because I actually know who she was before all of this. She's going to open her eyes, remember both sets of memories, and be so fucking confused, she'll hate all of us more for trying to force her to see anything different. And then she'll slap lover-boy there for being so handsy when clearly, she hates your guts right now."

I shot her the finger, but she was right. Sophie would hate that I spent the better part of a day holding her without her permission. If we ever lived to see the other side of this, I wanted her to know that even when she wasn't herself, I was always here for her.

"Bullshit," Blake called Serena out. "If you thought any of that you wouldn't've delivered her the drink that did all this to her."

"Kinda hard when lover-boy injects you with the hope she might be herself again."

"Excuses. Leave if you're so sure." Kim's reaction surprised me.

She and Serena were pretty tight, and I wouldn't want to see the two of them get into it.

"Not a chance. I fed her the drink. I need to explain my side of things."

I shifted my legs as my feet were going numb. "And if you're wrong?"

"Then I owe you a bottle of whatever your poison is. I'm not worried. I won't be wrong."

Loathing her confidence, we had a stare down. I quit first, refocused on Sophie, and indulged in the belief that she would wake up and love me again. Sophie was the only one in my sights as Jared coaxed Serena to deal the next hand of their game.

Caine and I didn't talk anymore but the guy stuck around, hanging out with the others, and giving me and Sophie a little space.

Dread settled like cement in my gut thinking Serena might be right.

26

JARRING IMPACT

Sophie

Curling into myself, my head was banging with a migraine that churned vomit into a froth I was surprised didn't bubble up and escape out of my nose. Hands-to-temples, I massaged them as I cursed my genes, my mother and far too many others suffering migraines as well. What triggered this one? The taste of whiskey settled on my tongue. Right, Serena snuck me a drink.

Oh, fuck.

The strikes of memory, Serena's worried face, then more faces, and Donovan telling me not to fight the memories, memories that came with so much pain. They planned this, they did this to me, brought on images that thumped behind my eyelids once I couldn't fight them anymore.

A feather of contact to my arm startled me. As it tried to turn me over, I grabbed the hand touching me, cranking it to the side until bones snapped and Serena wailed. I didn't know it was her, but assumed it was one of the ones who did this to me, and I was right.

I refused to let go of Serena's hand, keeping hold of it as I turned it over and forced Serena onto her knees. More bones popped. Serena's mouth opened wide, gasping, yet unable to scream.

Someone grabbed my wrist and called my name. Donovan was under me. The little creep must have been sleeping, in my bed, with me.

I thrusted my free elbow into his nose, and he let go of my wrist as blood burst from his face.

I shoved Serena by her broken hand to the floor before getting down and crawling over her, nice and close to my cousin, as she cradled her broken limb. "That's what happens when you drug someone and fuck with their head."

Jared and Kim muscled me away from her. Someone else grabbed me in some kind of hold with my arms behind my back. Donovan called my brother's name in warning a second before my skull met his face, his sunglasses flying to the floor. He shot off of me really quick, others whisking Serena and Adam away from the cell so their bones could be reset and healed. The process guaranteed to be as painful as the break itself.

Donovan stood. He, Kim, Caveman, and Caine were left, all looking at me like I was possessed.

I examined my supposed friends as potential targets, unsure of what they planned to do to me next.

Donovan braved a step towards me, earning him a backhand across the jaw, pitching him off-balance, and landing his ass on the bed behind him. Caveman surged forward but Donovan motioned for him to stop.

Caveman smoothed his hair. "This is insane."

Kim's eyes glistened with tears. She had no right to be upset after what she did to me. Some of the images were her memories.

"Don't touch her." Donovan stood and flexed his jaw as if I did some damage and enacted a puppy dog expression. "I convinced Serena and all the others it was essential to help you."

I stared at him. "They're all adults. You didn't coerce them into anything. Though the idea stinks of you. Another scheme to control me."

"That's not what I did." He took another step towards me into a right hook I snapped out before consciously deciding to move. This one didn't knock him down, just cut the skin beneath his eye as well as on my knuckles. He didn't move to protect his face, nor did he retaliate, not even when I straightened my fingers and jabbed him in the windpipe.

He hinged at the waist and grabbed onto his throat. No visible damage, all jarring impact. He raised another hand to Caveman, requesting he stay out of it, though even Caine looked like he wanted to step in.

Donovan cleared his throat and regained his height. "I thought—" He coughed. "I thought if you could see the *real* memories and not the ones the Soul Magic messed with, then maybe it could save you. I love you too much not to try everything possible."

"Save me? From what? From letting myself filter through one unhealthy relationship to another? Save me? Such horseshit."

I shoved Donovan backwards a step. He steeled and regained his balance, again, motioning for the others to let him handle me.

"That's not what you're doing." Kim found her voice, Caveman thrusting an arm in front of her so she didn't step too close.

"You know this is the damaged Soul Magic, Sophie. We're trying to help you see the truth." Caine was supposed to be on my side. Of all people to be persuaded.

"Truth? Come on, Caine." I turned back to Donovan. "Sorry to disappoint, but I'm not the idealistic little lady who thought tying myself to you centuries ago was the height of romanticism." I shoved him again, and again, he took the hit, straightening. "And you can let yourself be a punching bag, it doesn't make you a martyr. It makes you an idiot with a broken nose."

I wound up and hit him with a thrust of my palm into his face, the crunch of cartilage making the others cringe and Kim to hide a gag as I landed another hit to the solar plexus to drive home the point.

He went down to one knee at my feet. I've seen him been hit a hell of a lot harder than that and shake it off with a cocky, dimpled smile. The asshole was laying on the "poor me" routine extra thick for audience reaction.

He wanted to be the victim in front of the others to gain their sympathy. Stupid move considering he already had it and they and my family all spent hours pretending they wanted nothing more than to help me.

Caveman surged forward and grabbed my shoulder.

Energy shot from Donovan and a wall materialized, zapping Caveman's hand off me, evoking a growl from the big man as he was cut off from Donovan and me. He and Kim were stuck on the other side of the blacked-out divider that muffled the majority of noise from the other side.

A tingle of Donovan's power settled in the air around me, brushing up against me. Something about it was familiar, as I knew his power as if it were my own. Whatever this was, something in it was different. His soul glow didn't look different to me on the outside of the cells. Maybe he was changing it somehow like the Sovereignty employees were or how Joelly did.

Either way, power in a place where power shouldn't exist, wasn't right. Did Vincent know about this? These were his cells, he had to know if Donovan could still use within them. And if Vincent knew, did he set this up, too? I couldn't believe he would sic Donovan on me, though he did pressure me to search my soul for reasons to forgive Donovan.

Maybe he wasn't on my side as much as I thought.

27

CREATED AN OPENING

Donovan

Sophie's glare narrowed. "The cells are spellbound. How'd you do that?"

The strength of the ritual stone magic hummed inside me. I was done talking and done taking a beating. I ignored Sophie's emotionless question as a cannon blast of intuition bitch-slapped me, telling me without words what to do.

Determination clicked into place like I had unholstered a weapon. If it meant sledge-hammering the odd-shaped puzzle piece into a makeshift home, I was going to fix her.

I rushed forward. Sophie was ready and blocked me with a shove to the side, using my momentum to drive her knee into my gut. A huff of oxygen chased out of my lips as she pushed me to the ground, and then a swinging hit snapped my head backwards, the crushing blow coming from her steel toe.

A tingle of ritual stone magic converged on my chin, stitching up what must have been a gash, though I was too fuzzy to feel any blood.

Sophie's expression was remorseless disgust. Serena was right.

The experiment failed, and yet Sophie's anger made her feral-like, but sloppy. She'd fought some battles before, but her weapon was her magic, not bare knuckles. She could hold her own, but she didn't have her bag of tricks in here and I had much more experience to pull from. I wasn't fighting full throttle before as hurting her was the opposite of what I wanted to do.

I don't want to hurt her at all, but this was happening.

Before fully shaking off her hit, I saw her on the bed trying to find a weak spot in the wall I erected. As if I was stupid enough not to ensure it hit each wall and the ceiling and strong enough it didn't crumble even though my ass was warming the concrete floor.

I chose stealth while her attention was distracted, moving to my knees to try and catch her. She caught me and kicked at me; her boot meant for my chest. I snatched her foot and cranked it high to throw her off balance. She landed on her back with a thud on the thin mattress.

She kicked the other boot not in my grasp, hitting home with her combats in my beanbags. A cramp seized my groin with lighting strikes of pain into my gut.

I tried to hang on, but she snapped out her foot and hit me in the chest, sending me into the wall, my thighs too busy screaming to hold me up, and my tailbone hit the floor again.

"Dirty fighter, eh?" The cramp radiated with stinging tentacles and shuddered through my junk. My power took a lingering second to collect itself to dowse the pain.

"Like you can judge." She scrambled to her feet, planted a fighting stance as I was gaining some height.

Half-way vertical, Sophie sprung at me from the bed with her legs curled up, landing on my collarbones with all her weight. I went backwards and slid down the wall where I started.

Poised above me, Sophie used the leverage to wail on me over and over, her fists cutting. While it wasn't the first time I picked a fight for the sole purpose of getting good and bloody, I raised my arms to defend myself in a way she easily flanked and landed the hits she threw.

Even through half-hooded eyes, I saw all the blood landing on her and covering her knuckles. This was more pain I caused that she would feel later.

The ritual stone magic took over and healed as she hurt me, then seeped from every pore and flushed over my body in defence of her continued barrage.

Hands still up, nothing else came at me. Quiet dropped over the room and Sophie's oppressive shadow moved away from me.

A light huff and movement was Sophie suddenly seated on the ground with her back to the bed frame, eyes wide in a blinking frenzy, pulling in deep sucking breaths.

The ritual stone magic was still on me, around me, and in the air. I didn't see it, but I felt it. Was it doing something to her?

Whatever happened, it created an opening.

Here's my chance.

The itch of healing attacked my face and had me woozy when I sat up. I gritted through it, focused on a target, and grabbed her ankle. Before she could try and shake me off, I pulled her body across the floor to me. Whatever the ritual stone magic was doing to her, it made her compliant or something as she didn't fight me as I expected. Instead, she slipped down onto her back, her arms limp at her sides, and her eyes rolling and fighting for consciousness.

I leaned over her, inches from her face, and palmed her cheek. She reached for my arm without the energy to push my hand away. I thought about what I planned to do to end all of this and how exhausted she was. And while it was another intrusion on her, I couldn't live another day without knowing I did everything to repair the damage I had done.

Her lips parted widely in a soundless scream. The ritual stone magic that incapacitated her was now in my fingers caressing her face. I grasped the hand that tried to fight me off and held tight as the power flowed through me into her.

I didn't know exactly what it was doing to her yet knew stopping wasn't an option. The drive to reach deep and heal us was potent, keeping my hands glued to her even when she flailed her arms and legs, her boney knees clipping my ribs, as her voice caught up with the agonizing expression of terror in her eyes. Ringing echoes of her screams buzzed in my power-clouded ears.

Split in half at wanting to end her pain since she had been through so much already and knowing letting go would leave her half the woman she used to be, I pushed on needing her to be stronger than me, needing to heal the Soul Magic.

The flow of power backed up. It never abandoned what it was doing to her, but now it came at me, needling through me, digging deep into my chest. Sweat broke out over my body as pain bloomed, it humming to near numbness.

I refused to let her go.

I bent to her side, clutching her hand in a tight grip as I was overtaken.

A slow, cold burn grew into a volcanic heat engaging my whole ribcage and spilling into my bones. Her scream in my ears was now my own, the pain travelling up through my spine to my brain. Power crawled over my skull leaving fingers of fire in its wake.

The power channelled through me until nothing was left. I tried to hold on longer, but my body white-flagged it and I collapsed next to her.

Hands touched me. The pressure was salt on raw fire-scorched flesh. Voices spoke, worry in their tone. I couldn't catch the words or who was talking, and every breath was like making out with a fire-breathing dragon, licking flames down my throat into my lungs. I tried not to inhale, but the pain worked against me.

Pain. Everywhere pain.

Kim's voice was going on about something. Was Sophie okay? I tried to open my eyes and it took a few times for the fuzziness to subside.

Sophie was sitting up against the bed. Kim knelt next to her with a bottle of water in hand.

"Here." Kim brought the bottle to her lips. Sophie sucked some back and winced, palming her chest and her stomach.

I curled onto my side as a burning path cut down my throat into my gut, Sophie doing the same.

Perceptible silence peaked as I looked at them, now noticing Hall was standing in the room as well, before I locked eyes with Sophie.

"I felt that."

Sophie braced her hands on the side of bed, using it to sit on the edge.

"I felt that!" I sprung up onto my feet quicker than my body wanted me to.

Kim and Hall looked at each other and at Sophie as if unsure of how to react. Maybe she needed proof.

"More water." Sophie reached for the bottle from Kim.

I pulled a pocketknife from my pocket, yanked up my sleeve, and ran its blade along my forearm deep enough to draw blood.

Sophie gasped mid-gulp and almost dropped the bottle. She scowled at me. I held my arm out as evidence. She pulled up her own sleeve and revealed smudged blood and a clean slice in her skin.

Kim gasped. Sophie continued staring at her arm.

"It worked." My eyesight blurred, this time from tears I fought back so I wouldn't lose sight of her or the knife wound proving all the pain was worth it.

Sophie wrenched her shirt sleeve down to cover the bright red evidence of the connection's return. "It doesn't mean anything."

The confusion in my chest was all Sophie's. She didn't understand what was happening, but her confusion was layered in fear and resentment and something close to guilt, but also betrayal. In that moment, I didn't care what she felt or if every feeling was directed at me, I felt what she felt, and we were connected again.

I forced myself to swallow and fought to speak, my voice barely above a whisper. "This means everything."

DESPERATE FOR LIFE

Vincent

Humidity stippled my glasses, forcing their removal to retain visual alertness. I surveyed the deep recesses of my new environment, dark corners beyond reach, and promised such danger. This place was the same I last viewed Cora-Lynn. She was here, somewhere, watching.

My father gave me what I wanted. A sick rendition of a reunion with my wife, the singular wish atop my mind since the day I lost her.

Conditioned for centuries to hate me, and but a sliver of the woman I married, Cora-Lynn locked me in her sights, waiting for her opportunity to pounce.

How would others know of my imprisonment? Would my fate trickle through the ranks to internal contacts who could...could what? Probabilities of escape were infinitesimal, even smaller when considering my father would perform his due diligence in manipulating others to believe I simply abandoned the cause and left town on an extended unexplained absence.

No key and no avenue of escape from the cells meant outside

intervention was the single form of escape. Unless my father decided to make this a temporary torture attempt. My fate now lay within his hands.

The heavy air and earthy scent wafting from beneath my loafers as I moved in circles to peer into the depths of the tropical landscape was as real as any other place. No wonder Cora-Lynn believed she was in the grips of a tropical forest. No detail would lead her to believe otherwise.

Amazing what illusions could be pulled off in the confines of a ten-by-ten cell.

"Cora-Lynn?"

No response.

For all I knew, I could be in the crosshairs of a jungle cat sent to stalk me, though I was certain Cora-Lynn had found me.

"Cora-Lynn, I am not the Vincent you have seen all these years since my father took you away from me. I am no imposture." Silence returned besides the insects of the cell's imagination. "Come out so we may speak."

A slice of her lean body peered around the safety of a palm. A salamander crawled up the front of the palm, a creature so real I forcibly reminded myself of the falsity.

I opened my hands at my sides. "I do not wish to harm you." She remained hidden. "Please, love, I was led to believe you were dead the day my father struck you down. He captured you and kept me from the knowledge of your imprisonment."

What little visible part of her she deigned to show me disappeared again.

"Cora-Lynn, please."

I went to where I saw her. A solid form ran into my flank before I reached the palm. A feral cry rushed through the lips of the woman who never raised her voice at anyone. She pitched me to the ground with all the weight of her tiny, muscular body and landed on top of me, knocking the wind from my lungs. The ground may have smelled of loose soil, but it gave no differently than cement.

Coughing and sucking air was pain I fought to control as Cora-Lynn and her wild blue eyes were poised over me. All that blonde hair I remembered was gone, cheekbones jutting. She was malnourished, and bald. A stranger who saw me as nothing but a target.

She ran her fingers over my shirt before her expression pinched and she scurried away. She lowered into a defensive crouch on all fours like an animal tracking my every movement as I pushed up onto my elbows.

"Please, listen." I held out my hand in some attempt at reassurance. She flinched, too on edge as I attempted to reposition myself to better defend against another attack.

When she stared without further contact, I tried again. "I know you have endured fathomless torture, but this is the first time I have seen you in four hundred and sixty-two years."

She pounced forward like a territorial gorilla. I pushed backwards and up onto my feet, now in the same position as she. Cora-Lynn stopped her advance, sliding in the soil feet away from me.

"Cora-Lynn, please. The other times you saw me were an illusion. I was never—"

"I know."

Her first words spoken to me were severe in their manner, clipped and failed to soften that scowling expression.

"What do you mean, 'You know'?"

She straightened her posture, causing me to flinch at the quick movement. "The others could not be touched." She took a few steps to the side. I took a few steps in the opposite direction untrusting of her motives. "Anything closer and the others disappeared or moved with great speed. You are solid and clumsy."

I unfolded from my defensive position hoping she would not take advantage of my attempt to appear non-threatening, though of course she saw me as inept and not much contest.

Tears sprung to my eyes. I fought to blink them away, not wanting to lose sight of the woman I thought was long dead and knowing blinking could be deadly. We were in the same cell. Flesh and bone and within each other's reach. If allowed, she could end me.

I fought for the right words. "I would never hurt you."

"Impossible. Not now. However, you have. If not for you, I would be elsewhere."

I nodded. "I should have told you about Magics and their world sooner. I feared I would frighten you."

"You should have revealed to me much more." She crossed her arms. I settled with the fact she was content not to attack. "Son to a man who would scour earth's end to find him. In danger you left me unprepared to handle. When I hurt the man meant to harm you, I did so without touching him. That should not have been possible."

"You are special—"

"Do not mock me!"

I fell silent as her shaking fists clenched at her sides, eyes wide, lips in a snarl.

Not wanting to further anger her, nonetheless unwilling to stop, I tried again. "My magic will not work in here."

"What man are you without it? Useless. Weak."

I sighed. "My father would like nothing more than to watch us kill each other. Do not give him the satisfaction."

She gave an ugly laugh. "You could not end me."

"I would never attempt to, even given the opportunity."

She laughed again.

"Please, Cora-Lynn. The world outside has changed—"

"The world, Vincent, changes every day."

"This is not the world. This is a prison cell constructed by magic meant to punish you for crimes that were not your fault."

"More lies."

"No. This world changes because it is an illusion."

She went quiet. I hoped she was considering the truth of my words. "Does it matter if my world is a prison or an illusion when I cannot escape it?"

This answer came with hesitation, knowing my responses were

unsafe from being overheard by more than my wife. "I know Magics who have infiltrated my father's company and know many others who will fight for us. They know I came to find you and will not allow us to rot in here." Promises were more than I could keep but I needed her on my side, working with me and not against me.

"And these selfless others, they will release us from these illusions?" Her tone was bloated with cynicism.

"Some have greater power than even my father. Greater than me."

She scoffed as if I was an imbecilic child. "No one will save you. Your words mean nothing. Never have. All lies to cower behind. You and your father share more than blood."

"I am not my father." My voice now grew louder. I stepped forward until she tensed like a coiled snake in warning. "I have dedicated my life to destroying my father and this place where he imprisons countless other Magics like yourself. I know it is confusing."

I mistook closeness for familiarity and placed my hand on her shoulder. She smacked my hand away from her, thrashed jagged nails across my face, and took off into the brush as I was still bent over cradling my bloody cheek.

I tried calling for Cora-Lynn again, apologizing for overstepping, but Cora-Lynn remained elusive. Minutes dragged into hours without another sighting of her. I searched and searched realizing the cell must be sending me in circles.

Thunder rumbled in the non-sky above and water droplets hit my face, running into my scratches, and stinging them with the salt of my sweat. Every drop was so real and chilled me immediately. Rain fell heavy enough to force me to suspend my search in favour of shelter under thick, heavy branches as hours passed without reprieve. The onslaught of weather turned nasty and whipped up a beating wind.

Of all the reunions in all the lifetimes I envisioned when hoping to see Cora-Lynn again, never did I imagine this. She hated me.

Would rather end my life than have me touch her. No part of her spoke of the Cora-Lynn I married.

She knew I was who I claimed to be, nonetheless, that was not something that worked in my favour. She has had over four hundred years to loath me and to forget what I meant to her. Over four hundred years to dwell on the omissions that ruined her life, extending it centuries only to pay for crimes that were purely my own. I loved her with everything I was, searched for her in the faces of those on the streets I walked, and then adopted a mission to find her once discovering my father's hand in plundering her soul. Never could I have guessed she was alive, and I afforded no chance for her forgiveness, nor could I erase her time wasted in this cell.

If I remained a prisoner, we would spend an eternity with me chasing after her as she did everything to stay as far away from me as possible.

Immeasurable hours passed as the rain drizzled through the leaves and soaked the ground when sudden exhaustion overwhelmed me. A heartbeat ago, I was alert and now could scarcely lift my eyelids. Seconds before my eyes closed for good it dawned on me that it must be the next day and either the mutant who sent me inside or my father did something to force my unconsciousness so the illusion could begin anew.

When awareness resumed, the forest leaves were gone, and rock walls surrounded me. No dreams played out as I slept. No sense of time passing, yet I was rested. The illusion had changed, and my clothing was no longer soaked through, though they remained dirty. I found it disorienting to find no familiarity, and to think, Cora-Lynn endured this morbid surprise every day for an innumerable number of days.

Before leaving the small cubby of rocks surrounding me through the hole at my feet, I remained still and listened. An unidentifiable sound pinged off the rocked walls, soft rustling of bare footsteps telling me Cora-Lynn was close by.

Moving inches at a time, I slid to the edge of the opening at my feet and found myself in a smaller part of a larger cave. Where I slept was a small inlet. Light drifted in through seams in the ceiling. I had a feeling we would remain inside this day.

The crackling of a small fire constructed to one side of the cave grew as Cora-Lynn collected small branches to burn, though I could only guess where she found them. It is curious she was given the option considering my father would never allow an actual fire to be set in a cell.

Taking the opportunity her focus gifted me, I sat and observed her. Her determined walk, her silky movements, all so foreign. I tried and failed to find anything in this woman that spoke of my Cora-Lynn. The sadness that followed this was a despair my father no doubt loved to witness. Thinking of my father enjoying my misery was enough for me to suppress hatred for the man and to exit the inlet.

My loafers scuffed small rocks on the way out. Cora-Lynn spun and fell into a fighting stance. I lifted my hands noticing places for her to run and hide in this new environment were missing and assumed this was purposeful planning.

"I will remain here." I slid down the wall and settled onto the cave floor, wiping my hands of debris, and sitting with my knees bent.

"Why are you still here?"

I ran a hand through my mussed hair. "I, too, am a prisoner. I suspect until someone comes for me, we will have many days together. Truthfully, a swift rescue is slim so this may be longer than we desire."

She squinted at me, reserved on if to believe me or not.

For now, she was happy to ignore me and for hours that was exactly what she did. Keeping to my spot, I watched as she meandered the cave without letting me out of her periphery while she kept the fire up and stayed busy if only not to engage with me. All the while, I watched her.

Water dripping grabbed Cora-Lynn's focus, something that took me longer to identify, as she searched for the sound's origins. Not that

I was not parched, the water sounded like enough to clean myself up with.

Cora-Lynn grew anxious at the dripping. She paced and chewed on her thumb nail.

The water came in from a long two-inch gap where the ceiling met the wall. The gap where sunlight came in. The dripping developed into more of a stream and continued at a steady pour. As the water increased, so did Cora-Lynn's pacing. A caged animal with fear that emanated from her and wholly confused me.

I started to worry when a puddle of water started creeping my way, forcing me to stand. A roar sent water gushing from that gap in the ceiling and it became clear what was happening. There was nowhere for the water to drain and with it coming in as it was, we would surely drown.

Would my father end us so soon?

Water encroached around my ankles; my loafers soaked through. "Has this occurred before?"

Receiving no answer, Cora-Lynn was transfixed by the gushing water, and she pressed against the wall farthest from where it was coming in.

"Cora-Lynn!" I yelled over the water with the same result.

Then I saw it. That sliver I sought out all day, something to show me my Cora-Lynn still existed within this feral creature. I had all but forgotten, however, the expression on her face was one I remembered. A childhood accident led her to near drowning as she took a misstep and slipped into a fast-moving stream near her home. Her eldest sister ran for their father and he and her uncle fished her out downstream, leaving her with a lingering fear for water from that day forward.

The rain last night must have been to keep her on edge. She wouldn't drown from rain but would keep her thinking that may change. Yesterday it remained nothing more than rain, but today was different. The water gathered and deepened as it hit the backs of my knees with bone-shaking coldness. Cora-Lynn remained with her back against the wall, her arms hugging her body, chin shaking, eyes unblinking as she shivered.

I pushed through the water but when I approached ten feet in front of her, she scrambled away, falling into the water, and pulling herself up and against another wall looking at me as if I meant to drown her myself.

"I recall you nearly drowning as a child. Your father and your Uncle Sebastian saved you. My father will not kill you now. No matter what happens, you will survive this day."

Although the conviction in my voice was plain, her distrust for me was greater. For all I knew, this was the end, and I was not fully convinced otherwise.

The water grew higher and saturated my waist. Due to her short stature, it reached Cora-Lynn's chest. No matter how badly her muscles shook, she still refused to speak to me, yet completely alert, aware of the danger in front of her, and of where I stood at all times.

When her chin dipped into the water, she pushed up onto her tiptoes and tried clutching the rock wall. Her wet fingers slipped on the slick rock, her toes losing their grip on the floor only to dunk her whole face into the pool sending her into a panic.

Her fear cut through me. The part of me desperately needing to protect her still lived. "Let me hold you up!"

Not a flicker of her acknowledgement glanced my way.

She slipped a few more times, the water swallowing her before she bobbed up, gasping for air.

When the water rose above her nostrils and she could no longer remain above the waterline, her panicked eyes shot to mine. I captured the opportunity as permission, swimming to her, and hoisting her up.

Only in desperation for self-preservation did she tolerate the contact. No matter, it came with a bittersweet bliss, and I soaked in the feeling of her hard body. Not an ounce of fat on her and every rigid muscle now vibrated against the cold in adrenalized terror.

Two feet of clear breathing space above her head was all I could give her, and she clawed at the ceiling like a panicked animal. The rising water crested my chin, promising neither of us any breathing room in little time.

Above me, I found her looking down with a passing understanding that before long I would be submerged, and quickly after, so would she.

"It will be okay." My hoarse voice shook, sputtering water off my lips.

Her panic worsened. She scrambled to create distance between us, either so I would not drown her myself or to prevent herself from weighing me down, I was unsure.

I refused to let her go and hoisted her as high as possible.

When my nostrils were submerged, I held my breath. The rush of water muffled in my clogged ears. Seconds passed as my lungs screamed for breath that would not come, this not nearly as terrifying as Cora-Lynn thrashing against me, her legs kicking, arms flailing, and neither enough to save her from the suffocating water as it washed over her head.

Impossible clarity underwater showcased Cora-Lynn pinching her nose and panicking as bubbles escaped her lips in her struggle.

No oxygen to gift her. No ability to drain the cave. No spell to create sanctuary. Without power, I would watch her die. Again, Cora-Lynn was forced to face her biggest fear, and after years of torture, she was still so desperate for life that she clung to a man she hated, the liar who destroyed her life, and all I could think about was losing her again.

Cora-Lynn stopped thrashing, her body settling with dreadful calm. I pulled her to me, placing a hand on her cheek, unsure if she was seeing me or if those pale blue eyes saw nothing. My lungs burned so badly I contemplated inhaling the water to end the suffering.

If Alasdair was really going to kill us, then she and I could start our lives over. I may never find her again, but she would be safe and free.

I sent out a wish that my Charges would land on happiness and that they may alternatively find me one day as another Seedling trying to learn what it meant to be a Magic.

Before hopeful thoughts of them formed, a tumultuous whirlwind of water twisted our bodies into each other and the hardtoothed walls as I strangled my hold on her arm so we would remain together.

Slammed onto the rock floor as all the water was sucked from the room, I hacked until my lungs cleared and ached with every pull of oxygen while Cora-Lynn vomited water along its slick surface.

No longer requiring my help, and even less interested in my touch, Cora-Lynn pushed herself unsteadily to her feet and braced her weight against the nearest wall to separate herself from me, undoubtedly willing to forget her weakness in seeking my comfort.

With a swipe of my hands through my hair and rubbing my face, I coughed a few more times, wanting nothing more than to speak with her, but I saw she was not present enough to listen. Her thoughts remained in the water taking her under and to her near drowning as a child. Telepathy was unneeded in order to read this from her, her thousand-yard stare said it all.

Time passed, with no way to guess how long, before the dripping sound started again. Cora-Lynn's stare snapped back into the room as she was sitting against the wall with her knees drawn to her chest. Soon that dripping became a stream, and that stream began to gush, and I knew this was how we would spend our day—in hours of silence, clinging to each other, and brought to the brink of death by drowning only to be rid of the terrifying water to retreat into silence.

When the waters grew and forced Cora-Lynn onto her toes again, I watched from my position against the wall and prepared to witness my wife drown again.

29

COMPANY MAN

Sophie

Yup. There in the middle of my chest and riding through my veins was Donovan's roaring excitement for re-establishing the connection.

Of course, he couldn't let it be. The pushy son-of-a-bitch provided another prime example of forcing me to do something I didn't want to and to shove himself into the forefront of my life whether I wanted him in my personal bubble or not.

His enthusiasm might be because of our new mission, though I sincerely doubted it. Almost as soon as the connection was re-established, Bronya traipsed her eager ass into the cell and told us it was time to hit the road. When she saw Donovan and me bloodied and battered, she touched his arm. A simple gesture meant to capture his attention, but I still wanted to throttle her bloody.

And what do you know? With the connection alive and the magic Donovan used still reverberating in my bones, he was gifted the satisfaction of my knee-jerk emotional reaction. Though, Bronya knew of his touch-triggered Psychometry. And even in the cells meant to douse all power, you don't just touch people all willy-nilly like that. The dimpled smirk he gave me confirmed he caught the emotions I could no longer hide and was gleeful for it.

The tips of my ears burned with anger.

The prospect of a mission thwarted his happy dance, though I was still subject to every spine-tingling thrill that raced through him.

After a quick clean-up, strapping on our gear focused us both. Only once did the niggling sense of libido flare as Donovan enjoyed the sight of me fastening my tactical vest. We reverted into our roles on the Team, and I could finally ignore him.

Kim was in the room when Donovan forced the connection into working order, so it shouldn't have surprised me when she came barrelling across the lobby before we left. I couldn't get away fast enough before being caught up in a Kim-style bear hug.

"I'm so happy for you!"

I shook myself free. "Are you fucking kidding me?"

"Nope. I don't care if you're still pissed or still being poisoned or whatever. The connection being fixed is progress and I'm happy as a pig in shit that the bastard found a way to pull it off."

"I didn't want it fixed!"

People were staring and I knew that one of those people was Donovan. A sprig of guilt hit me, but it was his and only lasted a second before he remembered he wasn't guilty one bit.

Kim stared at me straight and smiled around a white-toothed grin. "Too. Bad. I'm not about to let you ruin yourself, so I'm revelling in this excellent news and telling the whole damn world."

"Excuse me?"

"What? Everyone will want to know."

I stepped in close to Kim, sensing Caveman behind her as he readied for the mission, he also prepared to protect Kim if needed. A part of me wanted to put him to the test. "I don't want to live every day tied to Donovan, tied to his emotions and his temper tantrums. I don't want to be half a person who gets lost in how they feel about everything and everyone, and I don't need you blabbing my business to the whole Coven like a petty old lady with nothing more important to do. You want to be a good friend? Keep a fucking secret for once."

With a proud chin, Kim held her own. "Like it or not, people actually give a shit about you, even when you're being the nasty little bitch you are now. We know it's the damaged Soul Magic poisoning you, but still. So, I'll be honest and tell you up front, as your friend, that once you leave here, I'm immediately going to your family and telling them the connection is back. Serena is still pissed you broke her hand and might not care. And to be clear, I don't give a shit about whether you're mad at me for it or not."

As much as I wanted to punch her in the face, taking on Caveman right now was not a personal goal. If I tried, Donovan would jump in and suddenly it would be about the two of them instead of Kim's meddling. Not to mention, Kim would give me a good fight and I had a mission with no time to think about how pissed Serena might be.

"Love you too, bestie," Kim called, blowing me a kiss and adding a joyous wave as I stepped into the elevator to leave the Creation.

Kim may be annoying, but I respected her honesty.

In the Denali, Lincoln drove as Ismail explained we heard word of more Magics' homes being torched. Our job was to verify intel, confirm the residences belonged to fellow Magics, and pray the body-count was low.

"Not only did Loring burn down the houses, but he did it in daytime in full view of the public."

"So what?" Caveman shifted his big body in his seat. "All that would do is give the police a witness statement and a description of a man they'll never catch."

"I would normally agree, except it went viral." Ismail pulled out his tablet and handed it to Jessabelle in the first row of seats.

Jessabelle held up the tablet so everyone could watch. What we saw was shaky camera phone footage showing Loring standing in front of a house next to a few other Magics with their backs to the camera person who was hiding behind the blinds of their house across the street. They caught it as Loring lifted his gnarled fingers and started the house on fire without the use of accelerant. The video had thousands of hits.

"We're working on taking it down," Lincoln explained, "but as you can tell from the video, which was recorded before nightfall hours ago, a lot of people have already seen and shared it. The exposure is monumental and even if we manage to remove it, someone could upload it elsewhere or may have already downloaded it and spread it around. We need the original."

"Why'd it take so long for us to get wind of this?" Caveman's tone was laden with accusation.

"Being stuck in a Creation hides us from anyone who wants to kill us as well as from useful contacts. We don't like it, but the Creation is where the boss wants us. The one who informed us of this threat kept calling leaving Vincent messages, assuming a non-answer meant he was already on the job. When he hadn't gotten back to them, they reached out to other contacts who eventually led them to me.

"More troubling was that the owner of the burning house is actually one of those people standing with Loring. They calmly strolled out of the house and watched as Loring torched their place, but they weren't the only ones inside. The others burned to death."

"Loring is a Puppeteer?" Donovan interjected.

"No, he's not."

Ismail jumped in. "My guess? We know Loring isn't a Puppeteer, but one of those standing with him is. It's not a common power, so that gives us a small list of Magics with the capability. Taking Loring's warning into consideration, one of the men with him is Evaristus's son and Loring is using him to go after other Magics who participated in Evaristus's death."

This surprised me. "I thought his kids didn't use the power like he wanted them to and died in the span of a normal lifetime?"

"His wife, your ancestor," he said, looking at me in the rear-view mirror, "definitely died when refusing immortality. Most of his childreñ, too, but not all of them. And even if they did, they still parented children with bloodlines that grew beyond his reach, most probably in hiding since he was stalking them all down when he could. His son, Issát, is still alive and possesses the same ability as his father. Maybe he decided to avenge his father's memory or maybe Loring is somehow controlling him. We don't know."

Great. Another family member I would have to possibly put down. Plus, how did the Team know any of this? Did Vincent? I needed to talk to him.

"Why couldn't they reach Vincent?" I would think Vincent would come to me immediately with something this big involving my family no matter how extended the relation. Or he would act quicker and send the Team to deal with it.

Lincoln drove through an empty intersection without stopping at a red light. "Doesn't matter. We need to remain alert. That wasn't the only house hit and there were also reports of a woman pushing over a telephone pole with her bare hands onto a house before it was set on fire. Loring is beyond hiding his need for schooling the Blind on our existence and there are cameras everywhere."

Lincoln's extra-vigilance lecture went on as my head was stuck thinking about Vincent and him being unreachable. I wondered how long it had been and assumed Lincoln knew what was going on and was keeping it to himself.

I did not like that.

We pulled up to a scorched house, not the one from the video, one more recent. All we saw was a charred shell dripping in water as fire trucks still sat there while exhausted Firefighters milled around poking at the ashes and intimidating the crowd with impatient threats of arrest and flimsy crime scene tape.

"Stay here." Lincoln climbed out and headed for the fire truck where others in uniform stood.

"We have contacts everywhere," Gregor casually stated. Apparently, at least one of those contacts was a fire inspector and, regardless of the restrictions, Lincoln had VIP access.

"How often does Vincent check in?" I asked Ismail.

He turned in his seat as if surprised I was resurrecting the topic. "Either he or a trusted contact on his behalf finds a way most days."

"And you don't find it odd that he's MIA? When was the last time anyone heard from him?"

Ismail glanced at the burnt-out house and towards Lincoln maybe hoping he would materialize and shut down the conversation. "A few days."

I got the feeling it had been longer than he was admitting to.

"How can we contact him?" My voice was flat and restrained.

"You can't."

"But Lincoln can, right?"

Ismail turned to me again, but didn't say anything, his way of politely telling me to drop it and an indication of my correct assumption.

I let it go since Ismail's hands were tied in loyalties to his boss. When Lincoln's ass hit the driver's seat again, I asked him the same questions.

"You don't need to contact him."

Not good enough. "He hasn't been heard from in at least a few days. If *you* don't, clearly someone needs to give a shit."

Lincoln started the Denali and began turning the beast of a vehicle around. "We do give a shit. If I was going to answer you, I would've the first time. So, shut it."

"Watch it," Donovan warned, which only pissed me off more, and didn't faze Lincoln.

When I started pressing the issue, jealousy flared from Donovan. Ridiculous, and I ignored it, but wasn't sure if I was angry about it, more so happy I was making him uncomfortable.

Lincoln could whine all he wanted, but I was relentless and added the fact that since Vincent was in the hive of the enemy, checking on him should be a necessity for the Team Vincent put together...on and on and on until Lincoln finally broke and groaned through a promise to do what he could once we were done with the mission.

I still felt like he knew more than he was saying, but I backed off since I got what I wanted.

For now.

According to the fire inspector who was up all night chasing every scene, the bodies found in the home from the video were of a young family, two kids under ten and the wife. The Magic, Stephen Oakley, who was led or turned Puppet and brought outside to watch, was missing and presumably captive, but the Blind were searching for him as a possible arson and murder suspect. Not that the Team could do anything about that. No matter if Stephen survived Loring, he could never return to his old life.

For whatever reason, he didn't seek a safe house or leave town, and Loring found out about his presence at the Creation takedown. Although the video showed nothing but his back, I had no clue who the guy was or what role he played in the field outside the Creation. My time in the field wasn't spent memorizing the faces of others waging war.

Lincoln rushed off to another scene, one older than the last. "Oakley got exactly what he deserved for being stupid enough to think he was untouchable, and now his family, his Blind family, died brutally. Oakley has no one to blame but himself."

The wreckage Loring left behind was a total of eight homes, a mix of houses, apartments, and townhouses all their overcooked bare bones displayed for the world. Some Magics were taken. Others were executed on the spot and died along with their families, pets, and house plants. Someone was always outside to watch the show before Loring and his posse took off with a new Magic on his team or at least a bump to his body count.

We didn't know why Loring or Issát took some Magics and left others. A good guess was that the ones taken had either connections or abilities Loring wanted.

At almost every scene, Lincoln would scope out the area, now void of activity besides smoldering husks of familial ruin, bringing Gregor or Ismail with him to be sure nothing at the scenes pointed to Coven activity.

Going beyond the crime scene tape was easy when done under the protection of a cover spell, so they couldn't remove much when they left. Some ritual items were found, a safe that held a family grimoire, though Loring destroyed everything Magic-related he deemed unimportant.

Sick of being cooped up in the Denali, as Lincoln always appointed himself to do all the work, by the fourth house, I stopped pretending to care and rested my head against the seat with my eyes closed. Not sleeping, but wishing I was anywhere else. I didn't even pay him any attention when Lincoln's and Ismail's doors closed, returning from another drive-by.

"Nothing in this place," Lincoln relayed as he started the Denali. "The owner, Thomas Saterlee, and his son, weren't home when Loring hit the place."

I gasped and popped up in my seat. "Whatthefuck?!"

Searching out the window, I realized we were on my dad's street.

Everyone turned to me in the back. Donovan jumped to open the door.

"Come on!" Donovan coaxed me to follow.

Staring at the open door for a confused second as Lincoln hammered me with questions I didn't hear, I was suddenly boots to asphalt, running across the street, seeing nothing but blackened wood and carnage. Nothing was left to identify the place as being anything remotely like my father's house.

Donovan broke through the strip of yellow tape, getting there before me as I stutter-stepped in breathless horror at my dad's destroyed home, one I hadn't been inside of for far too long. I didn't even know where my dad thought I was. I missed Christmas, Thom's favorite holiday. Did Adam call him?

Wait. Lincoln said they weren't home. Where were they?

"They were supposed to watching him," I said to no one.

The other cars lining the street were empty. Could the guards be invisible? I would have seen their soul glows, no? They would have seen Lincoln, made contact, something. Shit. No one was here.

"I'm so sorry." Donovan touched my arm.

I raced away from his sympathy and stormed back to the Denali where the others stood in front of the open doors.

I got in Lincoln's face. "Where's Vincent?"

"Step down, Sophie," he ordered with deathly calm.

Donovan come up on my side, Caveman on the other, both visible in my peripherals.

"Where is he?" I pushed Lincoln against the side of the Denali, his big body hitting with a thud. I didn't give two shits in a punch bowl about his fucking orders.

Lincoln flexed to come at me. Donovan struck first, hauling off and punching Lincoln in the face. A scramble of people yelled and grabbed my arms as I tried to throw hits of my own, my knuckles throbbing from Donovan's initial assault.

Throwing some extra *oomph* into shoving Bronya off me, I didn't have the satisfaction of laughing at her sprawled on the pavement as I reached for my Beretta and bullseyed the muzzle at Lincoln's pie-hole, the safety off, and my finger on the trigger.

Caveman held out a hand towards me. "Whoa, whoa, sweetheart."

Gregor was also in the way and both he and Lincoln froze and stared at the end of my gun, Gregor taking a slow step away from the line of fire.

"This is my father's and my brother's house. Vincent appointed Magics to guard them. Now, my dad and brother are gone, their place is torched, and they're completely Blind. So, I'll ask you again, you evasive prick, where the fuck is Vincent?"

Lincoln stared at my gun like it may go off any second. "He's imprisoned in the Sovereignty cells."

The others' voices hitched as I fought to process what he said. I didn't notice when I was no longer pointing my gun at his nose.

A flash of Vincent's enraged expression as he pled for us to join him in his rebellion blinded me. His father finally did it. Alasdair locked him away.

Was Vincent caught trying to find Cora-Lynn's soul? Did Chase overrule his father's sanction and order people loyal to him to take Vincent in?

I felt a pulling in my mind that concentrated in my eyes. Donovan was forcibly refocusing me as my inflection had him in a trance.

"What else do you know?" Caveman saddled up nice and close to Lincoln in clear intimidation. A part of me was happy to hear he wasn't among those keeping it from me.

Lincoln looked around. "This isn't the place."

Since it proved to be the only way to get Lincoln's lips flapping, I lifted my gun and stopped below his belt, Caveman backing off a step. "I'm about to shoot off your left nut as punishment for withholding this info from me. Make it the place or say good-bye to your boy's wingman."

Bronya scoffed behind me. "Let's be real, honey—"

I spun and lifted my gun inches from that little turned up nose, and watched as she straightened, holding her ground with a shitty poker face that said the opposite.

"I'd stand by as you shot her, babe, but your dad's neighbours might recognize you. Climb in and Lincoln will tell us everything. Won't you, Lincoln?"

Caveman chuckled but Bronya was unimpressed with the whole thing, especially when Donovan claimed to be dandy with me shooting her.

It was the first thing to make me smile all day.

Climbing back into the Denali, Caveman, Donovan, and I took the first row so we were closer to Lincoln in the front seat.

"Sitting here is drawing too much attention." Lincoln focused out the windshield, though I didn't see anyone. "I'm going to the next place on the list." He turned to me. "If that pleases Miss Gun-Happy?"

"I could use my disintegration powers if you prefer. I figured a gunshot wound was easier to heal." Lincoln stared at me. "Talk while you drive."

Pulling away from the curb, Lincoln was too quiet for my liking. Anxiousness railed through me, propelling me to act with drastic measures, until he finally spoke up.

"Our intel is solid but incomplete."

"Opposing concepts, don't you think?" Donovan's sarcastic response pretty well covered my thoughts and was far nicer.

"A Sovereignty contact heard from a Magic who isn't on our radar, yet privy to information he couldn't keep to himself. He approached our inside guy, knowing it would get to someone in the position to do something."

"And the intel is...?" I was growing increasingly impatient.

"The reporting Magic is stationed in the hallway of the cells' access wing. He doesn't go inside but says prisoners do. Sometime after the meeting with Miklos, Vincent entered this hallway and the door where the cells are *with* Alasdair Llewellyn. They're inside for some time and only Alasdair exited."

"How trustworthy is the Magic who went to our contact?" Caveman questioned.

"Seems like he's on the up and up. In the company for the last dozen or so years, working his way through the ranks of responsibility before being placed on this assignment over two years ago. No Tainted affiliations. He told our guy it was the first time he witnessed admittance to Vincent, and Alasdair made a point in telling him, in front of Vincent, that it was a one-time thing. When Alasdair left, he didn't stop to explain why he was alone, but he was."

"I don't get it," Gregor said from the back, "you're telling me a devout company man in a position of high-security is going to rat out his employer? A Magic that could imprison him within the cells he was hired to secure? What's this guy's motivation?"

Lincoln passed a slow-moving sedan. "Apparently, this is his way of keeping the cells secure. Like everyone, this guy knows Vincent's history with his father's company. Maybe even knows Vincent's only there now trying cases because he's being blackmailed. This Magic, however, knows about the army of supporters Vincent has collected over the centuries and assumes they'll unite to rescue him. Instead of having us bust the barn doors open and implode the whole set-up, he's willing to hand us the key so we can swoop in and walk out with Vincent while inflicting the least amount of collateral damage as possible."

"Sounds like a trap," Caveman decided, "engineered to 'out' the Team with us inside the walls where Alasdair and Chase can stick us in a cell with Vincent. I'm not about to hand myself over to the enemy."

"Why doesn't this guy release Vincent himself? He too stupid to open a door?"

"Think about it, babe." I was doing my best to ignore the fact Donovan was casually using 'babe' again. "He wants this to happen, but can't take the heat, wants his job to be secure in the end, and doesn't want to die in a rescue attempt. He needs us to create a spectacle and stage it like he did his best to guard his post."

"That," Lincoln agreed, "and the fact he's not the key holder of the cells. He guards the exterior access point where the cells are located. He doesn't even know what's on the other side of the door."

"Again, it's a ruse," Caveman enunciated. "You don't guard a door for over two years without knowing what you're guarding down to the last detail. Even if you trust your employer, you don't bank on trusting those you're guarding against. You need to know exit strategies, choke points, everything to ensure when shit goes down that you're prepared."

"Experienced taking exit strategies when shit goes down?" Gregor dug.

"No," Caveman said, drilling Gregor with a stare, "experience in infiltration and the personal protection of others. You won't see me walking into a situation I don't have a clear exit for. If I go down, it won't be because some spineless piss-ant wanted to protect his paycheck." Caveman turned to Lincoln. "I dropped an infiltration mission as a Recondite Magic in the Sorrel Compound when it came time to protect them." He motioned to Donovan and me. "I say we call this asshole's bluff and make him choose a side."

"Our contacts have lives—"

"Then he's not willing to do everything to ensure we free Vincent," Caveman cut Ismail off. "If things go sideways, which we have to be prepared for the inevitability, then he'll shove us in a cell before revealing his role in the ploy. No way I'll let someone's drive to live override my own. Force a choice. He picks it or kill the fucker when we do it our way."

We agreed we couldn't lean on this contact-of-a-contact to provide all the info we needed and would dig deeper before making our move, but this wasn't my current priority.

"There's no way Vincent would have left my family unprotected. He stationed guards on that house. So where are they? And where the hell is my dad and brother for that matter?"

"Here," Jessabelle handed me a cellphone. "It's untraceable. Make some calls." Then talking to Lincoln, she said, "Let's get this over with. Once we're done, we got a lot to do." Good to know someone felt a sense of urgency.

I was all for springing Vincent, hoping he was actually in the cells and not dead and buried or a soul in a fancy pickle jar once we found him, but I needed to find my dad.

Nowadays, no one needs to remember phone numbers because they're usually saved in your contact list. My dad carried a cell phone, but again, the number was something my brain refused to call up with any amount of confidence.

I asked for the number of the Prison Creation. There are only so many places my dad would go and Serena's dad's was the next logical place. It took people a bit to find Serena. She only took my call because I lied to the person who answered and said I was her mom.

She hung up as soon as she relayed her dad's number, still angry.

I called my Uncle Joe. To my semi-surprise, Uncle Joe handed my dad the phone.

Relief flooded me and I almost hung up. As the seconds before Dad came to the phone ticked by, I realized I didn't have an explanation for my absence and should have talked to Adam first to see what information he told Dad, if any at all.

Before my internal conflict resolved itself, a crackling came over the receiver and I heard my dad say, "Hey-low," in an all too familiar cadence.

Donovan was itching to comfort me. I did my best to appear steady enough not to need it and kept clear of eye contact with him. "Hey, Dad."

Pause. "Sophie?"

"Yeah, sorry. I went by your place. Are you guys okay?"

The sound of the receiver being shifted from ear-to-ear brushed as I could imagine he was sitting down, bracing himself, or relieved to hear from me, the pause longer than I liked.

"Last I saw you, you had a new boyfriend, was babysitting your ex's nephew, and then everyone at the mall passed out, though still no one knows why, unless you ask a conspiracy nutjob. No calls to check in, no calls around the holidays, and then you happen to drop by my place hours after it burned to the ground? Too many things don't match up here, kid. What kind of trouble are you in?"

"I...." I what? I couldn't tell him the truth.

"You called me, kid," he said when I didn't answer right away.

"Sorry, I know. I can't explain right now, but I'm okay. Adam's okay, too. I just wanted to check in and see if you guys were at least physically safe."

Silence stretched.

"Dad, if we could've been there during the holidays, we would have."

"Mhmm." Thom took in a deep breath. "We're fine. We were at a movie, came home to it on fire. Max and Scales didn't make it and neither did everything we own, but we're alive and have insurance." Max and Scales were a fifteen-year-old thirty-pound cat and my brother Ben's lizard. A tragedy but it could have been worse.

"Good to hear. Tell Ben I'm sorry about Scales."

"Will do. When can I tell him you'll see him again?"

"Umm...I don't have a precise answer to that."

"Right." Sometimes the disappointment in a parent's voice was worse than if they yelled at you. "If it's this new guy, I will kill him. You know that, right?"

"Dad, it's not...the new guy is...I can't...It's not like that." I felt Donovan's tenseness grow and I stopped myself from saying more.

"Can't explain it...I heard. Y'know Soph, I *can* handle your life better than you think, but you have to let me know what I'm up against or I've got nothing to work with."

For a second, I thought maybe Adam spilled the beans on the Magic issue, but he hadn't. It was simply my dad trying to put aside his disappointment and be supportive. I would have loved to tell him, but at this point, less knowledge was still better, and he would be in the wind now anyway since his place was totalled. The important thing was that they were safe.

"I gotta go, Dad."

"Mhmm."

"I promise that if there's something you can do to help, I'll ask. Right now, it's better this way."

"And I don't get to disagree?"

"Of course you do, I—"

"Does your mother know?"

Dammit! This was the type of shit I worried about most. Telling my mom wasn't easy but I did because Magic was a part of Mom's family bloodline. If it was from my father's side, Dad would have been sitting across from me in the horrible reveal conversation. Last thing I wanted was my father feeling less of a parent because my mother knew more than him.

In this case, deflection was better. "She's as worried as you are.

It's not personal. It's crappy but will hopefully be over soon. I'll call you when I can. Don't worry."

"No promises there, kid. But I do wanna hear from you soon. And tell your brother I'm not happy with him, either. Plus, tell your cousin to drop a line to her old man. Sounds like she's a part of this, too. Not that your mothers would tell us."

"I will." I wondered if they actually called our moms. Both couples were divorced and avoided contact since weekend drop-offs. Clearly, my mom didn't tell my dad anything, and Serena's mom didn't know anything, I didn't think. I should probably ask Serena. It was Aunt Karen's family with the power as well, and yet, I was almost certain Serena kept it a secret from her mom.

Saying good-bye wasn't easy. For all I knew, I wouldn't see my dad again and he would have a mountain of unanswered questions and possibly not even a body to look for answers.

This reminded me that I hadn't called my mother like I promised and hoped Adam had picked up the slack. He was sitting in the Prison Creation on his ass anyway, may as well be useful.

"You okay?"

The question was from Donovan as I passed the phone to Jessabelle. "No. Are we there?" Disappointment and rejection emanated from Donovan, but I kept my eyes forward at Lincoln.

"Yup." He pointed to the burnt-out house down the street. "While Gregor and I check this residence, I need someone to go there." He pointed to a dark red brick house with white shutters across the street. "It's to retrieve the original video from the guy who posted it."

"I'm going in." This stopped Lincoln like I knew it would, but I've been stuck in this car forever and needed to stretch my legs. "Donovan and I will knock on the door, pretend like we're some type of officials, undercover cops, whatever. Confiscate their rig and see who else he sent a copy to other than posting it online. Caveman can watch the back in case they make a run for it, and since they're clearly not a Magic or they wouldn't have posted the video, we can get in his head for what we need and bounce."

Not a bad plan. Plus, since Donovan enjoyed the fact I included him, he was on spot to plead the case, which is the only reason I included him at all. Lincoln didn't trust my judgement, but he trusted Donovan's. Having Caveman as back up, and them close-by if needed, Lincoln didn't have any justification to decline.

When we were walking up the sidewalk, Caveman spit into the grass. "Thanks for the inclusion. You don't need my help, but my ass was getting numb."

"No, prob. Why the fuck would they take the whole Team in the first place when Lincoln was going to do the job solo? Bullshit waste of our time."

"No kidding," Donovan agreed, "and thanks for bringing me, too, even though I know you didn't want to."

"Shut it, play your part, and don't make me regret it."

Even though I was rude, it didn't matter. The blip of excitement from him wasn't squelched one bit and Caveman gave a low chuckle as the two walked behind me. Ignoring them, I went up the three steps to the door and rang the doorbell.

"Whistle if you need me." Caveman quick-stepped and disappeared around to the back of the house.

"Who are we pretending to be?" Donovan asked as we waited.

Before I could answer, the door opened revealing a young guy, maybe eighteen or nineteen years old, hair flopping in his face needing the chop months ago, sporting not much muscle. Judging by his lacking soul glow, there was no power to make up for his reedy physique.

"Hi there." I did my damndest to appear grim and official. It wasn't as hard as it should have been. "I'm Detective Smalling. This is my partner, Detective Cockburn." Yup, that's what I said. "May we please come in and speak with you regarding a sensitive matter?"

The guy's forehead creased. "Why?"

"We have reason to believe that you possess a video of somewhat important content needing further discussion."

The guy peered over our shoulders, I assumed at the burned house across the street. "Ah...it's my parents' house, so you'd need their permission. They aren't here."

"Are you eighteen or older?" Donovan asked.

"No, I'm seventeen."

A blatant lie. We could read that without peeking into his brain.

"Your government-registered identification states otherwise. Are you refusing us access?" We weren't going anywhere, but if this guy didn't budge, I was going to introduce him to the wall behind him.

"No. Well, yes. I...Can I see your badges?"

Donovan took that one. "As undercover operatives we don't carry standard issued badges. We can go inside and contact our Lieutenant if you require confirmation."

The guy wasn't buying it. We could read from his mind that he was about to go on a tirade about his rights as a Canadian citizen blah, blah, blah.

As far as I was concerned, he had his chance. Over-playing the part of a government official sunk us into the quicksand of government legislation.

Breaking character, I pulled my knife, dug it an inch below his chin and into his Adam's apple as I held him by his too long locks, putting pressure on the blade while I pushed my way inside. He fought to breathe and not move his head.

"Jesus Christ...." Donovan closed the door behind us as I kept my eyes glued on the ones in front of me wide with fear.

I holstered my knife. "Thanks for your cooperation, sport."

He replaced my hands with his own, checking for blood. "Yo, psycho. You can't do that!"

I grabbed him by the shirt collar and dragged him into the living room to the right of the entrance and threw him onto a green couch straight from the nineties.

"Hey!"

"Shut it!" I yelled and pointed my gun at him.

When Caveman entered when hearing the commotion, the guy's eyes widened more, but he shut up.

"You've got interrogation duty," I said to Hall, using the guy's obvious fear of the six-foot-seven Viking to our advantage.

"Excellent." Caveman added a creeping grin purely for showmanship.

As we left Caveman to it, we searched the house hearing Caveman shout a commanding "Sit up straight!" like a drill sergeant with enjoyment for making the little fucker squirm.

The place was a basic three-bedroom family home, large living room, bedroom, and one bathroom to the right down one hall, one converted into an office, the other a home gym/hobby room unused for some time, collecting dust. The largest room was definitely a marital bedroom which meant the guy's space was somewhere else. Presumably the basement.

Going back to the living room we saw the guy pressed into the couch as Caveman was leaning over him, grilling him about who he shared the video with. Donovan and I strolled on past into the kitchen. Good size with eat-in dining. Through there we found a small mudroom that fit a washer and dryer, the door to the backyard, and another door that went to a basement.

Of course. Techy-nerd living in his parents' basement probably jacking it to porn all day or PVPing with his internet buds instead of using his computer skills for something more interesting and bring in a lot more moolah than any fool's gold he could collect online.

The place was a shithole. I wasn't saving the world at nineteen. Wasn't doing much of importance either, but I wasn't sucking off of my parents and wasting their dime on monthly online subscriptions and Doritos. Not to mention PC upgrades.

I didn't know a lot about computers but this one was clearly custom. A see-through tower gave us visual access to the internal components, which I guessed were supposed to be chubby-inducing to tech nerds. Pulling out the wires, Donovan didn't seem to know much either, but he knew enough to remove the hard drive so we could take it with us.

We headed upstairs where Caveman was still drilling the nerd who looked moments from pants-wetting freedom.

"We got his hard drive, it all we need?" I asked Caveman.

"I don't know," he eyed the guy. "Joel? Does your hard drive consist of the original?"

"Y-yes." He nodded emphatically.

"And you didn't copy it or send it to anyone else?"

He shook his head without looking away from Caveman.

"We're good." Caveman straightened and smiled at us, clearly enjoying his role.

We left without another word from Joel, but his mind was screaming about how we took his hard drive and cursing us for all the data he would lose.

Coming out of the house and walking to the Denali, we found Lincoln loading in a few important items from the house across the street that we didn't want the Blind finding. Since we hadn't used any magic while in Joel's parents' house, we were safe from that.

For all the guy knew, we were dickhead government agents, throwing our weight around and fucking him out of a hard drive. It was doubtful most people, including his parents, would even believe him and his complaints would end up buried in a subReddit somewhere.

30

INFORMATION CONTROL

Sophie

Next stop was a contact's place. This time we were all permitted to leave the vehicle. In a crappy apartment building not much different than mine, we found Jordan. His apartment was much swankier on the inside than you could have guessed from the exterior. Unlike Joel, Jordan was a techy-nerd with useable skills, beautifully white teeth, and good looks that weren't typical, but the kind that grew on you the more he talked. Plus, he wasn't an immortal, but he was strong, his soul bright and colourless.

Seeing that smile made liking him even easier as he was giddy at the thought of getting his hands on the hard drive. We handed it over and I took a seat near him as everyone found a spot to squat while we waited.

After plugging it into another rig, one of at least a dozen extras strewn around the place like a tech outlet with metal shelving units full of wires, components, towers, and monitors, Jordan tapped away on the keyboard that lit up with green LED letters disappearing under his swift fingers.

"What a weasel." Jordan shook his dirty-blond head as he typed. "Thought he caught something worth taking to the bank but was too stupid to hit the news stations and went for social media instead. Amateur."

I couldn't help but laugh.

Jordan glanced at me in his peripherals, his eyes hitting me for only a second, but his fingers didn't stop. "Want a drink?"

When Donovan's irritation fluttered, I knew my answer. "Whatcha got?"

That smile of his flashed again, his hazel eyes glittery from the monitor's light, and he paused his progress, boxes of info on his screen rolling through commands frozen, all looking completely cryptic to me. Opening a drawer in his desk between us, usually meant for files, revealed a built-in cooler stocked with drink and snack options.

"Fancy-schmancy."

"I know, right? Allows me hours of uninterrupted work and the chance to impress beautiful ladies now and then."

"Count me impressed." I opened the Coke he handed me as he cracked his own and we clinked them in cheers.

"Can you get this done?" Donovan barked at Jordan.

Jordan swivelled his office chair to face Donovan, the can still to his lips with his eyebrows raised. Unaffected, Jordan turned back to me. "Friend of yours?" Guess he picked up on Donovan's territorial chest-beating as easily as the rest of the room.

"Not particularly," I answered with a conniving lilt to my head as I stared at Donovan who was positively fuming.

"Might wanna tell him that," Jordan mumbled and gave me a wink that made me laugh at Donovan's expense.

"The hard drive?" Lincoln prompted, his voice on edge.

"I'll be done soon. I'm running a program to alert me in case the vid pops up somewhere else, plus a program to remove it. Seems like you've got more than Loring and these fires to worry about."

"Meaning what?" Caveman leaned against the wall.

"Gualichu has shown up at dozens of accident scenes and

random hot spots, some accidently recorded, and I've pulled some strings to fudge footage or have it expunged all together. Meaning, I haven't heard anything in regards to stopping him."

"Loring is—"

"Top priority, as he should be since Gualichu is a passive danger and not actively seeking targets...that we can tell. Don't forget, we have more enemies than Loring and less room to hide and devise plans against them."

"You'd rather hide than fight, I take it." Donovan meant this as a blatant insult.

"I'd rather be beatin' blood through my veins and do what I do for the cause the way I do it, which is not on the frontlines. I'm leaving the city very soon. I can do what I do from any country in the world. And while there are pockets of strife in other places as well, there's a concentration of activity here most will be lucky to avoid."

"Well, not everyone can handle it." Now that Donovan watched the flirtatious banter between Jordan and me, he was pissy.

I tapped my fingers against the can. "Judging by the strength of your soul, you could handle yourself just fine."

"Ah, so true, lovely. We all have our strengths. Mine's using my brain and my uncanny ability to access any and all information needed."

"Like the video."

"Like the video." Jordan smiled. "Plus, news sites, government institutions, databases on all sides, you name it. Control the flow of information. I have other strengths as or more dangerous than yours, but in the end, information control can prove more effective than a gun or exchange of power."

Stewing but staying quiet, Donovan didn't offer another retort. I could tell he was holding back but he was angry enough to make my heart pound and my knuckles ache from him clenching his fists. His anger issues didn't have to be mine, but it didn't mean I could escape them.

"Doesn't mean you have to goad him either," Caveman's rumble

of a voice invaded my head. *"Donovan's in love with you. If it were me, Mr. Smiley would be beaten senseless with his keyboard by now. Give the guy a break."*

I huffed and flipped up my mental barriers.

Since Jordan had everything under control, we left with a promise he would keep an eye out for sightings of our enemies and contact Lincoln with anything useful.

Jordan stopped me with his hand raised between us. "Jordan Chapman."

"Sophie Saterlee." I returned the handshake. While standing up he was a few inches taller than me and leaned in a little. At first, I thought he was going to kiss my cheek and I almost leaned away. Pissing off Donovan was fun, and Jordan was easy to flirt with, but having him so close put me on edge.

"Drink for the road?" he offered with a casual smile.

I accepted. He fished out another can of Coke from his desk cooler and I thanked him before leaving. It's not like I was going to date the guy, but it was nice that someone was remotely interested, someone clueless about my Soul Magic with Donovan and couldn't be scared off by the prospect. Of course, he would probably act differently if he did know but it didn't matter. Some harmless flirtation was exactly what I needed.

Back in the Denali, Ranlyn called Lincoln and changed our plan to return to the Creation. Instead, we were diverted to visit as many Magics' dwellings, safe houses, and hangouts, warn them about the severe danger they were facing, and see who was going to stay and fight and who was leaving town like Jordan was.

Caveman groaned and slumped in his seat between Donovan and me. "I hate politics."

"This isn't politics," Ismail argued. "This is about gathering numbers and warning those who think this'll blow over that it's about to get a lot worse, and they could be in direct danger."

"No," Caveman said, sitting up in challenge to Ismail, "this is about us showing face on any and all Magics' doorsteps and cataloguing who's on what side of the Mother Coven and challenging any of them unwilling to fight. Which will also put us in danger since we're supposed to be in hiding."

"Guess we can count Jordan off the list," Donovan mumbled.

"Him and most others. We've fought numerous times now, always promising things will improve, and instead they're worse. How exactly do you see these meet and greets going?" Before anyone could answer, Caveman replied to himself. "Expect slammed doors in our faces. If Ranlyn wanted Magics to feel safer or try to convince them our Coven is the right faction to side with, then he should have showed up himself. Another waste of time."

Unfortunately, Caveman was right. Having a Tactical Team show up at their doors or in their hiding places didn't make anyone feel better. Even with Lincoln doing his best to sound otherwise, everyone saw it as a propaganda circuit. Others who aligned with Miklos's side of things—who apparently didn't get the memo that Miklos was trying to reconcile—went on a rant about who was right and how we destroyed their sanctuary by reopening the Creation.

When I reminded them that Loring and Evaristus had broken into Diluculo far before we destroyed the Creation, it turned into another blame game, getting us nowhere, and only made me want to kill the ungrateful bastards who didn't recognize that ending Evaristus was far better than keeping the Creation intact.

Few people were happy to see us. Very few. And after more than a dozen stops, I was officially disillusioned with what we were fighting so hard to save. Our own people didn't give a shit about our past sacrifices or the ones we would soon make, so why risk our asses so turd-pilot Magics like them could sit back and judge why and how it was done?

Fuck that noise.

After hitting a place that flat-out never wanted to see us again and threw threats around like stale bread for the birds, we left and stopped in an empty church parking lot to take a breather. We noticed no place we went to consisted of Miklos or the others with him, so clearly we hadn't seen everyone, but we were hit hard with the reality of our enemies being on all sides and needed a time out.

Donovan's pre-paid rang and he answered cautiously as if he didn't know the number. I could only listen to half the conversation, and then less than half when he walked away from where we were stretching our legs.

Caveman leaned in. "It's a friend of Fox's."

"How do you know?"

"His mental barriers weaken with worry." He paused, listening for more. "The friend is concerned about Fox. Whatever they thought would help isn't and Fox's health is failing. The friend thinks Donovan should say goodbye."

"What's wrong with him?"

Caveman caught me up on Fox's failing health due to his role in the last fight. As angry as I was with Donovan, Fox was a good man. He may have wasted his time trying to save Donovan from himself, but he was a good Magic and an exceptional tattoo artist. It may have been the despair I felt rolling off of Donovan, but I suddenly felt sorry for him even though I didn't want to. His gaze flipped to mine. I realized he could sense my concern, so I did my best to lock down my sympathy.

He ended the call and returned to the Denali without saying anything, hiding the fact his pseudo-father was dying.

"Can you contact Rosemary?" The second Donovan returned, Lincoln was on him with the question. The look Donovan shot back was an apt enough answer. "We need to know what she knows and what she's heard," Lincoln justified. "Her contacts are much different than ours and can reveal more information than this round of visits can."

"Told you it was a waste of time," Caveman chimed in.

"Especially since we should be breaking out Vincent," I added.

"Just call her," Lincoln ordered adding a "please" as an afterthought.

Again, Donovan paced away from the group as he dialled his mother.

"She's happy to hear from him. Really happy." Caveman didn't lower his narration.

"I don't need to know." I really didn't.

Without acknowledging my complaint, he went on. "She knows about Loring going after Coven members and their families." He paused, listening. "Her flock isn't on Loring's radar since technically they're Tainted yet she's willing to put her life on the line to help us. By the sounds of it, she only stays with her flock because they're useful."

"No loyalty for the Tainted."

He chuckled. "Not likely."

I felt a stirring mix of emotions as Donovan spoke to Rosemary. A reserved happiness that shifted as presumably the topic changed. Maybe he was talking about Loring or was talking about how she was worried about him.

"Both, actually." Caveman heard my thoughts. I cursed my flabby barriers. "But he wasn't talking about Fox, he was talking about you. Telling her the physical connection returned, but that you still hate him."

Guess that explained it.

"Rosemary loves him and is worried, and even though she has her reservations about you, they're only because you're actively hurting her son. Gotta hand it to that woman. She may be Tainted, but she is willing to risk death by the hands of her flock to keep him safe."

Something in Rosemary kept her dedicated to Donovan, though it took her twenty-four years to reveal who she was and to give a shit about what happened to him. Donovan himself probably didn't want to admit that he cared about his mother, though he clearly did.

I reminded myself *I* didn't care, tuned out the conversation, grabbed the Coke from Jordan in the Denali, and cracked it open in remembrance of that smile.

"I don't trust her," Bronya said after Donovan explained his mother promised to pass on any info about Loring.

"She's not around for you to trust or distrust, so I don't give a shit what you think," Donovan snapped back. Bronya steeled herself against obvious wilting.

Overreaction or not, I enjoyed the trainwreck.

"Can it!" Lincoln scolded the both of them. "Do you trust Rosemary to be honest when it counts?"

Donovan's hesitation clearly didn't settle Lincoln's reluctant acceptance, but again, due to the connection, I had the inside track on the bastard's emotional compass and knew it wasn't a lack of trust that made him pause. He was pissed. Probably at Lincoln for asking him in the first place.

The guy can look at everyone with his charming dimples and bad-boy "I don't give a fuck about anything unless I'm killing it or fucking it" attitude, but I knew the real Donovan. Most of the time I'm dealing with the anger he hides and drinks away. Anger like this that makes him forgo talking or he would start throwing punches.

"Incoming!"

At first, I thought Gregor was right next to me until I realized his rigid tone was inside my skull. Not just mine, everyone snapped to attention and surveyed their surroundings for threats.

A dark-haired man emerged from behind the church. Even before his buddy, a longer-haired man with silver threaded through it, came around the other side of the church, the first guy's laser stare drilling its way through the night was unmistakable.

His soul glow told me what type of fuckery this put us in. "He's a Transmutator. Don't give him the chance to change forms."

Before the Transmutator and Silver Streak got to us, more of their friends sauntered up, but we still outnumbered the enemy. True to his nature, Donovan put himself in front, targeting their wild card whose form began to warble as if he would *shift* any second, moments before Donovan cracked him in the jaw, effectively halting the *shifting* process.

A jolt of pain shot through my knuckles, but Donovan was too preoccupied with the exhilaration of beating someone's face in to notice.

In that one punch, Donovan knocked the guy out and was in search of another target. Gregor went for Silver Streak as Lincoln and Bronya took on their own targets. Flashes of power struck across the parking lot as the enemy felt no reluctance fighting with the Blind in close proximity. All anyone had to do was open their windows, hope for good cell camera resolution in the dark, and we would be right back into fake undercover ops mode.

I twisted as a hit of magic flew my way. The skin of my palms left behind on the asphalt as my chin bounced off of the blacktop. I rolled, ready to dodge another hit. Caveman dealt with the asshole, saving me from a blast of fire that went haywire and hammered into the Denali's side panel.

"Motherfucker..." Caveman popped up to his feet and went after the Magic who nearly got us, a woman with the sneer of a jackal, gun holsters hugging her thighs.

I noticed that while I was down, our upper hand in numbers evaporated and we were now facing a handful more enemies.

Caveman's efforts to save me put Donovan's down as well. Two Tainted Magics were on him as he tried to keep his power usage low. Grabbing hold of the closest corpse and using them as a shield, Donovan avoided some hits but needed to drag his ass up off of the ground.

A boot to the jaw kept Donovan down and sent me back on the asphalt. My neck screamed. Shaking it off wasn't happening quickly enough and through spotty vision I saw one of them grab Donovan to drag him to "Who-the-Fuck-Knew-Ville" while the other one helped his comrade go after Caveman since his friend wasn't fairing as well against the brute.

"You okay?" Jessabelle's frenzied voice hovered over me but she was pulled into the fight before I could answer.

Didn't matter. I wasn't paying attention to anything but Donovan's struggle. With the connection restored, it was safe to say that if he died, then it was definitely over for me. And if he was kidnapped and tortured, I was along for the ride, too. So much for him wanting the best for me. He was more danger than safety.

The parking lot still strobed in and out, probably the reason why Donovan wasn't defending himself. Instead of screwing around, I unholstered my Beretta. Even though my shot was wild, I nicked the Magic trying to drag Donovan off. It probably only hit the elbow of his jacket, but it was enough for him to drop what he was doing.

The shot reverberated off the buildings around us. If people weren't looking through their windows yet, now they were rubber-necking it through dreary lids. And if not from that, the second shot that hit the guy in the chest definitely did it.

Another of their comrades going down and staying down whipped up a frenzy. Hits came harder, the enemy bringing their own hardware to bolster their natural strengths, guns popping off, fists hitting body parts filled the dark church's parking lot with grunts and *thwacks*.

Looking like a professor didn't match the violence he used when Ismail slit a Tainted Magic's throat open, threw him to the ground, and moved onto his next target.

Police sirens rose above our fighting. The enemy scattered, deciding dealing with the Blind was beyond the scope of their mission. Caveman threw a large knife from his belt and skewered a slow-moving Magic in the back of his balding skull with a champion throw.

"Get in!" Lincoln high-tailed it to the Denali as Caveman retrieved his blade.

We piled into the SUV and Lincoln peeled out, driving over a body or two as sirens grew closer.

We could kill every cop that showed up without much effort, though it didn't mean we should. Those civil servants were unprepared for what they were rolling up on, probably betting on a drug deal gone bad depending on what the caller reported. We couldn't exactly bind and memory alter every cop and Caine wasn't around to lend his persuasion gift.

We took corners that made my stomach filled with only Coke splash acid into the back of my throat and fizzle in my nose. Swallowing wasn't easy but at least, since it was late, we didn't have much traffic to dodge.

"This is what I get for trusting Tainted motherfuckers!" Lincoln took a sharp corner that pressed us into each other like a carnival ride. We all sported easily-healed superficial injuries. "You said your mother was trustworthy!"

Donovan gripped Lincoln's headrest and pulled himself forward. "Why the fuck would Rosemary send them?"

Taking another tight corner and hopping a curb, Lincoln manoeuvred around cement tree planters on the sidewalk. "Common-*fucking*-sense says she sent them!" A police cruiser was on our tail. Lincoln shouted above the sirens and rev of the engine.

Donovan's anger roared with his adrenaline-fuelled blood pressure. "Coulda' been Loring's people or some turncoats from all the pissed off Magics we visited."

Gregor chimed in from the back. "Loring would've been there, and I didn't recognize any of those pieces of shit."

"Rosemary wouldn't send people after her son." No one could make me believe that.

Donovan fished out his phone from his pocket and dialled. "Did you send your flock after us?" He screamed over the sirens and squealing tires as Lincoln pushed it up a hill.

I couldn't hear the other end of the conversation but knew how Rosemary answered. Donovan kept yelling about what happened. The cop's sirens blared as we weaved through the city. Ismail hollered directions to lose the heat, but we were still followed closely.

With all the noise and me getting sicker by the second as the Denali jerked around corners and swerved around cars and pedestrians, I couldn't think, and we were getting nowhere. Last thing we needed was a news-worthy high-speed chase. I didn't know if the

Niagara Region employed helicopters for such a reason, but it didn't matter. This needed this to end.

I lowered my window and pulled my body halfway into the breeze. Caveman grabbed hold of my belt. I thought he was trying to pull me in, but he anchored me as I trained my gun on the cruiser behind us, seeing there was now more than one.

I shot at the cruiser's tires hoping that even if I missed it would be enough for the cops to drop back. A couple squeezes of the trigger and the cops decelerated, their squealing brakes throwing smoke. The Denali jerked around, Lincoln yelling something as he fought to straighten the path.

Another pull on my belt—this time it was coupled with a wrench on my arm—and someone yanked me inside like a rabid dog at the end of my leash.

Bronya's complaints registered in my wind-rocked ears and were easily ignored.

Donovan was the one who dragged me in, having reached across Caveman. "Are you fucking insane?"

"Do that again and I'll kick you the fuck out of the car!" Lincoln swerved and ran through a four-way stop.

"Fuck you, Lincoln. See?" I smacked Donovan hands away from me. "The cops backed off, giving us room to get away."

"You could've killed them!" Donovan screamed over Caveman who leaned back in his seat. "Or some kid in their bed."

"I'm not that bad a shot."

"Doesn't matter. It's called ricochet for a reason."

Caveman pushed Donovan away from leaning over him and muttered, "Fucking children."

I ignored him. "Find someplace to hide this beast. We're better off on foot."

"Because you have experience fleeing from the cops?" Lincoln sneered.

"No, because I'm not a moron and we only have a couple minutes before they find their balls again. Can't you hide us and the vehicle under a cover spell or something?"

"Sit the fuck back, sweetheart."

Even pissed with his mom apparently still on the phone and screaming in his ear, Donovan smacked Lincoln in the back of the head hard enough for my fingers to sting. With no hands to spare and concentrating on not running us into a phone pole, Lincoln shook his head, mumbling something I didn't catch.

Whatever he thought of my tactics, Lincoln listened and sped into an empty driveway, cut the engine, and began spouting off a spell. After tense moments of silence, we listened to distant sirens as the cops continued the search.

"We can't hike to the parking garage from here." Jessabelle rubbed her hand through her short hair with a stitch of annoyance.

Technically we could, but it meant a good forty-minute jaunt or more and we weren't exactly inconspicuous in our gear.

Lincoln turned in his seat and raised a pointed finger at Donovan. "Touch me again and you and me are gonna have real problems."

"That so?"

"The only reason I don't drag you out and beat you like a temperamental child is because I'd be beating your psycho of a girlfriend, too."

"Suck it, Lincoln." He didn't give a flying fuck about my wellbeing.

"Not only wasn't it my mother who sent those guys after us, it was Sophie who got us away." Lincoln tried to interrupt Donovan, who spoke over him. "Yes, she was reckless and six circles of stupid, but they backed off. So, keep your goddamned comments to yourself or next time you'll get more than a slap to your thick skull."

"Can we get the fuck outta here?" Caveman's patience found its end.

"You three have fun," Lincoln said, motioning to me, Donovan, and Caveman. "I've had enough of all of you today. The rest of the

Team, come with me. You're from this city. You guys can find your way to the Prison Creation on your own."

The others filed out of the Denali and headed down the sidewalk, disappearing mid-step under a cover spell. Whatever their plan, it didn't include us.

Caveman threw up his hands. "How the fuck did I get stuck with you two? You realize standing up for either of you lands me in shit, right? I should let you find your own way back."

I snorted. "Like I couldn't?" If Vincent were here, he would have taken care of shit a lot better than Lincoln and we wouldn't be in this situation.

"Even if he was, Vincent could do fuck-all and you know it." Donovan had plucked the words from my head.

"He wouldn't have let Lincoln waltz off like a little baby."

"Enough!" Caveman's shout held nothing back and rang in my ears with power-driven command. "I can't listen to your childish bickering anymore. Both of you, control yourselves before this emotional clusterfuck you're stuck in has you murdering each other in the middle of the street."

I didn't know if it was a connection thing or not but I had enough of talking to Donovan anyway. "Look, as far as we know, Vincent has been in the Sovereignty cells for days while we dick around playing missionaries to the Word of Ranlyn, and again we sit here and do nothing."

Caveman shifted in his seat. "I hear you, but the three of us can't infiltrate the Sovereignty alone. We need the others. Divided like this is a direct result of Lincoln being on his last leg with the both of you."

I tried to get my point across. Donovan talked over me.

"No! No, I don't care how you justify it. You're both at fault." Caveman pointed at me. "You insisted on antagonising Donovan by flirting with that techno-weenie, then get high and mighty when you're called out for it." Then he looked to Donovan. "And I know you love her, but you're letting her fuck with your head like you're a teenage boy with his first crush. Hitting Lincoln for his snide remarks is juvenile and doesn't earn you points with anyone. Sophie can stand up for herself, especially when she's dumb enough to put herself in the position to have to."

"I can flirt with whomever I damn well please."

"See? Both of you are too busy screwing with each other to know you're making everyone's lives hell. Focus on the job or focus on each other, but we have multiple wars going on. Yes, Vincent is captive, Loring is burning our people, not to mention we have an Architect-riding demon on the loose. Both of you need to stop being selfish brats and move outta my way, cuz I need to get the fuck outta this car before I decapitate you both extra slowly for messing with my day."

Both Donovan and I opted to follow since we were mid-getaway anyway, but the point was crystal.

"Now," Caveman said, straightening his pants by tugging at his belt, "who wants to choose a car to boost?"

31

COMFORTING EXISTENCE

Sophie

We ditched the stolen green Dodge Neon Caveman hotwired and were steps from the Creation elevator when Donovan's pre-paid rang.

Caveman didn't narrate this time. We waited out the call in the parking garage, confident the police gave up on finding us.

Donovan hung up. "As I told the taint-jockey, one of the jackasses we paraded around to on our political tour flipped on us."

"Rosemary?" Caveman made a good guess at who called.

Donovan nodded. "Baxter Hesselark sent word about us hitting Magics' houses, so they followed us to each one waiting until we were done before attacking."

Oh, shit. "So, everyone we visited is on some watch list?"

Donovan tilted his head as if to say 'probably'.

"Great. We can thank Ranlyn for that."

When we stepped off of the elevator into the lobby, the rest of the Tactical Team was standing with Ranlyn and Veata. Glares flashed in our direction said it all, though I assumed they would have more to complain about.

The looks didn't stop me for calling our "I know what's best" leader out. "Don't look at us like that. This guy's a douche." I thumbed at Lincoln. "And you may as well have beheaded most of the Coveners yourself."

"Excuse me?" Ranlyn challenged.

Once Donovan described the conversation with his mother, Ranlyn's features stilled as his eyes unfocused. Clearly, he didn't anticipate this outcome.

"All spewed out of the filthy, lying mouth of a known enemy."

A rush of fury screamed inside of me as it barrelled through Donovan. The feeling of power over my skin begged to be released.

Lincoln found this amusing and his lips cracked into a provoking grin, hitching the sense of power around us up a notch.

"Piss on trees on your own time." Veata gave a slow blink, tired of their bickering. "Donovan, your mother is beautiful, talented, utterly evil, and unapologetically proud of it. Lincoln, you're worse than a crotchety old man who makes me glad all my husbands are long dead. Anne-Claire would be embarrassed by you." Her mention of Lincoln's dead girlfriend had him poised to lay into Veata, but she wasn't interested in hearing it. "Again, old man, stop talking."

I made a throaty noise, stopping myself from full-on laughter.

Veata's clouded eyes shifted to me. "Don't get me started on you, girl. You're a loose bag of nuts pilfered by half the neighbourhood squirrels."

"Point Veata?" Ranlyn wrangled her rant.

Veata *tsked* her co-Elder and shook her head. "No appreciation for the truth. Point being, just because the lot of you are spared unTainted souls, don't mean you are any more trustworthy than Rose-mary." She wagged a finger at Lincoln. "Every kill is in revenge for a woman who indulged in more ding-dongs than a hostess at a sausage shack." Her finger swung my way. "You're in the running for 'Psy-chopath of the century'." Next was Donovan. "You have the fury of a hurricane and the pinnacle of familial dysfunctions, not to mention the future you've spawned." Donovan steeled but said nothing. "And you," she side-eyed Caveman next to her and paused, "I like you." Caveman smiled. "Besides insisting on trying to knock boots with the redhead, you are perfectly level-minded, providing equal opportunity for all Magics to demonstrate their worthlessness and assume, unless proven, that you're better off trusting a rabid fox in a henhouse." Caveman dipped his head giving credence to her fair assessment.

She went on. "And like the Viking here, who has burned and pillaged more towns and townswomen then a horde of locusts in a corn crop, Rosemary has proven to me that when concerning her son, we would be best to trust her. A shift in that woman happened the moment she revealed her parentage to this boy birthed by evil, and somehow, seeing how he denounced that past has made her stronger."

Something like pride swirled in my chest, Donovan hiding it well from reaching his expression.

Veata thumped her cane on the ground like a commanding king. "Now, warn the good people you put in peril. Chances are this Baxter Hesselark who sent danger to their doorstep is long gone, so be useful for a spell and get on with it."

When it came to Veata, half of the time you could forget the woman was even there, unless she was snoring, but no one could ignore her ability to say it straight.

When the Elders left, we all stood in awe until Kim walked up.

She narrowed her eyes at us. "What happened?"

Caveman laughed and wrapped a muscled arm around Kim's shoulders. "They've all been Veata'd." He continued laughing as Kim stood confused, though I noted she didn't remove his arm.

Lincoln had enough and stormed off.

"To steal an honesty page from the Veata handbook, why haven't you two knocked boots yet?" I motioned between Caveman and Kim.

Kim's mouth dropped open as Caveman laughed harder. "I happen to enjoy the boots I'm already knocking, thank you very much."

"Don't worry, kitten." Hall wrapped his other arm around her. "I'll take my boots off first. Unless you want them to stay on, of course."

"Can it, Viking." Kim pushed at him, Caveman not moving an inch until he unwrapped himself from her, smiling the whole time.

Straightening her shirt, Kim huffed and crossed her arms. "Like you can talk. Now that the connection is active, how long until you two are hitting the sheets again?"

"As I recall, we barely ever made it to the sheets." Donovan spoke in our defense I never asked for. He caught my expression. "What? I'm not wrong."

I rolled my eyes and didn't comment.

Flashes of naked, sweat-slicked skin blinded me, forcing a gasp. A shudder raced up my spine. A chilled wall pressed at my back as I was held up off the floor by the hips. Suddenly the glow of the television strobed against our bodies while we were on the couch wrapped around each other. The edge of the kitchen island then dug into my ass.

"Whoa!"

The images were pulled away at Caveman's complaints as quickly as they hit me, leaving my heart racing and body tingly. I swallowed hard and fought to compose myself.

"Got an eyeful of parts of you I'd rather never see again." Caveman pressed his fingers into his eyelids. "And I won't comment on your dance partner." Kim backhanded his arm. "What? I said I wouldn't."

Donovan shrugged. "Didn't see any sheets, did you?"

Caveman sucked his teeth. "Not a stitch."

"Shut your face." A more creative insult was lost between gritted teeth, betraying my calm and inner struggle to resist Donovan's lust and amusement with himself.

He was grinning like a fool with a pair of dimples that caved and mirrored another set from those visions. I blinked against the sight of him and those dimples as a shudder hit me again.

"You okay?" I heard Kim's question but had my eyes closed and rubbing at my eyelids.

"More than okay." A deep chuckle came from Caveman. "Not thinking about Mr. Smiley anymore, are you?"

"Who's Mr. Smiley?" Kim asked.

Sweat hit the back of my neck, my breathing coming quicker instead of calming. My head swam and sparked nausea.

I needed to sit down.

"Sophie?" A delicate touch on my elbow was Donovan.

With the visions still swimming inside my brain, I couldn't handle the contact.

A flash of the Sorrel cells hit me. I shrugged Donovan away as a punch to my gag reflex had me taking off. I couldn't take another word from any of them.

The hitchhiking emotions from Donovan's visions and the buried ones they incited wouldn't fuck off quick enough.

Too much was scrambled inside my head. Memories on top of memories, ones I trusted, others I...I didn't know what to think of. Each wrapped with conflicting feelings and shit I didn't want to examine closely and didn't need the new mixtape of amateur porn rattling around in my brain.

I collided with others during my fight or flight escape, unable to follow a singular path as I grasped straws at finding solid ground.

Fuck that pompous jockstrap! Perfect example of his arrogant audacity. Suuurrree, go ahead, blind me with visions of us having sex. That'll make me want you again when sex was the reason I hated you in the first place. Stupid asshole.

Shaking off the desire to be wanted and the drive to be with Donovan, the love that filtered through the memories of lustier times had me wanting to projectile vomit Exorcist-style.

Stumbling to find somewhere without people all over me, I realized too late I was headed in the opposite direction of the cells. No fucking way I was passing by Donovan again to get to them.

Slamming into an office and shutting the door behind me

silenced the outside barrage, using a lock spell helped the inner noise, but wasn't enough to end it.

"Firefly?"

I gasped, spun towards the voice, and felt a choking power surge until I saw Olive in a high-backed office chair behind a desk.

A groan escaped. I tried to leave and couldn't open the door or focus enough to reverse my lock spell.

"Fucking Christ." I closed my eyes, still facing the door. Nothing could be easy. Not even being alone.

The hand on my elbow was tentative, but it may as well have been Donovan's. I flinched and turned, trying to step away, but hitting the door.

"Firefly, it's okay."

"Right. You don't even know what's wrong."

"I don't need to. Here...." Olive took a step away from me. "Come sit."

I didn't want to sit. Everything in me was screaming to move.

Olive sat in a shorter chair in front of the desk and patted the seat of the one next to it.

With an immoveable door in my way, I didn't have a viable alternative. I could break the thing down but didn't have the energy to fight Olive.

I sat and cleared my throat, feeling like I swallowed too much dry bread, and let go of a breath I was trying to hold in. Frenetic energy was fighting to pour out of me. Sitting was not helping.

"Beneath so much anger is such sadness, Firefly. Let it all go. You can't keep on like this."

"It's...." I couldn't verbalize what was boiling inside of me. That ball of thickness in my throat cut me off.

Olive held my hands. Not the light touch that made me want to flee, but a tight grip that somehow grounded me. "It's too much, whatever it is. To be free of this, you must let it out."

"I can't." I inhaled with sucking pain in my chest. "I can't...He's all over me." I rolled my shaking shoulders, shook my head, gripped

Olive's hands as tightly as I could, but nothing helped. Another quick breath was shallow and cutting, tears I never felt soaked my cheeks. "Nothing I do helps."

Olive leaned in closer. "You don't have to do anything. Feel as you need to."

"The connection—"

"Is a part of you. Not all of you. You haven't been able to be yourself in some time. Not your fault and not fair. Allow yourself freedom in this moment."

Falling apart was an agony I couldn't fight.

Olive let go of my hands so I could bury my face in them. She squeezed my shaking knee I couldn't keep still as all the tension and anger spilled from me.

This, this is why I didn't want to deal with myself. Most days, if I won the battle, I didn't feel anything. Other days, I felt everything and couldn't take it.

Donovan and his bright ideas forced everything through the pus-filled wound refusing to heal. Now, I was too overwhelmed to cauterize it shut and bury deep all the shit getting in the way of basic daily functioning. I can't do this. I can't keep this up.

Guilt flooded me until the skin between my shoulder blades crawled. Not my own. Donovan was somewhere feeling like a bag of shit and bawling along with me.

Conflicted, and too immersed within myself, I wasn't sure how I felt about his guilt. It had to be real or I would sense the lie, right? Whatever the case, I didn't want him in the background of my soul, taking up space and spinning my sadness into such grief. His guilt was too much when I couldn't shoulder my own.

Another squeeze on my knee reminded me Olive was on standby with comforting existence, remaining silent without trying to talk me through it or calm me down. If I had to have anyone around for this, I was grateful it was her.

I wiped some tears and sniffed back what I could. Olive handed me a few tissues from somewhere.

Sobs dissolved into shuddering breaths as I tore the worn tissue in my hands. An errant thought of not remembering the last time I wore makeup popped up. I was too busy doing something else, anything else. Checking a mirror was not a priority, nor did I give a fuck about what others thought of my face.

I managed a deeper breath and then a few deeper. The knot in my throat dissolved.

Donovan's apologetic fear replaced his guilt; he worried he screwed things up more. I was more comfortable with his guilt. The rest caused me too much sympathy for the guy, sympathy I didn't think the bastard deserved but that felt genuine when considering the sincerity behind his regret.

"I really hate this." Finally, I managed a few words, yet unable to look up at Olive yet. "I know I've been rotten lately."

"A lot has happened."

"Yeah, but it doesn't give me the right to be a royal dick." I gave a small laugh as I wrapped the unsoiled edges of the tissue around my fingers.

"Maybe not a royal dick, though Serena may think you earned the crown."

A bigger, snottier laugh. "I bet she would."

Quiet settled for a moment. "Is this crying a sign of good things to come?"

I chewed my lip, trying not to think of where the tears came from. "I don't want to feel the way I do."

"Well," Olive leaned forward with her elbows on her knees, "anyone looking at all you've been through would say it's compli-cated. At its base, this is much simpler."

I looked up at her in full, confused and defensive.

"Strong emotions are driven by pain and trauma. Regardless of the details or whose shoulders the fault lands on, you hurt. You're in pain. No number of guns or amount of yelling or hating everyone around you and lashing out at them will erase the resulting anger. It's a process running from only worsens."

Right. Olive knew a thing or two about processing trauma. She lost everything, even her mind, before pulling things together after her institutionalization.

"I had heard from Kim, somewhat, but do these tears and a willingness to listen have something to do with the connection between you and Donovan being fixed?"

I shook my head. "Not because of it, though it doesn't help."

"Are you sure whatever happened when he reconnected it didn't change something in you?"

"Why do you say it like that?"

Olive's lips pulled in a small smile. "Because your colour's better."

I thought about that. Clearly Olive meant my soul colour and not my complexion which was probably blotchy red with the makings of a Rudolph nose and red-tipped ears.

"I know you see what he did as a betrayal, but that boy cares about—"

"He wants me the way I was," I stopped her. "I don't feel the way I did, and I don't like being forced into it, which is what people are doing every chance they get."

Olive grabbed my restless hands. "And they will continue trying until they know it works."

My shoulders slumped further.

Olive laughed. "That's what happens when people care about you, Firefly."

"No, that's what happens when people feel jilted. They want to put Miss Humpy Dumpty back together with hot glue and positive thinking. And when that didn't work, they held me down and wrapped me in duct tape, then pretended it was for my own good."

Olive raised a finger, taking time to think about the next words out of her mouth. "I've never been one half of a Soul Magic pairing, but finding happiness and then having your world come down on you by the actions of someone else, being forced to live through something you dread with every piece of your being...*that* I understand."

I felt like a schmuck.

"You're not a schmuck."

Ugh. My stupid mental barriers.

"Your soul colour *has* changed, that I can see plain as day. Without seeing this damage to your Soul Magic, I can't tell if that's fully healed, but something has changed in you, and I think you would be doing yourself a service to allow Donovan to try again."

"What?"

Olive licked her lips and leaned in farther. "When I was told I was leaving The Royal I was sad because after years of being forced into that place, I had become accustomed to it. Being in the world was what I needed, even if at the time I wanted to revolt against leaving so that it didn't become another aspect of my life I had no say in. But I would have been wrong. Never can I erase my years in The Royal, just like you cannot change your time in the Sorrel cells or go back in time and discover why you loved Donovan *so* much that you'd go as far as to create the Soul Magic in the first place."

"It doesn't mean I have to put up with his bullshit now, nor anyone else's."

"True. And it doesn't mean they have to put up with your bullshit either."

Olive's smile coupled with her sugary use of "bullshit" made it impossible not to laugh, but I couldn't fully agree with her.

"Either way, we love you and want you safe, so in the meantime, while you're unravelling the questions of your universe, as family and friends we will support you, but expect brutal honesty when you need a kick in the arse to keep you in line."

I smiled. "Yeah, yeah."

"And Donovan, whether you want him to or not, will keep trying. That boy is no quitter. You are in control of your emotions. You feel his but yours are all your own. Stop fighting what's there and be honest about what is. That means with Donovan as well." I tried not to roll my eyes. "You think he's being a jerk, tell him. Too pushy? Make it known. That's simple communication." She waved a finger at me. "But do not tell me that your anger is the reason for your bad manners, especially with the Soul Magic damage mostly fixed. I've met your mother. I know you weren't raised to be disrespectful and you're too old to be using it as an excuse."

"I love you too, Olive." The hint of sarcasm lessened the sentimentality, but I understood what Olive meant.

Olive leaned in and kissed my cheek. "I love you, Firefly."

Seeing her crinkly eyes, I did feel guilty for being so absent from her and the other Ballard's lives since I was myself again without Nya piggy-backing my body. I wasn't about to tell them all I loved them, but I cared if they were alive or not and should have acted like that instead of ignoring them because focusing beyond my pain was impossible.

Olive's eyes narrowed on me. "You haven't called your mother."

Damn. For the next ten minutes Olive laid down the law about keeping promises since I hadn't talked to my mother yet, but stated that Adam and Serena kept Mom informed and made excuses for me the whole way through. Olive didn't forget to mention that I didn't deserve to have them cover for me, yet they did anyway.

Mom was still cooling her heels at Elizabeth's, doing everything she could to help, but Elizabeth was fervent about keeping Mom from participating in anything protection wise in case this released latent powers. This did, however, mean that Elizabeth was using hers. In what manner wasn't clear but I bet the next time I saw my grandmother I would see a very different soul.

I stood feeling more centered than I had in a long time. No telling how long it would last, but I breathed easy, and my head wasn't pounding anymore, even with all the crying.

We tried to leave, but the door wouldn't budge. I forgot I spell locked it. With a little concentration, I envisioned the door unlocking and a click told me it worked. I opened it wide for Olive.

"You know—" Olive put her arm around mine, "—most Magics have to recite a spell to accomplish that."

I shrugged, making Olive laugh, and I followed suit.

Kim, Caveman, and Donovan stood in the hallway looking at us.

Caveman surprised me by not addressing the obvious reason for Donovan's red eyes, but saying the Elders called for everyone to meet. Others streamed in the direction of the lobby behind them.

"I will round the troops." Olive reached up to hug me. I returned the squeeze hoping the unmentioned "thank you" was alive in my arms.

Disappearing in the opposite direction, Olive went to rally the Ballards. Chances were most were already in the lobby, but the aunts were slow-moving.

Making way for the lobby with the crowd, the hallway became congested, and we slowed.

Kim's attention on my left was noticeable without turning.

I sent a telepathic *"Sorry"* in place of eye contact.

Kim couldn't respond in the same way, but I could keep my mind open and filter through Kim's enough to hear when she came back with a surprised, *"Thanks. I can only guess at what happened in there with Olive, but I thought Donovan was headed for a breakdown."*

Through Kim's thoughts, I saw Donovan as he endured the crying jag along with me, unable to untangle himself from my strong emotions and stood in the middle of the crowded lobby a blubbering mess as Hall led him to the side of the room.

"Are you okay?" Kim thought.

"Probably not. As good as I can be, I guess."

Ranlyn and Veata stood before the coven in the lobby, reminding me Vincent should be up there and why he wasn't.

Keeping Vincent's capture a secret wasn't happening. The meeting was Ranlyn making sure everything was on the table to be viewed and scrutinized by the collective. Smart, but it wouldn't make everyone happy.

No one was surprised at hearing the destruction Loring caused but they were assured the Tactical Team and outside contacts were doing everything they could to keep their existence in the Prison Creation a secret. I thought of Jordan and wondered if he was already out of town. Like so many others, the Magics of the Niagara Region were fleeing to safer ground.

Standing amongst the crowd, I zoned out having already lived through everything Ranlyn was set to cover. Donovan stood in front of me next to Caveman to my right, enough I could see his profile. Telling my pride to take five, I reached for him with my mind hoping Donovan's was open. It wasn't. Not that I should have expected any different. After a minute of trying to breach his defenses, I gave up and tried something more direct.

I pinched my forearm. Hard.

Donovan grunted and looked down at his arm.

Reaching out again, I found that his mental barriers were still up, but I was able to scratch along the surface enough to announce my presence. He wasn't concentrating on Ranlyn anymore and able to answer.

"A little childish, don't you think?"

"You're just pissy I made you cry in front of Caveman."

He dipped his head to the side, peeking at me side-eyed before refocusing up front. *"Whatever. I was a dick, you left, and I bawled in front of an audience. I deserved it."*

His tone was guarded, not understanding that I was doing my best to keep things light. Not that I could blame him. It had been a while since I treated him as anything less than a pariah.

"I'm sorry," I finally managed.

In utter surprise, Donovan turned to me and stared, waiting for my expression to shoot him the punchline. When it didn't, he asked, *"What's changed?"*

I pressed my lips together, nodding my head enough to motion towards Ranlyn. *"Focus up front."*

He inhaled and turned to our Elder.

Now that I had started talking, I didn't know why I bothered because I had no clue what to say.

"Sophie?"

Dammit! Where was a portal to be sucked into when I needed it? Disappearing right about now would have been a dream.

A sharp pain in my arm had me cursing, Donovan giving me a taste of my own medicine in attention-grabbing.

"Bastard." Instead of our usual bout of name calling, Donovan returned a dimpled smile and raised brow. *"Fine. Keep looking forward. I'll talk."*

An eye roll of his dark eyes said he would comply with my terms as he faced front and crossed his arms again, waiting patiently, his nervousness wading within our connection.

Taking a few breaths before I began, I pushed passed my worry, unsure if it emanated from me or him. *"Okay, first of all, I realize I've been a cunt."* Donovan actually laughed, gaining Caveman's attention since Ranlyn wasn't trying out his one-man comedy show up front. It was a harsh word, yet one I earned. *"I've been a nasty, antagonistic, cunt and no one deserved this...not even you. Not most of the time, anyway."*

He stayed quiet.

"Regardless of my cunt-ish ways, I'm not happy about how you went about fixing the connection. I'm still not even happy there is one. I don't understand why we made the Soul Magic in the first place. Clearly, we were delusional or high, but we definitely didn't think about the consequences. Half of the time we've been fighting, I'd say I meant what I said. The other half I maybe wanted to say them but shouldn't've. Definitely not in the way I did. It doesn't take a Seer to know I'm miserable, but I'm this way for a reason and you can't make me be any way I'm not."

"That's not what I want."

"We beat the shit out of each other before you dragged me to that storage place."

"You were beating, I was defending myself. If I wanted to hurt you, I could've knocked you out. And for the record, it was Vincent's idea to bring you to the Amsterdam storeroom. I was following orders." I could hear the smile in his voice at the comment.

With that said it grew quiet. His anxiousness rose, unsure if I had finished and not wanting that to be the case.

I went on. *"What happened at the Sorrel Compound...I know it wasn't your fault. I know what Tobias did, and I know that because of it I fucked up our Soul Magic and turned this into a war. I just don't know what else to do. Like I told Olive, I'm not ready to be who I was before it happened and would appreciate it if you stopped forcing me to try."*

He was quiet for a good minute as this was absorbed. *"I'm not the same either, you know."* His inner voice was low and sombre. *"After the first time...."* He seemed to be at loss for words. *"Living with my sanity after the first Conception Rituals was basic survival and a loss of innocence at an age when I was too young to comprehend the full implications of what Tobias was trying to do. This time, not only did I lose the upper hand against that tyrant, but he got me on my back and fucked me in ways I wish I could get a grip on. Concentrating on you has helped me focus on something other than obsessing about my own traumatic shit. A delusional escape, I guess, but still an escape I needed.*

"Losing you on top of all of that has been unbearable. I may have been wrong to go at it the way I did but apologizing would be a lie. I was prepared to do worse for a long time until things were whole again, or something close to it. I don't expect perfection. Fuck, being with me at all is a step in the wrong direction. Believe me when I say I love you as you are. Even as a pain in the ass, you're everything to me. Thinking I was losing you was the most helpless I've ever felt."

A little numb, I stayed quiet as he talked, riding the storm of emotions each part of his speech delved him into. Nervousness, anger, regret, helplessness, and somehow acceptance, he felt it all. I was jealous for his articulation. If only I understood myself as well as he did himself.

"Please say we can work on it." Donovan's voice came out a plea. *"Say you don't completely hate me and being with me isn't the worst*

decision you've ever made. The only promise I can offer is that I won't ever give up on us."

Words can do a whole lot of things to a person. They can hurt, demoralize, confuse, encourage, empower, inspire, and sometimes they can steal the ones you thought you wanted to say, dragging them away like a corpse and disposing them with the other meaningless garble our brains kick up.

Donovan's words, spoken without his outer voice, without even facing me, completely decimated my resolve to keep him at arms' length. This time it wasn't his emotions impeding on my own, his were busy feeling equally hollow and desperate as he braced for an answer that may alter our relationship. He gave me the choice with a vulnerability I refused to endure. The strength it took to say all he said was more than I possessed. Hell, I couldn't even handle this conversation face-to-face.

A part of me wanted things to be as they were, but as he said, he wasn't the same either. The part I focused on was him saying he would never give up on us. Not just me, but us as a couple. In my past, I was used to doing most of the work to keep a relationship alive. With Caine, we didn't have a chance, but before him, fights like this meant we only remained together because I compromised a part of myself. Saying we could work on it together implied a joint operation. For me, even if people didn't grasp the reason, this made the difference.

I finally said, *"I don't hate you."*

Relief rolled through him. Donovan's chin dropped to his chest. Keeping his head down, he opened glinting eyes that shifted over his shoulder at me. They said so much, showing me that the time I spent torturing him wore him down. Waking up in the Prison Creation after Nya was killed wasn't that long ago but not a second passed that I didn't punish him for everything that went wrong. Be it the poison from the broken Soul Magic or just a plain ol' trauma response, he took it all.

Being the first time in a long time that I actually looked at him, searched his tired eyes or glanced at his unruly hair in need of a cut, I realized he was harbouring enough hope for the both of us and feeling like an utter failure. Now, this inkling of reciprocation left him in a cloud of surrealism.

When someone walked in between us, I realized Ranlyn had dismissed the meeting. When another body passed, I took an all-important step across a precipice that before seemed so wide an ocean could stretch its legs. He spun in time to catch me in an embrace. We pressed into each other like a hug couldn't display the right sentiment but was everything we needed.

"I've missed you," Donovan whispered as he held me.

I couldn't say it back because I hadn't missed him. I'd loathed him the whole time, so I settled for something more accurate. "I'm here now." It wasn't enough and didn't inspire love or even longing, but it was where I was.

A gasp and squeal from behind us was unmistakably Kim. That sound impossible to ignore. Donovan's chest rumbled against me as he had full view of Kim's joyous celebration behind me, but he wasn't about to let me go until I pulled away first.

He looked down at me still in his arms, and for a second, I thought he was going to kiss me. A flash of "Oh, shit!" went through me, but he didn't make the move, probably feeling my freak-out meter on the edge. I wasn't entirely sure where it came from, but he wasn't smiling any less, so I inhaled and turned to face my bestie.

Another high-pitched squeal. "Soph!" Kim replaced Donovan's arms with her own.

"Okay, okay," I said lightly and wiggled free.

"I'm so happy for you guys."

"I know, Kim. What happened to the days of you convincing me he was an asshole I should stay far, far away from? Those days had less squealing."

Kim answered with a greater squeal and bear-hugged me again, and this time I let it happen. I may have even laughed a little.

Caveman passed a few silent words over to Donovan but neither shared. I really didn't want to know and didn't ask. Since the lobby hadn't emptied too much, too many were in the way, essentially hiding us from view of the masses. Not that anyone could tell, but I dreaded attracting any attention to this development. Judging by the flutter of Donovan's heart, his thoughts were everywhere including looking into future possibilities of screwing the pooch.

For all I knew, I was wrong for going back to square one and had no clue where to go from here. I didn't feel like I used to before he hit me with whatever magic that was in the cell, but I did feel different.

"Wow," a voice said from behind.

We turned to see Caine standing with Ness, Felix, Derek, Jet, and Andy. Caine's eyes were resting on Donovan's hand comfortably on the small of my back, though he dropped it so we could turn.

"Paradise in check?" Caine asked with a genuine smile.

Donovan and I glanced at each other, then I looked at Caine. "Working on it."

No sense of insult filtered through from Donovan for me saying it like that, ready to jump up and down like a gleeful cheerleader but keeping himself in check.

"Seriously, glad to hear it."

"Thanks." I drove my hands into my pockets. Caine and I were friends, but he was still my ex and Ness's emotionless glare wasn't helping any.

Knowing it was needed, I fixed my attention on Andy. "Hey, kid. Sorry about before."

Andy shrugged.

"No, really. I messed up and owe you an apology. I'm not sure if your mom has told you, but sometimes adults are idiots."

This had Andy smiling.

"Hey, now," Jet pulled Andy in close. "We adults are super smart and perfect in every way."

"As if, Mom." He pushed her off with a playful shove. "I figured that out for myself."

"Oh really?" Jet's tone rose in jest, Andy laughing.

"Your mom's different. Smartest adult I know." I bobbed my eyebrows Jet's way, and she smirked. "If you listen closely, you might learn how she does it sooner than most kids your age. Imagine how smart you'd be."

Andy crossed his arms and angled his head at me, wearing a suspicious glare.

"No jokes, kiddo. Pinky promise." I crooked my finger at him. He gasped and grabbed my pinky with his.

Caine laughed. "I actually came over to see what was happening about getting Vincent out. Ranlyn was vague. Figured you guys might know more."

Jet patted Andy's shoulder. "And with that, let's see if there's something with chocolate in it in the cafeteria."

Andy gasped. "Cookies?"

"Or ice cream." Jet hurried him along. I assumed she was trying to keep the strategic planning around him to a minimum. Or maybe she didn't want to hear much about it herself. I wouldn't be surprised if she had her fill of this war.

I was ecstatic for something other than Donovan's and my relationship to concentrate on. "The Team will push for something now that Ranlyn has knowledge of what's going on. Regardless, I'm getting him back, so meet me in the boardroom. I'm going to find Ranlyn so we can brainstorm a plan."

Dread hit my gut when I went to leave. Donovan's dread. He wore a familiar expression, the same as Caine's the first day I met him in person at the hospital instead of in my dreams. He thought I would leave, and he would never see me again. I don't know what I looked like in these moments through their eyes, but whatever it was, it didn't inspire confidence in the men in my life.

"See you in there." Smiling was too much—he would see through it—so my words would have to do.

I needed to catch up with Ranlyn. As I left, Kim's squeal faded behind me, Donovan's complaints half-hearted as she celebrated more than anyone.

32

UNKNOWN CHAOS

Sophie

We sat around the big boardroom table, Donovan next to me, and not because it was the only seat left. The fact I was so close and not on the edge of wanting to attack him was odd. When I woke up, I wanted to physically rip out his guts. Hours ago, I didn't want him dead, but I didn't want him happy, and now, well, I wasn't exactly sure how "together" we were. What was a couple called when they were working on things? After the initial hug, I wasn't up for further physical contact, it still causing a part of me to recoil. He waited all the time I was with Caine. If he truly meant he was all-in, he could wait a little longer.

Ranlyn's voice broke through my reflection, his question one I didn't hear but should have. I refocused on the crisis at hand.

Everyone agreed breaking out Vincent was crucial. A Mother Coven Elder in the hands of their sworn enemy—even if it was family—left the rest of the Coven in a weakened state both strategically and politically. If reuniting the Mother Coven and re-establishing relationships where opening the Creation broke them, having a united

Elder Counsel was a critical step towards progress. Something Ranlyn and Veata both agreed on.

The method in which to do so was a bone of contention.

Do we go in guns blazing? Or utilize the Tactical Team and few others to infiltrate the Sovereignty in a smaller operation, slipping in and out before Alasdair and Chase knew they were one less prisoner?

According to intel, we have at least a few inside contacts, as normal, and now another who was selfishly driven to see Vincent far away from the Sovereignty cells before all hell broke loose and he was forced to defend his post with his life. Something he apparently had no faith in doing.

Our biggest concern was a small group walking in and never walking out. What if the contact's story was a ploy to trap us?

Caine, Ness, Felix, and Derek wanted to be a part of the operation, but Ness made it clear if we allowed Felix to tag along, she would tie him to a chair. Unfortunately for Felix, everyone else agreed. Ness and Felix never met Vincent. Why they wanted anything to do with it I assumed was all Caine. When Donovan contacted Caine inside the Creation, Ness and Derek were always close. Caine created his own band of comrades while inside and we could use their skills.

"I'm not letting my brother go, either." I looked to the kid. "No doubt you're talented, but the fact that I'm going is nearly laughable. The only reason they give me a gun is because Vincent made them."

"It's true," Lincoln's deadpan confirmed.

"Fuck you very much, Lincoln," I shot back with an impish grin. He responded by flipping me off.

Kim giggled. "As if you even need a gun. Don't worry, kid. You don't have to go to every party. I'm not."

"What? Yes you are." I glared at Lincoln, who shrugged. He didn't know anything about it.

"No, she's not," Hall argued.

"Not your decision, Caveman."

We debated this, but I lost since Kim wasn't fighting for inclusion, something that relaxed Hall for some reason. I was too wrapped with my own drama for girl-talk on the situation with Kim and Hall. Whatever fueled Hall's drive for Kim, he wasn't letting it go anytime soon.

To my utter irritation, nothing was happening immediately. Direct contact with our Sovereignty insider was essential before anything happened and a delay was expected as well as time to confirm their details and gather those willing to infiltrate the facilities. From what I gathered, getting inside wasn't as straightforward as we could have hoped for, and it may be detrimental to inform the Magic who offered to sneak us inside when exactly we were going, ensuring he couldn't set up a strike force against us. We needed his schedule and to confirm he shows up for work that day.

"Whatever!" Kim squealed, brimming with excitement. "We've survived the past year and rescued our fair share of Coveners. Plus, you two like each other again, which means we're on an upswing. May as well double and triple-check we've figured everything out. None of us are living on luck right now and Vincent wouldn't want anyone charging in and dying alongside him."

"We could at least get it together quicker. Y'know...before his father kills him."

Kim scowled at me. "Nice one, Negative Neil."

Hall leaned back, his chair complaining. "You don't know what it's like in there, kitten. Prepare, yes. Hesitate for the sake of hesitating? Not smart."

"I'm sure it's a worse hell than what we went through in Diluculo," Felix jumped in, more comfortable with the group than his sister who hadn't said a word.

"If the stories and what I've learned from Vincent are a third true, absolutely." I didn't envision Vincent in swim trunks sipping fruity drinks on a beach somewhere. Not unless the drinks were poisoned, the water was acid, and the sun could actually cook him alive. Ugh. I didn't like thinking of him in there at all.

"Okay," Donovan leaned forward in his chair. "Ranlyn, let us know when we have the missing info to make next steps a reality. And since the mission's delayed and this may be my only shot, I'm visiting Fox. Pretending the guy isn't on death's door won't keep him from dying."

Ranlyn straightened his posture as he stood in front of the group. "Donovan, we could be hours from going after Vincent in—"

"Be honest and say days. No way we're going in a matter of hours. And I might die trying to free Vincent, or Fox will die in the meantime. This wasn't a petition for permission, it was respectfully informing you." He turned to me. "Are you going with me?"

I didn't know what my face was doing, but he looked at me like I asked him to braid my leg hair, shock zinging the connection as to why I wouldn't immediately volunteer to go with him.

I understood Fox was important to him, but our window of opportunity to infiltrate the Sovereignty might happen while we were with Fox, and Vincent was more important to me. Fox was an amazing man, but he was sick. Vincent was being tortured—nothing could convince me otherwise as no one assumed anything less. Their situations were football fields away.

"Whatever." Donovan shot to his feet still without an answer from me. "Tell your guards to let me the fuck out of here or you won't like my exit strategy."

"I'll go with him," Hall volunteered. "Keep in contact. We'll be ready."

Ranlyn didn't answer either of them, though as far as Donovan was concerned it was a done deal with or without Hall. I knew that look. He was focused and unrelenting.

Five minutes later, Donovan and Hall were at the elevators and Liam, the elevator guard, lips moved in a spell. His pointed finger morphed into an ornate key he then stuck into a keyhole to bring up the car, an upgrade since Hall drugged the guard for us to check on the Ballard Family Estate. Once inside the elevator, Donovan knew I was standing in view. I felt his anger and rejection swimming around me while he fought the impulse to yell or drag me along with him.

The bubble of our reunion popped so loud my eardrums rang.

Once he was gone, I was pissed. He knew how important Vincent was to me. He didn't even give me the chance to talk about it without an audience. Again, in perfect Donovan style, it was his way or no way. No discussion, no compromise. Fuck you. See you on the flip side.

Kim huffed. "He'll get over it."

"*Pfft*. Fuck him."

Marching back to the boardroom where everyone still stood talking over the mission to retrieve Vincent, I couldn't sit, far too amped and restless as the voices of everyone talking around me didn't filter through my brain.

A knock on the door stopped all deliberation. Ranlyn told whomever it was to come in and Liam the prison guard entered.

"Excuse me. We just received word stating Loring has hit Clifton Hill."

"Hit Clifton Hill, how?"

"According to the news—"

"The news?" Ranlyn's voice rose, and Liam's already impeccable posture straightened, blue eyes steady and procedural.

"Yes, sir. The news stated that what they believed was a gang doing street magic for tourists was responsible. Once they gained a sizable crowd, the tourists all assuming it was a shtick, they attacked onlookers and cars there to see Niagara Falls and the Festival of Lights."

Everyone was on their feet.

"How many of Loring's flock are we dealing with here?"

"Unconfirmed, sir." Liam's regret for his lacking information was clear in his guarded expression.

Regardless of those missing details, we needed to be prepared for more than the small group that attacked us in the church parking lot.

I saw the Festival of Lights every year as a kid, and then continued with Ben once he was born. The bumper-to-bumper drive or cool walk through a small section along the Falls exhibited light displays with trees and winter scenes that had been up since its inception, kid and tourist-centered. Moreover, the festival was a place where Loring was guaranteed to find carloads of families and couples playing kissy-face looking at falling water and holiday twinkle lights. And Clifton Hill promised Loring more unsuspecting targets playing games and walking the cold street under an array of neon signs. Easy pickings and enough cannon fodder for a grand splash. Especially if the media was already there.

As we speed-walked down the hall to the lobby, Lincoln and Ranlyn strategized ways to remove the media from the equation. Cell phone blockers wouldn't be enough—though I was impressed they possessed the technology. We needed something more.

"What about Ethan Phillips?" A few others knew who Gregor was talking about. I wasn't one of them.

Ranlyn nodded and Gregor agreed to call while on the road.

Getting to Niagara Falls wasn't normally difficult but once we piled into a bunch of cars—all stolen from the parking garage to accommodate the Magics we could—we realized Loring's ploy created a traffic jam of people fleeing the city. We rode the shoulders, praying no one stepped out of their vehicles. Cops should also be locked in traffic or too busy to chase us down.

I held onto a handle in a red Bronco as Ranlyn drove like a maniac with Veata in the middle of the front bench seat and Lincoln in the passenger's seat. When we hit a curve in the road, Ismail's and Gregor's full weight pancaked me into the door.

"Hey! No seatbelts back here, speed racer!" Bronya yelled from the trunk as she and Jessabelle untangled themselves.

"Suck it up, princess," Veata called from the front bench seat. She didn't look to be having much fun either and Lincoln was doing his best to stay off of her lap.

Getting to the scene by the Niagara River Parkway in a car was impossible due to all the people escaping the area, abandoning their boxed-in cars in the middle of the road that ran parallel to the Niagara Falls.

We swarmed out of our vehicles and proceeded on foot.

Lincoln and Gregor lagged behind on their phones calling loyal Magics to act, including Miklos and his people. If the ex-Elder wanted true peace, he would show up with his team, represent the Mother Coven on Clifton Hill, and engage while the rest of us focused on the bottom of the hill on Dufferin Islands that hosted the Festival of Lights where Loring should be. Or at least where I hoped he would be.

Not only was Ranlyn sending Miklos into unknown chaos, but he also made him responsible for removing any exposure threat by disabling all camera crews, ensuring that Miklos will try his damndest to keep his flock's faces from the media.

Ranlyn worked off a theory that Loring would head to Dufferin Islands among the light displays. Once there, Loring could act like the twinkling lights were lit up for him alone, as they would spotlight a stage where he would perform one of his greatest performances.

Running through packs of panicked families towards the Dufferin Islands took time and endless frustration. More frustrating was beating the crowd, reaching our destination, and finding no sign of Loring. Many dead, half-dead, and others bloodied up and screaming next to the bodies of their dead/half-dead loved ones, but no Loring.

Backtracking took even more time. We ran into others from the Mother Coven from the Prison Creation as well as Magics from Kim's and the Ballard Sects.

"What's happening?" Caine yelled over the crowd as he, Ness, Felix, and others from the Sect kept up with me and the Team.

Jared was doing his best, but winded. Blake prodding him to keep running.

"Trying to track down the fucker," I yelled back.

I wasn't happy to see Adam and Serena but reminded myself they had experienced battle and survived.

Everything went dark. All the lights were cut. Cries rang out over the chaos of voices and car horns. Since the entire area was a constant source of buzzing florescent lights and electric energy, the sudden drop into environmental silence and blackness was disorienting.

"Our insider at the hydro company came through. This gives us an advantage and lessens the chances of attacks being recorded." Ranlyn's laboured voice directed the warning right into our heads.

Ethan Phillips must have been a hydro guy. It would be harder for the media to see in no-light conditions with any amount of undeniable accuracy, so camera phones were shit outta luck. Plus, this gave added bonus of making it easier for the Blind to hide. Negative side effect? None of us could see in the dark.

Moving as fast as we could against the fleeing Blind while Ranlyn was on his phone with someone, I followed since he seemed to know where we were headed.

We didn't have to go far before light leeched from between the trunks of the trees not far from Dufferin Islands itself where a three-hole golf course sat on the grounds of an old Tudor style mansion named Oak Hall. Soul glows lit up the semi-darkness far greater than the small, floating light spell casting a cool illumination on their faces. The others wouldn't see them well, but they saw enough to creep up to the treeline and halt, waiting for everyone else to prepare for a splash of an attack.

While a tingle of healing restored my lungs and stamina, a hint of intuition itched as I saw the soul glows in the distance. Something about this was all wrong. Not all of the people standing there showcased soul glows. Magics and the Blind were among the Tainted?

What was happening? Were they captives?

Taking a few more steps beyond the safety of our location, Ranlyn grabbed my shoulder. "Don't make me bind you, Sophie. There're too many of them to waltz in."

"You can't see what I can. Hang back a sec." A couple more steps closer gave me a better line of sight.

I watched a man with greying hair at his temples walk with deadly calm towards Loring and who I assumed was Evaristus's son, Issát. My ancestor was average in most ways, slimmer than his entitled father with the same thick, dark hair worn short and same narrow nose and olive complexion, though his face was a bit longer with only a short beard darkening his chin. His almond-shaped, shadow-rimmed eyes narrowed as he crossed the manicured lawn, his soul glow bright and unTainted. The silver of immortality and brightness of his soul glow upstaged his natural colour, yet a hint of sage green waded below the surface.

When the man neared them, he knelt at Issát's feet as my ancestor reached with long fingers and touched the man's shoulder. The man's head fell back, in pain or bliss, I couldn't tell. Light poured from his chest and settled over his whole body, grew brighter, and then plunged into darkness.

"Oh shit, doggy!" I scream-whispered and bit down on my lip.

"What'd you see?" Ranlyn was at my side, squinting into the darkness.

"My doucher ancestor released some Blind guy's magic and then Tainted him all with one touch." Surveying the gathered crowd of Magics with darkened souls, the implications hit me. "Loring doesn't want to kill them. He's having Issát create an army of Tainted souls."

33

MATTER OF TIME

Donovan

The drive to Beamsville to see Fox wasn't long, but I was restless to see him. The visit Fox paid me before he left was supposed to be some type of goodbye, so I wasn't sitting at his bedside, but I didn't give a shit. I wanted to be there.

Nothing on the radio was worth listening to. They droned on about gang activity on Clifton Hill. Probably moron teenagers who thought they were hardcore, showing how dense some in the next generation were.

I flicked off the radio, preferring to sit in silence. I should have drove. It would have given me something to focus on instead of wishing Hall would quit with the sight-seeing pace so I could see Fox while he was still breathing.

Hall shifted the boosted '99 Honda Civic into fifth gear and passed a bunch of cars in no rush to go anywhere. We got lucky with the winter tires.

"From full-on enemies to embracing like long-lost lovers in the midst of a crowd one minute, and then back to storming off in silence the next. I don't know how Vincent's dealt with you two all these years."

The guy must have had his internal dialogue set to thoughts of Sophie and me. As if he didn't have his own drama to focus on.

"Really, man?"

"What? I don't get you two. Something in those racy images you sent her did the trick. Not sure how, but it did."

"Nah. They made things a million times worse. Hence the epic, snot-filled breakdown. Nothing I ever say makes a difference. Whatever Olive said or did was the linchpin. When she came out of that office, she was halfway herself again." Sophie had every reason to hate the world. I had to remind myself that a push too hard in the wrong direction and we were back to insults and public domestics. Leaving things as I did couldn't have helped. I still couldn't believe she wasn't next to me instead of Hall.

Pulling up to Virgil's place was depressing yet ended the conversation with Hall. The Chestnut Court Townhouses weren't what I expected from a powerful Druid, but then again, Fox didn't live in a mansion or buy flashy things except for his motorcycles. The yellowed, brick townhouses were in rows of three, each weathered to a pukey pallor, Virgil's on the end.

I pounded on the door before Hall caught up. Heart racing, I pressed the heel of my hand into my chest to relieve some of the anxious discomfort as I waited for someone to answer the door, realizing that it wasn't *my* heart that had been adrenalized, it was Sophie's.

The door cracked open an inch with a screech, the light above flashing on and destroying my night vision. "Virgil?"

"Who's asking?"

"A guy with seared retinas, jerk-off. Open up." I added another fist to the door for good measure.

Virgil backed off and let us in.

I would have taken my boots off, but looking at the grimy floors, I opted to leave them on. Piles of random shit lined the hallway leaving little room to walk. A kitchen to our right had a sink and counters full of dishes, a stairway on our left led up into more darkness with dirty and worn carpeted steps.

Following Virgil deeper into the townhouse, we didn't walk as far as the living room, heading towards a set of stairs to the basement. I heard the snap of Hall's gun holster release. We were on the same wavelength as I enacted my power a hair below notice.

At the bottom, the basement was a whole other environment than upstairs, full of stuff up to our ears but relatively clean. Past a set of laundry machines it got even better, revealing an area more fit for living. The carpeted space was orderly, the furniture for comfort with a large leather lounger and matching deep couch facing a TV big enough to make me drool.

Behind the couch was a double bed in the corner. Did someone live down here full-time? The bed now swaddled Fox who was on his side sleeping. At least that's what I hoped he was doing. Oddly enough, the man I had known for years didn't look any different. Not until he opened his eyes. Shit. Kind of hard to miss the difference.

The whites of Fox's eyes were bloodshot, the dark colour of his irises paled out like Veata's but not as clouded.

Fox shot up onto his elbow as I came towards him, eyes wavering without focus, not really seeing anything.

"It's Van. You look like shit."

Fox's mouth moved in what should have been a smile, but failing to reach its target. Instead, he plonked down with his arm folded under his head. "Whatcha doing here, kid?"

"Virgil called. Said you might kick the bucket soon."

Panic and anger streamed through me, jacking my heartrate higher, forcing a deep inhale.

"What's wrong with you?" Even in his condition, Fox didn't miss a thing.

"Not sure. Something with Sophie, I think."

Fox's heavy brows creased.

"I, um, partially fixed the connection. Enough that we can feel each other again."

Fox managed a real smile. "Happy for you, kid. Told you it was only a matter of time."

"Yeah. Doesn't make her give a shit about me, but its progress." I still couldn't believe she wasn't here right now.

"Give it more time." Fox's voice was tired.

"Speaking of time...What about you? How much you got?"

"Oh, who knows?" He waved his hand. "Pass me my glass, would ya?"

I palmed a tall glass filled with golden liquid. "Molson?"

"Damn right. If I'm going down, I'm going down with beer breath."

I laughed. What a guy.

Sweat broke on my brow and down my back, my chest and lungs aching as if I was running. Was Sophie running?

I found Hall standing near the entrance of the living space. "Hey man, can you call Sophie and see what's up with her? She either took up fun running or something's going down."

Hall nodded and pulled out his cell as I turned to Fox, not wanting to waste any time with him, made uncomfortably difficult as I could barely suck in steady air.

"She alright?" Fox handed me the beer glass.

"I'm sure she's fine. Probably winded from cursing me to some low-level circle of Hell. Now, what's up with you? Virgil can't get you recharged?"

"Nah," Fox spoke slowly. "Seems like this Energizer Bunny finally quit."

That was precisely what it looked like—exhaustion, maybe strung out from partying too hard, but nothing more finite.

Is that how it would be? Fox's body would power down like a battery without its juice and then he was left a husk of the man who whipped me into shape and saved my ass at every turn?

Another example of the unfairness of life.

34

WOBBLY REBELLION

Sophie

"Call someone, Ranlyn, or you'll have to make good on your threat to bind me." Watching Issát release and Taint yet another soul while we stood around and contemplated next moves made me furious.

A forced metamorphosis to advance Loring's nefarious agenda meant anyone and everyone in his way was free game. No telling what that was or how far his manipulation could reach, although a good guess was this was his first generation of newly-turned recruits of many to come who would serve his every need.

Ranlyn asked to see the scene as I saw it in my thoughts. Hoping it would move things along, I allowed it, assuming he would have taken a peek either way and was being gentlemanly about it. Or maybe my mental barriers were getting better.

As another Blind's power was released and Tainted, I gave a courteous five-count pause so Ranlyn got a good eyeful of the damage Loring and Issát caused before I headed towards the enemy on my own, ignoring and sloughing off Ranlyn's attempt to stop me.

"Wait!" I was surprised it was Kim at my side and not Ranlyn.

"Not a chance. I can't stand around and watch soul after soul be turned. They don't know what's happening to them. Sitting on our hands is the wrong call."

"And going in alone is better? You're letting your anger cloud your judgement. Again."

"Damn right I am. It's fuelling the show, so rush back to Ranlyn and tell him I'm the distraction he needs until he materializes his sack and gets in the game." No way in an amusement park's septic tank was I watching Loring flush souls as we stood by rubbernecking at the disaster.

Since her plea was wasted, Kim gave up, and I assumed it was to play messenger. The smart move may have been to wait, watch, and plan, but facing Loring as many times as I have, I was positive the piece of shit would toy with me long enough for Ranlyn to cook up a plan worth chowing down instead of Tainting souls. And if not, then at least I wouldn't have to deal with Loring anymore because I would be dead. Win-win.

Assuming someone stopped him by my next life cycle.

Coming closer to flank Loring and Issát, something shimmered next to them. Was their light spell on the fritz?

The Apporter popped into view next to his Master with Tobias and Brandon at his side. Last I saw him, the asshole's skin was dripping off of him like I had thrown a vat of acid at him. I don't know how I did it, though the protection tattoos Fox did may have taken the lead. And now I wasn't close enough to see if there was permanent damage. A large and unapologetic part of me hoped there was.

My blood pressure ratcheted a few extra notches. Olson betrayed the whole Mother Coven. Tobias manipulated and used me to teach Donovan a lesson, and Brandon was nothing but a sick fucker with daddy issues. I wanted all of them dead and gone, but Loring was the biggest threat and earned death a thousand times over.

Tobias and Brandon's presence was as good a segue as any.

My voice boomed across the fairway before any of them saw me. "If only your son were here to see your hard work!"

All attention shifted my way. All save the woman on her knees who stared adoringly up at Issát, currently under his full control and as much of a Puppet as Issát's father turned so many others before her.

"Firefly!" Loring's welcoming tone had me cringing as I eyed Tobias.

Although the flare of power prickled my skin as flashes of the Apporter trapping me in my childhood school and then waking up in a prison cell blinded me, I kept myself in check, allowing it to simmer without bothering to hide its presence.

"Loring...." Instead of attacking, I remained casual to keep Loring doing what he did best—talking to hear himself talk.

No welcome extended from the Sorrels. No attempt at a hello from Issát either, though we shared a bloodline, even if it was diluted by innumerable generations. Keeping a safe distance from all of them, I remembered my mental walls and focused on fortifying them, making a concentrated effort not to pay any attention to Olson.

"Oh-ho, what you must see." Loring's cringy smile was filled with delight. His ruined form bent over a cane eyeing me as his toxic soul infected the air around him.

"You're looking better than the last time I saw you, Loring."

That ease in his features fell. Push any harder and he might dispatch of me too quickly. His feelings were not my concern, but Ranlyn needed more time. Provoking only got me so far.

In an attempt to cater to his ego, I followed up with, "Of course, the body doesn't dictate the Magic, does it?"

A nefarious smile pulled on deep creases in his face as he laughed. Never in all my life could I hear that laugh and have it not make my insides recoil. Swallowing bile wasn't easy, but my burning oesophagus distracted me from my anger.

"Have you come to witness the awe that is my new recruits, or have you decided to shake hands with the son of the Master you succeeded in dispatching?"

Issát's stare had been glued to me since I arrived, his heavy attention obvious to me without checking. Chances were he knew next to nothing about me or only whatever Loring rambled on about, which most likely included his views on Issát's father's death to further retain Issát's allegiance.

"As I heard it, you flew off when things got rough, leaving Evaristus to protect himself." I, again, reminded myself that offending Loring wasn't in my best interest. "Though, if you stuck around, you'd know I wasn't responsible for your Master's takedown." I slid a level stare over to Tobias. "Although, you seem oddly content with the father of the guy who did his best work when he ripped Evar apart like a Ken doll."

A flash of Magic hit me. A millisecond passed as I thought "too far" before I crashed to the ground like an ACME anvil dropped from the sky onto my head. This wasn't an attempt on my life, merely a swatting cat keeping its mousy pray in line.

The taste of iron spilled down my throat. A few teeth were knocked loose. Running my tongue across my lower set of chompers caused shooting pain through my gums. Healing took over since my power was still enacted.

I made it onto all fours in wobbly rebellion. To my surprise, Loring wasn't the administrator of this punishment, but Tobias himself. Either a warning of me slicing through a touchy subject or he was plain annoyed and hoped the smackdown would shut me up.

Cha'right, bud.

"And you wonder why Donovan isn't at your side." I licked blood off my lips as it drooled down my chin while Donovan's panic vibrated within the connection. "Of course, you still have Brandon." I stretched to my feet and wiped my face on my sleeve. "And yet, he's no replacement for your true heir, is he?"

Brandon took a wrathful step forward. Tobias stopped his son, the small move from Donovan's brother telling of Brandon's existing second-best complex.

"Donovan broke free of that leash. Too bad you require one to keep you from running headlong into traffic, sparky."

Having enjoyed my fun with the Sorrels, I refocused on Loring. "Releasing the general population's inner powers and then Tainting them. This is your endgame? A little flawed, don't you think?"

"Flawed?" Loring laughed. "In a world where humans endlessly seek an exceptional existence in their mundane lives makes perfect sense."

"If that were true, you wouldn't need to Puppet them first. Remove that control and every one of them would be running to the nearest police station. I passed most of them on the way here. They did not seem super stoked about your epic plan."

The edges of his mouth turned down in disagreement. "The persuasion is merely to ensure compliance. In times of great triumph, all experience the anxiety of change."

"Anxiety?" I paused, wasting more time. "So, instead of educating and convincing the world that Magics aren't a threat, that we could be your neighbour and you wouldn't know the difference, you overthrow the Blind's free will and force them into becoming Magics themselves, hoping they won't hate themselves enough to want to destroy what they are. You plan to have Issát visit the homes of seven billion humans and release all their souls one-by-one? I gave you credit for more intelligence than that. Was I wrong?"

A compliment, no matter how small or from the lowliest of creatures, gave Loring extra pride to puff up his chest with and straighten his crippled back those few crucial inches. Leaning on his cane didn't seem to matter, he found a way to look as pompous as ever.

"Issát and yourself are not the only Magics with the talent to release souls and Taint them, Firefly." He waved a gnarled hand with fingers that no longer fully extended towards the group in front of him. "Plus, this lot of cattle are purely experimental and not the first group to be given a new path. Others will follow. Others in formidable positions that will ensure the flock migrates to the Master, and will not simply follow, but will seek me out."

Master. Loring was his own Master since Evaristus's death. As Issát looked me over while keeping the woman Puppet adoringly staring up at him, I refused to see myself as anything like my ancestor. Not to mention the fact Loring just surprised me with insider information about my ability to not only release souls, but also to Taint them, something I would never attempt.

The scene of my faceoff with Loring in Pario blinded me. The Elders I met hours before were dead and thrown into a fleshy pile to rot while Aunt Lacey was barb-wired to a plank of wood, naked and bleeding to death at my feet. In desperation to keep Caine alive, untamed energy erupted from me. This energy shifted Loring's Tainted soul colour, altering it between its black toxicity to lighter tones before he took off.

The result of Caine living was all that mattered. I was too distracted by Aunt Lacey's heart-wrenching death to take note of what happened to Loring.

The memory disappeared. Loring was talking away without realizing I wasn't listening.

This wasn't an everyday "I remember when" scenario. With an infinitesimal drop of his chin and intense dark eyes, I understood Issát highlighted this event for me as proof I could do as he does.

Not only had Issát read my mind, but he also read my soul, tapped into the memory without ever touching me or moving from his spot, and simultaneously kept this new flock of Tainted Magics in his Puppeteer clutches. Then he somehow replayed the memory in my mind like planting a clue. All without overwhelming me or tipping off the others.

Did the memory he sent me mean he was on my side, and this was his way of letting me know exactly how to defeat Loring? If this was the case, the fact that he was releasing and Tainting all of these souls, plus the ones in the previous experimental groups Loring mentioned, meant Issát might be trying to manipulate me.

Shaking off the emotions the memory provoked and the question of where Issát's loyalties stood, I focused on Loring droning on about the life of Magics and how what he was doing would alter the world around us for the benefit of blah, blah, blah.

No matter how he boasted, Loring didn't do anything for the good of any Magic other than himself, and without Evaristus to tame him, this was Loring's heyday of self-actualization. A spoiled brat given free rein in the biggest toy store in the world.

Tobias and Brandon stood almost apathetically but I interpreted it as tiresome of their Master's rant, having probably heard the sermon too many times and were far happier with killing than teaching the new ways of a Loring-altered world. I grouped Olson with them as he had likely been enduring Loring's tirades for years.

"Now that you are here," Loring said to me instead of talking at me, "it would seem to be kismet that you should meet family that has seen the greatness of a plan such as mine and is willing to assist. With your abilities aligned with much the same as Issát's, I give you the opportunity to hasten the process and aid your brethren."

"Help? Loring, are you having memory issues? Or are you selectively forgetting that I've tried to kill you more than once? Sure, I didn't succeed, but I did try." Again, I was buying time in hopes Ranlyn would get his shit together. They already attacked me once. What were they waiting for?

Loring laughed. "It may surprise you to know you wouldn't be the first of those who once devotedly considered me their enemy to find themselves bowing and adopting me as their Master."

The visual this caused involved whips and ball gags before I knocked that horror aside and focused on what to say that didn't involve me making him think anything close to me on my knees in front of him.

"Is he one of the ones that's adopted you as Master?" I motioned to Brandon. "Bootlicker over there loves being collared, so it wouldn't surprise me."

Brandon's expression twisted. He jolted forward, throwing

himself into a long-jump leap. His light brown hair, piercing blue eyes, and near six-foot figure dropped into an opaque semi-existence as he came at me.

Vague notion of surrounding voices rose, yelling to stop him or egg him on, I didn't know. I was too filled with dread as I had a second to recall Donovan being able to ghost like this during high-octane battle. The move was highly effective for the ghost, not so great for the target.

Before gaining his full form, Brandon landed in front of me, swinging his arm down like an axe on my shoulder, ghosting through my body, and stopping in my chest.

Cramping agony railed through me. No scream escaped. Brandon gripped my lung, fingers squeezing, with psychopathic delight alive in his smile.

I grabbed his arm, still sticking out of my body. Without the strength to tear him from me, and knowing if I did that, I would kill myself, I fought not to remember the Apporter doing something similar to Caveman, and how easily it dropped the mountain of a man.

I bared down in search for my power. A flare of energy sparked across my back where Fox's tattoo work tingled.

A shocking force clocked me across the face. I saw a fist flying at me before the hit, my brain taking longer to register what happened as another fist rained down on me. My knees hit the ground as my power switched off with my surroundings, darkness taking over.

Orbs of light around me strobed in and out. Noise in my head was jumbled, yelling as my face throbbed.

Chest still aching, my head and neck a choir of pain, I was jostled around, gaining consciousness enough to see Tainted Magics hauling Brandon off me before he beat me to death. Brandon struggled against those trying to yank him off of me. If they were using their power, nothing registered with the guy. He scrambled away from them, adding a wave of power that laid them out, as he sprinted towards me and landed on my diaphragm, knocking the wind out of me.

I coughed and fought to breathe without being able to roll into the fetal position.

Loring was yelling, ordering Tobias to control his son and to teach him how to better fall in line or he would kill Brandon on the spot. Evidently, Loring wasn't about to let anyone but himself end me and wasn't happy Brandon wasn't more controllable as promised.

Brandon's hands sparked with energy like they had in threat the first time I met him in Donovan's kitchen. Primed and quick before my power could gain any ground, Brandon slammed his power-sparking hand down and around my throat.

Unrestrained gargles of agony spilled out of me as Brandon twisted my neck to the side with immense pressure. Not meant to suffocate me, but to break my neck.

Muscles twitched. Breathing cut off. Electrocution and drowning incapacitated me, my body bucking against my will as noises I didn't choose spilled from my lips.

Warmth bloomed throughout me. Its growth not alarming and yet the dread of possible death remained as Brandon still held me in the grip of his deadly hands.

The heat found speed and turned molten. It erupted from me, chasing away the electrocution in a bomb of energy. I stilled. An eerie silence settled over me until I gasped in a raking inhale, the air going down like acid-covered tacks.

Muffled moaning was my own. I was unable to hear properly, and every part of me ached. Small movements, even my chest expanding, was like wearing a suit of cactus spines.

I tried to see if Brandon was around, gearing up to attack again. I managed to open my eyes only to see glowing shapes zipping by. A few more blinks and I realized those shapes were Magics' soul glows. Ranlyn and the others were attacking. They were being met with force, though I couldn't focus on where Loring was.

My cousin, Chelsea, and her boyfriend, Elliot, from the Apish

Coffers, sliced down some of the newly turned Tainted. Easy since they had zero battle training and were no longer Puppets. They didn't know what was happening.

A burst of energy popped in the crowd: another new Magic being hit with their inner power in a rush. Not that it mattered. Chances were they were as dead as the others.

Chaos surrounded me. I struggled to roll onto my side and lift myself up mere inches to look around in the dark. Beneath me was a pool of black. I raised my hand up off of what was a manicured lawn beneath a layer of snow, and now a black goo smeared across my palm. I sat and froze at the sight of bodies around me, none of them moving. The light of power burst ignited the Oak Hills lawn, illuminating Brandon laying on the ground staring at me. I flinched, until I realized he was dead, his skin singed and melted like a ritual candle. A couple of other bodies not far from him had the same wax melting effect, though I couldn't have guessed who they were.

Managing to crawl to my knees, I brushed the blackness from my palm on my pants, looking down around me at a blackened blast zone of ash melting into the snow.

The heat I felt before I went unconscious. Not my disintegration power taking over, yet a greater and quicker impact before Brandon and the others could get away. Anyone who saw the light show must have thought I was also dead.

Holy fuck! I killed Donovan's brother.

A tingle of my healing power getting to work raced over my body as I struggled to rise to my feet. I would be battle ready in no time.

Now, where the fuck was Loring?

35

EXAMPLES OF CONSEQUENCE

Donovan

"What the fuck's going on?" On my knees in front of Fox's bed, my legs exhausted from Sophie running around, and then the hit of what felt like a vision, yet I couldn't see it. I tried to pull my phone from my pocket but couldn't focus.

Hall cursed in what sounded like Norwegian, dialling and unable to get a hold of anyone.

She was sassy once the sweating and running stopped. Then pissed off and confused. Now, she's recovering and maybe suspicious?

"You okay?" Fox's wild eyes tried and failed to focus on me.

"Fine." I swallowed the saliva filling my mouth, even though I wasn't the one who had been running. As much as the sensation was odd and awkward, I was still ecstatic to feel anything at all. Whatever she was going through, I was there with her instead of finding out after the fact.

"I can't get anyone." Hall kept shaking his head and dialling.

I didn't have to ask him to know his primary worry was for Kim, guaranteeing he called her first. Maybe she and Sophie were together. Them not picking up a phone was not a good sign. Though, cell phones didn't work in the Prison Creation. With all the running Sophie was doing, I doubted she was there, but the connection didn't come with GPS tracking.

"Get him a drink." Generous of Fox to boss Virgil around for me since I was busy cataloguing Sophie's shifting emotions, now antagonistic and calculating.

Could they have gone after Vincent without letting us know?

Come on, Sophie, what are you doing?

Virgil returned from a mini fridge with a beer bottle in hand. He opened it, and passed it to me.

I took a swig, but it didn't give me the relief I was hoping for.

"That girl of yours probably picked a fight with someone. Or is working out." Fox flopped in place resuming his arm-over-his-eyes position. "They got a treadmill where you are?"

"Probably. No. No treadmill." I fought to breathe deeply and think calming thoughts. Maybe it would help her.

Closing my eyes, trying not to fixate on the fact that whatever Sophie was up to probably could have waited for any other time when I wasn't trying to say goodbye to Fox. She had a breakthrough back at the Prison Creation. Maybe it wasn't enough.

A phone rang. Not Hall's. Virgil went to the side table next to the couch and picked up the receiver of an old rotary phone, doing some mumbling of his own as I watched Hall pace and redial someone. Probably Kim.

"Hold on a sec." Virgil put the phone down, grabbed the TV remote, and turned the enormous thing on, its light filling the room and forcing Fox to reposition to guard his sensitive eyes.

Virgil picked the phone up again as a news anchor team from CTV Toronto News talked about authorities' confusion over the reported gang activity causing serious harm and death to Niagara Falls seekers. In the top corner of the frame was a box that read

"BLACKOUT" in bright white letters against a black background. The one anchor gave a disclaimer about disturbing footage in a grave tone before that box expanded to fill the whole screen and rolled cellphone footage. The unsteady camera recorded a crowd of people standing around four others in the wide circle. The crowd gave the four performing some space as they...What the fuck?

Their magic tricks were too smooth, more than a sleight of hand or misdirection of a seasoned crowd-pleaser. When a trick involved the levitation of a concrete street planter not even a pulley system could manage without being blatantly visible, I knew what I was looking at.

After a round of applause, one of the female performers took center stage. "You have all been witness to a pinch of what you Blind humans could possess." The woman peered directly into the camera, happy to see the person capturing her show, and flashed a split-second conniving grin. "As the children of our Master Loring, you will become a part of a new reign where we all walk free."

Loring?

"All except you." She gave a flourish of her hand towards the confused crowd waiting for the next trick. "You lot are the examples of consequence for those who resist."

The onlookers appeared confused yet assumed it was still a part of the show.

The Magic brought her arm up to match the other one. Light built between her hands. When onlookers gasped, the Magic hit them with a jolt of energy, hitting the small crowd including the one live streaming. Screams rang out before the footage cut to droves of people running.

A familiar, orange-haired teenager casually walked against the stream of panicked tourists. His attention elsewhere, yet surveying the crowd, searching for something or someone.

"Shit. Gualichu." If the demon was there, it meant shit was worse than any TV camera could pick up.

"Where?" Hall leaned forward trying to see what I saw, the others asking questions I hushed.

The news team returned to the screen. The calm-faced commentators stated the authenticated footage caused great concern for those in the area and emphasized that no obvious weapons were shown in the footage. Emergency personnel were dispatched to the scene, but the attacks were against many others and numbers of the dead or injured continued to filter in as people overwhelmed emergency rooms, everyone having difficulty navigating the blackout.

"Loring's attacking the Blind. If whatever he's doing attracted the demon, then Sophie's there and figh—"

A slash of pain cut down my shoulder, my whole torso frozen in pain. I grabbed my chest and the side of the bed, scaring the shit out of Fox. He grasped my arm, talking. I couldn't answer him. It felt like my sternum was going to explode and toss my lungs into the pool of my knocked-over beer pooling below me on Virgil's floor.

No way Sophie wasn't taking on Loring. If he hit the public, she would be front and center.

I pitched forward on all fours, unable to rid myself of whatever this was.

Hall gripped my shoulder, leaning over me. "Is this Sophie?"

I managed a nod.

With her power unpredictable since Nya, facing Loring was a crapshoot. Especially if she went in alone. If this was how we died, at least I fixed the Soul Magic first.

A tingle of power and heat rose and skittered across my back, Sophie's back. Yes! Her tattoo was activating. Fox's power may have left him, but it was alive in her.

An unmistakable punch cracked against my jaw and laid me out, more keeping me there. I woke up to the others talking over me. More questions I couldn't hear with my brain rocked. The power Sophie was seeking was gone. My chest no longer felt close to implosion, but my face and skull ached like I suffered more than the hits I was awake for. Sophie took a beating.

Please, Sophie, find a way to fight.

Helplessness was overwhelming. I wanted to kill whoever did this to her. If it was Loring, he knew every hit was against the both of us and was likely toying with her.

A flash of fear raced through me, followed by energy. An electric current overwhelmed me, eyes rolling, jaw locked, muscles flexed, body bucking in agony, powerless to stop the simultaneous torture.

Something braced my head and shoulders, then grabbed my ankles. Hands were on me, voices around me, none I could do anything about.

Power deep within me ignited. Sophie's tattoos again? No. Ritual stone magic woke up, creating heat that radiated through my marrow, distracting me from the pain of the convulsions. Could the ritual stone magic reach Sophie? Could it save her from this?

Hope sparked until the warmth grew hot and then became unbearable, setting my insides on fire. Inescapable pain drove through me. Unable to move on my own, dowse the flames, or tell the others, glued to Sophie in fear and abject agony was not the reunion I pictured.

Magic boiled over, splashed, and rushed out of my pores. An unrestricted flow of energy streamed from my body, independent and urgent, continuing until unconsciousness won.

I tried to move, blinded and in silence.

Fuck me.

A twitch of muscles equalled spikes of pain. Nothing like the electrocution, though an agony that left me unable to move without consequence.

A tight grip and a pull on my shirt flared a panic of impending attack. Fox held me, his lips moving, but the pain he caused was overwhelming. The echo of his voice in my head didn't reach my ears, my hearing not up to par.

Opening my eyes to a strong shake showed me Fox's strained expression leaning over me again. "Y'okay?"

Still in pain, but not as bad, my healing power was doing its thing. I waved my hand as much as I could, and he let me go.

My ears popped. I groaned. "Hold up." I needed another minute of recovery.

When I could, I pushed myself up onto my elbows, joints cracking like I was an eighty-year-old man, the healing taking its time.

I managed to prop myself up onto my hip and caught sight of something black beneath me, a powdery grit on my fingers.

Around me was dark. A flicker and a buzz was a camping light in Virgil's hand, illuminating the room in strips of light. If I hadn't been in the basement already, I would have thought it had survived a fire. The couch was a tangle of springs and singed fabric, Fox's bed was now nothing but melted and twisted metal.

Oops. The TV didn't survive. Virgil took around, eyes wide in shellshock, surveying the destruction as Hall palmed his phone again, trying to call someone.

I sat up more, unsure if I should move. "What happened?"

Fox extended his hand for me to grab and helped me to my feet.

Ohmygod. I stepped back and looked Fox over. He was standing. Clearly strong enough to help me off of my ass. "Damn. Your eyes. They're normal."

Fox shook his head. "I don't know what happened to you or what that was when you, I don't know if exploded is the right word, but close enough. The other two took cover, but I was too slow. Whatever it was, it didn't kill me." He rolled his shoulders. "I'm recharged, feeling better than I have for the last decade or more."

He truly looked it.

Fox was still his portly and bearded self, but something from inside of him shone. Like he had the energy of a hyperactive yorkie alive inside of him.

"The ritual stone. Its magic must have healed you."

Fox shrugged. "No idea, kid, but I owe you. And the big guy still can't get a hold of whoever he's wearing out the numbers on his cell for, but you're still standing, so I'm assuming Sophie is too."

Assume? Fuck that! I needed to kno—Oh, there she was. As my anxiousness rose, I felt it as Sophie's shock filtered through, she in awe, more so since she hadn't experienced a proper taste of the ritual stone magic before.

If she was down at the Falls, she may still be in danger. Either she survived an attack or had doled one out herself. If Loring and his flock were still floating around, another confrontation was guaranteed and possibility imminent.

I needed to find her.

Fox landed a heavy hand on my shoulder. "I'm more than fine, kid. You should get out there and see what's doing."

He must have seen the worry plastered on my face. "You sure?"

Fox splayed meaty hands and looked down at himself. "I'm fine enough for you to go and to figure out the rest later."

"Shit, man." I wrapped my arms around Fox's big shoulders, filled to brim with relief. "I'll call you as soon as I can."

"Focus out there, Van," he said as he pulled away. "This stone magic is unpredictable shit. If it healed your Soul Magic—"

"Not all of it." If only.

"Even if it did a patch job, guarantee it can heal the rest and then some." He hit me in the arm. "And stay alive so I can tap into that shit if I need to. No telling how long this boost will last me."

"We'll test your powers later. See how they hold up." Virgil's voice was absent-minded, he was still surveying his decimated furniture. "You'll probably need a top-up every now and again."

Fox huffed and crossed his arms across his barrel chest, clearly not happy his talents and survival depended on me.

"Listen, I owe you anyway, big guy." I gave him another quick hug. "And I'd love to stay—"

"Get the fuck moving." Fox waved me towards the door. "Say hi for me."

"I will." I turned to Virgil. "I'll write you a check later." I headed for the stairs, Hall leading.

"Pen one out for me while you're at it!" Fox's voice threw back as we jumped over a mess.

Piles of stuff were no longer neat, the impressions of bodies now imbedded in the sides of boxes, their contents strewn all over the place. Hall and Virgil were only left unharmed due to Virgil's hoarding, and I reminded myself how close I'd been to killing innocent people.

The ritual stone power was strong, creating destruction without prejudice. Why the fuck didn't it roast Fox? All I could hope for was that the well of power was endless. If not, I'd be going through this end-of-life scene with Fox again and again.

I'd take all the time I could with the guy.

36

GROUND ZERO

Donovan

After some bickering, I jumped into the back seat. Ridiculous. Hall didn't want to chance taking a hit while driving if Sophie was thrown around. As if it couldn't have happened on the way to see Fox. At the break-neck, hold-the-fuck-on-tight, speeds we were travelling on the way to the Falls, a nudge on the elbow posed the potential to leave us a blood-soaked twist of metal ready for sale to the most morbid art collector in the region.

Fine. So, I was relegated to the back seat. As long as Hall kept the pedal to the floor and disobeyed as many traffic laws as possible, I would strap myself to the roof rack if it made him feel safer.

Without communication with Sophie, Ranlyn, or any of the Tactical Team members, we were still in the dark about what we were driving into. Only the video on the news and the Magics claiming the Blind would be given the privilege of possessing magic abilities provided any insight. Which was bullshit. Loring couldn't give them anything but early grave rights.

Sophie's power vibrated at a constant hum; she was fighting or looking for a fight. No way would she stand by and let others do the heavy lifting. She was running around and engaging where she could, frustrated, yet still alive.

A couple hits tripped her up good. I didn't fling across the back-seat, but I wasn't immune to the damage, it being a hit of magic or skinned palms against asphalt. What I did notice was that she didn't stay down long. She was determined to win and drove to beat her targets with vengeful enthusiasm.

Something close to pride jacked up in my chest, but was always doused in worry that she was one hit away from being killed before I saw her again. Selfish, but true. I needed to see her, needed to hold her again. The quick embrace in the lobby after we reached an under-standing was still fresh, yet unfinished business, and the euphoria of relief didn't last as long as it should have.

I should know by now that anyone pitting someone against Sophie's concern for Vincent would only get them steamrolled in disappointment. Apparently, I had a momentary lapse in common sense that blinded me in cock-numbing jealousy. Who knew what to expect from Sophie if the guy died, but I imagined a new zombie routine and the genesis of a revenge plot on every Llewellyn she could get her mitts on.

To reach our destination on any normal day would take thirty minutes from Beamsville to Niagara Falls. With a pissed off Viking railing on the horn, pushing the five-speed Civic to its limits, and peeking in his rearview at me like I was going to go nuclear again, we shaved off a good ten or more minutes before hitting a police roadblock.

Flashing lights ahead of us gave a clear picture of what we were rolling up to, making the decision to ditch the stolen wheels, and use the blackout to disappear beneath a cover spell and stroll on by.

Now that we were within the vicinity, our location meant dick-all because it was pitch-black and finding Sophie or Kim or anyone familiar in the mash of people fleeing the city or rubbernecking at the tragedy was impossible. The connection was no locater spell, and I didn't have the time or implements to pull off the concentration for one.

Heading up the hill, we agreed the best place to start was where we saw the footage on the news, thinking of it as ground zero. One thing our steps brought to light was that Blind law enforcement was crawling all over the place: reenforcing roadblocks, assisting the injured, directing emergency crews, moving along clusters of small groups flapping their gums about what happened and how they "saw it happen" instead of getting to safety.

From all of their minds, a small percentage actually witnessed anything, but from the looks of it, whatever someone did see, it was all over now. Ground zero was littered with body-shaped sheets of at least ten or more, presumably crews working to remove the dead from the outer skirts first and working their way in.

A large florescent sign for *The Great Canadian Midway* tourist trap was now scrap metal, storefront windows gashed with their insides a glittered mess crunching under our boots. Thousands of dollars' worth of damage and a body count you needed both hands and feet, plus a buddy's, to tally.

No matter what this was, what went down was a threat of exposure beyond concealment. Our hope laying in the hands of conspiracy theorists to do what they did best and flood the internet with their convoluted explanations until no one believed it was anything but what it looked like: bold new gang activity using a hidden devise to attack the audience and then wreak havoc on tourists for the thrill of causing chaos.

The speech the Magic gave would be dissected, resulting in nothing close to the truth considering they were clueless to who "Loring the Master" was.

I tried calling Rosemary, thinking maybe her flock showed in support of the plan to bring shock and awe to the tourist's haven. An automated voice told me the phone was no longer in service. Not switched off or busy, not in service. Something about that didn't sit well.

With no answers in the midst of the dead or Blind, the only viable option was returning to the Prison Creation in hopes that the others were there and not held up in another section of Niagara Falls.

I didn't like leaving, neither did Hall, but we weren't getting anywhere by staying.

Jumping into the stolen Civic and racing to the parking garage across from the city's bus terminal in no time, we walked off the Prison Creation elevator into more chaos.

The lobby was congested with Magics. Our height advantages afforded us a bird's eye view of who we were looking for.

One of which was blood-smeared and wearing a familiar expression.

I shouldered a path through the crowd to find Sophie at the guard's desk. She was giving Ranlyn shit about something. Stress bags under his eyes and as much dirt and blood shadowing his features as Sophie's, told me that whatever she was griping about was not on Ranlyn's radar.

Closer to the pair, I heard Sophie talking about Vincent as Ranlyn rounded the desk, pointing at something and speaking only to the guard. Sophie yelled above them, refusing to be ignored.

"We need to go in now! Those Sovereignty pukes didn't even show up—"

"And why would they?" Ranlyn finally snapped as he continued on with the guard.

"Are you alright?" I tried to gain her attention.

Fed up with getting nowhere with Ranlyn, she spun to me. "No. Vincent is still in the Sovereignty cells and Mr. I-Say-What-Goes," she said this louder so Ranlyn could overhear her, and he responded with a stern glare, "won't even consider the possibility that now is the perfect time to strike."

"Sophie," Ranlyn said her name with a tight tone speaking as he came out from behind the desk, "too many are dead already including some of your own Sect and the Tactical Team. If Vincent were able, he would tell you himself that infiltrating the Sovereignty with our losses is suicidal. Drop the subject."

Ranlyn walked away, disappearing within the crowd. For a moment, it looked like Sophie was going to go after him as she took off in the same direction, but Ranlyn was gone.

"Who's dead?" I tailed her with quick strides before getting cut off by a guy I vaguely remembered from the Mother Coven and losing Sophie for a few steps.

"Sophie!" I called to her. "Wait up."

She wasn't listening, forcing me to race around people to catch up and ask again.

"Your brother," she answered without facing me.

Brandon is dead? Wow, this news legitimately surprised me. "Did you kill him?"

She paused before answering. "Yes, but I don't know how."

Without elaboration, I realized she was moving towards the boardroom. Maybe I would learn more there.

My Sect had congregated, not that they did so on my word. In my mind, the Sect was Kim's, and she was standing at the head of the room, her mood displayed in her crossed arms as Hall stood too close and looked to be lecturing her. Those arms and the accompanying scowl told me she wasn't taking a bit of the lecture into consideration, she was just waiting for him to run out of steam.

That was until Hall wrapped her up in a tight, lingering embrace pasting an expression of shock on Kim before she lifted her arms to the length of his ribs and hugged him back. Hall stood, leaving his big hands on her shoulders, and saying something more before leaving the room all together.

Whatever the guy said left its mark. Kim was a statue staring after him until Gwen caught her up with a question and forced her to focus. Since she was an easy target, I could have delved into her brain and plucked the info for myself, but thought I understood the gist without the invasion.

Hall had it bad for Kim. I didn't get it, but it was what it was, and

Kim just found out the Viking wasn't all talk. No games, no bullshit pet names, straight-up, from the heart declaration of affection, and that expression Kim was stitched into as she half-listened to whatever Gwen was talking about, said she wasn't ready to hear what he said and was still recovering from a case of the what-the-fuck-just-happened?

Around the room was a mix of angry faces and wet cheeks. A swath of blood crossed Blake's chest like a long-healed wound seeped through his torn Ed Hardy shirt. He was among the angry, pacing the floors like he itched to get back out there. On a normal day, Jared would be right on him, playing the peacekeeper and calming his friend down, but not even he had it in him. He sat in a chair staring at those big mitts, and it took me too long to see his hands were covered in dried blood.

Kim calling the room to attention brought the big guy's head up, though the rest of the room took longer to settle.

Clearing her throat, Kim took a breath before beginning. Hall may have caused a stir, but this was all about the Sect, and she was having difficulty spitting out what needed to be said.

"We didn't expect to find what we did when we left here only a few hours ago and unfortunately Matt and Caitlyn didn't return with us."

Ah, shit. That's why Blake was pacing. Jared rubbed his hands together and dried flakes of blood crumbled to the table. The three of them were tight, and now the Chameleon and his girlfriend were added to the casualties' list.

No fighting-related deaths occurred since I joined Aunt Lacey's Coven. Since Sophie joined, all the Elders were slaughtered, Henry's life was taken by an over-zealous Apish Coffer, not to mention the injuries of many going uncatalogued, and now Matt and Caitlyn were gone. I knew I forgot important people, but with every-thing that was going on with Sophie, I could say with certainty that I didn't have a handle on the Sect roster. Something I should probably know.

Kim tried her best to tame the grief-stricken crowd demanding to know what would happen to Matt's and Caitlyn's bodies.

She lifted her hands to quiet them. "The Blind are already on the scene, but Veata is reaching out to Coven contacts in the local..." the word "morgue" was on her lips, but she opted for "...hospital that will contact any family and create a plausible cause of death fitting for their injuries. Made easier by the fact the attack was so public."

A deep, stout laugh came from Jared. "What story do you think they'll cook up to explain Matt's chest being ripped open? Rabid raccoon?"

Kim's head momentarily dropped, the visual too much.

"Cait was thrown over the Falls," Deidra spoke up, leaning against the wall. "They probably won't even find her until she's some disgusting floater. They'll assume she committed suicide."

Blake stopped pacing, crossing his arms to face off with Deidra across the table. "With all the dead and injured, plus the footage, you seriously think they would think it was unrelated? When you picking up your detective badge, Nancy Drew?"

In a rushing flush, Deidra threw off waves of heat, surprising everyone around her. Caine shifted his face away from the flare of temperature. With any powers, they were hardwired to emotions and Deidra was no different, Blake having pushed her further than she was willing to take.

Since her girlfriend Rachel died—shit, another Covener I forgot about—she was constantly on edge.

"She will be found," Kim yelled over them before Deidra went full flamethrower and baked Blake alive. "Unfortunately, she wasn't the only one thrown over and they've already sent for crews to retrieve them." A hard swallow punctuated the discomfort that gave Kim. "Fished-out" would have been appropriate but Deidra might have really gone nuclear.

"Will we know when they're funerals are?" I was shocked Denise asked or considered attending.

"Well...." Kim let out a heavy exhale and leaned into her arms on the table. "When the funerals are set, you can be informed...." Her pause spoke loud enough for Blake.

"Come on!" He went wild with the hand gestures. "You can't stop us from going. This is a prison but we're not criminals."

When Kim's head bowed again, I stepped in. "Seeing as how our enemies are still out there, know our faces, know the faces of our dead, they'll be graveside waiting to pick you off. You'd be putting their families in way of Loring so you can slap on a tie and throw some dirt."

Jared stood so fast it flew his chair into the wall behind him, the flare of power unmistakable.

Before I could show the pup who the alpha dog was, Caine popped up from his chair and shot Jared the hairy eyeball with a flare of his own strength. "Sit!"

When Jared's gnarled features relaxed, he sat, retaining eye contact with Caine. Caine sat as Jared did before releasing him from his persuasion. Jared blinked in the midst of confusion at what happened and looked down at his chair as if questioning why he was sitting.

Speaking softer, Caine said, "Listen carefully, and don't make me do that again. We all fought tonight, we all lost Coven members. You have no idea what it means to stand up there and pretend to have all the answers."

Caine did know. Not with this group, but he was their leader in the Creation for months and it weighed on him to lose so many.

"If you want to leave, do it now. We won't hold it against you." I raised an eyebrow at Kim who straightened and nodded in agreement. "Tonight only proves Loring's getting bolder and doesn't give a shit if the Blind know about us or who gets caught in the crossfire. You'll have to flee the province. Shit, I'll pay your travel expenses. Just do it now before shit really hits the fan, and your window of opportunity is nailed shut. If your heart's not in this fight, you may as well off yourself before we have to fabricate another bullshit story to explain your death to your family."

"Like you can talk." Blake shot a pointed finger at me, then eyed Caine, remembering Caine's threat, and settling both hands on his hips to lessen his intent. "Where were you when Loring was ripping us apart?"

"Not available! By the time I could get there, I'd gone through whatever electrocution and stabbing and beatdown as Sophie and missed the party." I took a step closer but didn't round the table and give it a new finish with Blake's face like I wanted to. "And if that was your way of testing my allegiance to this Coven or the fight against Loring, then I suggest when you run, that you run farther than the neighbouring province and never step over the border again."

As Blake internally shrank while managing to look steady, no one took me up on my offer to hit to the road on my dime. Something that surprised me as most looked willing to jump ship.

Kim took back the reins. "I know this sucks. Right now, I hate this job. I hate not knowing what to do or what to say. Obviously, if you need a good rant, I'm here to listen but don't expect anything profound. Trust that I will keep you informed about everything," she counted them on her fingers, "Coven plans, Loring's location, funeral arrangements, the fuckin' laundry schedule if you need it. Just promise me that you will allow the Elders and those in charge the belief that you are one hundred percent behind them. The Coven's divided enough as it is."

She took a heavy breath, squaring her shoulders while retaining her composure as she held the Coveners' attention. "As Donovan said, take the out if it's truly what you want, but do it now. If you stay, be helpful and stop with the petty complaints. Show some initiative. Help with food, cleaning, organization, entertainment, anything to keep everyone else motivated and ready to fight when the order comes in."

For someone claiming for a loss of words, Kim sure said exactly what the Sect needed to hear. When I'd walked in the room, everyone was so stuck in their heads, they were hell-bent on impulsive revenge or close-to-medicated break downs.

Kim looked over at me and I gave a subtle nod. As much as that chick chews on confidence for breakfast, this move was a tidbit of insecurity the old me would have exploited and called her out on. Not tracking the reason for the change, I didn't know how doing so would help me in the end. Kim was keeping the Sect rallied and I sure as shit didn't have it in me to fulfil the job description.

Satisfied Kim and I did all we could and said everything we needed to say, the room emptied.

Kim approached me and Sophie, who had stayed invisible the whole meeting probably obsessing about Vincent and pissed at Ranlyn. Caine joined the three of us.

"Besides my brother, did any other heavy-hitters go down?" I asked Kim since Sophie was silent.

Kim's eyes flashed to Caine and back. "Not too sure on their side, but on ours, Jessabelle didn't make it."

"Really?" This came out part-surprise and part-disbelief that a fighter as seasoned as Jessabelle was killed.

Kim nodded sympathetically.

"How?"

"Some Blind ran and hid in the dinosaur mini-putt place. Jessabelle followed a Magic who was tracking them." She gave a small head shake. "When Lincoln found her, he knew the Magic who did it because she had been bled to death."

"People bleed out when they've been injured. What's the difference?" Caine asked.

She answered on an exhale. "Because the Magic can control the body's inner functions including blood flow. Jessabelle, plus all of the Blind she tried to protect, were in puddles of their own blood, it was coming out of their pores, eyes, ears, noses. Like squeezing a sponge. He drained them of their life-source in the time it took Lincoln to run down the street."

And that's what we were up against.

Our Sect wasn't nearly as talented. The fact only Matt and Caitlyn were snuffed out was a fucking miracle.

"Kassie too," Caine said to Sophie.

Her already bleak expression didn't shift, but I felt a rise of something. Guilt maybe? Sophie and Kassie, her Soul Seeing cousin, were far from close, but she was still family and the Ballard Coven had lost their first in this war.

Sophie stiffly nodded.

Of all people, why did it have to be another Soul Seer? For Sophie, seeing souls was her air-raid siren, her warning against all she was up against. Could Kassie tell who she was fighting? Did she realize what their soul colour meant and knew she was destined to lose? Sophie said the Ballard Tome left out so many soul colours. Sophie didn't know them all and was far more open about the gift than Kassie. Why was she exposed in the first place?

Kim and Caine went on to explain that Ness and Felix kept a lot of our allies under cover to better engage the enemy, attack, and move to their next target effectively, the team of Illusionists aware of their weaker members and focused on them to increase chances of survival. Kassie was supposed to have been with them.

Maybe she was playing hero. Not her style, but you never know. Could have been overconfidence, which Sophie seemed to think was more plausible.

Sophie said her cousin Chelsea and her boyfriend didn't make it either. She witnessed their downfall, so the Ballards logged big loses for such a new coven. As it was, they only had a dozen or so members left, and half were too old not to feel the aches and pains of that night for the next week, even if magically healed.

Leon's limb loss, making him the only three-legged Transmutator I had ever met, should have been enough for the other Ballards to stay put in the Prison Creation. No way Kassie or Chelsea and her Apish Coffer barnacle had stood a chance against the mayhem of Loring's flock. Sophie and I would likewise be dead if we didn't have the luck of the ritual stone magic.

Done with the recount, Sophie stormed out of the boardroom.

Caine watched Sophie leave and then turned to me. "You're not following?"

"I don't know that she wa—"

Kim gave my shoulder a small shove. "Go, you idiot."

"Idiot? I didn't see you chasing after Hall."

Kim rolled her eyes.

"That's what I thought." But I did leave in search of Sophie. She would be searching for her family, and while she didn't ask for my support, I wanted to be there in case she needed it, even knowing she may tell me to fuck off instead. The cafeteria didn't peddle sympathy cards, so I didn't have much else to offer her or the broken Ballard Coven.

Passing the cafeteria, I saw Adam, Serena, and a destroyed-looking Kevin, Sophie's cousin and brother to the now deceased Chelsea. Sophie wasn't with them. I didn't need their questions and had no answers or words to help them, so I kept on walking.

I spotted Sophie standing in a line formed at the cell console. Apparently, everyone wanted privacy to sleep and shower off the tragedy.

I approached her as she stood wearing an impatient scowl. "You okay?"

She turned her scowl on me. "Stupid question."

"Fine, yes, it is. How is—"

"Your mother was exiled from her Coven."

"What?" That's one way to deflect the conversation. "Is she here?"

"*Pfft.* Are you high? Why would Ranlyn let an ousted Tainted Coven Leader in here? Even if she fought for our side, which she never would have done without you, she carries around her Tainted soul proudly. People here would drown her in cafeteria mashed potatoes." Sophie huffed at the line of people using the console and mumbled, "What the fuck is wrong here, people? Push the button, enter the cell."

The line moved forward a step. I followed. "Well, where is she?"

Sophie crossed her arms and huffed again, her irritation flooding the connection. "How would I know? The woman has her own seedy contacts. Plus, she's beautiful. Someone'll take pity on her." The anger this engaged in my gut cramped in her own as she shifted uncomfortably. A small victory of sorts. "I don't know what to tell you. She could be anywhere."

"How do you know they exiled her?"

"Come on!" she said loud enough for those using the console to hear. "It's self-explanatory."

I grabbed her elbow. "Sophie."

"I heard you." She pulled out of my grip. "Rosemary's number two, which I'm pretty sure is Rodney from The Chiff's brother, didn't appreciate her protecting his target instead of fighting next to him. They rumbled. She beheaded the fucker with a piece of some metal sign thingy. Since others saw it, she split."

Giving up and shooting Sophie glowers as they left, Sophie finally stepped up to the console and started searching for someone.

Protecting a target? "Was she protecting you?"

"Yup. Of course she was. Another thing she can hate me for, though I never asked her to sacrifice her sassy ass in the first place. I had it covered. But she won't kill me and risk your life, so I'm inclined to use her up until she proves unusable. Now move." Finding what she was looking for, Sophie engaged the cell system. I glimpsed the console before the name disappeared and saw she was now in a cell with Olive.

With Sophie preoccupied with everyone but me, I hit my own cell. After a scrub down, I called to check on Fox, who was still healthy. He and Virgil were testing his powers, seeking limitations, and which abilities caused more of a drain than others. After giving him a quick rundown of the events in the Falls, Fox apologized for not being able to be there, though I wouldn't have wanted him to be. Plus, I hadn't been there either. And while Sophie said Brandon was dead, I hadn't heard anything about Tobias.

Without adding anymore ball-blushing emotion Fox hated, I

agreed to call soon and left the conversation feeling good at least one person in my life was doing well.

No wonder my mother's phone was dead. She would have pitched it to stop them from tracking her. I wouldn't be able to contact her until she was safe and found a way to contact me. Between her and Sophie, those women were going to put me in a straitjacket. Chances were I was headed there anyway, but they were ushering me in to the padded room.

DEVASTATED

Sophie

"Olive?" Sitting on the bed in deep thought, my great-aunt startled at my voice.

"Sorry, Firefly. I didn't hear you come in."

I chuckled. "They need to build a knocking system."

Olive tried, but her smile was limp.

I sat next to her on the bed. Before I could say anything, we embraced each other. I let the tight hold linger until Olive straightened and used a tissue to blot her cheeks.

"Lewis is taking care of contacting their parents," Olive said without lifting her swollen eyes, shaking fingers looking for a clean piece of tissue. "We're deciding on what to tell the family. There're still snowy roads and with their injuries...maybe a car crash? I don't know. No one outside of the coven knew they were still in the region. Thought they were staying with friends out west or on vacation somewhere. Same with Kassie." She shook her head unable to finish, another tear falling down her cheek.

"It may feel like a gross deception, but a car crash or illness may be the closest thing their minds can accept. And relatively easy to fake unless they want to view their bodies." Closed caskets were likely a must. I didn't see the final conditions of all of them and didn't have to to know it was not something their parents would ever get over if they had to identify their remains.

"The truth would be too much to expect in this case." Olive sniffled. "I know that, but it still doesn't feel right. And when I heard, a blip of thought that we could hold a celebration of life for all of them at the estate fluttered into my brain." She shook her head. "As if I could forget the estate is no longer standing."

"It's still there. Not whole and not about to become whole in time for a something like that, but the spirit of the estate is still there."

Olive's head whipped up, her bloodshot eyes meeting mine. "It is?"

I nodded. "It was callous of me to return and tell everyone about the estate the way I did. I'm sorry. I wasn't—"

Olive grabbed my hands. "It's fine, Firefly. You were not yourself. What of the estate's spirit?"

As quick as Olive was to dismiss my behaviour, I planned on apologizing again later. "Well, it was still there when the place was rubble and still recognized me. Even when Nya possessed me, it was there, faintly sad and helpless when I was aware enough to actually feel it."

"And now?"

I exhaled, not wanting to say it. "Devastated."

Olive pursed her lips and hung her head a bit, more tears falling.

"I wasn't able to reassure it, not that I was in the right headspace to even think about doing something like that, because Miklos showed up and everything became about him and...I don't know. If the estate's spirit is still there, that has to be good news, no?"

Olive swiped at her wet cheek. "One can only hope, Firefly."

I held Olive's hand tighter. "We can rebuild."

"You can rebuild."

"Wha—? I'm not letting you give up. You've spent too much time away as it is. The estate wouldn't want that. And if this life is anything like my past one, I may not be around long enough to see it standing again. You have to keep on. If I'm gone, the estate will find another heir."

"No, I think you will outlive me. As you should. And one day, if we can rebuild, maybe I will still be around to see you and Donovan marry in the garden."

"Oh, I don't know if anyone has enough years in them to wait for that." I laughed, but it was true. As soon as Olive mentioned it, my chest tightened with anxiety at such a thought. We may be better off than we were a day ago, but we weren't that good.

Olive returned my laugh, but again, it was devoid of true happiness. Her heart was too weary.

"I think, for now, I will settle for a nap, if you don't mind."

"Of course not." I sprung to my feet, meaning to leave, and then rethought my quick exit. "Can I get you anything? Or do anything while you rest?"

Repositioning herself on the mattress Olive gave a hollow smile, her eyes still red, probably prepared to continue crying the second I left. "The shoulder was more than enough, Firefly. Though, if you could deliver Ferdinand to one of your aunts, I could gain more uninterrupted time alone."

"Ferdinand?"

Olive pointed to a dark red glass container attached to braided rope on the small desk. "Ferdinand, the Pompeii Worm. Like, Ferdinand Magellan, the Portuguese explorer who travelled and named the oceans, one where a worm such as a Pompeii Worm would find lovely hydrothermal vents to cozy up in."

"Umm. Okay then. Those ladies were certainly thoughtful with their naming practices." After being in Donovan's brain a couple of times, Ferdinand the Pompeii Worm was definitely an explorer.

Olive gave a tired nod. "I was meant to feed him and ended up here."

I carefully gathered the glass, seeing the Pompeii Worm curled into a tight ball inside the container in some kind of liquid. The aunts did see the creature as a pet and pets get names. I didn't even know they brought the worm with them. It must have already been packed in case they needed to leave.

A flash of the pain it caused while tunnelling into Donovan's head left a phantom ache in my brain. Without this little creature, others wouldn't have known the fight to infiltrate the Creation was worth it. Guess we owed it as much as we could give to a little worm.

Olive thanked me again and laid down, her back to me before I left the cell.

Worm container in hand, I stood, surprised at how quiet it was. The air of grief was heavy in the main lobby. People were scarce, resting like Olive. Those in the lofty space moved slowly, some unchanged from the fight, walking in a daze at more heartbreak or exhaustion from getting our asses handed to us again.

We took a chance when we opened the Creation. I didn't give anyone much of a choice, and I didn't regret it. Now, Loring was free, and this wouldn't be the last time the world would be subjected to his merciless schemes. This was my fault and I needed to find a way to limit the death toll and make him pay.

ABOUT THE AUTHOR

S.J. Cairns creates paranormal romance fantasy from her hometown in Southern Ontario, Canada. When S.J. is not plugging away at her laptop on her comfy couch, you can find her chasing around her three-year-old daughter alongside her husband of over twenty years or working in true chaos at local homeless shelters and an anti-human trafficking safe house.

Website: www.sjcairns.com
Facebook: www.facebook.com/SJCairnsauthor
Twitter: www.twitter.com/SamiJoCairns
Email: samijocairns@gmail.com